About the

Damien Owens is the author of four novels — *Dead Cat Bounce, Peter and Mary Have a Row, The Bright Side* and *Little Black Everything*. The latter two were published under the pen name Alex Coleman.

He is also the creator and writer of *Trivia*, a television comedy/drama which ran for two series on RTÉ.

Damien has contributed comic material to a number of other television and radio programmes, and to numerous magazines and newspapers in Ireland, Britain and Australia.

He lives in Dublin with his wife, two daughters and a small animal that is most likely a cat. His hobbies include laughing at inappropriate moments and worrying. He does not have a man cave.

MARRIED TO A CAVE MAN

MARRIED TO A CAVE MAN

DAMIEN OWENS

Unbound

This edition first published in 2017

Unbound

6th Floor Mutual House, 70 Conduit Street, London W1S 2GF

www.unbound.com

ISBN (eBook): 978-1911586852

ISBN (Paperback): 978-1911586845

Design by Designer

Cover image:
© Picture Library

Printed in Great Britain by Clays Ltd, St Ives Plc

MIX
Paper from
responsible sources
FSC® C018072

To Ailish and Eimear

Dear Reader,

The book you are holding came about in a rather different way to most others. It was funded directly by readers through a new website: Unbound.

Unbound is the creation of three writers. We started the company because we believed there had to be a better deal for both writers and readers. On the Unbound website, authors share the ideas for the books they want to write directly with readers. If enough of you support the book by pledging for it in advance, we produce a beautifully bound special subscribers' edition and distribute a regular edition and e-book wherever books are sold, in shops and online.

This new way of publishing is actually a very old idea (Samuel Johnson funded his dictionary this way). We're just using the internet to build each writer a network of patrons. Here, at the back of this book, you'll find the names of all the people who made it happen.

Publishing in this way means readers are no longer just passive consumers of the books they buy, and authors are free to write the books they really want. They get a much fairer return too – half the profits their books generate, rather than a tiny percentage of the cover price.

If you're not yet a subscriber, we hope that you'll want to join our publishing revolution and have your name listed in one of our books in the future. To get you started, here is a £5 discount on your first pledge. Just visit unbound.com, make your pledge and type CAVEMAN17 in the promo code box when you check out.

Thank you for your support,

Dan, Justin and John
Founders, Unbound

Special Acknowledgments

Nathan Finn
Emma Gillies
Lily Ledwith
Ray Nolan
Liz Nugent

Super Patrons

Paul Bond
Stephen Bond
John Bond
Michael & Anne Bradley
Cormac Bradley
Trish Byrne
Peter Cosgrove
E.M. Dillon
Martin Fanning
Mel Gallagher
Shona Greenwell
Nina Gustin
Adrian Harte
Rachel Killeen
Hilary Lennon
Barry Lyons
Ciara McCluskey
Alan McCormack
Paraic O'Donnell
Faith O'Grady
Peter O'Kelly
Richard Osman
Sinead Owens
Claire Owens
Joanne Kelly Owens
Kate Saunders
Darren Smith
Rikke Vader
Richard Walshe

Prologue

2005: Redmond and Nancy

As he wandered towards Jupiter, pint in hand, Redmond Cole had a word with himself. The pint was his fourth of the day. There would be wine with dinner and a long night to negotiate after that. Drinking to relax among strangers was one thing, but if he didn't take it easy, he'd be on his arse by nine o'clock. People often assumed that he must be able to hold his booze because of his unreasonable height – he wasn't far off six foot five – but people were wrong. His drink-holding abilities were entirely average. His hangovers, however, tended to be world class. All those dreadful mornings, hugging the toilet bowl and begging for the sweet release of death...

He walked past Venus, and saw that it was mostly older ladies – aunts, he guessed. Neptune was all couples with young kids. Likewise Mars. He slowed as he approached Saturn. The blonde in the pink dress was sitting there. He knew that because he'd heard her telling someone as he tried to pretend that he wasn't scoping her out at the bar. She had a boyfriend, of course, or a husband – a male companion, at least – but that was immaterial. Even if she'd been single and desperate, she wouldn't have given him a second look. Redmond didn't think he was ugly; he knew he didn't frighten small children in the streets. But he was nothing if not a realist. The height thing wasn't for everyone, for a start. And then there was the hair, or rather the space where it had formerly thrived. (It was a peculiar feeling, and not a pleasant one, to look in the mirror every day and see your forehead apparently growing.) The blonde in the pink dress was so far out of his league, she might as well have been a different species. Every man at her table, he saw, was smiling at her inanely, delighted with their luck at being seated across from such unfathomable hotness. All of the women were smiling at her too, but their eyes were wild, searching for flaws. The blonde's boyfriend/husband was sitting almost in her lap, and had his arm around her shoulders. It was part protective gesture, Redmond guessed, and part boast. Feeling another deep stab of the spiritual pain that attended all of his encounters with extreme female beauty, however remote, he picked up the pace and headed for Jupiter. All of the seats there were filled, except for his. It was obvious, even from afar, that none of the occupants knew each other. These were neither close friends nor relatives of the main players. They'd named the table after a gas giant but they might as well have called it 'Odds and Ends'.

He picked his way around to the empty space and got himself situated. The name card on his left said Simon Hanratty. Redmond offered his hand.

'Simon, I see? Redmond.'

'Hello.'

They shook. Simon was a little older than Redmond, maybe mid-thirties. He had bushy hair and appalling breath.

'So, bride or groom?'

'Gillian,' Simon said. 'We practise the law together. You?'

'I'm one of Donal's. I mean, I used to be. We were waiters in the same restaurant one summer. I haven't seen him for ages. I was kind of surprised to be invited, to tell you the truth.'

Oops. That was the fourth pint talking. He mentally kicked himself, hoping Simon wouldn't pick up on it.

'Oh? You think he's hard up for friends, is that it?'

'No! God, no. I didn't mean that. I meant, I'm flattered, that's all.'

Bloody lawyers. *Hard up for friends* was exactly what Redmond had thought. It was the only reason he'd come. Donal was a nice guy, but he was shy to the point of requiring professional help. Being a waiter had almost killed him. It didn't seem likely that he had acquired a large posse in recent years; it was amazing enough that he had acquired a wife. On the morning when the invitation arrived, Redmond distinctly heard the sound of a barrel being scraped and knew that he had to step up.

'Are you here on your own?' Simon asked.

'Yeah. I am, yeah. Probably a few singles at this table, eh? We're all expected to—'

'Oh, I'm not single.'

'Right.'

'Engaged, actually.'

'Congratulations.'

'My fiancée couldn't make it. She practises the law too.'

'You really like saying "practises the law", don't you?'

'*Excuse* me?'

Redmond's smile slid off his face. Okay. He had established that Simon wasn't blessed with an exceptional sense of humour. Good to know.

'Just a wee joke,' he ventured.

A long pause. A blank stare. Then: 'Hm.'

There was a lot of information packed into this single syllable. Redmond heard *You are not funny, I am a very important man*, and *Please minimise your interactions with me for the remainder of the meal*.

On Redmond's right, two women were chatting amiably. They'd been at it when he sat down and didn't sound like they would be stopping any time soon. He stared at the floral arrangement in the centre of the table and sipped on his pint. It was a relief when Simon joined in another conversation on his left; sitting in solitary silence was somehow less embarrassing than sitting in silence with someone else. After a couple of minutes had crawled by, he became aware that the conversation on his right was petering out. He half-turned, hoping to invite a greeting without looking desperate. It worked.

'So,' the nearest woman said, leaning forward a little to catch the corner of his eye. 'You're Misc. too?'

'I'm sorry?'

'This table. It's for all the guests who don't fit in anywhere else. Misc.'

'Oh! Right. I was thinking Odds and Ends myself.'

'What do you make of it? This business of naming tables at weddings?'

He shrugged. 'I was always comfy enough with numbers myself.'

'Me too. There's no Uranus, I noticed.'

'Correct. I bet they knocked some people off the invitation list because they didn't want to add that as a table.'

'Yeah. Gillian's very proper. I couldn't see her taking some elderly uncle aside and saying, "Are you lost? Head for Uranus."'

She was better looking than he'd thought when he spotted her outside the church earlier, Redmond realised with mounting delight. The short red hair and trouser suit combination had made her seem a bit androgynous from afar. But up close he saw that she was just the sort he usually fell for – out of his league, yes, but not comically so. She was tall, too. Very tall. He remembered making a mental note of it, just before being distracted by the blonde in the pink dress. His own height was unlikely to count against him, so. On the contrary, maybe she was one of those women who was desperate to find a partner she didn't have to bend down to kiss. Maybe, when it came to men, that was her overriding concern. Maybe she'd be willing to look past, say, a receding hairline.

'So, did—'

'You seem fairly normal and nice. Are you? Are you fairly normal and nice?'

He rubbed his chin, pretending to think about it. 'Hmm. Define "normal".'

She leaned closer. Whisper-in-his-ear close. She smelled like vanilla. He held his breath. She said, 'You just met that guy beside you, right? I saw you shake hands.'

'Yes.'

'I mean, he's not some good friend of yours that you haven't seen for years?'

'Total stranger.'

'Okay. Confession time. I'm supposed to be sitting where you are. You're supposed to be here. Girl-boy, girl-boy? I swapped the cards. I'm sorry. But I got talking to your man earlier and, Jesus Christ. I couldn't take a whole dinner's worth. I just couldn't.'

Redmond turned his head towards her. Their faces were only inches apart. He screwed his up in pain and spoke through barely parted lips. 'Did he say anything about "practising the law"?'

She slapped a hand over her mouth and sat back, snorting with laughter. 'Oh boy,' she said after a moment. 'I did the right thing. I definitely did the right thing.'

Redmond shook his head, pretended to be disgusted. 'You owe me, though. Big time. You'll have to ignore that woman on your right and keep me talking for the whole thing. Why should *I* suffer?'

'That's only fair.' She raised her glass. 'Deal.'

He reached for his pint and they clinked. 'Deal. Redmond, by the way.'

'I know. I saw it on your card when I was palming it.'

'Palming, eh? Very subtle.'

'This isn't my first wedding. And my name is Nancy.'

2006: Dooley and Julie

Julie Gallagher was in a bad mood when she boarded the train to Cork. She was on her way to visit her oldest friend, Rose, and she couldn't stand Rose. They'd been close in primary school, a little less close in secondary school, and not at all close in their university days. Since then, they'd dutifully visited each other in Dublin and Cork, finding less and less to talk about each time. But it wasn't just the lack of frequent contact that made the encounters increasingly awkward. Rose had changed. Or else Julie had, slowly becoming a better judge of character. Maybe Rose had always been boastful, self-centred and mildly racist. It just hadn't been obvious in primary school, where she had fewer opportunities to brag about her salary or drone endlessly about her landlord trouble or volunteer with a shrug that she thought Chinese people were 'shifty'. As she opened the bag of Maltesers she'd scored in the station, Julie made herself a promise. If Rose wanted to see her in Dublin, that was fine, just about. She'd hold her nose and get on with it. But this would be her last trip south.

The man sitting opposite looked up briefly as she crunched her first Malteser, then returned his gaze to the Stephen King he had propped up against the edge of the small table between them. She considered offering him one, then decided against it. What if he took it as a sign that she wanted someone to talk to the whole way? Too risky. She tried to make herself comfortable and let her thoughts wander where they may – to work, to her mother's dodgy ankle, to her need for a new kettle, to the well-dressed fiftysomething who'd whistled at her on Baggot Street and then followed half a pace behind issuing compliments and grinning inanely until she rounded on him and told him to fuck off.

Across the aisle, a middle-aged woman was sitting alone, staring emptily at the floor. There was something crumpled about her, Julie thought. It wasn't her clothes or her hair; it was more fundamental than that. She looked as if she was on her way to, or running away from, the most dreadful encounter of her life. Every so often, she would close her eyes and tilt her head back, her hands joined before her as if in prayer. Then she'd snap out of it, rub something – an elbow, a wrist, her forehead – and go back to staring. They'd been under way for almost an hour when the woman's phone rang. She made a sound like a tyre losing air and reached into her handbag.

'Tim,' she said flatly when she answered, eyes now closed again. Julie turned to look out of her window, trying not to appear nosy. But she snapped around again when the woman issued a tremendous sob and dropped her head onto her free hand. There were no follow-up sounds for what felt like a full minute. If you didn't know better, Julie thought, you might conclude that she had fallen asleep. Then a second sob, even more violent than the first, made her shake like a soaked kitten. The man with the book didn't seem to have been paying any attention but now he caught Julie's eye and tilted his head ever so subtly at their fellow passenger. Julie gave him a *Don't ask me* look.

'Okay,' the woman said then. 'Okay... Okay... Thanks. Thanks for letting me know. I'll talk to you tonight.'

She hung up and put her phone away. And then she began to cry in earnest, steadily and consistently. Further up the carriage, necks craned and heads appeared. Julie was conscious of a general murmuring but not of any specific words. The man opposite calmly put his book away and eased himself out of the seat. Without ever standing fully upright, he swung his arse across the aisle and squeezed into the one opposite. The crying woman was startled and looked at him as if she half-expected him to brandish a knife. He placed his hand on the back of hers, saying nothing. Julie held her breath.

'Are you okay?' he asked. An Australian accent, soft.

'Not really,' she replied.

'Anything I can do to help?'

'No.' She dabbed at her eyes with a tissue that Julie hadn't seen her produce. 'You'd laugh if I told you.'

'I promise you I wouldn't.'

She considered for a moment, then took a deep breath and plunged. 'My dog died.'

'No! That's terrible. Did you just get the news?'

'That was my husband. He was hit by a car this morning. I had to leave. I knew he'd be put down. And he was.' A pause. A frown. 'Not my husband – the dog.'

'What was his name?'

'Barney. He wasn't a purebred or anything. Tell you the truth, you had to look twice to make sure it was a dog. Ugly as sin.'

'Have you got a picture?'

'Yeah. Yeah, I have.' She got her phone out again and after a moment's swiping and tapping, handed it over.

The man nodded. 'That's the ugliest dog I've ever seen in my life,' he said, and the woman actually laughed.

'He was smelly too.'

'The full package.'

'He sure was.'

'We always had cats when I was a little lad. Back in Sydney? Must have had six or seven over the years. I was never really that bothered. Could take them or leave them. But then this stray showed up. My mum started feeding him and he just never left. Skinny thing, every colour a cat could be. Black, white, grey, orange. Like someone made him from spare parts. We called him Frankencat. He was kind of an arsehole, to be honest. But, I dunno, I just took to him? Couldn't tell you why. We had cats that were way nicer looking, cats that were more playful, cats that were *a lot* friendlier... I didn't give a damn. I loved that little bastard. One day, he just wasn't there any more. We never found out what happened. Maybe he was run over or got poisoned or something. Maybe he found some other family to mooch off. I cried for a week. So, yeah. I get it.'

Julie popped a Malteser into her mouth and realised that she already had several in there. She must have been unconsciously shoving them in as she hung on every word.

'I'll tell you a funny story about Barney,' the woman said, finally removing her hand from under his. It turned out to be not in the least bit funny, but telling it seemed to do her good. Julie stopped paying such close attention. A calm certainty had enveloped her. She didn't need to hear more. The woman with the dead dog wasn't going all the way to Cork. She got off at Thurles, giving the man a long hug and thanking him for his kindness. He returned to his original seat and put his nose back in the Stephen King. When the train was moving again, Julie said, 'Excuse me?'

He looked up. She had an excuse now to take him in properly. He was pale for an Australian, with a halo of fuzzy blonde curls. There was something of the dandelion about him. Grey eyes and high, fine cheekbones. Not gorgeous. But not bad.

'I saved you a Malteser,' she said. 'For your good deed.'

She slid the bag across the table. He smiled and took his reward. 'That's very nice of you,' he said, the Malteser now lodged in his cheek.

'I overheard,' she said. 'Obviously. Poor old Frankencat.'

'Oh, there was no Frankencat. I made him up. We never had cats. I'm allergic, actually. I had a goldfish for about a week before I fed it to death. I'm not from Sydney, either. I don't know why I said that bit.'

Julie nodded slowly. 'Kind, but sneaky too,' she said. 'Or maybe just a compulsive liar.'

'I'll take "kind but sneaky", thanks.'

'Are you on holiday or—'

'Yeah.'

'Touring around?'

'Been all over Europe, working my way west. This is the last stop. Back to Oz in a couple of weeks.'

'Will you be in Cork for long?'

'No idea. I'm keeping it loose.'

'I'm going for a couple of days. Visiting a friend. Let's have a drink while I'm there.'

He blinked at her. 'Are you asking me out on a date?'

'I'm asking you to go to a pub with me.'

'Like, on a date?'

'We'll see.'

'Wow. This has never happened to me before.'

'So, what do you say?'

'Are you joking? Have you looked in a mirror lately? I say yes.'

Julie ignored the compliment. She was used to them. 'Good.' She stuck out her hand. 'I'm Julie.'

He grasped it but didn't shake. His hand was warm and perfectly dry. 'Vincent. Dooley. Vincent Dooley. Everyone just calls me Dooley.'

2008: Leo and Deirdre

Colm, this one was called. You could argue that he had a kind face, Deirdre thought, trying to be kind herself. But the main thing he had going for him was the fact that he was number ten of ten. Another couple of minutes and she'd be done. She could traipse home via the chip shop and throw herself on the couch, content in the knowledge that she had tried.

'What would you say is your biggest fear?' Colm asked. His voice was high-pitched and nasal. Everything he said sounded like a piss-take.

'My biggest fear...' Deirdre said, casting her eyes to the pub ceiling and pretending to find the query fascinating. Speed dating, she had found, was even more like interviewing for a job than regular dating was. You didn't have a conversation – questions were thrown at you and you tried to come up with answers that made you sound impressive. If what you said had some truth to it, that was a nice bonus. But it wasn't priority number one. The real answer to this question, for example, was *My biggest fear is living and dying alone and unloved*. She sure as hell wasn't going to say that, even to Colm, who she found as attractive as a balloon with a face drawn on it.

'Centipedes,' she said. 'Or millipedes. Anything with too many legs.'

Colm's tongue made a brief appearance to moisten his lips. He leaned a little forward, causing Deirdre to lean a little back.

'My biggest fear is you not putting a tick on that card.'

She was tempted to mock-vomit or at least roll her eyes. But she didn't want to be cruel. She squeezed out a giggle.

'You've got a lovely laugh,' Colm said.

Deirdre squinted at him, all pretence at good humour evaporating in an instant. 'What's next? Are you going to say I'm "jolly"? Because I swear to God—'

'What? I don't—'

'Jolly! It's what people say when they're trying to be kind to someone who's…' She selected a term. 'Struggling with their weight.'

'No! Christ, no! You're not f… I wouldn't say you're—' He slumped. 'I just meant you have a nice laugh, that's all.'

To be fair, Deirdre thought, he did seem genuinely disturbed by her accusation. Feeling a little embarrassed, she dropped her eyes to consult the cheat sheet of fallback questions she'd culled from a website.

'What would be your dream holiday?' she asked, hoping to sound conciliatory.

'Easy,' Colm said, recovering. 'Disneyworld, Orlando, Florida.'

'Really?'

'Without a doubt. Big Disney fan. Always have been.'

'*Really?*' she said again, hoping he would realise that she'd meant it both times as an expression of disbelief, rather than interest. He did not. As he began to list his favourite Disney characters and what made them so 'magical', she was seized by an urge to get up and run away, regardless of how little time was left on the clock. She stayed put only through a massive effort of will, which was most sorely tested when Colm said, 'The fact that Goofy isn't traditionally cute is the very thing that *makes* him cute'.

And then it was over. The woman from the speed-dating company rang her little bell and began her wind-up spiel. Deirdre wasted no time. She said goodbye to Colm and, even as the hostess was still speaking, handed over the card on which she had ticked no names. She raced to the exit, certain she could feel curious stares boring into her back. It made her walk all the faster. When she reached the door she burst through it like someone escaping a burning building. To her horror, she heard – but mostly felt – an impact on the other side that was somewhere between a thump and a crunch. After freezing for a moment, she stepped gingerly outside where she was sure she would find an old lady bleeding from a massive head wound. Instead, she found a man of approximately her own age bent over and clutching his right hand with his left.

'*Shit!* Are you okay?'

'Yep,' he said. 'Just a bit… in agony.'

'Is it your hand?'

He gave her a long look. 'Yes.'

'Sorry, sorry, of course it's your bloody hand.'

'Bent my finger back. It'll be grand in a minute. I'm sure.'

'Sorry, I'm usually more careful. I was in a hurry to get out.'

'Well, I'm in a hurry to get in, so…'

She stepped aside and gestured to the doorway with a flourish. 'Sorry. Again.'

He gave her a nod and a quick smile. 'Wish me luck,' he said, and pointed to the poster in the pub window.

'Wait, are you here for the speed dating?'

'Yup.'

She winced on his behalf. 'You missed it.'

'What?'

He pivoted and gave the poster a better look. '8.30? Oh, for…' He rubbed his good hand over his face. 'I had it down for 9.30.'

'You didn't miss much,' Deirdre said. 'If that's any comfort.'

'You were in it? On it? Doing it, whatever?'

'Yeah. Wasn't a great success. Mind you, I suppose you'd have been looking for different qualities than me. Boobs and that.'

He nodded that this was so. 'I'm gutted I missed it. That's a lie. I'm relieved. Mostly. I've never been to one. Had you?'

'No. I only went so I could say I'd tried.'

'Yes! That's my attitude too. I don't expect it to work, I expect people to stop telling me I'm not making an effort.'

'Exactly.'

They nodded in concert.

'So, did you look up questions on the internet or did you wing it?'

'Bit of both. Anyone who got an internet question from me wasn't doing well.'

'Go on, then. Let's hear one.'

'We're going to do a speed date standing on the street, are we?'

He shrugged. 'I came all this way and I've probably got a broken finger for nothing. Might as well get my feet wet, at least.'

Deirdre chewed a nail and regarded him afresh. No heart-throb, but not all that hard to look at. Clean shaven, which she liked. Limp sandy hair, the sort you could do nothing with. Big blue eyes. A touch of the Luke Skywalkers about him, maybe. Just a touch, mind. His T-shirt said 'Wilco'. She assumed that was a band.

'God, my internet questions were all so rubb— Oh! This isn't mine but I thought it was pretty good. What is your biggest fear?'

He answered without hesitation. 'Never meeting anyone and spending my whole life alone.'

She waited for him to laugh it off, but he didn't. After a moment, the smallest suggestion of an embarrassed smile appeared. She stuck out her hand.

'My name is Deirdre,' she said.

He took her hand, winced a little, then shook it very gently. 'Leo,' he said.

2011

1

'Mammy! Lookit! Mammy, lookit! Mammy! Mam! Lookit! Mam! Mam! Mammy! Mam!'

Nancy Cole continued staring at the toaster. Its contents were about to pop. As soon as they did so, she would turn around and bear witness to whatever it was that had so excited her older son. Until that moment came, she wouldn't move a muscle.

'Mammy! Mammy!'

This was something she had only recently started doing – inventing little rules, lines that she wouldn't cross. One day she had found herself vowing that she wouldn't swallow her latest mouthful of tea until her younger son stopped banging his xylophone with her good spatula. She wound up drooling down her chin and almost choked to death while attempting to stifle a sneeze, but she held out. You didn't have to be a trained professional, she knew, to see what was going on here. These were attempts to exert some small measure of control. A darker personality might have resorted to self-harm; Nancy stared at her toaster.

'Maaaammmmyyyy!'

The toast popped. As ever, both slices cleared the device entirely and flopped on the counter-top like landed fish. Free at last, Nancy spun around. She immediately regretted not having done so sooner. Aidan, it seemed, had been painting the wall behind him with Weetabix.

'No!' she cried, grabbing a cloth and dashing across the lino. 'No, no, no! Anything but Weetabix! That stuff dries like conc—'

The words died in her throat in the moment when her bare left foot slipped on a discarded bib and rammed with some speed into the table leg. She lost her balance somewhat but not enough to bring her crashing to the floor. That she wound up there anyway was due to the fact that her knees buckled (and her stomach flipped and her eyes bulged) as a bolt of bright white pain shot up from her toes to the crown of her head and back again.

'Mammy falled,' Aidan noted, in the flat tone of a newsreader reporting a nil-all draw.

A couple of seconds went by before Nancy's brain diverted enough energy to her limbs to enable her to move. She tucked her legs underneath her body, grabbed the edge of the table for support, and hauled herself upright. Almost as soon as she was vertical, Luke picked up his Fireman Sam plate and flung it at her face, grunting like an Olympian unleashing a discus. It was made of thin plastic, but it certainly didn't feel that way when it connected with the bridge of her nose.

'No!' she said, rubbing this fresh injury. 'Please, honey! No throwing plates! No throwing anything, in fact.'

Luke's head dipped a little. He wasn't into the whole language thing yet, but knew a rebuke when he heard one. Nancy hobbled over to the wall and got to work on the Weetabix.

'I think we've talked about this before, Aidan, haven't we? Sweetie? About the Weetabix on the wall?'

The boy looked away. 'Nyuh,' he said.

For a three-year-old, Nancy mused, he was quite the politician. She didn't have the strength to press him on the issue. Her foot hurt. Her nose hurt. She was so tired she could feel it in her hair.

'Exactly,' she said and went back to cleaning the wall. 'Nyuh.'

Redmond was having a shower. He had finished washing and was standing perfectly still, his eyes closed, his arms folded. The shower nozzle was as high as it would go on its rail and still it pointed at his sternum. To wet his head, he was obliged to squat like a sumo wrestler. The water was not merely hot – it was just shy of scalding. This was a matter of policy. It wasn't a proper shower, in Redmond's book, if it didn't hurt a little.

'My key strength, Bill,' he said, 'is my tenaciousness... my ten... acious... nicity... tenacity. My key strength, Bill, is my tenacity.'

He frowned. Tenacity? He was sure that was right, but it didn't *sound* right.

'So often in work, as in life, it's tempting to say, "Okay, I give up. This is just too hard." But I always stick at it. From the day I started working here, my motto has always been…'

He frowned harder still and shook his head. This was exactly the sort of slip-up he had to avoid – launching into a sentence without having a clear plan for where it was going. He tried again.

'I always stick at it. I grab on and I won't let go, no matter what.'

An image came to mind: a small dog, grimly humping its master's leg and resisting all efforts to dislodge it. This, he knew at once, was the end of the 'grabbing on' analogy. If he used it in front of Bill now, he would picture the dog and perhaps, for the first time ever, he would laugh in the Big Man's presence. A bubble of anxiety swelled in his abdomen. Why hadn't he been more methodical about this? He'd known the date and time of this meeting – this interview – for over a week. He could have prepared potential answers properly, on paper, maybe even role-played the thing with Nancy. Instead, he had told himself that it was good to keep it loose and fluid, to have some ideas, but not to tie himself down to any specific forms of words. And now look. The interview was mere hours away and he was standing in the shower trying desperately to think of anything, anything at all but a dog humping a leg.

Five minutes later, he had dried himself off and dressed in the marginally nicer of his two suits. There had been a long period when he ritually examined his hairline every morning, assessing the damage and adjusting his prognosis. But those days were gone. The rot had stopped. He was one of those semi-fortunate men, it seemed, who would be forever balding without ever actually going bald. Halfway down the stairs, he paused and patted his pockets. No phone. He turned and stepped back, not to the master bedroom or to the boys', but to the smallest one, across the hall. The box room, Nancy called it. Redmond went along with that, but privately he knew it as the Game Room. The games were of the video variety and all told, between discs, cartridges and downloads, he had somewhere north of 700 of them. They filled every inch of the limited shelf space and still they tottered in piles on the floor, the desk, the windowsill. He had his fair share of hardware too: a SNES, a Wii, a PlayStation 3, a DS, an Xbox 360 and a *killer* PC.

This last was his darling, his love, his sweet, sweet baby. He had built it himself from parts and was sometimes frightened by how much it meant to him. These machines were useless, of course, without displays, and Redmond had three, all crammed side by side on the desk that just about fitted between the walls: the PC was hooked up to a 24" monitor; the PS3 and the Xbox sat beneath a 27" TV; the SNES and the Wii had to make do with an old portable CRT that had a dodgy speaker and was prone to suddenly turning everything green. Redmond never felt even the slightest twinge of embarrassment about his games and the equipment on which he played them. But he had to admit that, given the choice, he wouldn't like anyone from work to see any of his figurines or posters. The latter tended towards the garish and the former could easily be confused for a child's action figures – which they most certainly were *not*. (They were superbly crafted memorabilia that married exquisite attention to detail with a rich sense of gaming heritage.) Most people, he felt sure, would understand that a person who liked video games was liable to have a lot of them – but they might look askance at, say, his 12" Master Chief with 18 points of articulation.

His phone was on the desk between his keyboard and the fifth gaming mouse he'd bought in the last 12 months. He snatched it up, took a moment to straighten his framed poster of *Metal Gear Solid 4: Guns of the Patriots*, and left.

When Redmond stepped into the kitchen he was pleased to see that Luke immediately gave him a huge grin and the frantic windmilling of one arm that was his version of a wave. He responded in kind and then, as he cleared the doorway, noticed that there was a crisis afoot. Crises were not rare, of course, but this one was happening in silence and that, somehow, seemed to indicate that it was serious.

'What's wrong?' he asked, jockeying to get a better look at what was going on. Nancy was on the floor, wrestling with Aidan. It wasn't immediately clear if she was trying to hold him down or haul him up. 'Nancy?'

After a moment, she got him where she apparently wanted him, on his back, splayed across her lap. She pulled his jaw open and poked a few fingers in there. Aidan squealed in horror.

'Something in his mouth,' she said.

'What? What is it?'

No reply. More poking. Aidan, Redmond now realised, wasn't squealing in horror – he was laughing. His teeth closed down on his mother's fingers but she didn't give up. And then, at last, she held her prize aloft. It was a a triple-A battery.

Redmond snorted. 'A battery! Dude! If you're short on energy, have a banana.'

Nancy gently pushed Aidan off her lap. He sprang to his feet and ran off down the hall, laughing. She got to her feet and peered at her husband.

'He could have choked. He could have choked to *death*.'

'It was a pretty good joke, though.'

'Oh no it wasn't.'

'Oh yes it was.'

'Oh no it— This is panto, Redmond. We're doing *panto*.'

'Oh no we aren't.'

He thought that was funny too, but it didn't earn him a smile either. Not many of his lines had, of late. He'd never kidded himself that Nancy found him hilarious, but she usually had the energy to fake it. Should he say something, he wondered? She wasn't herself these days and he was beginning to get a little worried. Before he could decide one way or the other, Aidan returned to the kitchen at full speed, announcing at extraordinary volume that he was a helicopter. Redmond swept him up and waved him through the air, making the appropriate noises, before crash-landing him back into his chair.

'What do you think, boys?' he asked. 'Do you like the suit? Do I look promotable? I tell you what, Luke – if Daddy lands this job, you might get that new nappy you've been harping on about.' He turned to his eldest. 'And you, my friend – well, I'll buy you all the batteries you can eat.'

'*Redmond.*'

He held his hands up in apology. 'Scratch that. Batteries are off the menu.'

'Sit down,' she said. 'I have more toast on here.'

'You know what, don't worry about breakfast for me today.'

'What? Why? It'll only take a minute. You've got loads of time.'

'Actually, I was thinking I might try that new café by the butchers. I need a few minutes of peace and quiet. Get my head straight for the interview.'

Her face seemed to run through several different expressions in under a second. 'Peace and quiet? Oh, yeah. I think I've heard of that.'

He sensed trouble. 'Is it okay with you? If I split?'

She shrugged. 'Yeah.'

'I just… Is everything all right?'

'With what?'

'With you.'

'Why wouldn't it be?'

'That's what I'm asking.'

She smiled but only briefly and not at all convincingly. 'I'm fine.'

A long pause. 'Okay.'

'Off you go, then. Boys, say bye-bye to Daddy.'

Aidan and Luke made several loud noises each. Redmond skipped across and bent to kiss each of them on the forehead, wincing a little at the strain on his back. 'See you later. Be good for Mammy.'

He stepped back to Nancy and kissed her too, then stood there waiting for a second. She didn't take the hint. Again: worrying.

'You're not going to wish me good luck in my interview?'

'Oh! I forgot. Sorry, sorry. Good luck. You'll be great.'

'I hope so. I've never got the impression that I'm Bill's favourite.'

'You'll be great,' she repeated flatly.

He hesitated. Should he make a renewed effort to weasel it out of her? No. He'd asked and she said she was fine. What else was a guy supposed to do?

Redmond had been gone for no more than five minutes when Nancy realised that this was bin day and she'd forgotten to tell him to put them out (he never remembered on his own). Gritting her teeth against this minor annoyance, she flounced out through the back door and did the necessary herself. It was recycling week, which was some consolation – those bins were always lighter. The sky was only lightly clouded and it wasn't cold. For Dublin in June, that counted as a beautiful day. On her way down the front path for the second time (Compostable), Nancy caught the eye of the tubby woman who'd moved into the eyesore across the street a few months back – Deirdre, was it? Denise? She was on her way to work and didn't look at all thrilled about it. Not for the first time, Nancy entertained a terrifying notion – what if Deirdre/Denise had no problem with the way her new house looked? Its previous owners had painted it a shade of delicate pink that might have worked in the midst of other pastels on a beautiful coastal road but was completely ludicrous in a suburban cul-de-sac. Worse, they had covered the facade with every architectural adornment imaginable, with no regard for style, period or simple common sense. It looked like the sort of house a six-year-old girl would design if you left her alone with a book on architectural history and an unlimited supply of sugar. Nancy had always assumed that the place would undergo a major makeover if and when someone was desperate enough to buy it. So far, though, no joy. Maybe it was a money thing. She'd seen the husband mooching about during the day and got the impression he was out of work.

She nodded hello at Deirdre/Denise, deposited the bin at the kerb, and turned back towards the house. Just then another neighbour emerged. This time it was Julie from next door. As ever, she was dressed like one of those women in commercials who run major corporations and don't have time for headaches.

'Good morning,' Julie called across the low wall that divided their homes.

Nancy pulled her tatty old dressing gown a little tighter around her waist. She had long since stopped being self-conscious about her height but encounters with Julie always made her stoop a little. They also made her wonder if her left ear stuck out, if her eyes were the same size, and if the hair that she had spent several years growing out, having decided it was a beautiful flaming red that deserved to be celebrated, was in fact plain old ginger after all.

'Hiya.'

'Hi Nancy, how are you?'

'Couple of broken toes and a broken nose so far. But sure it's only eight o'clock. Plenty of time yet for a spinal injury or maybe a nice skull fracture.'

Julie stared, still smiling, but clearly lost.

'I'm grand,' Nancy clarified. 'How's Nicola? Is she over that bad dose?'

'Nope. Poor wee thing. Look at the cut of her.' She waved up at the first floor. Nancy saw that Julie's husband was standing by the bedroom window with Nicola in his arms. Even at this distance, it was obvious that the little girl was still heavy-eyed and encrusted with mucus, as she had been for a week or more. Nancy waved up at her dad and breathed the word 'Dooley'. She had trouble saying it out loud, no matter how many times she was instructed to do so. It was ridiculous. The man's name was Vincent. By contrast, she said 'Julie Dooley' as much as possible, in her head at least. It felt like a tiny consolation prize.

They'd been neighbours for a couple of years now, not close but always on good terms. There had never been so much as a 'Please turn the music down' from either side. Nancy didn't know for sure but she suspected that the Dooleys were in the same boat as herself and Redmond, property-wise: they'd bought into this little early-nineties development in Artane thinking it would suit quite nicely as a foot on the ladder, then watched in deep shock as the economy imploded, leaving them with no chance of moving on any time soon.

'You'd want to hear her in the middle of the night,' Julie said. 'She sounds like she's gargling mud, God love her. Anyway – I'm late. Gotta run.'

'Me too,' Nancy said. 'I left Ronnie and Reggie on their own. Say hi to the real world for me.' In her head, it had been a cheerful farewell, the sort of line that barely registers on the recipient. In reality, it had come out sad and defeated and... small. She forced a smile and went inside again.

Half an hour later, Nancy was attempting to have a shower. The boys were in the bathroom with her, of course. She had already issued nonspecific warnings to both of them – just vague entreaties to be good and careful and stationary. Now, as she poked her head out from behind the curtain for the twentieth time, she saw that it was time to get specific. Aidan was sitting on the floor, with a bag of cotton balls, and had apparently popped a few into his mouth; his cheeks had gone hamsterish. Luke was on his knees by the toilet, looking for all the world like a tiny drunk who was about to lose his post-pub kebab. All the while looking her right in the eye, he dipped a finger into the water and sucked it.

'Luke! What have I told you about drinking from the toilet? Aidan, gimme. Please. Gimme. Give that to Mammy...'

She leaned out to grab the bag of cotton balls and immediately felt the bath mat slip a little underneath her. There was just enough time for her to lament the fact that not slipping was the thing's only responsibility in life before it gave way completely and shot up the side of the bath. She pitched forward like someone diving into a swimming pool, taking with her not just the shower curtain but the pole from which it hung. It was some consolation, she supposed, that she missed punching Aidan in the face as she landed. There was little else to celebrate. She'd bashed her knees against the edge of the bath and her left wrist, which had taken most of the impact, hurt like hell. Although they hadn't suffered fresh violence, her toes seemed to be throbbing with renewed enthusiasm too. Then there was the whole dignity thing. Half-covered by wet shower curtain, arse in the air, it was hard to feel like a big success. For a moment, she couldn't move. The problem wasn't physical. She simply felt exhausted, in the literal sense – not merely tired but utterly depleted. Dragging her legs out of the bath and and getting to her feet seemed like an impossible task. You might as well ask her to be at the source of the Amazon by lunchtime. But matters were taken out of her hands. As she lay there, scarcely able to pant, she heard a sound that she recognised as Aidan beginning the process of choking to death on a cotton ball. Sighing deeply, she crawled forward to save his life again.

Next door, Dooley sat in the front room with Nicola in the crook of his arm. He was still in his boxer shorts and didn't expect to get dressed any time soon. Nicola was asleep – or at least she was more asleep than she had been since 4.30 that morning. She still had one eye half open and every couple of minutes her entire body was shaken by a wracking, wet cough. Both nostrils dripped incessantly. In the first day or two of her illness, he'd been obsessive about wiping her nose and top lip when they needed it, which was constantly. But he soon thought better of the practice. Even though the tissues he used claimed to be 'sensitive' and 'gentle', he began to feel that he wasn't so much tidying his daughter up as flaying her alive. Now he intervened only when the amount of snot on her face threatened to render her unrecognisable.

He wasn't feeling great himself. When his shushing and cooing had finally borne results, he'd lowered himself on to the sofa with little attention to his own comfort. His shorts had ridden up alarmingly, but he'd been so relieved by the prospect of peace that he had ignored the issue. Now, 20 minutes later, he was experiencing a sensation that could only be described as testicular strangulation. Three times he tried to fix the problem by gently raising his hips and tugging desperately amidships, but to no avail.

1

He was just beginning to worry that he might be doing himself real and lasting damage when Nicola's eyes suddenly flew open. She stared up with the sort of expression that he himself might have reserved for, say, the appearance of a live grenade, and drew breath to voice her displeasure. Dooley took immediate action. He sat her upright, leaned closer and smiled as broadly as he could, given the fact that his balls were several inches away from their natural habitat. It made no difference. She screamed for all she was worth and then immediately segued into a deep, sorrowful sob.

'Oh, mate,' he said. 'Ah, now. Shushhh. Shushhh.' On the bright side, the fact that she had moved from partially to fully awake meant that he could at least stand up. He did so, simultaneously moving the warm, sticky bundle to his shoulder in a well-practised move that was part lift, part swing. The situation in his shorts immediately resolved itself, and he moaned with sweet relief.

'Let's go for a little walk, what do you say? Yeah? Would that be nice, Nicola? A little walk? Okay, then. Off we go.'

There wasn't a lot of scope for pacing in the Dooleys' front room but he made the best of it. It made no difference. If anything, Nicola's cries grew ever more raucous. After a mere five minutes, he gave up and returned to the sofa, this time taking special care with his intimate arrangements. With a heavy sigh, he picked up the remote control and stabbed at it with his thumb.

'Oooh, look, Nicola, look what Daddy found. Jeremy Kyle!'

Dooley hated all of the morning talk shows and their ringmasters, but he reserved a special dark place in his heart for Jeremy Kyle, who struck him as being representative of everything that was wrong not just with television but with humanity in general. A host, but also a parasite.

'What is it today, do you think? Let's see here…'

He watched in silence – his own, at least – for a few minutes until all the major players in the drama had spoken up for themselves.

'Okay,' he said then. 'This woman? With the scary eyebrows? Her name is Carol and she's really, really mad. One day she… Oh, wait, this is Anthony, this is her boyfriend. Well, he *was* her boyfriend. They'd been together for five years and everything was going really well. They had four kids and they were thinking of getting married. But one day Carol came home and found Anthony going to town on her grandmother. Not her mother, mark you, her *grandmother*. I know! I was shocked too. The woman's only 50-odd, but still. That's her there on the end. Looks a bit like Gene Hackman. Carol wasn't all that stoked, as you can imagine.'

Nicola's breathing was still heavy and ragged but the screaming had stopped. Dooley lowered his voice and continued.

'I know it's hard to credit – I mean, look at him – but Carol says she still loves Anthony. She forgives him and she wants them to go back to normal. Did I mention that she's pregnant again? Yeah, she's pregnant again. Anthony says it's probably not even his – he reckons she was still having a go on her old boyfriend, Carl. And anyway, even if it is his, he's not interested because – get this – he's in love with the granny. Head over heels. What's that? Does she love him back? It's hard to know. She said she does but she kind of laughed when she said it. Between you and me, Nicola, I think she's just delighted to be on TV. Put it like this – I don't think he'll be the one picking her nursing home.'

He looked down and saw that she had settled considerably. As her eyelids drooped, he resumed his commentary. Five minutes later, she was asleep. Not daring to move in case he disturbed her, he let his head fall back and stared at the ceiling.

In undignified moments like these, Dooley often imagined what would happen if someone from his pre-parenthood days walked through the door, someone from back home or just an Irish friend he hadn't seen in ages. How would he appear to them, he wondered? Would they see a devoted father who deserved credit for slipping into the role of house husband, having cheerfully accepted that his wife had vastly superior earning power? Or would they point and laugh at this pathetic perversion of manhood, slumped in his underwear before Jeremy frigging Kyle? Not that he had any serious doubts himself, of course. He was quite comfortable with his choice. He loved looking after his daughter and any imaginary figure who thought him less of a man for doing so could go fuck himself. Still, though. It was curious. If he was all that proud of himself, why did these scenarios occur to him in the first place? Worse, why did they make him feel anxious? It was conditioning, he supposed. The weight of human history and whatnot. He could tell himself that this was all perfectly fine, and he could genuinely mean it, but there was always going to be some ancient part of his brain squirming in horror because he was staying by the fire while his wife went out to hunt. It was just a matter of shouting it down, he supposed. There was nothing else for it.

So that was what he did. He sat there, staring at the ceiling, holding his little girl, shouting himself down.

Meat is Murder was not Leo Dunlop's favourite album. It wasn't even his favourite Smiths album (that honour went to *The Queen is Dead* – of course). But in the half an hour since he'd discovered it missing, it had assumed near-total control of his mind. He could hear every boom and splash, every trill and chirp. He could see every inch of the cover – not just the general layout, but the details of his own specific copy (it had a badly bent lower-left corner and some unknown idiot had tested a pen on the back, just to the left of the barcode). If someone had burst in and asked him his name, he might well have mumbled 'Steven Patrick Morrissey'.

It was here somewhere, that was the really annoying thing. If there was a chance that he had simply lent it to someone, he would have been able to let the subject drop and get on with his life, such as it was. But he hadn't let anyone borrow a record since 2009. The last one to be wrested from his grip was *The Soft Parade*. He'd given it to Garrett Knowles, a former colleague who was forever claiming that, any day now, he was going to 'get into vinyl'. Leo had never been all that taken with Garrett but when the record came back missing its inner sleeve and sporting two major scratches – two! – he had only just resisted the urge to do violence. So, no: *Meat is Murder* was properly missing. But it couldn't have gone far. As he surveyed, yet again, the packed shelves on either side of his front-room fireplace, Leo found this brute fact to be of little comfort. The problem with a misfile – and that, surely, was what he was dealing with here – was that you had no idea where to look. If the record wasn't where it was supposed to be, it could be anywhere. He had started out by searching on either side of the Smiths section and when that failed to produce a result, above and below it too. No joy. Thereafter, it was anybody's guess. For want of a better strategy, he'd spent 30 minutes doing a succession of quick passes, tilting his head to the right as he scanned his entire collection, Abba to The xx. He had to wobble on a stool from the kitchen to get a good look at the top shelves and more than once had imagined slipping and cracking his head open on the stone mantelpiece below. It wouldn't be a dignified death. He could just imagine what Deirdre would say to his corpse.

He had no option now, it seemed, but to drop the quick passes routine and do a fingertip search. It would take time – potentially, lots of it. According to the spreadsheet he'd been forced to employ to keep track, he owned 1867 records. This was more than could comfortably fit in the available shelf space. Searching through 1800 records was bad; searching through 1800 records that were jammed together like playing cards in a pack was much worse. The upshot was that his plan for the afternoon ahead lay in ribbons. Admittedly, that plan had been to listen to records, stare into space and maybe sleep for an hour or two – same as every other day, an unhelpful voice in his head observed – but that wasn't the point.

He scratched his belly through his Joy Division T-shirt and climbed back up onto the kitchen stool. This was bullshit, he reminded himself yet again. What was wrong with him? Why couldn't he just say, *Oh well, I can't put my hands on it right now, but it'll turn up?* Ten minutes later, the combination of craning his neck, peeling sleeves apart and general irritation had conspired to give him a dull, muddy headache. He considered quitting – he even climbed down from the stool for a moment – but he just couldn't. No album left behind, he told himself, and settled in for the long road ahead. He was halfway through the Fs and ready to put his fist through the wall when his mobile rang. It was Deirdre.

'Hiya.'

'Hey.' Her voice sounded thin and brittle. He waited. But apparently 'Hey' was all she had called to say.

'So,' he said by way of a prompt. 'How's it going?'

'Ehhh… It's not going great.'

'No? Why? What happened?'

'Ah, just… Y'know… I had one of those mornings. Baby talk.'

'Louise?'

'Louise.'

'Banging on.'

'I'm not complaining. Honestly. I'm not.'

She felt the need to do this every time, he had noticed – to establish at the outset that her unhappiness was decent and honest and not in any way the product of a defective soul.

'I know you're not, love.'

'And God knows, if the day comes—'

'When the day comes.'

'If the day comes and it's my turn, I'm sure I'll be every bit as annoying. Not annoying! I mean…'

'I know what you mean.'

'I mean, excited.'

'Excited, yeah. Of course you will. So will I. What was it this time? A scan?'

'Nah. Equipment. They've been stocking up.'

'Bottles and that.'

'The whole bit. Bottles, steriliser, car seat, bath… She must have named 20 things and we got the full rundown on each and every one of them. What she wanted, what she definitely didn't want, all the places she tried, price comparisons, the conversations she had with the shop staff… Everything. She was at it all morning. Jadwiga had all these questions, comments. I just sat there with this stupid pretend smile stuck on me gob. Felt like I was going to burst into tears at any minute. I still do.'

Jadwiga was the Polish girl who shared a large office – it was really more of a corridor, Leo recalled from his one visit – with Deirdre and Louise. The very mention of her name caused him to twitch. There was more than a hint of the Scarlett Johanssons about her. He shoved her image out of his mind and gave voice to the first thought that replaced it.

'Did you ever think maybe it would be better for you if you joined in?'

'Sorry?'

Oops. Deirdre was porcelain these days. Speaking in haste had been a mistake. But there was no backing away now.

'Maybe if you got involved, asked a few questions. Made a few comments of your own. It might, I don't know…'

'What?'

'Take some of the pressure out of the situation. For you, I mean.'

'How?'

'All I'm saying is it can't do you any good, when Louise starts going on about her baby, if you just sit there pretend-smiling. Driving yourself crazy. Maybe if you chipped in a bit, you'd feel less… intense.'

In the silence that followed, he dared to hope that he'd got through to her; that she would see how she couldn't continue to wig out every couple of days because a woman at her job was pregnant. But when she spoke again, he could tell that she was doing so through her teeth.

'What exactly do you think I should say, Leo? Where exactly do you think I should "chip in"? Because, I don't know if you've noticed, but I don't have a lot of experience with buying baby gear and cooing over scans and picking out names. It's not really in my wheelhouse.'

'I'm sorry,' he said quickly. 'Let's just forget I ever said it. Look, do your best to get through the day. We'll have a nice cuddly night. Get a Chinese in. Watch something stupid on the telly.'

'Cuddly night' was a phrase of Deirdre's invention. She knew that he wasn't crazy about it, to say the least. He hoped that using it would be seen as an olive branch.

'You know I had a bad week last week. Fucking *gained* a pound. And anyway, we can't afford deliveries at this time of the month. So no Chinese.' Without drawing fresh breath, she added, 'How's the job search going today?'

Now it was Leo's turn to grit his teeth. 'Nothing new to report today.'

'No?'

'No.'

'Okay.'

There was a long pause. For some time now, they had been doing little fly-bys on the subject of his ongoing failure to find work. Perhaps this would be the moment when they finally had a Proper Conversation about it. He braced himself. Would he be able to lie convincingly? Or would he roll over and admit the dreadful truth – that he had basically given up and rarely bothered checking the job sites any more?

'I'll see you later, then,' she said.

Leo resisted the urge to literally sigh with relief. 'See you later. I love you.'

'I love you too.'

They hung up.

Redmond regularly had days when he achieved next to nothing at work and, all things considered, might as well have stayed at home. Sometimes they were days that he accidentally frittered away, chiefly by amusing himself on the internet. Sometimes they were days that he deliberately marked out in advance as occasions when he might get away with skiving off. Sometimes they were days when he was simply paralysed by a foggy sense of despair – *this* was what he was doing with his life? Selling insurance? The fucking joke job? What happened to becoming an astronaut? Today had provided him with a fourth category: days in which he fully intended to work but found that he simply couldn't. It was the interview, of course. As soon as he took a seat at his desk, he was overcome by a sense of dread that robbed him not only of motivation but, apparently, basic motor functions; it took him three attempts to type his password correctly, and his password was PASSWORD. The photograph by his monitor wasn't helping. It was the only known picture in which Luke and Aidan were together, smiling, and free of disgusting substances (there were hundreds that scored two out of three). All morning long, he tried to avoid looking at it. Each time he accidentally glanced in its direction, he imagined himself telling them that he had made a balls of his interview and, regrettably, had failed to win promotion. The fact that in real life they wouldn't understand a word didn't seem to enter into it; the fantasy was appallingly vivid. His quivering voice, their sad little faces... *It's all right, Daddy. We can start eating every other day.*

By the time his slot rolled around, he had worked himself up into something that he hadn't previously thought possible – a frenzy of inactivity. He was drying his palms on an ancient napkin for perhaps the thirtieth time when he saw Declan Dinkins slipping towards him. Stealthy movement was Declan's big thing. Redmond had heard him referred to as 'the ghost', 'the ninja' and – his own personal favourite – 'the shadow'. Sooner or later, everyone at the Blanchardstown HQ of First Celtic Insurance found themselves clearing the ground and shrieking because they'd turned around to find him standing six inches away, smiling his watery little smile. There was nothing malicious about him, but the word 'creepy' had been known to get an occasional airing. Redmond thought that unkind.

'Here you go,' Declan said. 'I told you I'd bring it back. Didn't I tell you I'd bring it back?'

He threw a USB stick onto the desk.

'I hope there's no porn on it,' Redmond said. 'Because last time, I could tell that one of those midgets wasn't into it and, frankly, I found it upsetting.'

Declan glanced around. 'Jesus, don't even joke. Did you hear about Philip?'

'Which one?'

'Baldy Philip.'

'They're both kind of baldy.'

'*Hughes.*'

'Right. No, I didn't hear. What? Porn?'

Declan leaned in, which was hardly necessary. He was something of a short-arse and they were already practically eye to eye. 'Hot water. Very hot water.'

'How can there be hot water, never mind varying degrees of hot water? I thought you were supposed to get chucked out straight away? Do not pass Go?'

'Yeah, well. Philip's not just anyone, is he? He's Bill's BFF. I heard they were related, actually.'

'No way.'

'Not properly – Bill's wife's cousin is Philip's mother's sister-in-law's auntie, some shite like that. Speaking of Bill – your interview's today, isn't?'

Redmond consulted the clock on his monitor. 'Ten minutes.'

Declan bit his lower lip and nodded. 'None of my business and all… But I just don't get it. I don't get why you would possibly want that job. You know what a pain in the hoop it's going to be. Late nights, weekends…' His voice dropped to a whisper. 'And working for the Big Man directly? He's a fucking cold sore. He'll grind you into the carpet and he'll laugh while he's doing it. Margaret has her moments, God knows, but no one wants her dead. You've heard Bill's team in the pub. Some of them have got pretty advanced plans. Body disposal and whatnot. I mean – they've *really thought about it.*'

'I know he's not all that—'

'And for what? Three or four extra grand?'

Redmond sniffed. 'Two.'

'Two grand!'

'Keep your voice down, for fuck's sake. I'm not supposed to even know that. Susan told me.'

'Redmond, I'm starting to worry about your mental health. Two grand, fuck me…'

'All right, you've said your—'

'It's not as if—'

'Declan. Zip it. You don't understand. You're not even married yet.' He sat forward and gestured at the picture of his boys.

'It's different when there are kids involved. Nancy does her part and I do mine. That's the deal. Smiling at the likes of Bill and telling them you'd be delighted to work an occasional weekend is something you just have to suck down. There's bacon to be brought home.'

Declan exhaled with force. 'I didn't like that "yet" in there.'

'Sorry?'

'You said I'm not married *yet*. Don't go running away with the idea that it's inevitable.'

'It is. Three years? Pushing 30? You're screwed. Then you'll see what's required of a man.' He squirmed. It had come out like something from a 1950s commercial for cigarettes.

'We'll see about that. Anyway – I'm sorry, I didn't mean to, y'know...'

'Don't worry about it.'

'Good luck with it. Don't forget to picture him naked.'

'Jesus.'

Declan nodded and moved soundlessly away, as if on castors. Despite his every intention, Redmond suddenly pictured Bill in the nip and shuddered from head to toe.

Deirdre Dunlop had seen at least one movie and read more than a few books in which the boss's assistant wound up on all fours in his office. It had never been her cup of tea, really, no matter who she envisaged in the role of boss. Not even Michael Fassbender himself could make the idea seem particularly erotic. Still, she'd always prided herself on being the live-and-let-live type, and wished nothing but the best to anyone who gave it a whirl. Now, shuffling slowly across Mr Fallon's floor, she was beginning to loathe the entire concept and to think less – a lot less – of anyone who fancied it a good idea.

'Thanks again for this,' Mr Fallon wheezed. It was the third time he had thanked her.

'Don't mention it,' Deirdre said, also for the third time.

'I could kick myself. I'm such an eejit.' She stole a glance at him. He was on his hands and knees too, on the other side of the desk. They were looking for his wedding ring, which was missing and presumed lost in the ludicrous depths of his shag-pile carpet. Like herself, Mr Fallon had never been thin – she sometimes wondered if that was why she liked him – but he had swelled alarmingly of late and, finding the ring uncomfortable, had taken to leaving it on his desk during office hours. Its subsequent disappearance had a whiff of inevitability about it, in Deirdre's opinion, but Mr Fallon was shocked to his core and hadn't been at all comforted when she pointed out the obvious – that the thing couldn't have gone very far and it was only a matter of time before they found it. He claimed to have already spent half an hour looking before he called her in to help. What if the ring had embedded itself into someone's shoe? It could be anywhere by now. Mrs Fallon would have a fit, not least because she'd been badgering him to get some exercise every day for the past six months. Deirdre had gently explained that for one thing, it was a wedding ring, not a drawing pin; it couldn't 'embed' itself in a shoe or anywhere else, and for another, no one had been in his office all morning.

'That's three paper clips I've found,' Mr Fallon said. 'And two five-cent coins. I really think if it was here, I would have found it by now. It's gone. Gone forever.'

'Found it.'

'No!'

'Yes.'

'Really?'

She held the ring aloft between thumb and index finger. Her boss's face was overrun by a smile as he began the long and difficult process of getting to his feet (after a few seconds, Deirdre found it kindest to look elsewhere).

'You wonderful woman,' he said. 'I'm going to double your salary.'

She stood and handed it over. For a moment, she allowed herself to hope that this might turn into a genuine discussion of her remuneration which was, in fact, pretty miserable. But no.

'I looked there,' he said, as he jammed the ring back onto the plump sausage of his finger. 'I looked *right there*.'

'I don't know what to tell you.'

'Well, thanks. Seriously. Thanks. I know it's not exactly part of your job description, this. You have enough to be doing out there.'

Deirdre glanced involuntarily at the door behind which Louise was no doubt holding forth. 'It…' she began. 'It…'

Mr Fallon raised one of his bushy eyebrows. And Deirdre burst into tears. Her hand flew up to cover her mouth and she found herself taking a step back. Then another. And then a third. She only stopped when she backed into the little round table that he used when he had more than one visitor in the room.

'Oh!' he said, looking as shocked as she felt. 'Deirdre, are you all right? Sit down, sit down.'

'I'm fine,' she said through her tears.

'You are not. Sit. Sit.'

Deirdre considered her options. It was either sit down here and endure his questions or step back outside, a mess, to Louise and Jadwiga. It was no contest. However awful the next few minutes with Mr Fallon would be, she didn't doubt that he would keep this whole thing to himself. Louise would email the whole company about it before she was back in her chair.

'Okay,' she said and sat down.

Now that he had achieved his immediate goal, Mr Fallon seemed unsure of how to proceed. He stared at her, slightly bug-eyed, for a few seconds before snapping out of it and placing an awkward hand on her shoulder.

'I have whiskey here somewhere,' he said. 'Maybe a wee—'

'No, thanks, Mr Fallon. Honestly.'

'Are you sure now?'

'Yeah.'

'Um… I'll sit down, will I?'

He moved around to the opposite side of the table, declining his chance to settle right next to her, and took a seat. A few terrible seconds passed.

'Was it something I said?' he ventured.

She managed a smile and then realised that he hadn't been joking. He was really asking. 'No. Nothing you said.'

His relief was obvious. 'Right. Okay. Right. Something... to do with work?' This time she didn't immediately allay his fears – she genuinely didn't know how to respond. 'I'm not enjoying this pause,' he said.

'Sorry, sorry. It's nothing to do with work.'

'Really?'

What could she say? That his beloved plumbing supply business was such a stupefyingly tedious enterprise that she was sometimes overcome by an urge to scream? That she regularly had nightmares about being lost among the lumpen grey boxes of the Santry industrial estate where it was based? That while he personally was a sweet if slightly absent-minded presence, his sons Liam and Francis, who did most of the real work these days and were poised to take over entirely when he retired, had a combined IQ of 150 and the combined charm of a cornered mink? That she could possibly put up with all of the above if it wasn't for the fact that Louise Cawley, her fellow PA and one of the most awful human beings she had ever met, had recently announced that she was pregnant?

'Really.'

'All right. Then it's none of my business. But if you ever need someone to talk to... Eh...'

He looked away. His nerve seemed to have failed him. He wanted to make the offer, Deirdre guessed, but he wasn't quite able to get the words out. What if she actually took him up on it? But he had nothing to worry about. She had no intention of doing so. The very thought was ridiculous.

'Things are a bit tough these days,' she said and then only just stopped herself from looking around to see who had spoken.

Mr Fallon recoiled as if she'd slapped him. 'I see,' he said then, frowning hard. They shared a moment of ridiculous silence.

'I'm sorry, you don't need to hear—'

'No, go on. Go on. Please.'

She swallowed. 'Well... You know Leo's out of work and all.'

'Yes. The estate agency closed.'

'It was a property management company.'

'Property management. Flats and that. Yes. Sorry. Sure you know as well I do how tough it's been for us here. One minute we were... Anyway. Never mind us. You were saying.'

'We didn't think it was going to be a long-term thing. Maybe because we'd only just moved. Maybe we didn't think we could possibly be that unlucky.'

'No.'

'But that was six months ago. More like seven, actually. And there's still no sign of anything out there for him. It's... difficult. For both of us.'

Outside, someone laughed. Jadwiga, by the sound of it. The skinny bitch. Mr Fallon waited for her to continue. She didn't want to. But she didn't want him to think she was an emotional lightweight, either.

'But that's not it, really. Not the main thing.' His frown grew heavier still. He shifted his weight in his seat, as if physically bracing himself. 'There's also... We've been trying for a baby. Trying, and not succeeding.'

'I see,' said Mr Fallon. His face reddened with astonishing speed. Deirdre was reminded of a documentary she'd seen about a weird species of octopus that could disguise itself in a flash. 'Well...'

'I'm sorry, I'm sorry. I shouldn't have said that. You don't need to hear about all this.'

She started to get up but he waved her down. 'Sit, sit. Please. Look. I'm not going to pretend that I'm an expert on... women's... business. But I have two ears, haven't I? If you think it would help to talk about it, talk away.'

'That's really nice of you, Mr Fallon.'

This was one of those tender moments between them – there had been perhaps two dozen – when she was sure he was going to smile and say, 'Please, call me Eddie'. The smile arrived, but the invitation did not. At this stage in their relationship, she supposed it never would.

'I'd imagine this hasn't helped.' He nodded at the door, behind which a foetus was quietly growing.

'No. No, it hasn't. Don't get me wrong. I'm very happy for Louise.' This was a lie. Her colleague's pregnancy made her feel nothing but bitterness and anger. She hated herself for that, of course, and wasn't surprised to find that it did no good.

'She does go on about it a lot, though, doesn't she?' Mr Fallon said. 'I mean, I'm sick and tired of hearing about it and I'm not even in your... boat.'

Just nod, Deirdre told herself. *Don't join in. That could only end badly.*

'And those printout things,' Mr Fallon went on. 'Of the baby in the womb? We didn't have them in my day... What do you call them?'

'Scans.'

'Scans! I've seen more pictures of Louise's baby than I ever saw of my own, and it's not even born yet. I wouldn't mind but it doesn't even look like a human yet. She showed me one, and I'm not kidding you, it looked like a croissant. I said I couldn't get over its beauty, of course, but all I felt, really, was peckish.'

'She's just excited,' Deirdre said, grabbing her chance to look mature and fair-minded. 'I'm sure I'd be the same.'

'I suppose you've done all the... you know... the tests and what have you?'

It cost him a lot to get this question out. His expression was that of a man struggling to get a wardrobe up a staircase all on his own.

'We have, yes. All of them. They can't find anything wrong.'

'Well then!' Mr Fallon was suddenly beaming at her – relieved, she supposed, that the conversation would not be taking a turn for the gynaecological.

'Well then what?'

'There's nothing wrong?'

'I wouldn't say that.'

'But you just told me—'

'I said they can't *find* anything wrong. That doesn't mean there *is* nothing wrong. I mean, if there's nothing wrong, then where's my fucking baby?'

A silence descended. It lasted, by Deirdre's estimation, an hour and a half and only ended when it was punctured by a shriek of laughter from outside. Louise, this time, no doubt cracking up at one of her own jokes.

'Sorry,' she said. 'I shouldn't have sworn. I know you hate swearing.'

'Oh, come on. I know I'm an old fogey but I'm not made of glass.'

Deirdre nodded, trying to work out how it had come to this – dropping an F-bomb on poor old Mr Fallon, a man who had once given a stern lecture on gutter language to a courier who'd referred to his van as a 'piece of crap'. One thing was for sure: this conversation was not making her feel any better. It should never have happened and now it was over. Her remaining challenge was to get out of it with some semblance of dignity – ideally, before he told her she could always adopt.

'Look, Mr Fallon, I'm sorry I embarrassed you with all this moaning. Especially the baby stuff. You don't want to hear that. Can we please just forget that this whole thing ever happened?'

He nodded. 'Whatever you want. I must be even more useless at this than I thought I was.'

'You're not useless. Like I say, I should never have opened my mouth.'

'Are you sure you're all right to go back out there? Maybe you'd like to head on home for the day?'

'No, thanks. I'm grand, honestly.'

She made a fresh move to rise and this time, Mr Fallon made no countermove. The door was six feet away. Getting there reminded her of one of those anxiety dreams where you make no progress no matter how fast you run.

'Deirdre?'

She looked back. 'Yes?'

'Don't forget – you can always adopt.'

With a tremendous effort of will, she kept her expression neutral. 'Yeah. That's true. Thanks a lot, Mr Fallon.'

She stepped out and gently closed the door behind her. Neither

Jadwiga nor Louise looked up from their computers. The three of them were in and out of their respective bosses' offices all day – Jadwiga worked for Liam and Louise worked for Francis – and paid no attention to each other's movements. This was good news, Deirdre thought. It gave her a chance to slip past them and on into the loo, where she could fix her make-up and, in all probability, immediately ruin it again with another cry.

Blackbird Clinical Research was housed in an immaculate three-storey building in Malahide. It looked, Nancy had often thought, like something from a stock photo – a marketing droid's idea of a 21st-century facility. The only criticism she had ever heard levelled against it was that it was a little sterile. But even that was hardly damning. There were worse words in the health industry than 'sterile'.

At 11 o'clock that morning, she pulled into the visitors' car park and killed the engine in the 2002 Fiesta that Redmond called 'the Mum-mobile' and she called 'the Heap'. Aidan and Luke were both asleep in the back. She didn't expect this state of affairs to persist and planned to stay no longer than five minutes.

It was not her first time paying one of these visits. On each of the previous occasions, she had managed to get her strange fix without bumping into any former colleagues and she was determined that she wouldn't break her streak now. She'd done some thinking – of course – about what was behind all this. Each time, she'd concluded that it was perfectly natural to want to keep in touch with people from the past. It wasn't bad, as excuses went, provided she immediately shouted down the mental voices who were so keen to remind her that she wasn't keeping in touch with people, she was sitting quietly in her car outside a building where she no longer had any business.

Aidan stirred in his seat, then issued a squeal of discomfort. Nancy breathed a gentle 'Hushhh' and might have immediately sent him back under if he hadn't suddenly unleashed a tremendous fart. She was watching in the rear-view mirror and saw how his eyes flew open in panic. He looked all around him in shock, as if to say, *What the hell was that?*

'It's okay, honey,' Nancy said. 'We're in the car. Everything's fine.'

He stretched and yawned and started to take his surroundings in properly. 'Where we going, Mammy? Where we going inna car?'

She turned to face him. 'We're not going anywhere. Remember Mammy told you we were going for a little drive? Well, we did. You fell asleep. And now we're going home. In a few more minutes.'

'I had a dream!'

'Yeah?'

'I was magic. I magicked a dinosaur to be my new friend and then he was my new friend and we were friends together but then he stood on an old lady and she got squished.'

'Oh no! Was she hurt!'

He looked puzzled. 'Mammy! It was a dinosaur. She got squished *dead*.'

Was this a bad sign, she wondered? Dreaming about violent death at his age? It was hard to imagine that it was a *good* sign. Should she say something? If so, what? This was exactly the sort of dilemma she'd always imagined she would breeze through when she became a mother. Then again, she'd imagined all sorts, once upon a time. On this occasion, she was spared from making a choice by the sudden stirring of her younger son.

'Hi, Luke! Hi, sleepyhead!'

He yawned and peered at her as if he had never seen her before. There was a moment when it could have gone either way. But then he grinned and slapped his thighs in delight.

'Good man!' Nancy said, relieved by his good humour. 'When we get home we'll have a—'

Someone knocked on the passenger window. Nancy's heart ricocheted around her torso as she turned awkwardly to see who it was. While practically any option would have been bad news, there were several that had the potential to truly horrify. One of them was Trish Kennedy.

'Well, hell-*oooo!*' said Trish Kennedy.

She'd changed her hair colour since Nancy had last seen her. But she was unmistakable. No other woman in Dublin – possibly in Europe – wore quite as much make-up. She favoured an amount that was actually unfeminine; it made her look like an enthusiastic but unskilled drag act.

'Trish!' Nancy screeched. 'Oh my God!'

She hoped the 'Oh my God' would sound like common-or-garden surprise but really it was of the *I can't believe my shitty luck* variety. She wound down the window and, with tremendous effort, forced the corners of her mouth towards her ears.

'Hey!' Trish smiled. 'What's the story? What are you doing here? Are you stalking someone?'

Nancy's fake smile faltered. It took her just a beat too long to come up with her excuse.

'Heh! No, as if! Luke's nappy needed changing. I was passing here, so I thought, y'know… I thought I'd pull in. And change it. The nappy.'

Trish nodded slowly. 'I see.' She peered in at the boys and adopted the manic smile of a person who was not used to children. 'Hello in there! I'm Trish. I used to work with your mummy. Slightly above her, really. Do you like football? I bet you do. Who do you support? Manchester United?' Silence from the back seat. 'Do you like sweets? I bet you do. What's your favourite? Chocolate buttons?' More silence. 'Not really talkers, are they, Nancy?'

'Well, Luke can't really talk yet. He's only a baby.'

'What's the other one's problem?'

'*Problem?*'

'Just shy, I suppose. Anyway! How's motherhood treating you? You look wrecked – I hope you don't mind me saying.'

Nancy simply ignored that. 'So – how are things inside? All go?'

'Worse than ever. I never get a minute to myself. It's especially bad this week. The barbecue's Friday evening and muggins here offered to help organise it.'

'I used to love the Blackbird barbecue,' Nancy sighed. 'The BBBBQ...'

'We'll be up in the roof garden, as usual, smart casual, if you feel like getting out of the house.'

'Um... I don't think so, thank you.'

Trish almost choked. 'I was *joking!*'

'I know!'

They re-fixed their smiles and each looked at a different something in the distance.

'Well,' Trish said then. 'It was nice to see you again after all this time. But I'd better get back in.'

'I'd better get on too. Like I said, I only stopped to change the nappy.'

As soon as the words were out, she realised that repeating the lie had weakened it still further. Trish's eyebrows came together.

'I believe you, Nancy. It's perfectly plausible. Bye-bye now.'

She waved at the boys and took her leave. Nancy ground her teeth together as she watched her go. She felt as if she must be visibly glowing with fury.

'Mammy,' said Aidan. 'Was that lady a clown?'

A couple of seconds went by before she realised what he meant. The make-up. She hooted with laughter and slapped the steering wheel. Was it worth getting out of the car to go around and give him a hug? She decided not, but it was a close-run thing. Trish, she noticed then, had stopped by the fountain at the front of the building to speak to a security guard. There had been two such employees in Nancy's time, the unfortunately named Tom and Gerry. This was neither. He was a much younger man, plump and sweaty and elaborately moustachioed. She had spoken to him briefly the previous week and had found it hard to escape the feeling that she had wandered onto a Peter Kay set. He and Trish seemed to get along pretty well, whoever he was. She watched for a couple of minutes as they chatted and giggled. Neither seemed keen to get on with their day. Her desire to get the hell out of there fought with her reluctance to drive past Trish. Eventually, she decided that enough was enough and pulled out of her space.

'We going home?' Aidan asked with a distinct note of hope in his voice.

'Yup. Home now.'

As they approached the fountain at which they would take a right, Trish leaned out of her conversation, waved, and blew a kiss. *Who blows kisses, for fuck's sake?* Nancy thought, as she blew one of her own. At that moment, the security guard spotted her and immediately began frantically waving both arms over his head. Nancy assumed that something was wrong with her car and although she couldn't imagine what it might be, the guy seemed convinced that her life and the lives of her children were in immediate danger. She braked hard and wound down her window. He trotted across. Trish followed.

'Howiye,' he said. 'C'mere, you didn't happen to drop an umbrella here the other day, did you?'

Nancy's breath left her. 'The other day? Here? Oh no, that wasn't me, I haven't been around here in ages. You must have—'

'The little fellas were roarin'? Both of them? D'ye not remember? I pulled my funny face?' He hooked his fingers into the corners of his mouth, pulled his lips wide apart and crossed his eyes. The effect was more terrifying than amusing – as it had been first time around. 'You told me I was only making it worse? No? Jaysus, you've an awful memory, missus.'

Trish, Nancy saw, had raised a hand over her mouth in an attempt to hide her growing smile – or at least, in an attempt to pretend that she was trying to hide it. There was no point in continuing with the lie. It was only making things worse.

'Oh yeah!' she said. She almost slapped her forehead but cancelled the move just in time. It would have been overkill. 'Yeah. Ha. I was here, that's right. Funny how the mind… the human brain… It's not my umbrella.'

'Ah. Sorry. My mistake. Not to worry.'

She realised she was revving the engine and eased off on the accelerator. 'Okay!' she trilled. 'I'm off, then. See ya. See ya, Trish.'

Trish grinned broadly. 'Bye-bye.'

Nancy turned the wheel and squealed away so violently that Aidan hooted with delight, as if he was on a playground roundabout. She drove white-knuckled for five minutes, simultaneously cringing and fuming. Still, she thought, as the fog lifted and her muscles relaxed, at least she had learned something interesting: the company barbecue was coming up. She had no intention of doing so, but she could, in theory, show up and see how everyone was getting on. See how business was going. See if they were letting people go these days or, y'know, hiring.

It was just a thought. Not a plan. Just a thought.

Julie Dooley swivelled to and fro in her chair and looked at the faces of her assembled juniors. She saw genuine fear there. Sean, Niamh and Paddy. Combined age of about seventy. Some imperishable part of her felt that she still belonged on their side of the desk – on the side of youth, the side of fucking up. She fought against it.

'Okay,' she said. 'First of all, I don't want to hear a single word about whose fault this is. Not one word. It's all of our fault and it's none of our fault. There'll be plenty of time for post-mortems later.'

Sean spoke up at once, as she had suspected he would. He was a good copywriter and a decent enough guy but he had proved on multiple sensitive occasions that he was incapable of prolonged silence.

'Julie, I think I should point out—'

'Niamh, if Sean says another word before I've finished talking, I want you to grab his scrotum and pull it up over his head. I want to see him wearing it like a swimming cap.'

She delivered the line with just the right amount of levity – enough to let them know that she wasn't about to have them all fired on the spot but not so much that they felt entirely off the hook. It drew a grin from Niamh and an eye-roll from Sean. Only Paddy, a timid individual who had possibly taken the comment literally, remained bug-eyed and stiff.

'I can do that,' Niamh said. 'No problem. No problem at all.'

'The only thing I want you doing for the rest of the day is finding out everything there is to know about this Canadian campaign that we have apparently copied.'

Paddy rose on his toes, a sure sign that he had plucked up the nerve to say something. 'We already have the basics, it—'

'I don't want the basics, Paddy, I want everything. I'm not talking about where it ran and when, I'm talking about who the creatives were, who the account manager was, where they worked afterwards if they moved on. I want to know if it won any awards, I want to know if it was featured in any trade papers, I want to know when it first appeared on the internet, not just YouTube, I mean anywhere.'

The door opened and halfway through the process was knocked upon. It was David Flynn, the head of Account Services, and Julie's boss.

'Don't mind me,' he said, as if any of them could possibly conceive of such a notion. Julie did her best to pretend that his appearance had no effect on her train of thought.

'I don't have to keep going, do I? You get it, don't you?'

Niamh and Sean nodded solemnly, each of them stealing unsettled glances at the new arrival. Paddy nodded too but his was frantic rather than solemn – an attempt, Julie guessed, to appear extra-conscientious.

'Well, go on then,' she said. 'Get to it. And yes, we will all be staying late tonight.'

The three of them shuffled out and Niamh gently closed the door behind her. David stepped across and sat on the edge of her desk. He almost always chose this position when he came in to see her. She regularly lost several minutes of her life staring into space and wondering about it. What, if anything, did it mean? Sometimes she concluded that he was asserting dominance. Sometimes she concluded that he was favouring her with a casual, friendly approach. Sometimes she concluded that he was trying to look down her shirt. The last conclusion made her feel excited but simultaneously lost and confused. It reminded her of the way she had felt as an 11-year-old when she found herself oddly fascinated by Take That, even though she had no interest in music.

'It's tough at the top,' David sighed. His look was sympathetic but experience told Julie that there was a challenge there too.

'I bet it is. It's definitely tough in the middle.'

'Ha. Yeah. So – I just thought I'd pop in to see if you're on top of this thing. But I see that you are.'

'I am. Yes. We're going to—' Her mobile rang. It was Dooley. 'Excuse me a second, I'd better take this, I'll have to call him anyway... Hello?'

'Hiya.' His voice was thick was fatigue, as it often was. 'How's it going?'

'We'll get to that. How's Nicola now?'

A yawn. 'More or less the same. Bad this morning, bit better since lunch? But still not great.'

'Poor wee lamb. I wish I was there to give her a cuddle.'

'Yeah.'

'Listen: I can't really talk but I was just about to call you. Something's come up here and I'm going to be home late.'

A silence. 'Okay.'

'I'm sorry.'

Another silence. 'I know.'

'So, how was your day otherwise?'

'Otherwise? You mean apart from looking after Nicola? There is no otherwise. I tried calling Mum and Dad earlier but they were out. Unless they've taken to hitting the sack at 7pm, which wouldn't surprise me.'

He climbed up on his latest hobby horse, his fear that his retired parents back in Wangaratta were getting old before their time. Julie looked up at David. His expression didn't change as he slowly raised his right hand and did the 'Yap-yap-yap' gesture. She put her own hand over the phone to conceal her giggle but her timing was off.

'What's the joke?' Dooley asked.

'Sorry?'

'I heard you laughing. Is someone with you?'

'No! No. It's just me.'

David pulled a face and slid off the desk. He pointed a thumb at the door, mouthed the word *Later* and tiptoed across the room in a parody of stealthiness. Julie had to look away in case Dooley heard the fresh smile in her voice.

'You sound tired,' she said to him then. 'I hope you're looking after yourself.'

'I'll be all right,' he replied, obviously cheered by her concern.

Just before he closed the door, David gave her a barely perceptible wink. She blushed and told her husband to squeeze in a nap if he could.

The first thing Redmond heard when he closed the front door behind him that evening was the shrill, piercing shriek that Aidan employed as a laugh when he was especially tickled by something. It was not a mellifluous sound – far from it – but it was one that his father loved. As he stepped down the hall, he heard Luke joining in with a breathless, hiccup-like cackle. This too was an indicator of extreme giddiness. He felt his mood lighten just a touch – but then, as he entered the living room, he gasped and stopped mid-step. Nancy had dropped dead. She was on the floor, supine, immobile, eyes closed. Luke was sitting beside her, leaning against the sofa, banging plastic bricks together. Aidan had his paints out and had covered every inch of his late mother's arms and face with thick, meandering lines. Having exhausted the available real estate, he was in the process of lifting her T-shirt and getting to work on her tummy. It was the sudden twitching of same as the first brush was applied that let Redmond know she was still alive after all. None of them had noticed his arrival. He stared for a few seconds before making his presence known.

'Hey,' he said.

Aidan and Luke screeched in fresh delight. Nancy opened her eyes and tilted her head to look at him upside down.

'We're painting,' she said flatly.

'I see that, yeah.'

The carpet was barely visible through a layer of discarded toys.

His own policy, when he was in charge, was to let them all lie there until the end of the day and to do one big clean-up at bedtime. But Nancy's was to tidy up as they went along. Usually. Picking his steps with care, he tiptoed across and kissed the crown of Aidan's head, then scooped Luke up into his arms.

'Bit… messy, isn't it? The paint.'

'I don't know what to tell you.' She wasn't trying to be funny, it seemed. She looked genuinely perplexed. 'He said, "Mammy, why don't you lie down and let me paint you". I didn't have the energy to say no, somehow. Plus, I really fancied the "lie down" part.'

He took a seat on the sofa and bounced Luke on his knee. 'So. I had my interview.'

Nancy hauled herself up into a sitting position and placed her hand on his knee. 'Sorry. I should have asked. How did it go?'

'Not… well.'

'What happened?'

'You've never actually met him, have you? The Big Man?'

'Bill? No. Just heard the horror stories. He's not even big, is he?'

'Nope. That's a nickname. Started by him, I think. Anyway, the point is, you have to know what he looks like to get the full effect. You know Jon Hamm?'

'Ohhh, yes. Yes, I do.'

'Right. Well, imagine Jon Hamm inside out. I mean – pug-fugly.'

'Plugufally!' hooted Aidan.

'*But,*' Redmond hurried on, 'really well dressed. Spends a fortune on it.'

Nancy frowned in confusion. 'I've never heard you passing remarks on how another man looks.'

'Well, he started it.'

'He what?'

'I was only in there for about 20 minutes and, I swear to God, half the time was spent on my clothes.'

'You're joking.'

'Nope. I hadn't even sat down and he said, "You know what my problem with you is? You're scruffy." I honestly thought he was having a laugh.'

'Jesus.'

'For a start, he says, you don't shave every day.'

'You don't.'

'I know I don't! But so what? Once in a while I skip a day! That should stop me getting a job?'

'All right, take it easy. What else?'

'He wanted to know where I got this suit. So I told him. Marks and Spencer. He pulled a face, like, all disgusted. Then he launched into this speech about how a man's suit is his calling card, blah blah blah. How can you be excellent, he says, if you don't *look* excellent? Bear in mind this is coming from a guy with a face like a foot.'

'Did you speak up for yourself?'

'What do you mean?'

'I mean, did you tell him you wanted a proper interview and he was talking crap?'

'Of course I didn't! He's the *boss*, Nancy.'

'So, what, you just sat there and took it?'

Redmond forced himself to breathe for a couple of seconds. 'I moved the conversation on as quickly as I could.'

'And how did the rest of it go?'

'It didn't go well, did it? I was all... put off.'

She shrugged. 'So that's that then. Forget about it. Lots of people are losing their jobs. Not getting a promotion isn't the end of the world.'

There was no point in this conversation, Redmond realised. He had been *humiliated*, that was the point. But she just didn't get it. It was part of a pattern with her. Nothing that happened to him at work was a big deal, no matter how awful. If he came home and said he'd been tarred and feathered for missing a target, she'd tell him it was always good to get feedback.

'Yup,' he sniffed. 'I'll do that. Right, I'm off upstairs for a bit.'

She gave him a look. 'You're only just in the door.'

'I feel the need to shoot someone's head off,' he said.

He deposited Luke on the floor and picked his way back through the toys, conscious of the silence behind him.

Fifteen minutes later, Redmond was engrossed in a *Call of Duty* multiplayer match. Although he always bought the latest incarnation of the game, in times of stress he tended to go back to *Call of Duty 4: Modern Warfare*. He firmly believed that it had the best maps and the best weapon-balancing, but none of that was as important as the comfort element. It was the video-gaming equivalent of an old pair of slippers.

'Sniper!' he yelled into his headset. 'On the roof, on the roof, by the... Yeah, you got him. Good one.'

A stranger's voice hissed in his ear. 'Cheers, mate. Got lucky for once.' A Scot, by the sounds of things – and refreshingly adult. Redmond had fully expected the response, if one materialised, to be high-pitched and astonishingly foul-mouthed. He stepped out of the hidey-hole from which he had been surveying the ruined street and turned left down an alleyway. An enemy player was a matter of feet away. Lacking experience, the guy raised his sub-machine gun to aim. Redmond knew better. He went for his knife, which was always the faster option at close quarters. Half a second later, he was moving off down the alley, leaving his foe sprawled behind him with an opened throat. *Fuck you, Bill*, he thought, as he had after every successful engagement. It was then that Nancy appeared in the bedroom doorway. He glanced up as she folded her painted arms and leaned against the frame. He gave her a moment but she stayed silent.

'What's up?' he asked.

'We have to talk.'

'About what?'

'Can you pause that thing?'

'Not really. It's multiplayer.'

She gave it a few seconds. Then: 'Redmond. I'm trying to talk to you here.'

It was no good. She wasn't going to give in. He pressed pause and swivelled a little to face her.

'What's up?'

'I've been doing some thinking,' she said, 'and I want this room back.'

He hesitated, wondering if he had heard correctly. 'I'm sorry, *what?*'

'We'll need another room for one of the boys eventually and in the meantime, we need a spare for… guests.'

'Guests? What guests? When do we ever have guests?'

'Well, we don't. Maybe we should.'

'What? Like who?'

A small shrug. 'I don't know.'

'This… I mean… I haven't a clue what you're talking about. You're not making any sense.'

To her credit, she looked briefly unsure of herself. 'And what if we have another child?'

Redmond almost choked. Had she lost her reason entirely? 'Nancy, I've had the snip. You had me done, like a cat. Remember? Because I certainly do.'

'Yeah, but you hear stories. Spontaneous… reversal.'

He didn't reply at once. This was moving from shocking to worrying. 'Nancy. Come on. Where is all this coming from?'

'All what?'

'You haven't been yourself for ages. I caught you crying that time and you said it was because the cross-eyed lad got voted off the island, but I'm not stupid.'

'I'm fine. I just want this room back.'

'But we had a deal! The first day we came to see this house, I looked in here and said, "Gaming room," and you said, "Fine, it's too small to be anything else." Don't deny it!'

'I'm not denying anything. I'm saying I've changed my mind. Okay? I'll give you a shout when dinner's ready.'

She left. Redmond slumped in his chair and glanced at the screen. He was dead, of course.

'Hello? Leo. Hi. Hello?'

He was lying down with his headphones on and his eyes closed. She'd lost count of the number of times she'd come home and found him asleep but this time she knew he was awake; his right foot was steadily tapping. There were records lying all over the place, as there were every day.

'Leo!'

No response. Lacking other options, she poked him on the thigh. He bolted upright and stifled a scream.

'Jesus! You scared me.' He removed his headphones.

'I've been standing here for ages. You didn't hear me.'

'*Meat is Murder*,' he said. 'I thought it was lost but it turned up. Under the sofa. I must have kicked it there at some point.'

She really had nothing to say about this turn of events. 'Right.'

'How was your afternoon?' he asked.

She shifted his feet and sat down. 'It wasn't fun, Leo. I couldn't wait to get home.'

'Aw. Well, you're here now. And tomorrow's another day.'

She nodded and waited for him to go on. But he didn't. Apparently, that was it. These were his words of comfort. She considered telling him about crying in front of Mr Fallon but quickly decided against it. What was the point? He already knew she'd had a bad day. That should have been enough of a prompt.

'Did you look into the paint?'

'Hm?'

'The *paint*, Leo.'

They'd always said that there was no point in trying to fix the front of the house piecemeal. When they had the money, they would take care of it all in one fell swoop, paying someone who knew what they were doing to knock off its various extrusions and paint the thing a more socially acceptable colour. It had become increasingly obvious, however, that the problem with their plan was the payment part. Several times recently, Deirdre had raised the possibility of getting cheap paint and having Leo de-pink it, at least. Not only had he never managed to investigate prices, he never seemed to remember that they'd even discussed it.

'Oh. No. Forgot.'

She started counting to ten and had made it to four when he said, 'Pasta okay?'

'Sorry?'

'Pasta for dinner?'

'I suppose.'

'Would you rather have something else?'

'Like what?'

'I dunno.'

'Pasta's fine,' she sighed.

He placed a hand on her thigh. 'Are you all right, chicken? Anything you want to talk about?'

Ah. This was better. And *chicken*. Leo wasn't the sort of guy who used pet names. He frowned on anything 'mushy' or, worse, 'lovey-dovey'. It was an attempt to win her favour. Now that she thought about it, he'd used 'cuddly night' earlier too. Guilt washed over her, and affection too. He did his best, bless him.

'Nope,' she said.

'Okay. If you're sure. I'll get started.'

He got up and left for the kitchen. Deirdre pursed her lips and stared at her feet. *Nope?* What the hell was that about? Did she want to talk things through or not? Best not to think about it, she told herself – like the Chinese she now wished she'd agreed to. Best to just put your head down and keep on keeping on.

When Julie turned her key in the front door at 8.30, her only goal in life was to pour a large gin down her throat as soon as was humanly possible. As she stepped into the hall, she saw Dooley stomping towards her with a bawling Nicola in his arms.

'Ah, Lord,' she said, 'is she still up? Poor poppet.'

Dooley raised their daughter out before him like a ticking bomb. 'Here,' he said, even more loudly than was necessary. Julie took Nicola from him and squeezed her close.

'Babba,' she cooed. 'Shhh. Shhh. Mammy's here.'

Nicola calmed down at once, nuzzling close to Julie's neck. Dooley's eyes widened. He shook his head in disbelief. 'Right. Great. Of course.' He turned on his heels and marched down the hall into the kitchen. Julie followed.

'Come on, don't feel bad. It'd be the same if I was here all day and handed her to you.'

'Would it?'

'Of course it would. It's just the novelty. Jesus, she's a bit hot, Dooley. Have you taken her temperature?'

'Thirty-eight.'

'That's not great.'

'It's nothing to panic about. I think she's made herself hotter with all the screaming.'

'And she's definitely not hungry or—'

'I've fed her, changed her, walked her around, everything. I think she's just exhausted by this bloody cold. I know I am.'

'Well, I've got her now. Go and relax in front of the… What are you doing?'

He had opened the door to the cupboard that housed their meagre collection of spirits.

'I'm getting a drink. A very well-earned drink.'

He withdrew a bottle of Jack Daniel's, found a glass, and poured a measure that, to Julie's eye, fell somewhere between 'generous' and 'asking for trouble'.

'I was just about to have a drink,' she mumbled.

Ever since Nicola's birth, they'd had a clear agreement that only one of them could drink alcohol at any given time. It was one of a broad range of safety measures that they'd introduced in that first rush of baby-mania. Most of these directives had fallen by the wayside over time but this was a point on which they'd remained utterly puritanical. 'What if there was an emergency and we needed to drive to the hospital?' they'd said on more than one occasion before congratulating each other on their commitment to excellent parenting.

'Oh,' Dooley said.

He looked longingly at the glass but didn't raise it to his lips. Julie felt for him. In all fairness, he did look pretty dreadful. His posture was that of a newly released galley slave and he appeared to have aged several years in the course of the day. Standing under the harsh kitchen light, he even seemed to have lost some *hair*. At the very least, his curls looked markedly less springy than usual, as if their battery was running flat. She patted Nicola on the back and dredged up a smile.

'You go ahead,' she said.

'Are you sure?' he asked and before she could answer, knocked the whole lot back.

'Wow. You *have* had a bad day.'

'Worst ever. I'm not kidding. First half was tough but manageable and then...' He raised his hand and mimed a plane going down.

'You're not alone. We had a disaster at work,' she told him. 'A total disaster. The crisp campaign? With the hedgehogs? It turns out that something very similar ran in Canada a few years back and... Never mind.'

He realised that she'd noticed his lack of interest and tried to make amends, raising his head and actually standing a little taller. 'No, go on.'

'It's all right. I'll tell you some other time.'

His relief was obvious. 'Okay. Sorry, I'm just zonked. Right, I'm going to have a bath.'

'Okay. Go on. Grab a *Cosmo*, light some candles, drop a few rose petals—'

'What's that supposed to mean?'

'Jesus, Dooley, it was a joke.'

He shook his head wearily. 'Sorry. Sorry. Have you eaten?'

'Yeah. We got pizza in.'

'Right.'

He poured another drink, just as large as the first one. Then he kissed her, and rested his forehead against Nicola's shoulder. 'You almost killed me today, mate,' he said. 'It's a good thing you're gorgeous.'

Julie watched him trudge off down the hall and then, as he climbed the stairs, she watched his hand move up the rail and finally disappear from view.

'It's just us girls,' she whispered to Nicola, who squirmed in her grasp and reached up to grab the lapel of her jacket. 'Will we go and have a wee sit down? Would that be nice? Of course it would. And then when you get all settled, you can go down for a wee snooze? You come with Mammy, there's a good girl.'

With her free hand she grabbed a glass and a bottle of gin, and headed for the sofa in the front room.

2

'Oh my actual God,' said Louise as she popped another Gaviscon. 'The heartburn's getting worse. I didn't think it *could* get worse. I said that to you the other day, didn't I, Jadwiga? I said the only consolation I have, heartburn-wise, is that it can't possibly get any worse. Do you remember? I said that, didn't I?'

'You did say that,' Jadwiga agreed. 'I remember. I remember you saying it.'

'And now lookit! What's it got?'

'Worse?'

'Worse.'

Deirdre looked from one to the other, smiling weakly, and hoping that she wouldn't be obliged to contribute any actual words. Louise's latest bout of complaining about the trials of pregnancy – there was at least one every day – had been going on for ten minutes and showed no sign of ending any time soon.

'And last night – I must tell you – last night, I was up... Ask me how many times. Ask me how many times I had to get up to make water?'

'How many?' Jadwiga said.

'Six! I'm not kidding. *Six.*'

Deirdre managed to slowly shake her head, as if she was shocked to learn that numbers even went higher than five.

'It's not just the getting up. It's the trying to get back to sleep. You can't! Not when you're this uncomfortable. Look at me! I'm enormous!'

Jadwiga looked personally offended. 'Oh, no, Louise, no! This is not true!'

It *wasn't* true. She was only five months gone. If it hadn't been the first thing she said in every conversation, no one looking at her would even guess that she was expecting.

'Oh, look at the time,' Deirdre said. 'I have to get going.'

'The smells thing isn't getting any better either,' Louise said, pulling a face. 'Cormac made chilli last night and I had to go upstairs and breathe into a scented tissue. Honest to God, my stomach was *rolling*.'

'I don't like the smell of chilli either,' said Jadwiga. Deirdre guessed that she was trying to empathise, but it was not a wise move. Sure enough, Louise shot her a look – it said *I'm more disappointed than angry*.

'I'm not talking about not liking it, Jadwiga. I'm talking about the tiniest sniff of it makes you want to puke your shoes up.'

'Okay then,' Deirdre said. 'I'm off.'

'But you don't actually vomit, do you?' Jadwiga asked.

'Well, no, but only because I get out of the way as quickly as I can. Mark my words, one of these days I'll be trapped somewhere with a bowl of chicken soup and… Where are you going?'

She'd managed to observe that Deirdre had risen and was putting on her jacket.

'I told you,' Deirdre said, faking, this time, a smile. 'I have an appointment at the dentist.'

'Oh. Right. See you later, then, I suppose.'

'Yup. Shouldn't be too long. Just a check-up, fingers crossed.'

'Goodbye,' said Jadwiga. It was a peculiarity of her excellent English that her farewells always sounded so formal. It was never 'Bye' or 'See ya' – always 'Goodbye', delivered in a tone that was never particularly sunny and often (as now) tended towards the doom-laden.

Deirdre nodded and slipped away, wishing the word 'doom' hadn't occurred to her.

Leo took a sip of his coffee and exhaled with some satisfaction. He wasn't a huge fan of caffeinated beverages but the lattes he had in Dr Vinyl on Wicklow Street always seemed to hit the spot. It was the location rather than the drink itself, of course. He knew that.

'Very nice,' he said.

Jeff Collins, owner and manager of both Dr Vinyl and possibly the most extravagant beard in Dublin, nodded thoughtfully, and smacked his lips. 'I'm not going to lie. Mine's just okay. I wish I could be more effusive. But I would be lying.' A brief shrug. He regarded the paper cup with suspicion. 'New place?'

Leo was a regular visitor to the shop and never showed up empty-handed. Jeff was a serious coffee fiend.

'No, same joint. I think they've changed the cups, that's all.'

Jeff sniffed equably. 'Something in the material, maybe. Some chemical fucknology.'

It always shocked Leo a little when Jeff showed off his creative swearing. He was English and, although he most certainly didn't look it now, had apparently enjoyed quite a privileged upbringing. He never talked about his past – and Leo didn't pry – but there had been occasional oblique references to boarding schools and horses. His accent was that of a 1950s BBC newsreader. It always made Leo over-pronounce his own gerunds.

'Maybe. So, listen – I'm not stopping. I just thought I'd see if there was any news on the The The?'

'Sorry, no. I've got my eye out, don't worry. And I've alerted my spies in every corner of the globe. No promises, as ever. But I'm quietly confident.'

'Good, great. Okay. I have to get going.'

'Already? Really? When you said you weren't stopping, I assumed you meant "for more than an hour".'

'Ha. No, I have an appointment. Dentist.'

'And yet you still brought coffee. Bless your heart.'

'Yeah, well – I really want that EP.'

'And you shall have it, my friend. Are you in pain?'

'Sorry?'

'Dentist?'

'Oh. No. Just a check-up. Let's hope so, anyway.'

'All right. Well, good luck.'

'Yeah, cheers. See ya.'

He turned and headed for the door, trying to keep his eyes dead ahead in case a sleeve caught his eye. Life wouldn't be worth living if he was late.

Doctor Larishi had a kind face. Somehow, that was important to Deirdre. It meant more to her than his medical reputation, which was impeccable, or the padded comfort of his consulting room at the Rotunda hospital, which was considerable. She thought about him 20 times a day and every time she did, she saw him in exactly the pose he was adopting now – leaning forward, hands clasped before him, head slightly tilted, the features of that sweet, kind face arranged in an expression that seemed to simultaneously offer both hope and consolation.

'Well,' the doctor said. 'Here we are again.'

He was Pakistani, she thought, but she wouldn't have bet her life on it. Indian, possibly? Or some other country in that neck of the woods? Geography had never been her strong suit. Neither had biology, ha ha.

She nodded solemnly. 'Yes.'

'Not a bad day,' Leo added. He was always keen to sound casual, she'd noticed, as if they were dealing with a sofa salesman or an electrician. In the waiting room outside, he had flipped breezily through a magazine, finding something on almost every page that he felt she might like to marvel or laugh at. Each time he elbowed her in the ribs, she almost snapped at him, but didn't. What stopped her was the suspicion that he was every bit as wound up as she was and was merely playing Joe Cool for her benefit.

'A very nice day,' Doctor Larishi agreed. 'And an important one. It's been a long road for you both, I know. We've tried several approaches. Clomid, IUI… We've hoped that nature would take her course but, as is often the case, she has stubbornly refused to do so. Our arsenal of small arms, or relatively small arms, has been exhausted. It is time, in short, to bring out the big guns.'

'IVF,' said Deirdre.

'IVF. Yes. Correct. IVF. I know we mentioned it at our first meeting, just as a possibility that we might one day face, but now I'd like to walk you through what will happen, should you decide to take this route.'

Deirdre felt, more than saw, Leo leaning forward slightly in his chair. Was he genuinely trying to pay close attention? Or was he merely faking it while in reality wondering how he could get his hands on some rare Japanese version of an album that no one normal had ever heard of? She felt guilty for thinking this – but still made a mental note to test him later. Personally, she had nothing to learn. She'd long since educated herself on what was involved. Nevertheless, she hung on Doctor Larishi's every word, hoping to hear that, why, just this morning there'd been an exciting new breakthrough that rendered their getting pregnant all but inevitable. No such luck. There were ifs and buts aplenty but the bottom line was that IVF, more or less, give or take, assuming this and supposing that, was a 50-50 proposition. And their last chance. There were no more options after this one.

'Thanks for that,' she said when the doctor had finished speaking. 'And the answer is yes, we will be going for IVF. Long protocol. Single embryo transfer. Five-day blast.'

Doctor Larishi's eyebrows did a little dance. 'It's a big decision,' he said after a pause.

'I know. But I didn't just start thinking about it today.' Her tone was blunter than she had intended it to be. She thought it prudent to add a smile but it felt so obviously bogus that she immediately cancelled it.

'Even so, perhaps you would like to take some time to disc—'

'Yes,' Leo said. 'That's a good idea. We'll take some time to discuss it.'

'Not necessary,' Deirdre said, keeping her gaze straight ahead. Once again, she faked a smile and, once again, cut it short, feeling ridiculous. The ensuing silence seemed to have a physical weight. Doctor Larishi looked from one to the other. His default expression of kindly good humour had been replaced, she noted with dread, by something that was probably just concern but looked a tiny bit like irritation.

'I'm still trying to lose weight,' she said, quickly. 'Not having much luck. But I'll keep trying. I got a rowing machine to go with the exercise bike, secondhand but still pretty—'

'Deirdre. You know what I think about your weight. Are you

a little bit over? Yes. Is it affecting your fertility? No. That's not one of your friends talking, hoping to make you feel better. That is my considered medical opinion.'

'I keep telling her,' Leo chipped in. 'She's perfect as she—'

'Oh, be quiet,' she said. She'd hoped it to sound like a jovial deflection of a compliment. But as Doctor Larishi pursed his lips and briefly averted his gaze, she knew that it hadn't come out that way. It had come out the way she really meant it, which was *Shut up.*

'We offer counselling services here, as you know,' he said then. 'I think it would be a good idea for you to book a session.'

'Not necessary,' Deirdre said. She flinched as she realised that she'd used these words twice in this brief conversation. On the plus side, the shock prevented her from fake-smiling a third time.

'There's nothing to fear, Deirdre. It's just a little chat. You can go together or if you'd prefer… separately.'

Leo reached across and patted her arm. The gesture surprised her so much that she flinched. His hand withdrew. She followed it with her own, a second too late, and clasped hard. This, she felt sure, did not look great from the doctor's point of view.

'Okay,' she said before he had a chance to add anything she didn't want to hear. 'Counselling it is.' And there, after all, was her third fake smile. She let this one persist.

'I hardly need to add,' David said, breaking an uncomfortably long silence, 'that this is to go no further. Not yet. I'll let you know if and when that changes.'

Julie nodded solemnly. 'No, God, no, of course not.' Another couple of seconds ticked by. His invitation to lunch had been last minute and sprinkled with intriguing terms like 'word in your ear' and 'bit of privacy'. She'd assumed that he had intelligence of the utmost drama and urgency, and would have felt thrilled to be invited even if his chosen venue had been Burger King. The fact that it was Azalea 141 only sweetened an already delicious proposition. Azalea 141 – around the agency, the name was invoked more than spoken – was a relic of the Celtic Tiger, the sort of restaurant that seemed to exist solely to remind the vast majority of the population that they were, at some fundamental level, failures. It was on Merrion Square, not far from the office on Fitzwilliam Street. Julie had never eaten there, although she had often inhaled deeply while walking past. If she'd been asked to speculate, she would have guessed that David's news was about a change at the top or perhaps even a buyout by one of the multinational players. But no. All he had to tell her was that one of Dublin's oldest and largest bakeries was unhappy with its current agency and was likely to jump ship before they were all very much older. There was nothing to be done just yet – his source was a long way from impeccable – but she should 'start thinking about it'. It wasn't glamorous work but the bakery's annual spend was huge. Julie had assured him she would and asked some obvious questions, each of which had elicited the response 'I don't know'. Now the subject had apparently been exhausted, and they hadn't even received their starters yet.

'I won't breathe a word,' she added, just for the sake of saying something. It was a poorly chosen phrase, she decided as soon as she had issued it – like something you might hear in a tree house. What was next, crossing her heart and hoping to die? Panic swelled in her chest. She had to say something – anything – that would make her sound like a grown woman and not a 12-year-old whose friend had just told her she fancied the boy from three doors down.

'You know, David, you could have told me all this in the office,' she said. 'Don't get me wrong. I'm more than happy to have my lunch here. But I have to wonder if there's something on your mind besides Callahan's Bakery.'

Tonally, this was a dramatic over-steer. She sounded, in her own head at least, like Kathleen Turner doing an impression of Jessica Rabbit. Was it too late, she wondered, to go back to being a 12-year-old in a tree house?

'You got me,' David said. 'There is something else on my mind, as it happens.'

He looked into her eyes and she felt her toes clench. Christ, was he actually going to… say something? He didn't really think she was *game*, did he? Should she explain about the over-steer? Apologise? Promise to be more careful in future?

'It's about Caroline. I need some female advice.'

Caroline was his girlfriend of a few years' standing. Julie had met her at a couple of Christmas parties and had formed no strong opinions on her either way. She was neither excessively loud nor notably quiet, neither particularly friendly nor unusually aloof. Physically, she was like one of those composite photos you sometimes saw on the internet: 'Average Human Female'. The only remarkable thing about her was that she had snagged David, who was – without wishing to be unkind – some way out of her league. More than once, Julie had caught herself assuming that the woman must be a magician in the sack.

'I see.'

David made a microscopic adjustment to the position of his fork. 'Okay, first of all, you're probably wondering why the hell I'm bothering you with this.'

'Uh—'

'The truth is, Julie, I don't have many female friends. Tell you the truth… I don't have *any* female friends.'

'Right.'

'I used to have. I used to have loads. But gradually, you know…'

'Let me guess. You slept with them all?'

'I was going to say that things became complicated between us. But, basically – yes.'

Julie shook her head in mock disapproval. 'Silly boy. You should have kept at least one aside. For emergencies.'

'I know. I was a fool.'

'So. Go on. Tell me. What's the story with Caroline?'

'It's—'

He looked behind her and smiled. Their waiter was closing in. With the care and attention of a man handling a baby while trying out rollerskates for the first time, he deposited her smoked salmon mousse.

'Thank you,' she said and only just stopped herself from adding *Now hurry up and fuck off again*. David had opted for the rabbit terrine. When both dishes were safely tabled, the waiter extended a little finger and began to point out the many little touches that made them different from any salmon mousses or rabbit terrines that they may have encountered in lesser establishments. Julie nodded throughout his little speech and even forced a little 'Oooh' at one point. Eventually, the waiter retreated.

'Well,' David said. 'This looks lov—'

'You were saying? About Caroline?'

'Right. Okay. Look. Caroline and I have been together for three years now, almost. Living together for a year or so. And we've been very happy, most of the time. But she's starting to get a bit… y'know… itchy.'

'Itchy?'

'Itchy. Marriage-wise. Nothing's been said, nothing concrete, anyway. But there have been hints.'

'Ah. So she's a traditionalist.'

'Yes. Exactly. A traditionalist. Which was news to me.'

'You'd never talked about it?'

'Only as a punchline. We talked about moving in together for a long time before we did it. *That* was the big move, as far as I was concerned. I didn't know that was only the semi-final.'

'That's an interesting way to put it, David. So you think love is some sort of tournament? Like the World Cup?'

'Right, so we're doing psychoanalysis? Should I lie down? Are you going to drag a couch in?'

Julie took some mousse. It was merely pleasant, which was somehow intensely disappointing. If it wasn't going to be orgasmic, she would have preferred it to be awful.

'I'm not sure what we're doing. You said you wanted female advice. So, go on then – hit me with a question.'

'Okay. I… Hm. I'm trying to think of a way to phrase it that won't make me sound like I'm in a Jennifer Aniston rom-com. In the Jennifer Aniston role.'

Dooley had grown up with three sisters and now, obviously,

lived in a female-only environment. He was comfortable talking emotions and relationships. Julie often thanked the gods that she hadn't been lumbered with an insensitive lout. Still. David's discomfort was refreshing. It was just so *male*.

'Would you like me to hazard a guess?' she asked. 'Save you the embarrassment?'

'Please.'

'I think your question is "How do I know if she's really the one?"'

David's chin hit his chest. He made fists and rocked back in his chair. For a moment, Julie thought he had choked on his rabbit. Then she realised that he was merely being horrified.

'Am I to take it from your acute discomfort,' she said, 'that I'm on the right track?'

'Not really, no. I'm squirming because I'm a man. This entire conversation is a form of torture.'

'This entire conversation was your idea.'

'I know, I know. All right, look: I'll put it simply and bluntly and you can just tell me what you think. Deal?'

'Deal.'

'Okay. I don't want to get married. It's not that I don't want to get married to Caroline. I don't want to get married to anyone. Ever. But I don't want to split up with her either. What am I supposed to do?'

'What have you got against marriage, then?'

'So we *are* doing analysis…'

'Hey, if you're going to have this conversation with Caroline, my woman's intuition tells me that she just might want an answer to that one.'

He nodded thoughtfully, went to work on his terrine and didn't answer for so long that she thought she might have offended him somehow. Then he scratched the tip of his nose and shrugged.

'I just don't think it's… necessary. We love each other. We live together. All things being equal, in a couple of years' time, we'll start a family. Why do we need to apply labels to it? Why do I have to be a "husband"? Why does she have to be a "wife"?'

'That would be all fine and dandy if she felt the same way. Given that she doesn't, let me tell you what's she's going to hear if you say that. She's going to hear "I'm not sure about all this and I want to keep my options open". I guarantee it.'

'That's exactly what I'm afraid of.'

'You can hardly blame her. You say you want to be with her permanently. Right? If that's true, who cares about a silly little label? Okay, you think it's unnecessary but so what? Would it kill you to have a label applied if it meant keeping her?'

'Well, maybe it won't come to that. Maybe I can get her to come around to my way of thinking.'

'And maybe she can get you to come around to hers.'

He shook his head, then stared at the condiments for a moment. 'I have two brothers, Julie, and a sister. All four of us are of the same mind: we will never get married.'

There was a certain weight to his tone – as if he was hoping he would have to say no more. Julie didn't miss the implication.

'Mum and Dad not great role models, then.'

'Individually – salt of the earth. Together – 9/11.'

'Are they still around?'

'Still around, still married, still sniping at each other from opposite sides of the room after 48 years. It looks to me like a kind of hell.'

She said the obvious thing: 'But why should your marriage be a disaster just because theirs was? That makes no logical sense.'

'Logic doesn't come into it. If the only person you'd ever seen do a bungee jump had wound up as a fucking *stain*, how would you feel about bungee jumping?'

Julie tried to look unfazed by all this intimacy, but it wasn't easy. Was she really his closest female friend at work? No, not at work – closest, full stop. She longed to press pause and chew it all over. But that would have to wait for later.

'I don't know,' he went on. 'Sometimes it feels so hard being in a long-term thing. Just too bloody messy, too complicated. You find yourself pining for the days when something's all new and fresh and exciting.' He took a sip of his sparkling water and fixed her with a look. 'Do you ever get that, Julie? Wanting something new and exciting?'

Her answer came tumbling out, the words running into each other like the strokes in a drum roll.

'Me? Ah, well, you know, my parents had a pretty good time, marriage-wise, still have, for that matter, and I'm quite happily married, thank you very much, so, no, that doesn't really, doesn't really come up, for me.' She swallowed. 'Although, mind you, everyone wonders, don't they, now and again, you can't help it, can you, human nature and whatnot.'

She took a long drink of her own. He was still looking at her. She could feel it. But she kept her gaze elsewhere.

'Well,' he said. 'I don't think we're going to solve my problem today. But thanks for listening. How's your mousse?'

She fell on the opportunity to swerve. 'My mousse,' she told him gravely, 'is *incredible*.'

Dooley tightened his grip on Mr Tiger and ever so slightly shook him – vibrated him, really. His intention was to simulate rage.

'Do my ears deceive me?' he said in the high, almost hysterical tone that he gave to all of Mr Tiger's pronouncements, regardless of context.

In his other hand he held Mrs Owl. Her voice was low and somewhat husky. An argument could be made, he knew, that he had given each of them the other one's natural register. But that ship had sailed. Swapping now could only lead to confusion in his audience.

'Please, sir,' said Mrs Owl. 'Begging your leave to explain my current predicament.'

Dooley increased the intensity of Mr Tiger's vibrations and, for good measure, bounced him on his knee (but not too hard; some of his stitching had come loose and he was in danger of losing stuffing). 'I'M NOT INTERESTED IN YOUR EXCUSES, YOU MISERABLE WRETCH. I WILL HAVE MY RENT OR

YOU WILL FIND YOURSELF IN WANT OF A ROOF BY NIGHTFALL.'

Mrs Owl recoiled in horror. 'Please, sir, Mr Tiger, sir! Another day or two is all I ask! My boy suffers with a terrible fever! If you put us on the street, he will surely perish!'

Nicola was at the opposite end of the sofa, propped up between cushions. She was transfixed.

'That is no concern of mine. Perhaps your boy's demise, if it came to pass, would teach you a valuable lesson about responsibility and respect for contracts freely entered.'

Mr Tiger's bouncing became ridiculous, and Nicola lost it. She cackled in delight, clapping her pudgy little hands together as she rocked from side to side. Dooley cracked up too, then dropped the toys to the floor. Nicola pouted, confused and disappointed.

'We'll see Mr Tiger and Mrs Owl again tomorrow,' he told her and reached across to scoop her up. 'Now. Let's get you a little bit of nosebag.'

'Goo!'

'You're damn right, goo. What do you think – chicken and vegetable? I know you like—'

The front door opened. He squinted in its general direction. It could only be Julie but her appearance now seemed as unlikely as that of, say, Kanye West.

'Well, hello!' she said as she entered the living room. 'How's my little princess?' She skipped across and took Nicola from him.

'What's wrong?' Dooley said immediately. 'Why are you home?'

Julie laughed as Nicola cooed and patted her face. 'I'm pretty sure I live here?'

'But you're early. You're never early. You're never even *on time*.' This last sounded a little more like a challenge than he'd intended. He braced himself for a cool reply.

'Well, that's true, I suppose. What can I tell you, I just felt like taking off.' She rubbed noses with her daughter, who blinked and gurgled with delight.

'Oh? That's not like you.' Once again, he had accidentally employed an accusing tone but once again, Julie let it slide.

'I don't know, I had such a good day and I just thought, why not quit while you're ahead?'

'Well, hurray for that.'

'Yeah. Doesn't hurt once in a while.'

For a moment, they watched Nicola tugging at the toes of her onesie.

'So, what went your way, then? Did you make someone cry in a meeting?'

'It was nothing in particular. Nothing major. Just… generally. Just a good day, that's all.'

'Cool. I haven't even started dinner. I was just about to get something for her majesty.'

'I'll do that.'

'Which?'

She shrugged. 'Both.'

He pulled a face. She never cooked after work. 'I'm suspicious now. Good day… or head injury?'

'Oooh. Solid effort. Eight out of ten from me.'

'Well. I'm not going to say no, am I? Thanks.'

She stood and headed for the kitchen. 'Come on, then, Nicola. We'll leave Jerry Seinfeld here to put his feet up.' Dooley made a big show of doing just that. A thought occurred. Would it be pushing his luck? He decided not.

'I was thinking…'

Julie paused and swivelled. 'Yeah?'

'I might duck in next door later. See if Redmond fancies a beer.'

'What, are you asking *permission?*'

'Uh. Kind of?'

She shifted Nicola's weight, freed a hand and made a gesture. 'Permission granted.' As she left the room, Dooley sat properly again – he wasn't really a 'feet up' kind of guy – and marvelled at this wonderful development. Whatever it was that had made her day at work, he wished it would happen more often.

At some point in the last few years, Redmond reflected, television had become obsessed with cake. He wasn't a big TV-watcher, never had been, and was unable to pin down the chronology. But he felt sure that there had been a time, relatively recently, when you could flick around the channels all night and never see so much as a jam sponge. These days it wasn't unusual, in the course of your surfing, to come across three cake-based shows in a row. It was one of those phenomena that he pondered every so often, failed to understand, and eventually gave up on, safe in the knowledge that a bored columnist would provide him with a theory one of these days.

Tonight he had decided, for the first time, that he would give one of these programmes a shot at the title. The one he'd chosen was about a firm of Italian-American bakers whose pudgy boss was constantly anticipating disasters that never materialised. The worst thing that had happened in the 20-odd minutes Redmond had been watching was that some pink icing had turned out a little *too* pink. Even this minor snag had been edited and scored to feel like something akin to the burning down of the entire business with the loss of several lives. One of the junior bakers was telling an unseen interviewer that having carried a large cake up four flights of stairs she now felt qualified to work for NASA when Redmond's doorbell rang. He ignored it. The only people who called to the door at 8pm were salespeople, pollsters and other assorted yahoos. Ten seconds later, it rang again. This time, Redmond sprang from his armchair. Salespeople got *one* ring. That was the rule. He thumped towards the door, already preparing his line of attack: children sleeping, time of night, take a hint, and so on. When he swung the door open and saw Vincent Dooley standing there he had to quickly readjust his features, which were already set to Snarl.

'Dooley! Sorry, I thought you were a salesman or something.'

'Redmond, how are you? I am selling something, actually. I'm selling good times.'

'Pills, eh? How much?'

'I was thinking more along the lines of pub.'

'Ah, I can't, man. I'd love to but I can't. Nancy's got a taxi over to her sister's for a wine-tasting evening, ie a wine-drinking evening. The boys are asleep but I probably shouldn't leave them on their own.'

'Yeah. They might get all their mates round for a party.'

'Exactly. I'd come back and find the place wrecked.'

'Oh well. Another time.'

He looked genuinely disappointed, Redmond thought, as if a long-cherished dream had died. 'Listen. Listen: *I* have beer. I might even have crisps. Sure, come on in.'

He stepped back. Dooley grinned and even seemed to bounce on his toes a little. The poor bastard was desperate. 'Yeah? You don't mind drinking when you're looking after the boys?'

'I'm not saying we should get stocious and run around naked. I'm saying, we'll knock a few back, tell some lies. Come on. I'm watching a show about cake.'

'It's not that I don't understand the pressure she's under,' Dooley said. 'I do. Of course I do. When we decided to go this way, with me at home, it was the first thing she said. That it was going to get worse if she went full tilt at her career. I mean, it was already pretty bad, when she was a junior in there.'

Redmond hit his beer. 'Sure.'

'I just never thought it would be *this* bad. She's late home three or four nights a week. And I don't mean ten minutes. I mean two hours? It's always something. And it's never the same something twice in a row. She was home early tonight, weirdly enough, and I thought she must have been fired.' He stared at the can in his hand, fiddled with the ring pull. 'Ah. Fuck it. You know what it is, really? What it is, really, is I don't feel like any less of a man because I stay at home with my daughter. I feel like less of a man when I *complain* about it, the way I'm doing now. I worry Julie's going to come in some night and cheer me up by giving me extra money to get my hair done.'

Redmond had been nodding along attentively. But at this, he

laughed, a single cracking 'Ha!' that, somehow, seemed to echo. 'Sorry.'

'Nah, don't apologise, mate. It's ridiculous, I know it is.' He drank. 'And we're doing the right thing. God knows, I was never going to make my fortune in the call centre.'

'Oh? I thought you were in IT, before?'

'Nooo. No. I was always in customer support, one kind or another, back home and for a while when I moved here. Management, y'know, but still – never going to retire at 40. I suppose I'll be back there again, one day.'

'You don't sound too thrilled about it.'

'Meh… I never had any real ambitions, work-wise. Just drifted into this and that. Tell you the truth, looking after Nicola was my suggestion in the first place. I *liked* the idea. Still do, when it's not making me moan like a big blouse.'

They attended to their drinks in silence. The TV was still on but they had long since turned the volume down. Cakes had given way to tattoos. A bedraggled blonde woman was tearfully presenting a photo of her grandmother to an enormous man with a shaven head and an astonishing array of facial piercings. Redmond was uncomfortable. He had no idea what he had done to earn this new role of confidant, and he wasn't sure that he liked it. He was quite fond of Dooley. But they were neighbour-friends, not friend-friends. Was he supposed to offer something personal of his own now? He weighed the notion in his mind and decided to go for it.

'Get this,' he said, making what he immediately realised was a poor attempt to sound casual. 'You know my gaming setup?'

'Yeah. I believe you may have mentioned it in every single conversation we've ever had.'

'Right, right. Well, Nancy has suddenly decided that I can't have the spare room any more. She wants to put a bed in it. Assuming one will fit. I'm being turfed out.'

'That's too bad.'

'It's *absurd*, is what it is.'

Dooley shook his head sympathetically. 'I can't say I get the video game thing, but I *do* get the space-of-your-own thing. There's something fundamental about it. For blokes.'

'*Correct. A space.*'

'I don't know where it comes from, but it's there, isn't it, at the base of your brain? I feel it too. A man cave, they call it.'

'Hm? Who does?'

'People. You've never heard that? Man cave?'

'I don't think so. Is it an Australian thing?'

'Look it up. There's whole websites. It's like a, whaddayacallit, a subculture. Some people go nuts. They have crazy game set-ups like yours or a room devoted to a footie team or movies or, I don't know, fucking *swords* or – or! – a pub. That's a big one. Loads of people have man caves done up like a pub. Pool tables, dartboards, jukeboxes. That's what I'd have, if I could.'

'A pub? In a bedroom?'

'Well, no, that wouldn't work. A lot of the ones I've seen are in those big basements they have in American houses. Or in, y'know, garages.'

Redmond sucked noisily at his beer. He nodded, thinking. 'Garages,' he said.

'Garages, yeah.'

More beer. More thinking. '*Garages.*'

Dooley blinked at him. 'Am I not saying it right?'

'*I've* got a garage!'

'Congratulations. So have I.'

'I'm saying, I could move my gaming stuff in there!'

'Oh. Right.'

'It's not like we ever put a car in there. We couldn't, even if we wanted to. It's too full of crap.'

'Well. It might be okay now but what about the winter? Wouldn't you… you know… freeze to death? Sometimes I think I'll freeze to death in what you people call summer.'

'Nah. I could get a gas heater or a little fan job. It'd be toasty after ten minutes.' His mind raced. He felt an urge to get up and pace around like a character in a cartoon. 'Jesus, this would be perfect. Nancy would get her spare room for the guests we never have and I'd get to keep my stuff. She couldn't possibly object.'

'I—'

'There's an old sofa in there that we never got around to throwing out properly. Not a damn thing wrong with it. Just a bit grotty. A few squirts of Febreze would sort it right out. And most of the rest of the stuff is useless. Paint cans with a half-inch of paint, horrible old pictures that we took down but didn't throw out. Dusty old knick-knacks. That foot spa I bought her for her birthday that she never used. I bet I could get those shelves 80, 90 per cent clear. There'd be plenty of room. Is that beer dead?'

'It is indeed.'

Redmond took the empty can from him and went to the kitchen to get more. The baby monitor crackled into life just as he passed it. He froze. But it was just a minor coughing fit. Luke, by the sound of it. He grabbed fresh beers and returned to the sofa.

'Okay,' he said. 'I've just had a thought.'

'Yeah?'

'You can tell me to fuck off if you like.'

Dooley cracked open his can. 'Nervous now.'

'First of all, let me assure you that I have many more beers. There's no danger of us running out.'

'*Super* nervous.'

'Here it is: I could get extra brownie points, it occurs to me, if I gave this thing to Nancy not, like, as a vague idea but as a done deal. She gets home, y'know, and it's *done*. I get to say that I took her concerns so seriously that I leaped – *leaped*, mind you – into action at the first opportunity. Can you see where this is going?'

'Yes, Redmond. I can see where this is going.'

'What do you think? Will you give me a hand? I'm not saying we could get the garage all set up but we could get the bedroom cleared out. Squeeze my gear in there any old way for now.'

'What about the boys? We'd wake them up.'

'Well, we'd have to be careful. And so what if we do wake them up? They always go back down pretty quickly. What do you think?'

Dooley nodded slowly, mulling it over, or at least pretending to. 'When I was standing outside, you mentioned crisps.'

'Fuck, I forgot! Yes. There are crisps. Both normal and Pringular.'

'All right, then.' He extended his hand. 'It's a deal.'

They shook on it.

On the day when Nancy said goodbye to Blackbird Clinical Research, there had been fewer than 90 staff. Looking around its rooftop garden now, she felt sure that those numbers had held steady, and possibly even increased a little. This was a good sign, given that there wasn't so much 'news' these days as there was a daily report on the latest round of redundancies and closures and scalings-back. It emboldened her, gave her hope – as did the white wine, a third glass of which she was currently draining. Fiona Slattery, her sole companion, was only halfway through her first. They were small glasses, Nancy had told herself at the outset. Now she wasn't so sure.

'Childcare's crazy expensive,' Fiona said. 'Would it even make sense? Money-wise?'

Nancy shrugged and looked around for the nearest wine waiter. 'I don't know.' She caught the eye of an alarmingly pretty teenage boy (was he wearing *make-up*?) and attracted his attention with a small nod. One of the benefits of being tall.

'What do you mean you don't know? You haven't thought about it?'

The teenager arrived and offered his tray. Nancy took a glass and promised herself that she'd be cautious with this one. The waiter bowed a little, as the catering company had no doubt instructed him to do but, as he turned to leave, somewhat undermined the effect by sniffing loudly.

'It's not about money, Fiona. It's about me not losing my frigging mind.' She took a large mouthful of wine, then remembered her promise to herself and, bizarrely, almost spat some of it back. Nerves. Her nerves were getting the better of her.

Talking to Fiona had been so pleasant at first. They'd had a few laughs about the old days and lamented the fact that they hadn't kept in touch as well as they might have, each assuring the other that it was their fault. Nancy was reminded of how much she liked this woman and, before she'd even had time to wonder if it was a good idea – this was towards the end of glass number two – she'd confessed her reason for attending the company barbecue. That was beginning to feel like a mistake.

'Well,' Fiona said, 'I have to say I'm surprised.'

'Really? Why?' She knew why, of course, but she thought it might be useful to hear it expressed. It would give her some idea of what she was up against.

'Come on. You were pretty loud about it, weren't you, when you left to have Aidan? "Young kids need their mum at home", "No child of mine will be dumped in a crèche". That's certainly the way I remember it. All gung-ho.'

Nancy affected innocence. 'Gung-ho?'

'Confident. And vocal. Very vocal. I'm not having a go, I'm just—'

'All right, relax, I'm pulling your leg. I know what I was like. This is the whole problem, isn't it? I'm doing a complete one-eighty.'

Fiona raised one shoulder. 'Meh. Who cares what other people think, though? Right?'

'It's easy to say that when it's not you they're thinking it about. And, anyway, I'm more worried about me than other people. I feel like a… well… Ach, never m—'

'Hypocrite?'

Nancy frowned. 'I don't think I'm being a hypocrite. Hypocrisy is saying one thing and doing another. I said one thing and now I'm saying the direct opposite. It's not great, but it isn't hypocrisy.'

'What then?'

'I feel like a *failure*, Fiona.'

'Explain.'

'I couldn't do it, could I? I couldn't make myself…' Her throat felt like it was closing over. When she spoke again, her voice was a wet croak. 'I couldn't devote myself entirely to the kids.'

Fiona briefly grasped her forearm and gave it a small comforting squeeze. 'Ah, now. Don't get upset. What does Redmond say?'

Nancy shook her head and sighed. 'I haven't told him any of this.'

'You're kidding.'

'He doesn't even know I'm here tonight. Told him I was going to my sister's for a wine tasting.'

'Wait, wait. You're going back to work and you haven't talked it over with your husband?'

'I'm not "going back to work". I'm investigating the possibility of going back to work. If Martina says there's a chance I can get my old job back, then I'll talk to Redmond.'

'You don't think maybe you should talk to him first?'

Nancy felt her grip on her wine glass tighten. Here was the crux of the matter. There was a good reason why she hadn't spoken to Redmond. It was the same reason why she hadn't investigated the cost of childcare. The fact was, the one-eighty she'd mentioned was really more of a ninety. She still believed that her children should have a parent at home – she just no longer thought that it had to be her. It wasn't merely a question of her returning to work. Redmond would have to quit. But there was no need, she decided, to say any of this to Fiona. She had said too much already. A change of subject was called for.

'Maybe I will. If I can get him out of the spare bedroom. He's still in there, you know. The little box room, with all the games? Remember how I used to complain?'

'I can't say I do.'

'I'm pretty sure I complained all the—'

'No, wait, his fort, you're talking about?'

'His what?'

'Fort. You used to say he was like a little boy making a fort. You thought it was cute.'

'I don't think so, Fiona.'

'I'm pretty sure—'

'Well, it's a lot worse now. It's like a shrine. He has three or four console things, a huge computer. *Hundreds* of games. Posters, books, little action figures—'

'Action figures? You mean… dolls?'

'You can't call them that. You must never, ever call them that. Oh, don't get me started about that bloody room. I know he works hard in a job he doesn't like, but I work hard too, for Christ's sake. And at least his job, no matter what he thinks of it, features conversations with adults. He doesn't have to sing 'Wheels on the frigging Bus' 25 times a day and pretend to be impressed every time someone gets their own name right. He gets to go to the toilet on his own! And then he comes home and disappears for…' She took a deep breath. 'Like I say – don't get me started on that bloody room.'

'I didn't. Nancy. Look. It's been a while since we laid eyes on each other and a long while since we had a proper conversation. So you can tell me to mind my own, if you like. But it sounds to me like you're getting a lot of stuff mixed up in your head. Maybe you should slow down a bit and—'

'Oh! She's here.'

Martina Price, Nancy's old boss, had arrived and was drifting through the crowd, smiling and nodding like a politician. Trish – car park Trish, as Nancy thought of her now – was by her side. She was smiling and nodding at the same people, a second later.

'Jesus,' Nancy said. 'Martina looks *great*. She looks younger than she did when I left.'

'Runs marathons now,' Fiona said. 'On top of the yoga and swimming.'

Nancy shook her head in wonder. She raised her glass to her lips and was only a little surprised to find that it was empty.

For the next hour and a half Nancy and Fiona floated around the rooftop, sometimes drawing closer to Martina, sometimes pulling away, and always avoiding Trish. Nancy was delighted to see some of her former colleagues and either bored or horrified to see others.

They were all surprised by her presence, naturally, but seemed to buy her white lie that she had 'caught wind' of the barbecue and thought it might be fun to 'come and say hello'. As her conversational horizons expanded, her wine consumption slowed to a more sensible rate. Fiona, however, went the other way. It was as if drinking was something she had never tried before but was quickly getting the hang of. Her gestures became more expansive and her tongue loosened to an alarming degree. She told one audience of her discovery that her teenage son had rather narrow tastes in internet pornography, limiting himself almost exclusively to sites that featured Japanese girls dressed as nurses. She told another that her brother had been arrested for credit card fraud and that the stress was keeping her awake at night – not that she was getting much sleep these days anyway, on account of the menopause. Nancy started to worry that she would soon spill beans that were not hers to spill. It was this, rather than any sudden increase in courage, that made her decide to take the plunge. They were in the middle of a large circle at this point. The focus of conversation lay elsewhere along its circumference.

'I'm going to go for it,' she said to Fiona out of the corner of her mouth. Martina was talking to – or rather, at – two men. Nancy vaguely remembered one of them as Mick something. 'Come with? Please?'

'Yeah, go on then.'

'Great. You try and distract those two, Mick and… I don't know the other guy.'

'He's another Mick. Only been here a few months.'

'Right. You take the Micks…' She squinted and frowned, offended by her own unintended wordplay. 'You take the Micks and I'll peel Martina away.'

'Take them? Take them where?'

'Where? Helsinki.'

Fiona stared. 'I'd forgotten how sarcastic you are.'

'I don't mean physically take them anywhere, do I? I mean, engage them, occupy them, *frigging* distract them.'

'You're being snippy, Nancy. Don't do that.'

'Sorry. Sorry. Butterflies. You ready?'

'Lead the way.'

Without a word, they stole away from their companions and headed in Martina's direction. She was at the edge of the roof, resting her elbow on the barrier that had always struck Nancy as being dangerously low. As she approached, Nancy found herself thinking how awful it would be if she were, somehow, for some reason, to give her a little push. She slowed.

'What's wrong?' Fiona asked.

'Would you believe I'm telling myself not to accidentally shove her in case she falls to her death?'

'Well. It's always good to think ahead.'

Nancy caught Martina's eye and tried not to read too much into the fact that she wasn't rewarded with a fond look. It had been a long time, she told herself. Her hair was longer now. She'd lost weight (and not just by giving birth). Perhaps she was unrecognisable.

'Hello, all,' Fiona said. She wasn't quite slurring but the drink thickened her voice somewhat. 'Mick. Mick. Look who I found, Martina. It's only Nancy Cole.'

'Hi, Martina,' Nancy said, much too loudly. 'How are things?' It was like being presented at court. She almost curtsied.

'Things are fine,' Martina said. Her lips twitched but Nancy wasn't sure that a smile was the result. There was a moment's silence. Fiona, to her credit, immediately applied herself to the problem of the Micks. 'The food's amazing, isn't it?' she said, inserting herself and neatly dividing the group. Left more or less on her on with Martina, Nancy found herself grinning inanely and shifting from foot to foot.

'So,' Martina said after what seemed like a full minute. 'This is a surprise. What happened – you were just passing and smelled the hot dogs?'

'Good one! No. Actually, I ran into Trish the other day.'

'Is that right?'

'Yeah, just… y'know… out and about. She mentioned that the barbecue was on. I must say, it's a lot posher than it was in my day! No caterers then! I remember Graham used to be in charge of the cooking. He was always trying to educate everyone, wasn't he? And it worked! I still do that thing of making a little dent in the middle of burgers.'

'Hm.'

'Because they tend to expand, don't they, in the centre? So your toppings wind up rolling off?'

'Hm.'

Nancy's plan had been to do a little small talk. That no longer seemed like an option. She gathered herself. 'Martina, listen... I have to admit, I had a bit of an ulterior motive for coming here tonight.'

'Really.'

'Yeah. I've been doing some thinking and I've, well, I've decided that maybe the time is right for me to consider returning to the workforce.'

'Oh? Are your kids going to school already?'

'No, Aidan's just three now and Luke's only—'

Martina stopped her with a raised hand. 'Wait, wait, I'm confused. You were absolutely sure that a mother's place was at home with her children during those first few years. Weren't you? Have I got that wrong?'

'I did say something like that, yeah, but—'

'Yes. That's the way I remember it. I was wondering, because I pride myself on my excellent memory.'

'Look, I—'

'Know what else I remember? "She's a hard-hearted bitch with a spreadsheet where her womb should be." I'm paraphrasing, but that was the gist. Ring any bells?'

'I don't, I—'

'You said that about me. To Trish. When I came back to work after I had my third. She told me so at the time.' She tapped her temple. 'I filed it away, Nancy. Never thought I'd get a chance to use it but still. *I filed it away*.'

Nancy felt as if she was drowning. It took her a moment to

form a reply. 'I really don't remember saying anything like that but, okay, you got me, maybe I used to have a different attitude to—'

'My hopes rose when I saw you here tonight. But then, when you started waffling on about barbecue techniques, they fell again. I thought, "God, she really is here just to catch up with everyone. That's just sad." So I'm delighted, obviously, that you've brought the job thing up. Honestly, you've made my night. I'm sorry to say, however, that we don't have any vacancies.'

She walked away.

Nancy stood in the centre of the living room, gently swaying. After fleeing the barbecue she'd tried to walk off her horror, as if it was a slight muscle pull. Dublin being Dublin, she had been obliged to pass by a number of pubs. The fourth was the one that had lured her in. It was an old man's place, all coughs and whiskers. No one had bothered her – or even noticed her, it seemed – as she perched at the end of the bar and knocked back an indeterminate number of vodkas. Later, the taxi driver who ferried her home had opined that she was 'fucking stupid' to be tottering about on her own in her condition. For all she knew, even he could be a sex maniac. The appropriate response to this, she was dimly aware, was to say that she should be able to roam the streets as drunk as she liked in total safety and that the sex maniac problem should be laid at the feet of sex maniacs. But the correct formulation of words had eluded her. Instead, she'd improvised with a small grunt.

Redmond was nowhere to be seen. There was nothing unusual about that in itself. It was late. The empty beer cans, though. There were more of them than she would have expected to see and, furthermore, they seemed to have been deposited in two distinct groups. He wouldn't have gone to bed and left them lying around. She struggled to come up with a scenario that would account for these anomalies. Nothing suggested itself. Mind you, she mused, she wasn't on top of her game, mentally (after paying her fare, she'd told the taxi driver to 'Keep changing'). She did a bit more swaying, then started for the kitchen, where she intended to drink as many pints of water as she could manage to force down, which, in all probability, would be one. She'd managed three large swallows when she heard a thump and then a sort of scrape coming from the garage. A thought blossomed: *sex maniac*. She grabbed a knife from the block, dropped it, swore and, bending to pick it up, bumped her head on a drawer handle. Upright again and brandishing her weapon in the direction of the garage door, she heard two more thumps and then... whistling? She rubbed her sore forehead and slammed the knife down on the counter. *Redmond*. What was he at? She stomped across the kitchen and threw the door open. Her initial impression, as her eyes swept around, was that she must have sustained some sort of brain damage in the bump. The garage, as she knew it, was gone. In its place was Redmond's gaming room. Except it wasn't his gaming room. It was a weird dream-like version of it, scattered and only half complete.

'What the hell is this?' she said.

'Heyyy!' Redmond said. 'You're back.' He spread his arms. 'So! What do you think?'

'You're supposed to be looking after the kids.'

He gestured to the corner, where the baby monitor was plugged in, its green light gently pulsing. 'They're grand. I'm just—'

'You'll wake them!'

'No, I won't, I'm being very careful. How was the wine tasting? Pretty successful by the sounds of it. Did—'

'Redmond, what are you *doing?*'

'Okay, listen. This thing about the spare bedroom. I got thinking. Wouldn't it work out perfectly for the both of us if I moved my gaming stuff into the garage? You'd get the spare room for your, whatever, and I'd get a space I could really go to town with. It's not like we use it for anything else. Now I know what you're going to say – I'd be too cold in here in the winter. But I'd be fine, honestly! I could get a little fan heater or one of those gas yokes. I know it's hard to imagine now because it's such a mess but I've got the old sofa, the TV's going over there, I can get some

better shelving, throw out all the crap, put a few posters up and...
Nancy? You don't look all that impressed.'

She turned and walked away. Sixty seconds later she was in bed
with the duvet pulled over her head.

3

Every so often, Eddie Fallon got it into his head to write a company-wide memo. Deirdre dreaded these occasions. For one thing, the memos were always whiny and passive-aggressive in nature. For another, Mr Fallon was a singularly awful writer who compounded his awfulness by being constitutionally unable to accept help. 'You're here to take dictation, not to dictate,' he snapped at her one day when she pointed out that 'loyalness' wasn't a real word. The subject of the memo on that occasion had been sloppy parking. There had also been missives on sloppy timekeeping, sloppy dressing and sloppy desk-tidying. Today's was possibly the worst ever. It was about sloppy toilet maintenance. Mr Fallon had paid a visit to the gents that morning and returned with fire in his belly. 'I appreciate that the soap dispensers don't always dispense with the greatest accuracy,' he fumed. 'And I know we're all busy people. Once in a while, we might be in such a hurry that we'd walk out and leave a little soap dribble on the sink. Fair enough. I understand that. I *get* it. What I do not understand, what I do not *get*, is how a grown man can urinate all over a lavatory seat – all over a *floor*, sometimes – and just walk away from it. I don't care how busy he is! And then there's the toilet tissue. The toilet tissue, Deirdre! Sometimes, I go in there and it's like we've had one of those space parties they used to do in New York.' She'd been in his office for almost 40 minutes, almost all of which time she had spent listening to him ranting (and trying to work out what a 'space party' might be – she eventually concluded that he meant 'ticker-tape parade'). Now, at last, he seemed ready to release her.

'Yeah,' he said and nodded, more to himself than to her.

'Yeah?' She hardly dared to hope.

'Yeah. Okay.'

'Okay?'

'Yeah. Send it.'

Mr Fallon, to Deirdre's ongoing amazement, refused to have

a computer in his office. He had a company email address but, if asked, wouldn't have been able to say what it was. Deirdre operated it for him from her desk, and used it almost exclusively for sending his anti-sloppiness memos and receiving spam about amazing financial opportunities (and penis problems – too small, too sensitive, entirely nonfunctional…).

'Right. Will do.' She closed her notepad and started to get up.

'Listen. Before you go.'

She caught herself sighing as she sat back down and only half-managed to stop it. The truncated sound that escaped her was akin to a gasp, and alarmingly sexual. Her cheeks flushed. 'I really don't think you can make this any clearer,' she said quickly, hoping to cover her embarrassment.

He shook his head. 'No, I just wanted to ask you how you're, you know… doing.'

'Oh.'

'Is everything okay now?'

How *male*, she thought. She'd told him she was in despair, but that was days ago; it was bound to have blown over by now, surely? It was not immediately obvious to her how she should respond. She still couldn't quite believe that she'd opened her mouth in the first place. On the other hand, it might not hurt to hear herself say some things out loud.

'Well,' she began, and exhaled deeply. 'There has been a development, actually.'

'Really?' He sat forward a little, looking genuinely relieved. Excited, even.

'On the baby front.'

He beamed and slapped the desk with both hands. 'Fantastic news! Congratulations! I knew—'

'Wait, wait. I'm not pregnant or anything.'

'Oh. Sorry.' He joined his hands together, as if to provide a solemn counterpoint to the desk-slap. 'What's the development, then?'

'Um. We're going to go for IVF.'

His eyes narrowed ever so slightly. Half a second later, when he remembered to smile, he looked like someone experiencing mild toothache.

'Great! That's great. Great.'

She stared at him, hard. His eyes flicked away.

'What?' she said.

'What?'

'You pulled a face, Mr Fallon.'

'No, I didn't.'

'Is it a religious thing?'

'Excuse me?'

'Religion. Some people object to IVF because of their religion.'

'I didn't know that. I've never even heard of that.'

'What is it then? There's obviously something.'

He sat back and briefly closed his eyes. 'All right, look. I didn't want to say this to you the other day but you're not the only person I know who's had trouble in the whole fertility, uh... arena.'

'Is that right?'

'My niece. On my wife's side. Her brother's kid. Ruby. Tried and tried, for years. Married young, too. I believe age can be a factor? Anyway, the time came when the doctor recommended UVF.'

'IVF.'

'IVF.'

'And?'

'And it didn't work.'

She waited for him to add something meaningful. He didn't.

'Is that it? Mr Fallon, I know it doesn't always work. Did you think I didn't know that?'

'It's not just that it didn't work. The *stress* of it, Deirdre. Hoping and hoping and then getting crushed. They had three, three, three, what do you call it... goes?'

'Rounds.'

'Rounds, yes. Three rounds. It took forever. Ruby was nearly mental by the end of it. *Mental*. And then they just shrugged and said that was it. It hasn't worked, so goodbye and good luck.'

He looked at her as if he had made an important point and was confident that she couldn't refute it. Rage swelled within her, so pure and intense that it changed the taste in her mouth.

'I don't understand,' she said, chewing each syllable. 'I don't understand why you're saying all this to me. Are you trying to help? Is this you *helping?*'

'I'm just saying—'

'Don't bother? Give up?'

'No!'

'What then?'

'Deirdre, I wasn't going to open my beak! You made me! You said I pulled a face!'

She was deterred but only briefly. 'Well, okay, maybe so, but still. This isn't what I want to hear.'

'I'm not trying to put you off. Honest to God, I'm not. It'll probably work for you! I'm sure it will! Just make sure you go in with your eyes open, that's all. Ruby didn't. She was so convinced it was going to work. She thought she was guaranteed a baby. That's all I'm saying.' He shook his head sadly at the memory of this poor deluded woman's folly.

'I doubt it,' Deirdre said.

'Doubt what?'

'I doubt your niece was convinced it was going to work. Believe me, a woman in my position knows the statistics, knows you're a long way from "guaranteed" a baby. Being a man and so not great at understanding emotions, you probably got confused and thought desperate hope was confidence.'

He squinted at her. She cracked a small smile to show – or rather, to pretend – that she was pulling his leg.

'Just get your head right,' he said. 'Before you go down this road, that's all. You and Leo, both of you.'

'Hm.'

'Go into it strong, together, with your eyes wide open.'

'Hm.'

'Okay? We're still friends?'

'Of course.' She pushed back her chair and got out of there at a pace that was just shy of jogging.

'Look, Nicola, tennis racquets!'

This was Dooley's third such exclamation. The previous two had been 'Look, Nicola, dumb-bells!' and 'Look, Nicola, basketballs!' She hadn't responded to either of those but the racquets elicited the exuberant shaking of all four limbs with which she typically indicated interest or pleasure (or, it had to be admitted, digestive distress).

'I know! I'm excited too.'

They were in All Star Sports. It was not Dooley's natural shopping environment, and he knew that it showed. He half-expected one of the perky youngsters who were bouncing around in bright pink polo shirts to approach and ask, not if he needed help with anything, but if he was lost. When he finally found what he was looking for (in the darkest, dustiest, presumably least-visited corner), he imagined the staff all nodding in unison, happy that a small mystery had been solved.

'Here we are,' he said. 'Now. These are called dartboards and... Jesus! Whoa. They cost a lot more than Daddy would have guessed.'

Nicola spat up. Dooley grabbed a wipe from the bag and dabbed her chin clean. As he did so, one of the pink shirts appeared at his side. He was even younger-looking than his colleagues. Still a teenager, Dooley guessed by his wispy facial fuzz. Tony, his name tag said.

'Hey, uh, sir. Anything I can do for you?'

'Yeah, mate. You can lift my jaw off the floor. Thirty-four Euro for a dartboard? This is just a thing you throw darts at, right? I mean, it doesn't do anything else? It just hangs on a wall and gets hit by darts?'

Tony swallowed and did some rapid blinking. His mouth fell open but no words emerged. Dooley felt bad for the guy.

'Sorry, man,' he said, patting him on the shoulder. 'I'm just surprised. I thought they'd be cheaper, that's all. Times are tough, y'know? It comes with darts at least, doesn't it?'

'Uh...'

'It doesn't even come with *darts?*'

'Just the board. I'm really, really sorry.'

His eyes went slightly wild. Dooley thought he might actually be in danger of crying.

'Right. Well, it's hardly your fault.'

'It isn't! Honestly, it isn't!'

'You just work here.'

'Exactly! And this is only my third week.'

'Well, if that's what it costs, that's what it costs. It must be a pretty *good* dartboard, at least?'

He paused, giving the boy a chance to impress him with his salesmanship, maybe gain some confidence. But Tony not only failed to take advantage, he actually sighed and shrugged. Apparently, he had gone from anxious to bored in the blink of an eye. Dooley did a little sighing of his own, then grabbed the (surprisingly heavy) dartboard and the cheapest set of darts he could see. He set about balancing them on the handlebars of Nicola's buggy. Without another word, Tony simply wandered away.

'Management material,' Dooley said to Nicola. 'They're lucky to have found him.'

'Gah!' she said, in what he chose to believe was enthusiastic appreciation of his sarcasm.

Outside in the shopping centre car park, there was an alarming moment when the buggy rolled over some small obstruction, causing the dartboard to become unbalanced. It shifted forward and was on its way to doing Nicola serious harm before he grabbed its leading edge with little more than his fingernails. His legs turned to rubber. They always did when it came to daughter-related injury – or potential injury – but this was worse than usual. Having to tell Julie that Nicola had been hurt on his watch would be awful. Explaining how it happened ('I bought this dartboard, see') would be tantamount to suicide. Then again, he reflected as he reached the car and popped the boot, he was almost certainly in serious trouble anyway.

'Getting pretty full in there, Nicola,' he said. Two slabs of Carlsberg, one of Heineken. A bottle of vodka. A bottle of gin. A bottle of tequila. Two bottles of whiskey. Three bottles of red, one of white. Four multipacks of crisps. Three jumbo bags of salted peanuts. A box of 24 pint glasses, a box of 12 whiskey glasses. Six shot glasses. The biggest cooler box he had ever seen, never mind owned. An old-school Jameson mirror. Two framed 'Guinness is Good for You' posters (he hated the stuff but it seemed fitting). And now a dartboard. It was a meagre beginning, but it was something. Helping Redmond to set up his gaming space had been a chore at first. But once the heavy lifting was done and the process turned creative – this should go here, that should go there – he'd found it fun and started wondering why he shouldn't have a go himself. He slept on it and woke up 90 per cent convinced. Then Julie congratulated him on the thoroughness with which he had cleaned the fridge. She all but patted him on the head and seemed hopeful that his day had been made. He had no doubt that she meant well. But her compliment gave him that final ten per cent. He was a man and, dammit, he should have a man cave. In the garage. A little pub.

He hunkered down and planted a kiss on his daughter's forehead.

'This is going to be great,' he said. Nicola spat up again.

Declan Dinkins took a bite of his tuna melt, chewed, swallowed noisily, shook his head, glugged on his sparkling water, swallowed noisily again. 'The way I see it, this is a test.'

'A test?' Redmond said.

They were in a booth in McCaffrey's, the nearest pub to the office. It was, by common consent, a dump. Why they had chosen to go there for lunch, Redmond couldn't quite say. Then again, he wasn't sure why he was having lunch with Declan anywhere. They rarely ate with one another and never alone. Today, they'd just happened to find themselves leaving the building at the same time. Without either one ever designating it a plan, they'd drifted towards McCaffrey's together, Redmond imagining all the way that the height difference made them look like C-3PO and R2-D2. Once situated, they'd rapidly bored each other with office talk, then fallen into near-silence. Redmond had broken it by bringing up the only subject on his mind. And that, he was already starting to believe, had been a mistake.

'A test,' Declan said.

'Of?'

'You. Your resolve. But don't worry. There's nothing at stake except the entire rest of your marriage.'

Redmond smiled. Declan did not. Redmond stopped smiling. 'Go on, then. Let's hear it.'

'You bent backwards here, am I right?'

'Well—'

'You did, Redmond, you bent backwards. She told you she wanted to take over your room for no good reason—'

'Guests.'

'Guests, whatever. Nothing important, anyway. You could have said no. You could have said no fucking way: I work all day long with morons and sadists and when I come home, I'm entitled to kick back a little bit. But you didn't. You dug deep and you got *resourceful*. You found a solution that's simple and practical. Now. How does the missus respond? Does she say, "Oh, that's a good idea, my darling dearest! Why didn't I think of that?" No. She does not. She slopes off in a huff.'

'Like no huff before it. This is way worse than the time I said I'd do her mother.'

'Right. So now you face a choice. How are you going to react? Because, let me tell you, if you roll over on this, you might as well cut your balls off and hand them to her.'

Redmond pushed his plate away, dragged it back, pushed it away again. 'The way you're talking, Declan...'

'What?'

'You're talking like Nancy's my enemy. She's my *wife*. Y'know – I love her and stuff.'

'Nah, man, nah. Don't get me wrong. I'm not saying you have to escalate the thing. I'm not saying you have to scream and shout and get all aggravated. You can do this quietly and gently. Peacefully. But you have to do it.'

'Do what, exactly?'

'Stand up for yourself!'

'Hm.'

'For this one small thing that you know you deserve.'

'I do deserve it. I do.'

'Damn right you do. Gandhi.'

'Excuse me?'

'The little Indian lad. Toga sort of thing, flip-flops—'

'I know who he *is*.'

'I'm saying, that's your role model here. Quiet, gentle, peaceful resistance. You don't want any trouble. But your cause is a just one.'

Redmond chewed on it for a moment. 'Gandhi... Yeah.'

'Just think what he achieved. They made a movie and everything. David Attenborough.'

'Richard Attenborough.'

'Whatever.'

Redmond stared at nothing in particular. 'Gandhi,' he said again.

Nancy had a vague impression that Starbucks was evil. You weren't supposed to go there. Something to do with global warming? No, that didn't sound right. Mistreatment of dirt-poor workers abroad? Nope. That wasn't it either. She took a sip of her vanilla latte, then another. Maybe she'd imagined it. Or maybe it was nothing to do with morality. Not evil – just powerfully uncool. That rang a bell. She looked around at the other customers. Were they cool? She had no idea. Take the young woman on the stool by the window. She had long dirty blonde hair but was shaved bald at the sides. Her clothes were really just a collection of holes held together by thin strips of material. She had no piercings, not even earrings, but was wearing so many metallic bracelets that she jangled every time she took a drink. Did other young women sigh with envy when they watched her go by? Or did they roll their eyes and wonder how she dared to leave the house? There had been a time when Nancy would have had the answer on the tip of her tongue but now she had no idea about the trendiness or otherwise of the baldy/holey/

jangly look. For all she knew, her own ensemble – a beige fleece over €15 jeans – was all the rage. But that seemed unlikely.

'Mammy?'

This was Aidan, who was on the chair opposite hers, his little legs folded up underneath him. Luke was in a high chair beside her.

'Yes?'

'My straw comed out.'

'Yeah? Just put it back in, there's a good man.'

He pouted. 'Unh.'

'What? You know how to put a straw in a juice box, Aidan.'

'But I want *you* to do it.'

'Why?'

A shrug. 'You do it.'

Nancy considered her choices – argue for a little while and then reinsert the straw, or just reinsert the straw. Why prolong the inevitable? She took the OJ from him and did the necessary. As he threw himself back into the task of slurping his remaining juice, she turned her attention to Luke, whom she had pacified with a square of chocolate from her handbag. As was his custom, he'd squeezed it to the point of liquefaction in his tiny fist, and smeared the result in the general vicinity of his mouth. She did her best to clean him up with a baby wipe but he reacted with a familiar combination of horror and violence. It may have been rendered goo-like and spread all over his lower face, he seemed to think, but it was still *his* chocolate, and he had plans for it. Just as she plucked a second wipe, she noticed the woman at the next table. She was older, but not old. Fifty-ish. Nicely dressed and fully made-up. Not a hair out of place. And she was staring. It was a stare of such intensity that Nancy almost burst out laughing. Before she could form another thought, the woman lowered her tea and said, 'Your son is making quite a lot of noise.'

'Excuse me?'

'I said, your son. He's being very noisy. With his drink.'

Nancy deliberated for a moment. On the one hand this, on the other hand that... *No*, she decided with a firmness that surprised her. *Not having this. Not today. Not in the mood.*

'Oh, I heard you. I wasn't asking you to repeat yourself. I meant it more in a "I can't believe my ears" kind of way.'

The woman produced a thin smile, which was somehow more menacing than her stare. 'You can't believe your ears? Really? You don't think other people are entitled to peace and quiet?'

'Listen. Maybe you were under the impression that this is your own kitchen and that we have all somehow invaded it, but I've got news: you're in a public space. Other people are allowed into it. Some of those people have young children. And some of those young children may occasionally make noises that adults might not like. Am I going too fast for you? Any questions so far?'

'Well, you've cleared one thing up for me, anyway,' the woman said. 'I can see now where he gets his manners from.'

'There's nothing wrong with his manners. He's *three*, that's all.' Aidan, unfortunately, chose this precise moment to produce his most astounding slurp to date. Nancy half-expected to see the sides of his head cave in. She hesitated. Her intention had been to follow up with a defence of her own attitude but the mega-slurp had robbed her of all momentum. Instead, she opted for the semi-conciliatory move of grabbing the empty juice box and placing it out of reach.

'Muuuum,' Aidan whined.

'I think it's empty now.'

'It isn't empty!'

'Aidan.'

'It isn't!'

'Please—'

'*There's juice in it!*'

He growled, then swept his forearm across the table. It was some consolation, Nancy supposed, that the only item he caught was her spoon, but still. By some weird accident of acoustics, it made a noise like a drum kit falling down a flight of stairs. Everywhere, heads swivelled. Nancy expected some sort of *I-told-you-so* from her neighbour but the woman merely looked down into her teacup and gently swirled it. There was something of the Bond villain about the gesture; it was slightly chilling and wholly infuriating. Nancy pretended not to notice and dived down to her side to retrieve the spoon. On her way back to the vertical she breathed in and immediately realised – there was no room for doubt – that Luke needed attention in the nappy department.

'Oh!' she said. 'Come on, little man. Let's get you sorted out. Time we were going anyway.'

Her tone was light and breezy, she hoped. Unshaken. Not stirred. But in truth, she was delighted to have an excuse to take her leave early.

'I have to change Luke,' she told Aidan. 'Up you get, sunshine. Do you need to go too?'

A scowl. He had a thing about being asked this particular question, especially outside the house. '*No.*'

'Okay. Maybe you will when we get in there.'

'I won't!'

'Stop shouting, Aidan.'

'I'm not shouting!'

The maintenance of a light and breezy tone was rapidly becoming impossible. She busied herself with gathering their stuff and transferring Luke to his buggy, then gave her eldest a look that told him his interests would best be served, at this point, by silent cooperation. Aidan climbed off his seat – it took him about 20 seconds – and they all trooped off to the coffee shop's only toilet, an outsized affair that catered to males, females and wheelchair users alike. As they reached the door that led to it via a short corridor, a young man emerged. He held the door open for them but wouldn't meet Nancy's eyes when she nodded her thanks. She took this as a sign of guilt and steeled herself for what she would find when she went through the next door, into the cubicle. But the air in there was surprisingly breathable. She undid the latch for the changing table, lowered it down and wiped its surface, then lifted Luke from the buggy. As she swung him up and laid him on his back, his brother stepped under the hand-dryer and screamed when it began to pummel him with hot air. Nancy was so startled she almost cried out herself. And then the boy burst into tears. He'd been paralysed by fear, apparently, and hadn't moved away from the dryer. It was blowing his hair down into a ridiculous bowl cut. His eyes were like cue balls, searching the room for some hint as to how he might escape this dreadful predicament.

'Just move away!' Nancy roared. Was the dryer getting louder? How was that possible?

'What?' Aidan screeched.

She turned back to Luke and quickly secured him in place with the changing table's grubby straps. Her haste seemed to upset him. His expression clouded and then he too began to wail. Muttering darkly, Nancy skipped across and gently moved Aidan away from the wall. The hand-dryer ceased hostilities but her son remained semi-hysterical. She held him by the shoulders.

'Aidan, love, it's all right now, you have to—'

'You shouted at me!'

'I had to shout because of the noise!'

'You shouted at me a few times!'

'What? When?'

'In the… yesterdays.'

She took this to mean 'the recent past'. Guilt gripped her hard. Had she?

'I'm sorry, honey, if I did. It wasn't your—'

On the changing table, Luke issued a teeth-rattling scream and, to Nancy's horror, managed to half-sit up. She hadn't done one of the strap buckles properly. With a strangled yelp, she dived back to him. As she worked to correct her mistake, he bucked his hips then swung his left arm. He hadn't intended to hit her – she assumed – but that was of little consolation when one of his fingers entered her eye and pushed it half an inch into her skull. The pain was immediate and profound. Perversely, it hurt so much that she didn't even cry out. Instead, she staggered backwards, gasping for breath, and stood on Aidan's toes. He screamed bloody murder and hopped about for a few seconds, then slumped in the corner and went back to merely sobbing at the top of his lungs. A brief hiatus followed, during which Luke thrashed about, crying, Aidan rocked back and forth, crying, and Nancy simply stood there, afraid to move in case she invited fresh disaster. When the time seemed right, she approached her younger son as one might approach a house of cards. She'd changed thousands of nappies in her time, she reminded herself. It would take more than excruciating pain and partial blindness to stop her changing this one.

'Okay,' she said. 'Let's get this done.'

To her relief – and, at this point, surprise – it went reasonably well. She got urinated on, of course, but she retained the use of her remaining good eye, which was nice. The nappy wasn't even all that disgusting; more of a shart than anything. Luke even stopped crying, although Aidan most certainly did not, despite her constant coos of sympathy.

'Mammy,' he moaned, as she finished up with Luke. 'Mammy…'

'Two seconds, Aidan. Almost done.'

'Poo, Mammy.'

'Just get on the toilet and—'

'No. Poo. *Poo*.'

She snapped her head around and saw that he was pointing at his jeans. 'Ah, Aidan!'

'No shouting!'

'I'm not shouting!'

His crying increased in both intensity and volume. 'It's okay, honey, shhh, it's okay,' she said, tugging Luke's trousers back into position. 'Mammy will get you cleaned up and we have spare… Ah, *Christ*.' Aidan had been relatively easy to toilet-train and hadn't had an accident in a long time. Not ten days previously, she had decided that she could save some room in her overflowing bag by no longer packing a spare set of trousers and underpants for him. He looked up at her, his little face twisted in disgust that she would soon share. *I could just run away*, she thought. *I could just leave them here and run away. I'd never be able to live with myself. But the option is there. Italy, maybe. I could find a job on a farm or in a vineyard. Simple manual work. Undemanding but spiritually rewarding. My lack of Italian would make me mysterious. 'Who is she?' people would ask. 'Who is this strange, pale woman who appeared out of the blue? She seems so troubled and yet there is great wisdom in her eyes.'*

'Okay, Aidan. Listen. Listen. We have to get you cleaned up but we don't have any other trousers for you. Or pants.' She stepped across and got down to his level. 'Will you stand up for me, please?'

He did so. 'I can't have no trousers,' he blubbed. 'I can't have no pants.'

She removed his shoes and started to work on his buttons. 'Well, maybe it'll be all right. Maybe your trousers won't be so bad. We could ditch the underpants and... Oh. Right.'

The briefest of glances amidships told her that, no, it would not be all right. No shart, this. It was a full Code Brown. And not... neat. It wasn't easy to keep her face from screwing up in horror but she did her best. She was able to get the trousers off without making a sound but issued a series of small squeaks as – with the merest tips of her fingers – she removed the underpants. Her only consolation was that Aidan stopped crying as she rendered him semi-naked. There was no way in hell she was going to attempt to wash the soiled items, so she stashed them in the bin. It would be poor form, of course, to just leave them there, stinking the joint up even more; on her way out, she'd have to tell a member of staff that the bin-emptying schedule would have to be adjusted.

'Right then!' she said with as much positivity as she could muster. 'Follow Mammy over to the sink. Come on, there's a good man.'

She took his hand and averted her gaze as he waddled unhappily across the room with her. Then she knelt down and set to work. Baby wipes were the best tool for the job but her supply was limited and soon exhausted. They weren't flushable either, so they went in the bin too, making a terrible little mountain on top of the trousers. By the time she gave Aidan a final sponging-down with damp and wadded toilet paper, he'd been rubbed red-raw and was whimpering afresh. Her knees hurt. Her lower back hurt. Her cleaning hand hurt. Her eyeball *really* hurt. She got to her feet and examined it in the mirror. It was bloodshot and watery but apparently whole. A knock came to the door as she gingerly prodded and stared.

'Just another minute!' she called out. 'Sorry about this!' She turned to Aidan. 'Right, shoes and socks.'

He threw his arms wide. 'But the people will see my bottom! And my willie!'

She tugged his jumper down as far as it would go, which was not very. 'Hm. That's no good.'

'No good,' he agreed miserably.

'Look, here's what we'll do. You can wear Mammy's fleece and—'

'No!'

'Why not?'

'Too big! And for a lady!'

'Bigness is the point, Aidan. It will cover your… bits.'

He frowned, caught between catastrophes. She removed the garment and began trying to get him into it, which proved difficult. There was another knock on the door as they wrestled, louder this time, more insistent. Nancy didn't respond because she didn't trust herself to be civil. Eventually, Aidan was be-fleeced. He looked ridiculous, even with the sleeves rolled up, and she thought it perfectly reasonable when he started crying again. Her intention had been to march him into the nearest shop and buy new clothes. But that plan was rapidly losing its appeal. Simpler and better, she decided, to just leg it back to the car and put this whole business behind them. She gave Aidan one last high-pitched, obviously unreliable assurance that he looked 'grand' and turned back to Luke, just in time to see him squinting and turning purple.

'Don't you dare!' she shrieked but it was too late, he already had. That small first nappy, she realised with a dizzying lurch, had been a mere messenger, a herald of things to come. Redmond referred to this sort of thing as a 'John the Bapshit'. Ordinarily, she thought that was a pretty solid joke but her husband's sudden presence in her mind now made her jaw clench all the tighter.

'Aidan. Stand in the corner. Don't move. Please.'

He nodded and relocated. She set about Luke's second nappy

feeling vacant, disembodied, lost in an ecstasy of irritation. There were more knocks on the door. She ignored them. When she was finished, she tried to lift Luke without first undoing his straps. The resulting jolt made him start crying again but she offered no apology. She was afraid to speak in case nothing came out but a howl. Instead, she wrangled him into the buggy, grabbed her bag, and flicked her head in the direction of the door.

'Going?' Aidan said from the corner. 'Are we going... outside?'

'Yes,' she managed to say. 'We're going.'

She opened the door and sent Aidan ahead, before following with Luke. The woman from the next table was standing there. Nancy glared at her. The woman glared back. And then she looked from crying child to crying child, pausing momentarily to take in the older boy's outfit. Her nose twitched and she frowned in disgust.

'There are other people waiting to use the facilities, you know,' the woman said. 'Not that your sort ever consider other people.'

Nancy punched her in the face.

One day, early in his unemployment, Leo made a decision. He hadn't asked for all this free time but damn it, he was going to use it. Specifically, he was going to get fit. He'd always been able to eat whatever he liked without putting on much weight – a fact that Deirdre threw in his face every so often, as if he did it deliberately with the intention of annoying her – but he had never been one for exercise. As a result, he looked reasonably healthy but could run perhaps 20 metres before collapsing in a reasonably healthy-looking heap. A narrative took shape in his mind. By the time he returned to the workforce – and it would be a matter of weeks, surely – he would have become addicted to the runner's high that he'd heard so much about and would be well on his way to his first marathon. In some versions of the fantasy, he not only ran a marathon but became addicted to *that* and skipped happily through two or three of the things every year for the rest of his life, traversing the globe as he did so.

None of this came to pass. He went out running three times, although 'running' was perhaps not the word for it. 'Jogging' wasn't quite right, either. Leo's style was more akin to a sort of falling forwards, clawing at the air, without ever actually toppling over. His first two forays ended within a quarter of an hour. Both featured dry-heaving and a great deal of attempted swearing (he'd lacked the breath to really get anywhere with it). The third lasted a matter of seconds. He pulled on his tattered gear, slammed the front door behind him and plodded as far as the footpath before issuing a loud 'Fuck this' and going back inside.

In all the months since, he had never regretted the decision – it was a sign of maturity, he regularly mused, that he could be so honest with himself about his limitations – but he did sometimes wonder if he was right to have thrown the baby of exercise out with the bathwater of running. When he noticed that he'd started spending several hours of every day not just inactive but *asleep*, he produced a Plan B – 'nice long walks'. That was what he invariably called them, even though they were never long and, if he was honest, rarely nice. Dragging himself around the local park once in a while was a long way from running multiple marathons, but it was better than nothing, he felt sure. And even if its health benefits were almost nil, it fulfilled one other important purpose. It allowed him, when questioned by Deirdre about his day, to report something that wasn't a lie about frantically searching for a job. That being said, he tended to lie about the walks too, inventing encounters with peculiar strangers, dangerous animals and the like, in the hope of making them – and by extension, his current lifestyle – sound more colourful. Late at night, he worried that if his unemployment stretched from months into years he would wind up telling her how a nice long walk had been interrupted by an alien abduction.

Today, as he closed the front door behind him, he was already working on a story about an enormous golden retriever that got away from its owner and knocked over an old lady, who later proved to be a colossal racist. He pocketed his keys and set to work on untangling his out-and-about earphones (as opposed to his enormous staying-in headphones), which, as ever, had apparently spent their time in his jacket pocket getting drunk and playing Twister. There was activity across the street, he noticed. The Australian man was clearing out his garage. He had introduced himself at one point as 'Dooley'. Leo wasn't sure if that was a nickname or what. Australians, in his experience, put 'y's on the end of everything. Maybe his real name was Dool. Their eyes met and they raised their hands in simultaneous salute.

'Hi,' Leo called out.

'Hey there, Liam,' Dooley replied brightly. He sounded very pleased about something. Leo hesitated. He was fine with the idea that neighbours didn't have to be best buddies, but he thought they should probably get each other's names right. This was as good a time as any to set the record straight. He went over.

'It's Leo, actually. Not Liam.'

Dooley's face fell. He looked genuinely upset. 'Oh, shit. I'm sorry.'

'It's all right, no harm—'

'I was sure it was Liam.'

'Not to worry. I've been meaning to ask – "Dooley". Is that—'

'Surname, mate. It's Vincent but I've always hated Vincent. I've been Dooley since I was old enough to talk. Even Julie calls me Dooley.'

'Wait, your wife's name is Julie? Julie Dooley?'

'I know. It's not ideal. She's fine with it, though. She reckons it's good branding.'

There was an ugly pause. Leo began to regret having made a move. He could easily have gone on wondering about 'Dooley' and answering to 'Liam' for the rest of his life. It was only partially broken and he'd tried to fix it. Now look – bouncing on his toes and staring at nothing, unable to think of a way to leave. He said the only thing that he could think of.

'Tidying up?'

'Yeah. Well, not so much tidying up as clearing out.'

'Going to start parking in there? No one does, do they?'

'Ha, that's true. No, though, I'm not clearing it out for the car.' He tickled the end of his nose and smiled. 'Believe it or not, I'm going to make a pub in there.'

'Is that right?'

'Well, not a *real* one, obviously. I mean, I'm going to… Do you know what a man cave is?'

'Ah. Making yourself a hidey-hole.'

Dooley grinned. 'Exactly, yeah. Starting out small, you know, but I've got big plans.' A high-pitched sound came from the garage. Leo thought it was a cat at first but then noticed for the first time that Dooley's baby was in the corner in a sort of rocking chair contraption.

'Oh, I didn't see himself there.'

'It's a girl, actually. Nicola.'

'Sorry.' Should he try a small joke? He decided to go for it. 'Still, you probably feel better about the Liam thing now.'

'Heh. I do and I don't. It's kinda sad, isn't it? The way neighbours are now?'

Leo fidgeted. He hoped this wasn't going in a touchy-feely direction. 'Hm.'

'My parents knew everybody all around us when I was growing up. And – *knew*. Not just to say hello to. Knew all about their jobs and their health and what their kids were up to, the whole bit.'

'Well—' Leo began. He wasn't sure that was such a great way to live. It certainly didn't appeal to him personally. But saying so now seemed like a bad idea. He just nodded and issued another 'Hm'.

'The only people in this street we know anything about are Redmond and Nancy next door and we're not exactly bosom buddies with them either. Do you know Redmond? Tall guy? I mean – *tall?*'

'Can't say I do. I've seen him coming and going.'

'Nice bloke. I have the odd beer with him. And I owe him for the pub idea, actually. He's fixing up his garage too, for his games.'

'What, poker?'

'No, video games. Xboxes and PlayStations and what have you. He's mad into all that. Don't see the appeal meself.'

Leo shrugged. 'We all have something, I suppose. It's music with me. Vinyl.'

'Yeah?'

'Yeah.'

'What sort of stuff are you into?'

'Oh, anything and everything. I suppose I'm an 80s guy at heart. Older R.E.M., Pixies, The Smiths. The usual suspects. But I'm not fussy. I've even…' Again, he hesitated. But this time he forged ahead. 'I've even bought stuff I have no intention of listening to just because I liked the sleeve.' He smiled, hoping he hadn't sounded ridiculous.

'I bet the wife loves that,' Dooley smiled back.

'She does, yeah. She's never done congratulating me on my record collection. "If anything, it could be bigger," she's always saying. "Are you sure you're spending enough money on it? Is there no way you could get it to take up more space?" Uh… that was sarcasm.'

'I suspected as much, yeah. Well, listen, if space is an issue, you could always jump on the bandwagon, ship everything out to the garage.'

'Ha, no, not for me. I like my comforts too much. I did think about the wee bedroom but that's…' He shrugged. It was earmarked for a nursery and had the status of a shrine. Deirdre complained if he so much as stored a bag in there. 'It's not a runner.'

'Hey, I'm not planning on having an uncomfortable pub. And Redmond's basically making another living room in there. There are ways and means.'

'I suppose so. But we have other priorities, house-wise. As you can imagine.' He cast a thumb over his shoulder. Dooley glanced across the street.

'Let me guess. You're not wild about the pink?'

'Not wild about the pink, not wild about the… any of it. But we just don't have the budget. At the moment.'

'Fair enough. But you wouldn't need to drop a lot of cash on a music room – cave, whatever. You'd need to sort heating of some kind, but apart from that it's just a matter of adding an armchair and whatnot. Step one, in any case, is to clear the bastard out.'

This last, Leo suspected, was a hint that the conversation was over. 'Probably not a good idea for me,' he said, 'but I wish you all the best with it.'

'You'll have to come over for a drink when it's done,' Dooley said. 'I'm making a bar and I got a dartboard, look.' He gestured behind him.

'Nice,' Leo nodded. 'Pool table next.'

'Yeah, exactly.'

'Oh. I was joking.'

'This is no joking matter, my friend. Deadly serious business.'

There was that grin again. He looked so happy, Leo thought. Good for him. 'Okay, then. Better leave you to it.' He leaned around and waved at the baby – pointlessly, he immediately realised – and then continued on his nice long walk.

Most days on his way home from work, Redmond made a small concession to society's inexplicable insistence that he keep up with the current affairs over which he had no influence, and listened to the drive-time talk shows. Or at least, he tried to. Sometimes they featured a politician or other blowhard who was simply too awful to stomach. And sometimes he just couldn't be arsed. In the event of either disgust or apathy, he would throw on one of the three CDs that had been in the car forever and then spend the rest of the journey reminding himself that he needed new CDs.

Today was different. A series of long, soul-crushing client calls had robbed him of thinking time in the afternoon and now he needed to concentrate. The Gandhi approach was the correct one, he felt sure – but he needed to flesh it out. For a start, there was the question of how to bring the subject up. After her initial storm-off a couple of nights ago, he'd expected Nancy to explain in some detail why she was so upset about his move to the garage, and for that explanation to lead to a major argument. But neither explanation nor argument had materialised. Instead, he had been treated to a weekend of barbed comments and long silences. On several occasions, he'd looked up to find her peering at him with suspicion and faint disgust, as if he was something she'd found growing in her armpit. The net effect was to make him think better of raising the subject himself. Getting her to open up now without sounding like he was spoiling for a fight might prove tricky. And what about the specifics? It was all very well having an attitude in mind but if he didn't come up with some good lines to throw in, he could wind up just standing there looking serene while she mopped the floor with him.

These and other similar questions occupied him fully for the duration of his journey. When he finally pulled into the driveway and killed the engine, he realised that he couldn't recall a single traffic light, a single stop sign. Tactical deliberations and safe driving didn't go together, it seemed. Still, he had made some decisions and settled on a few choice phrases. He felt calm. He felt self-possessed. He was certain his cause was a just one.

Aidan was in the hall, slamming toy cars into the skirting board. When the door opened, he looked up and smiled but didn't say anything. Redmond scooped him up.

'Hey, handsome! Whatcha doin'?'

'Crashes,' Aidan said.

'Yeah?'

'Yeah.'

He didn't sound like himself, Redmond thought. Muted. 'Did you have a fun day today?'

'Uh-huh.'

'What did you do?'

A small shrug. A guilty look. He'd been up to no good, no doubt. Had landed himself in trouble. The door to the kitchen was open but there was no activity down there. Redmond gave the boy a squeeze and stepped into the living room. Luke was on the floor, on his side, doing his best to bite the leg off a stuffed giraffe. Nancy was on the sofa. She was sitting stiffly upright with her arms folded and didn't so much as turn her head in his direction. This was almost a relief. He'd expected to find her like this. A warm welcome would have put him on the back foot entirely.

'Nancy,' he said softly, by way of hello. He was pleased with how it sounded. Gentle. Warm. Dignified. (In the car, he'd been briefly tempted by the traditional Irish 'Well?' but had concluded that it was too low rent.)

She didn't move a muscle. 'Hi.'

Redmond lowered Aidan to the floor and picked up Luke who, to his credit, seemed reasonably pleased to see his old man. 'Lukey-dukes! How are you fixed for tickles, huh? Any tickles in there?' He ran his fingers across his son's ribcage, eliciting cackles and wriggles, before returning him to his giraffe. Nancy remained motionless. Okay, he thought. Show time. He joined her on the sofa.

'I think we should talk,' he said, slowly and steadily, fighting against the nagging urge to do an Indian accent. 'The last thing I ever want to do is upset you. And I don't just mean about the garage. I mean, in general. It kills me when there's any kind of tension between us. I just want to understand—'

'Mammy had a fight with another mammy,' Aidan said, matter-of-factly. 'She hitted the other mammy and the other mammy hitted her.'

Redmond snapped his head around and stared at him. Aidan seemed to understand the meaning of the look, which was *What the fuck?* He nodded solemnly in confirmation.

'Jesus Christ,' Nancy sighed and rubbed her face with both hands. 'Little snitch.'

'A fight?' Redmond squeaked at her.

She was all motion, suddenly, shifting her weight and flicking her hair. 'Don't get all excited. I hit her, she hit me. Two hits. There weren't even proper punches. It wasn't the Rumble in the Jungle.'

'A physical *fight?*' He hadn't known his voice could go this high. He was in Bee Gees territory.

'You're blowing this out of—'

'A *fight* fight?'

'Stop saying that! Yes! A fight!' She got up and strode off into the kitchen. Redmond sat there for a couple of seconds, stunned, before he got up and skipped after her in what was (he couldn't help but think) a most un-Gandhi-like fashion.

'You weren't even going to tell me?' he asked. Nancy was standing in the middle of the room with her back to him. She didn't reply.

'Well?'

'No, Redmond, I wasn't.' She spun around to face him in a manner that reminded him of a soap opera's opening credits. 'It was no big deal. There's no—'

'No big deal? Are you fucking *high?*'

'Keep your voice down!'

'Nancy. Tell me what happened.'

She fumed for a long moment, her nostrils flaring. Folded, unfolded, and refolded her arms. Fumed some more. Then her expression changed and, at last, he thought, she seemed ready to begin. But no.

'I'm going for a bath,' she said. 'Get your own dinner. Sort the boys out.'

She brushed past him and strode off down the hall. For the second time in a minute, he froze, then sprang to life and chased after her.

'Nancy! Nancy, come back,' he spluttered as he took the stairs two at a time.

'Stay with the boys,' she said and closed the bathroom door in his face.

He started knocking on it and then immediately upgraded his knocks to thumps. 'Nancy! Nancy, for Christ's sake, open up! I'm your husband! You can't get into a fist fight and not tell me about it!'

'Leave me alone!'

He thumped some more. 'Nancy! Nancy!'

'Stop banging the door!'

He did so. 'Come out. Please.'

'No.'

'Well, talk to me, at least. What happened?'

When she didn't immediately reply he guessed that he was finally getting somewhere and that his best move was to shut up and wait.

'It wasn't my fault,' she said after a few seconds. 'I was... goaded.'

'Start at the start,' Redmond said gently. And she did. He didn't interrupt. Nor did he point out that talking through a door was completely ridiculous. Clearly, she needed some sort of barrier. He felt a little like a priest taking confession.

'Were you hurt?' he asked when Nancy fell silent. 'Was *she* hurt?'

'No. And no. I've never thrown a punch. I was going for her nose, I think, but I just slid off her cheek. She was worse. I took a slap on the ear, that's all.'

Despite his best intentions to keep things conciliatory, Redmond couldn't help but say, 'Jesus, Nancy, in front of the boys.'

'I *know*, don't rub it in.'

'Did anyone else see?'

'No. It was right outside the toilet in that little corridor thing.'

'So what happened then?'

'I don't know, we just... Look, we were both in shock, I think. And not because we'd been hit. Because we'd done some hitting. I know I was, anyway. And she was... white. Eyes like saucers. So we both just stared for a second. Then the door to the coffee shop opened and this young one came in. We all stood there for a moment, then she said something about a queue. I said I wasn't queuing. A bit more silence. Then the other woman said she wasn't queuing either in a, like, in a sort of whisper. I was in such a state I almost pointed out that she hadn't actually made it into the loo, so really, she *was* queuing. The girl looked at us like we were nuts, just standing outside a toilet for no reason, not speaking. Anyway, I didn't know what else to do so I... left. The end.'

Redmond let the story's conclusion hang there for a moment.

Then he said, 'Nancy, come out, please.' He expected a delay, for effect if nothing else, but she unlocked the door immediately. She wasn't crying but her eyes were wet. He gave her his most beatific smile and they fell into a hug.

'Nancy. You haven't been yourself for a while.' She said nothing but he felt her head give the smallest of shakes. 'Is there anything you want to talk to me about?'

'We have to get back downstairs to the boys, God knows what—'

'They'll be fine. For a few minutes, they'll be fine. Tell me. What is it?'

'Nothing.'

'It's not nothing. Is it?'

'It's *nothing*.' She stepped out of the hug and started down the stairs. 'We can't leave them alone like this,' she said as he descended. Redmond followed her down. When she had satisfied herself that the boys were not in mortal danger – in fact, they hadn't moved an inch – she retook her original position on the sofa. Redmond joined her there.

'Are you okay now?' he asked under his breath.

'Yes.'

'You don't want to talk—'

'No.'

He considered pushing her but decided there was little point. If she'd wanted to tell him what was bugging her, she would have done so already. There was no reason, he supposed, not to return to his original plan. He chewed his lip, trying to remember the opening line he'd settled on.

'Listen,' he said then. 'There's something I want to say. The last thing I ever want to do is upset you. And I don't just mean about the garage. I mean, generally. It kills me when there's tension between us. I just—'

'What?'

'Sorry?'

'This is what you said the last time you sat down beside me. Exactly, I think. Like, word for word.'

'I don't think—'

'Have you *rehearsed* this, this, whatever it is?'

'No, I—'

'What are you up to?'

'I'm not up to anything, Nancy, I'm just trying to *talk* to you. *Jesus*.'

She squinted at him. 'Go on then.'

He could feel his Gandhi-ness ebbing away and took a moment to collect himself. 'Look. About the garage—'

'What about it?'

'Well, you didn't seem to be all that... pleased.'

'Oh, you noticed. Well done.'

'And I don't understand why.' A noise escaped her. It was a distant cousin, Redmond supposed, of a laugh. 'I mean, you wanted the spare room freed up, right?'

'I did say that, didn't I?'

Her tone was troubling. Redmond felt sure that she was not only giving him enough rope but bringing in a stool. 'So, what, have you changed your mind?'

She shook her head. 'Typical.'

In Redmond's experience, the appearance of the word 'typical' was always a bad sign. It meant that his latest sin, whatever it may be, wasn't being considered in isolation but instead represented just another tile in a rich mosaic of failings that she'd been contemplating for some time.

'What does that mean?'

'Nothing.'

'Oh, no. Don't give the typical/nothing combo. Come on. Spit it out.'

She rolled her eyes, then looked away towards the kitchen. Redmond contemplated his next move but he didn't get to make one. Nancy snapped her head around again.

'All right. All right. Since you obviously can't work it out for yourself, I'll tell you. It's not about the *room*, Redmond.'

'What? What's it ab—'

'It's about you spending all your spare time blasting aliens or slaying dragons or whatever the hell it is you do in there, instead of helping out—'

'Instead of *helping out?* Are you taking the piss? I help out plenty. You *know* I do.'

She exhaled loudly. 'All right. All right! Instead of keeping me company. There! You're the only adult I get to talk to from one end of the day to the other, for Christ's sake. But you come home, you say a quick hello to everybody, and then you leg it upstairs. I have to call you down for dinner like a fucking ten-year-old.'

'Nancy! Language.'

'Weekends are the same. Every chance you get, you're up there. How long have I been asking you to look into that damp patch on the kitchen ceiling? Or to paint the bathroom? Or to get rid of that bloody bush in the back garden?'

'I don't see wh—'

'You've no time to do any of that, have you? But you spot a chance to change your gaming setup and suddenly you're Philippe fucking Starck. Just *bursting* with ideas and enthus—'

'Fucking start!' said Aidan, brightly.

Redmond threw his hands up. 'Are you happy now?'

She tossed her head but said nothing. Her outburst had left her out of breath. She was almost panting.

'Right, then,' Redmond said. 'You've said your piece. Now you're going to listen to my… piece.' His nose wrinkled up. That wasn't brilliant. But he had to push on. 'I'm sorry you think I don't spend enough time with you. And I will do better on that score. I promise. But you can't just demand that I drop my one outlet for relaxation. I work very h—'

'Here we go. The only person in the world who does any work.'

'I didn't say—'

'Typical. This is… You didn't even listen to anything I said, did you? You just sat there waiting for your chance to start droning on about how *terribly* hard you w—'

'Okay, okay, okay.' He got to his feet. 'There's no point trying to talk to you. No point. None. It's pointless.'

'Never mind talking, how about you try *listening* for once? If you… Where are you going?'

He was halfway to the door and turned with a flourish that, even as he was making it, felt slightly camp. He tried to compensate by deepening his voice for his exit line.

'I'm going to the garage,' he said, 'to blast aliens or slay dragons or whatever the hell it is I do.'

The traffic lights went green and, for the third time in a row, not one car was able to cross the junction before they turned red again. Julie swore and raised her hand over the horn. But she didn't bring it down. Other drivers beat her to the punch; their indignant hooting sounded so ridiculous and pointless that she segued, instead, into some quite inventive swearing. She was not usually an impatient driver. Most days she wouldn't even have raised the hand. Most days a delay like this one would barely have registered on her consciousness. Her current frustration stemmed, at least indirectly, from the fact that it was Oliver Rice's birthday. Oliver was Kennedy Joyce's head media buyer and one of its longest-serving employees. Julie had always tried hard to like him purely because he was gay. She knew that was ridiculous and would never have admitted it to anyone, but her embarrassment was far outweighed by her fear of appearing homophobic. Oliver wasn't malicious or even unpleasant, just quite astonishingly dull. If you so much as said hello to him in a corridor, he was liable to pin you to the wall and keep you there for 20 minutes while he gave you a scene-by-scene summary of the movie he'd watched the night before or described in appalling detail the relative merits and demerits of the three dishwashers that had made it onto his purchasing shortlist. Speaking to him was always like pushing that first domino. No matter how gentle your nudge, the result was a long and complex cascade that was going to play itself out whether you liked it or not. When she'd overheard, mid-morning, that it was his birthday and that a few of her colleagues were taking him out to lunch, she had immediately begun to work on her excuse.

Meeting with a client? Too easily disproved. Medical appointment with daughter? Too recently used. Half an hour later, however, David had perched on the end of her desk and asked if she was going. She flapped about a bit and said she hadn't decided – what about him? He raised an eyebrow and said he'd go if she did. She feigned exasperation at his childish machinations and shooed him away. She'd think about it, she muttered, as he headed for the door. But no thinking had taken place. It was a done deal.

The lunch was every bit as awful as she'd feared it would be. Buoyed up by being the centre of attention, Oliver outdid himself, treating the table to a series of anecdotes, each more rambling and pointless than the last. Easily the worst of the bunch was the tale of his most recent holiday, in which he and his partner Gordon had toured New England in a rental car, apparently stopping in every single town they encountered, and then entering every building in that town, where they spoke at length to every person they met. Just hearing about all of these towns and buildings and people was bad enough, but Oliver had also filled his iPhone to the brim with photographs and videos of almost zero interest. Every so often, he would illustrate some mind-numbing point by swiping to the appropriate place and passing the device around his stupefied companions, whose nods and smiles grew increasingly forced as time wore on (and on and on). The New England story, excruciating as it was, did at least allow for some interaction, as others chipped in with their own experiences of rude hoteliers, airplane micro-friendships, struggling with menus, and so on. Eventually, the chip-ins became more frequent and expansive, and conversational momentum was wrested from the birthday boy. A theme emerged: Best Holiday Ever. Deborah Garvey swooned about her honeymoon in Rome. Ian Lyons waxed nostalgic for his long-vanished youth, or at least the single weekend of it that he'd spent in Amsterdam with a Spanish fitness instructor. Trevor Hegarty became visibly emotional as he recalled taking his little girl to Disney World after she'd recovered from meningitis.

When she sensed that it was her turn to say something, Julie threw in a few lines about her first time in Paris and quickly passed the conversational buck to David. He thought about it for a moment – or perhaps pretended to, Julie wasn't sure – and then declared, 'Dog-sledding. Arctic Circle. 2005.' There were some snorts around the table before everyone realised that he wasn't joking. The trip was a whim, he explained. One night he'd happened upon a documentary about people living in extreme environments – deserts, jungles and whatnot. Something about the segment on life in the far north spoke to him. Three weeks later he was tethered to a pack of huskies, zipping across a frozen lake in the Swedish province of Lapland. No one around the table had been particularly energised by tales of Rome or Amsterdam but now the questions came flying. David neatly dealt with them all, even the stupid ones. Yes, he saw the aurora borealis. Yes, it was as beautiful as you'd hope. No, there were no hotels. They'd stayed in extremely basic cabins. No, the dogs were not his favourite part. His favourite part was the unearthly quiet. No, he wouldn't do it again but only because it had been perfect the first time and he didn't want to spoil it. Yes, it had been physically tough. Yes, he had liked the isolation. Yes, he had done a lot of thinking. Yes, it was cold in the Arctic Circle. Julie was amused to see Oliver grow increasingly irritated as focus drifted ever further away from him. But amusement soon took second place to another more primal sensation that gripped her as she imagined her boss out there in his Action Man gear, communing with nature and living hard, all frost-toughened skin and new beard growth. That sensation was lust and it robbed her of her breath. She dropped out of the conversation entirely and spent several minutes lost in idle fantasy (the roaring fire, the thick fur rug...). Her glances at David grew longer and eventually merged into a basic stare. He caught her eye at one point and she blushed like a schoolgirl. It would have been a thoroughly enjoyable interlude if she hadn't suddenly found herself wondering what domestic chore Dooley was tackling right at that moment – was he wearing rubber gloves? – and hating herself for it. Back at the office she had spent the afternoon oscillating between lechery and shame, and even now, sitting in the car, she didn't know whether she wanted sex or a good cry.

Traffic on the other side of the junction suddenly cleared. The lights turned green and she finally drove off, but not as quickly as she could have.

She found Dooley in the kitchen. When he turned to greet her she was relieved to see that he wasn't wearing rubber gloves or, worse, an apron (he'd never worn an apron in his life, as far as she knew, but that hadn't stopped the thought occurring). He was, however, crying. Julie issued an involuntary sigh and hated herself all over again.

'Onions,' he said by way of explanation as he planted a peck on her lips. 'I'm a bit behind with dinner. Good day?'

'Yeah!' she said, radically overcompensating with the enthusiasm of her tone.

Nicola was in her high chair staring with great intensity at a plastic spoon. Julie undid the buckles and scooped her up for a cuddle. 'And how's my little pixie?' she cooed. 'Did *you* have a good day?'

'Yes, Mammy, I did,' Dooley said in the high-pitched baby voice he sometimes affected for ventriloquism purposes. Julie wasn't in the mood but she forced herself.

'Yeah? What did you get up to?'

'I went out with Daddy and we bought supplies for the pub he's making in the garage.'

'*Did* you? Good girl.' She nuzzled her daughter's nose. 'And did—'

'No, really,' Dooley warbled. 'Daddy's making a pub in the garage.'

Julie stared at him, waiting for some kind of explanation. 'What?' she said when none was forthcoming.

'Daddy's making a pub in the—'

'Jesus, Dooley, stop doing the voice!'

He cleared his throat. 'I'm making a pub in the garage.'

'I heard that bit. I just don't know what you mean.'

'Well—'

'How can you make a pub in a garage? A *business?*'

'No! Of course not. I shouldn't call it a pub, really, it's just, like, a bar, a home bar. Just… somewhere to chill out.'

She blinked at him. 'You mean, a man cave?'

'Yes! A man cave. I didn't know you knew what that was.'

'I saw a thing in a magazine. It looked kinda… sad.'

'Mine won't be sad! Look, look… Wait a minute.' He turned the heat down on his onions. 'Come on, I'll show you.'

He skipped over to the door that led to the garage. Julie readjusted Nicola's weight in her arms and dragged herself along in his wake. She half-expected to find the garage transformed into the sort of thing she'd seen in the magazine piece. But there were no neon lights, no jukebox. No pool table, no stuffed moose head. If Dooley hadn't told her it was going to be a bar, she wouldn't have been able to guess. All he had done, really, was a bit of a clear-out. There were maybe ten bin bags piled high by the door.

'I've only just started, obviously,' he said. 'Picked up a few bits and pieces today. Mostly booze, to be honest.'

She followed his gaze to the enormous cooler in a corner that had previously been occupied by ancient carpet offcuts.

'And a dartboard,' she said, nodding at the wall.

'And a dartboard, yeah. Got some glasses too. I'm going to get some timber—'

'I don't know, Dooley. I don't like this.'

His head popped back on his shoulders. 'What? Why not?'

Julie made a strange noise with her lips. It was a good question. She'd walked in, been relieved to find that the place wasn't unrecognisable, then actually quite *pleased* to see it so tidy, and then… What? Something at the back of her mind had stirred and groaned, but she couldn't quite say what it was.

'Nicola has a nappy,' she said, which had the advantage of being true. 'We'll talk about this later.'

'We can if you like,' Dooley said. He stomped his foot. 'But I am your husband and you will obey me.'

This was an old running joke that started when they were deciding on their wedding vows and marvelling at how things were done back in the day. It was getting tired now but, still, it usually made Julie smile. Not this time.

'Nappy,' she said, and left him there. Just as she turned away, she saw his face transition from fake domineering to genuinely wounded, and felt as if she'd kicked a puppy.

Dinner was a dish that Dooley called 'Pasta Thing' – a bog-standard tomato sauce with whatever came easily to hand. Almost any ingredient could wind up in Pasta Thing, depending on how experimental he was feeling or, more usually, on how badly they needed to do a grocery shop. There had been no experimentation today and the cupboards were reasonably well stocked. Hence, bacon, mushrooms, green peppers. Julie learned that the meal was ready when Dooley stuck his head into the front room, where she was playing with Nicola, and jerked a thumb over his shoulder. For a few minutes they ate in a silence that would have been perfect if not for their daughter's occasional snuffle. Still feeling small, Julie was determined that she would be the one to break it, but somehow she couldn't find an opening. Dooley, it seemed, had no interest in conversation. Everything about him, from his refusal to catch her eye to the alarming speed with which he was shovelling food into his mouth, said that he was seriously pissed off. Eventually, she gave up on finding something pleasantly bland to say.

'Are you bored, Dooley?' she asked.

He froze for a moment and then looked at her. 'With our marriage?'

'What? No! Jesus! With *home*, with being at home! Is that what the garage thing is about? Are you looking for something to do?'

To his credit, he didn't snap at her, as she'd half-expected he might. She saw his features relax slightly, as he gave the question proper thought. 'I don't know,' he said after a moment. 'Maybe.'

She tilted her head and nodded, reminding herself of a psychologist who has seen a patient embarking on a useful train of thought and is keen to encourage further exploration. 'There's nothing wrong with that,' she said. 'Perfectly understandable.'

'Yeah, I… Yeah.'

More nodding. 'But if you're bored with being at home, don't you think you should find something to do that, y'know… gets you out of the house? Maybe something outdoorsy?'

'Outdoorsy? What do you mean, outdoorsy? Bloody *golf*?'

'God, no. I don't know, something… maybe… a bit… adventurous.'

The final traces of anger disappeared from his face. All that remained was utter bafflement. 'Mountain-climbing, that sort of thing? Do you think I should leave Nicola with the neighbours and take a crack at Kilimanjaro?'

She pushed some pasta around. 'It was Oliver's birthday today. At work. Oliver Rice?'

'The boring guy.'

'The boring guy.' Dooley had met him at a Christmas party one year. Despite Julie's warnings, he'd allowed himself to be cornered and endured an hour-long lecture on the correct approach to take with car salesmen.

'We all went out for lunch, a whole gang of us. And we got talking about our favourite holidays.'

'Yeah?'

She took a moment to wipe some drool from Nicola's chin. 'None of us had anything particularly exciting to say, except for David. He told us about this trip he took in Sweden. Way up in the Arctic Circle. Dog-sledding with huskies, out in nature all day, out in all that drama and beauty – and it wasn't comfy either. Stayed in these log cabins along the way with not much more in them than stoves and beds. Some of them didn't have electricity! He saw the aurora borealis and everything. He said there were days when he didn't say more than a handful of sentences from dawn until bedtime and—'

'Julie. You're losing me.'

'I'm saying, you could tell from the way he talked about it that it really affected him. Made an impact. Y'know?'

'No. I don't know. I honestly don't. You come home, you piss all over my pub idea, you stride off, and now you're babbling on about huskies.'

'Well…' she began and then dried up. She was sure she'd had a point. But it seemed to elude her now.

'Oh. I get it. You wish I'd do something manlier, be a bit more like the mighty David, is that it?'

'Noooo!' Her face did something funny as she said it. She had no idea what it must look like; she only knew that she had never used that muscle configuration before. It simultaneously felt like a smile and a frown, with a bit of horror thrown in. After a long moment in which Dooley simply stared at her, she could feel panic being added to the mix.

'What do you mean, "the mighty David"?'

'I mean you're always going on about how great he is.'

'That's ridiculous.'

'I don't really fancy Kilimanjaro, though. Maybe just abseil off a nice cliff somewhere? Or cross the Sahara on my own? Wrestle a bear? Would that do?'

'Dooley—'

'I'm sorry I'm such a disappointment to you, Julie. I'm sorry I'm just a boring stay-at-home half-man and not, y'know, not Indiana bloody Jones.'

'Oh, stop it. You're *imagining* things.'

He fumed in silence for a moment then shoved his chair under the table. 'I'm going out to the garage,' he said, quietly. 'I'll probably be a while.'

Julie said and did nothing to stop him. After he was gone, she sat down again and pulled Nicola close. The room suddenly seemed so airless and still. Her throat felt irritated, her tongue too large. *You're always going on about great he is.*

Was she? She genuinely hadn't noticed.

'Sorry,' Leo said. 'It's a bit cold.'

Deirdre nodded. 'Maybe a wee bit.'

'I spent too long getting the salad together. Stupid.'

She dropped her fork on her plate. The clatter made him jump. 'I shouldn't be eating this anyway,' she muttered.

'Lasagne? What's wrong with lasagne?'

'Are you joking me? It might as well be chips and a battered sausage. Y'ever see Garfield, the cartoon cat? Really likes lasagne? He's not famously thin, is he?'

'No.'

'No. He isn't.'

Leo hadn't even made the lasagne. Deirdre had, a week or so ago. He'd merely heated it up (and then, apparently, let it cool). It was beyond him how she could be mad at him for serving something that she herself had cooked, but here they were. No doubt she would spend the rest of the night upstairs on her rowing machine, pull a muscle, and blame him for that too. She'd been relatively cheerful when she left for work that morning. Something had clearly upset her. He pondered. Would it do any good to investigate? Probably not. A general enquiry, perhaps…

'How was work t—'

'Fine.'

He was reminded of a cat swishing its tail in preparation for taking firm action of some kind.

'Anything on the websites?' she said then. She meant the job websites, which he had briefly scanned, and not the record websites, which he had pored over for a couple of hours.

'No. Not today. I gave up and went for a nice long walk.'

'Hm.'

'Yeah. Listen to this: I was in the park, over towards the pond? This young fella came along, a teenager. Chinese. Walking his dog, this huge golden retriever. It must have seen something, a squirrel or something, because it just took off, right, your man had no chance of hanging onto it. Nearly took his arm off. There was this little old woman just in front of me and it kind of glanced off her as it shot past. Didn't knock her down or anything but she got a bit of a shock. Well! You should have heard the language out of her.' He paused to allow Deirdre to express interest of some kind. She didn't. He forged ahead regardless. 'She pointed at the dog guy and started shouting all this abuse, really racist stuff, chink this and slitty-eyed that and why don't you go home and eat a cat and all sorts. Awful stuff altogether. I couldn't believe it. I probably should have said something but she was so tiny and old and frail. So I just walked on.' He paused again. No input. 'Do you think I should have had a go at her?'

She shrugged. 'Dunno.'

Leo took another bite of his dinner. Clearly, this was a dead end. He felt irritation blossoming in his chest. What was the point of fabricating these elaborate lies about how interesting his day had been if she wasn't going to play ball? The easy thing to do would be to say to hell with this and go listen to some music. But that could lead to real trouble. It had done so many times before. No. He would cheer her up with pleasant conversation or die trying.

'I had a chat with your man across the way as I was heading out. Vincent? Dooley?'

'Yeah?'

'He was clearing out his garage.'

She nodded. 'That's something we should do, actually. We still have boxes and boxes of shite in there since the move.'

Leo was encouraged. These were whole sentences. 'That's true. You know why he's doing it? I'll give you a million guesses.'

'No idea.'

'Guess.'

'Leo—'

'He's making a pub.'

'He's what?'

'Not a real pub, now, just a sort of hidey-hole. He's making a wee bar, hanging up a dartboard, that sort of thing. Invited me over for a look when it's finished.'

'Huh. What does his wife think about that?'

'He didn't say. I'm sure she's fine with it. Why wouldn't she be?'

'Because maybe she doesn't want her husband disappearing for hours at a stretch when there's a baby to look after?'

'Sure he has the baby all day.'

'So? She's at work all day.'

They were getting off-track, Leo thought. Not only that, this felt like dangerous territory. Keep it light, he told himself.

'The guy next door's at it too.'

'You're kidding me. Is it going to be all joke pubs around here?'

'The other guy isn't making a pub. He's making a den sort of thing, somewhere to play his video games.'

'*Men*. Bunch of bloody children.'

Leo flinched. It didn't sound as if she meant this jovially. It wasn't *Hee hee, what are you like?* It was *You all deserve to die*. 'I don't think video games are really a man thing any more, if they ever were. Lots of women—'

'I'm not talking about video games, I'm talking about this building-a-little-fort bullshit.'

'They're not forts, they're man caves.'

Yet another eye-roll. '*Man caves*, for God's sake. Pathetic.'

'Huh? There's nothing wrong with wanting a little space for yourself, is there?'

'Well, how come women never get a little space to themselves? And how come when *men* get one they use it for pointless guff like video games or playing pub?'

'Hang on. You have our spare room for your exercise gear.'

'Oh! Are you saying that's pointless guff?'

'What? That was your phrase! I never—'

'I suppose we do have women caves, now that I think about it,' she said. 'They're called kitchens.'

'Holy shit. *I* spend more time in the kitchen than you do.'

'I made this lasagne, didn't I? All you did was heat it up, badly.'

'That was a week ago. What have you made since? I'm not complaining, I'm the one with the time, that's fine, I'm just saying – it's a bit rich to pretend that you're chained to the cooker night and day.'

She made no reply. He felt a brief rush of elation at this small victory. But it soon gave way to fear. It had never been a good idea, even in better times, to win an argument with Deirdre, however small. She seldom took it well. It was wise to choose your victories carefully. Too late, this one didn't strike him as a particularly wise choice.

'I'm done,' Deirdre said, after a prolonged pause during which Leo fancied he could hear his own blood rushing about. 'I'll leave the clearing up to you, since you're the expert.'

He had no idea what that was supposed to mean and, in fairness to her, Deirdre didn't look too pleased with it either. Something about the set of her mouth as she stood and turned away told him that it had sounded better in her head. But he didn't challenge her. Damage limitation was the name of the game now. Instead, he stood too and started gathering plates, keeping his eyes down, not looking up again until he heard her footsteps thumping up the stairs.

'I'll cheer her up with pleasant conversation,' he whispered to himself in a mocking falsetto.

The downside to listening to music in the dark with headphones on, in Leo's experience, was that it was all too easy to fall asleep and then, on waking, to find yourself flailing around in a wild panic, convinced that you'd gone blind and deaf. This time, the sensory deprivation was compounded by the eerie feeling that he was under some sort of attack. He woke not merely flailing, but karate-chopping and kicking the air all around him. It was only when he caught the headphones cable and yanked them over his face that he realised he'd nodded off. Deirdre was standing over him in the gloom, statue-still.

'I thought you'd never wake up,' she said. 'I've been poking you for ages.'

'Jesus. I thought I was being assaulted. What time is it?'

'Just after 11.'

He yawned. 'Are you done exercising?'

'What, you think I've been at it for four hours?'

He had heard her rowing with the predicted vigour earlier,

before he slipped on his headphones. It certainly hadn't sounded like she intended to stop any time soon.

'No,' he said meekly. 'I suppose not.'

'I did a bit. Had a shower. Read for a while.'

'Right.' Was an apology in the offing? She sounded reasonably conciliatory.

'Anyway,' she sighed, 'we have to have sex.'

'Sorry?'

'It's time. The calendar doesn't lie.'

Here was the thinnest of thin ice. Hadn't they agreed to start IVF, once the small matter of counselling was behind them? Hadn't they basically given up on getting pregnant under their own steam?

'Um,' he said.

'What?'

'Nothing. It's just...' There was no good way to ask the question. No matter how he put it, she was bound to take some sort of offence, quite possibly at something he hadn't even worried about yet. 'I didn't think you'd want to.'

'Why wouldn't I?'

Because the last time we spoke, you looked like I made you feel physically sick and then you stormed off in a filthy mood? 'I just... I didn't think you were in the form, that's all.'

She spread her arms then let them slap against her hips. 'Well, okay, I'm not exactly raring to go here but we have to, and that's that.'

Here was his chance. If he was going to say something about IVF replacing 'have to' sex, then this was the time. He looked up at his wife and cleared his throat. 'After you,' he said and gestured in the general direction of the stairs.

If anyone had told the teenage Leo Dunlop that there was such a thing as too much sex, he would have stopped masturbating just long enough to tell them they were crazy. Sex, it had seemed to him then (and indeed, for much of his twenties), was like money. You had to work hard to get any at all, and you never got anything like enough. The idea that you could have *too much* was a philosophical impossibility, a nonsense, a division by zero. But all that was before Deirdre or, more specifically, before the nightmare of 'trying'. In the early days, of course, it was fun. They were going to have a baby and the way to do it was by having lots and lots of sex. *Result*, Leo had thought. The months went by, however, and no babies showed up. Desperation crept in. Their sexual activity became frantic to the point where both complained of bruising. Any sense of fun and adventure disappeared. It was as if they'd jumped from a plane, Deirdre sobbed one night. At first, it was exhilarating. But they'd been tugging on their ripcords for a while now and the ground was coming up fast. It was time to admit that they were having 'trouble'. And so, books were bought and websites consulted. Diets were changed and underwear preferences adjusted. A thermometer appeared even though no one was ill. Crucially, timing became everything; constant sex gave way to rigidly scheduled sex. It felt to Leo as if they had shifted strategy from carpet-bombing Deirdre's eggs to performing surgical strikes upon them. He found the latter approach even less enjoyable. At least with carpet-bombing, you could pretend that nothing particularly unusual was happening – you were both just sex maniacs, that was all. When there were particular dates on which they 'had to' do it, there was no escaping the fact that something was fundamentally wrong. It was unnatural, and powerfully unerotic. The atmosphere in the bedroom, which had already undergone so many transformations, now became medicinal. Performing his timetabled duties, Leo felt like he had been charged with some minor health-maintenance task, like teeth-polishing or ear-syringing. And still, once a month, she would enter the room, damp of eye, and give a little shake of her head. Not this time either. Sex by appointment became so disagreeable to Leo that his first thought when Dr Larishi used the term 'IVF' was that the unpleasantness was over, at last. They could go back to having a normal sex life, neither impossibly manic nor stringently regulated. And yet here he was, slipping under the duvet to join his wife, not out of love or even lust, but because today's date was one of those circled in the cheap little diary that she kept by her bedside.

'Are you all right?' she said.

'Yeah. Fine. Why?'

'You're pulling a face.'

'No.'

'All right.'

'I'm not.'

'I said, *all right*.'

She had been lying on her left side, facing him. Now she flopped onto her back and stared up at the ceiling, as he was already doing. They lay there in appalling silence for some time.

'Did something happen today?' he ventured. 'You're in awful form. Anything I can do to—'

'Nothing happened. Come on. Let's get on with it.'

He took a deep breath. 'Deirdre, listen. Listen: do we really have to? I just don't… feel like it.' There had been many occasions, of course, on which he hadn't felt like it. But he had never, not even once, given voice to that fact.

'Well, neither do I. Obviously.'

'Okay. So—'

'But what difference does that make? We have to do it, so we're doing it.'

'Why, though? Why do we have to do it?'

She propped herself up on her elbow. 'Remember how we said we'd quite like to have a baby? For that to happen, we have to do a sort of special hug. It's—'

'But we're going for IVF.'

'So?'

'So, haven't we… given up on… on the, uh, natural… method?'

She bit her lower lip and nodded slowly. 'Right. Right, I get it.'

'What?'

'You're gutted because you thought you were finally off the hook. You wouldn't have to do this horrible job any more.'

'You said you didn't feel like it either!'

'Will I go and do another hour on the rowing machine? Switch to the bike? Maybe if I lose another half a stone, you might fancy me then?'

Leo took a moment, determined that he wouldn't lose his temper. 'I do fancy you, Deirdre,' he said then. 'I think you're beautiful. It's got nothing to do with looks. How could you even say that?'

She went back to ceiling-staring. Leo cursed his own boldness. He could have just gone along with it. He could have just kept his mouth shut and climbed aboard. But oh, no, he had to open his stupid gob. He reached across and, somewhat ridiculously, stroked her hair.

'Deirdre, come on. Come on. Don't get all mad. I was just wondering, that's all. I thought maybe going for IVF meant we didn't have to do it when we didn't feel like it. Nothing to do with anything else. Okay? Deirdre?'

She didn't reply immediately; she just lay there thinking and breathing heavily. He wondered if he should stop stroking her hair. If her next contribution was another barb, he would look pretty silly.

'I just thought…' she said after an eternity. 'I just thought it couldn't do any harm to keep trying naturally as well. Y'know? Maybe we'll have a last-minute miracle. And anyway, we won't be starting IVF for a while. We have to do the counselling thing first.'

'Sure we'll fly through that,' he said. 'We'll just lie and say we never argue.' This raised a smile, he was relieved to see. 'You're not worried about it, are you?'

'A bit, yeah. I didn't like the look on Doctor Larishi's face the other day. He seemed to be… concerned.'

'Nah. It'll be grand.'

She reached over and took his hand. He moved closer and snuggled in alongside her. Were they going to have sex or not? The question seemed to have been left dangling. He still didn't want to. If anything, his mood was worsening. It did that a lot these days, out of nowhere.

'Deirdre?'

'Yeah.'

'I want to say something but I want you to listen to me and not just get all angry straight away.'

She raised a hand to her head. 'Oh, Jesus.'

'See? You're preparing to get mad and I haven't even said anything yet.'

'All right, all right. Go on.'

'Well, that last day in the clinic I said you were perfect the way you are, y'know… weight-wise. And you told me to shut up.'

'Hm.'

'But I really meant it. And you heard Doctor Larishi. He said it has no bearing on whether or not you can get pregnant.'

She joined her hands in front of her and closed her eyes for a moment, thus briefly taking on the appearance of a laid-out corpse. 'Did it ever occur to you,' she said then, 'that I want to lose weight for me? You know? Maybe it has nothing to do with what you think or fertility or any of that? Maybe I want to lose weight because I want to lose weight? I'd tried umpteen times long before we even met.'

'I know. I know that. But it used to be just something you talked about once in a while. There was no… desperation.' He paused to gauge the atmosphere and deemed it safe to continue. 'If I thought you wanted to lose weight for the sake of it, I'd be behind you all the way. But you don't, do you? You want to do it because you think that even if it made a tenth of a per cent of a difference in fertility, it'd be worth avoiding crisps and sitting on that rowing machine every night for the rest of your life.'

Her hands parted then came together again. She sighed. She shifted her weight. She cleared her throat. But she didn't say anything. He took that as confirmation that he was on the right track.

'Listen,' he said. 'Why don't you just knock it on the head? Ditch the lettuce. Sell the rowing machine and the bike.'

No response.

'I think it'd be a good idea,' he continued. 'I really do. Give yourself a break.'

Still no response.

'And who knows, maybe we could use the room for something else.'

'What?'

'The spare room. If you got rid of the bike and the rowing machine, I'm saying, we could use—'

'You mean *you* could.'

'Huh?'

She propped herself up on both elbows. 'You want one of those man cave things? Is that it?'

'What? No! Where did you get—'

'That's what this whole thing has been about? All this thoughtfulness and concern? You're letting on you're worried about me but, really, you just want the fucking *room*.'

A dozen responses, ranging in tone from the nasty to the marriage-ending, fought for access to his voice. He beat them all back and spent a moment trying to get some air into his lungs, which seemed to have at least partially collapsed. When he was sure he was in control again, he spoke quietly and slowly. 'That's not true. I wasn't thinking of anything in particular. I just want you to be happy.'

'This all makes sense now. I come in from work and you're all excited about the pub and the game thing across the street...'

'I don't—'

'...and next thing I know, you're telling me it might be a good idea for me to clear out of the spare room? So you can move all your records in there?'

He lost his grip on his tone. 'I never even mentioned my records! For fuck's sake!'

'When we moved here, you said you could put them all in there and I told you no, you weren't having a whole room for that. You've just been waiting for your chance to bring it up again. Admit it!'

'Deirdre. I have zero interest in putting my record collection in there. If I was going to put it anywhere, I'd put it in the garage. I could soundproof the garage. Drop the headphones and finally get myself huge speakers.'

'So you *have* been thinking about it!'

He began to deny it but was given pause by a sense of genuine puzzlement. Had he? A fleeting thought or two during his nice long walk, perhaps. Did that count?

'I honestly haven't,' he said, chewing slightly on the second word. 'But you know what? I am now. I might as well do something nice for me. Because I'm getting nowhere trying to be nice to you.'

He turned away from her and stared furiously at the wall. After a moment she turned the light out and, judging by her movements, turned to face the opposite wall. One question had been settled at least, he thought. They sure as hell weren't going to have sex.

4

'She cut off their tails with a carving knife,' Dooley sang with no real fidelity to the original tune. 'Did you ever see such a thing in your life as threeee bliiiind miiiice?'

He was sitting on the floor of St Michael's community hall, part of a large human circle. Nicola was propped up between his outstretched legs. Attendance was particularly good today; there were maybe two dozen parents, some of whom had brought more than one child. Each of them wore the same fixed smile as they sang, trying to convince their offspring that they were all having the time of their lives.

Sometimes Kay, the exhaustingly enthusiastic woman who ran the Gymboree, played extended versions of nursery rhymes containing lyrics that Dooley had never heard in his life. This, however, was the canonical 'Three Blind Mice'. As the music faded away, she paused the battered CD player by her side and began to clap. All around the circle, parents and some of the toddlers joined in. Dooley grabbed Nicola's wrists and slapped her hands together, much to her grumpy bewilderment.

'Yaaay!' he cheered, hoping to make up for her lack of interest. Most weeks she was the youngest child present but today she didn't even make the top three. There was a baby boy a few spaces to their left who could barely support his own head. Even though his mother was rocking him on her lap as gently as humanly possible, he still looked deeply concerned to find himself in this bizarre environment. Dooley felt for the woman. Her manic stare and stained tracksuit bottoms told him that she was under a lot of pressure. Evidently, she had taken the cause of that pressure to a Gymboree for which he was plainly too young, purely to get out of the damn house for a couple of hours. In fact, now that he looked around, Dooley realised that only half the kids present met the 'two and up' requirement that Kay mentioned in her flyers. He wondered how many parents really believed that their younger children would get something out of it and how many had decided, like tracksuit woman, to come along anyway for the sake of their mental health. He further wondered which group he belonged to.

'It's almost time to go home now,' Kay said and pretended to rub a tear from her cheek. Some of the parents issued a mournful 'Aw'; a few of them seemed to really mean it. Two girls who had been dancing with great abandon all morning looked terribly upset. A little boy beside them raised a clenched fist in delight.

Kay winked. 'But there's just time for one more song!' She said it in the manner of Mick Jagger announcing that they could squeeze in 'Satisfaction' after all; the tune she had in mind soon proved to be 'I'm a Little Teapot'. It was, in her defence, a popular choice. The children who were capable of independent locomotion legged it into the centre of the circle, where they lifted and poured for all they were worth. When the song ended, Kay stood and announced that it was time to put the instruments away. Weirdly, this was a part of the event that the kids all seemed to adore. They toddled around the room collecting the plastic whistles, drums and xylophones that they'd spent the previous hour scattering, and then deposited them – often with great violence – in an enormous plastic bin.

'How about that farmer's wife?' said a voice behind Dooley. He swivelled and saw that it belonged to Paula, a mum with whom he sometimes found himself chatting.

'Who?' he said, getting to his feet and gathering Nicola to his chest.

'The farmer's wife. In 'Three Blind Mice'? They're physically handicapped, these little guys, and what's the first thing she does when she sees them? She grabs a carving knife and gets mutilating.'

'Right. Yeah. What a bitch.'

'*Total* bitch.'

'Well, did Charlie have a good time?' Charlie was Paula's three-year-old. Dooley had no idea what Charlie was short for. Charlotte? Charlene? She was a girl, at any rate, and a perpetually busy one. They watched her now as she raced about grabbing instruments as if each one attracted a large reward.

'She did,' Paula said, 'although we did have a little incident along the way.' She gestured to her legs. There was a large wet patch on each thigh.

Dooley nodded, sympathetically. 'You wet yourself again?'

'Actually, it was Charlie this time,' Paula said, deadpan. 'She was sitting on my lap.'

'A likely story.'

'I think it was just the excitement. 'Mary Had a Little Lamb' always sets her off.'

'It's a classic for a reason.'

'Yup. And how's herself?'

'Nicola's grand,' Dooley said, taking the opportunity to remind her of his daughter's name. She had serious trouble remembering it, for some reason. This was perhaps the fourth time he'd found himself having to slip it in. He leaned a little closer to Paula and lowered his voice. 'Sometimes I feel bad for bringing her here. She's obviously far too young to join in.'

'Don't be silly. Sure, look at that little fella.' She nodded in the direction of the tiny baby Dooley had noticed earlier. 'He hasn't had his cord cut yet.'

Dooley snorted. 'Yeah, I spotted him, all right. I suppose Kay knows full well that a lot of us are here for something to do.'

'Not me,' Paula sniffed. 'I'm pretty sure Charlie's a musical genius and I want to get her off on the right foot.'

'Yeah. The way she was banging that tambourine with a trumpet earlier... I had goosebumps.'

Clean-up was almost finished now. Charlie dropped one last item into the instrument bin and started to run back towards them. She had only taken a few steps when, from her left, she was struck by a blur. The impact spun her around with such force that she landed on her back, and not gently. There was a chorus of gasps from those adults who had witnessed the collision. Paula took off at once, muttering 'Shit shit shit shit shit'. The blur, it transpired, was a boy called Christopher. As Paula began to attend to Charlie, Christopher's mother appeared and dragged him to his feet.

'Is she okay?' Dooley asked Paula as he arrived beside them. 'He hit her pretty... Oh, Jesus!' Charlie had turned towards him, revealing a face whose lower half was covered in blood. Paula shot him a look.

'Oh, that's not so bad!' he said, trying to smile for the little girl's benefit. 'Bit of a bash on the nose, that's all.'

Christopher's mother, meanwhile, had established that he was unscathed. 'I'm so sorry,' she said to Paula. 'I've told him a million times to slow down, or at least look where he's going.'

'Accidents happen,' Paula said flatly.

'I'll get some tissues,' Dooley said and skipped back over to his bag. 'Shh, pet,' he whispered to Nicola as she began to squirm and mumble in his arms. 'Not a good time.' He didn't have any tissues, it turned out, so he grabbed some baby wipes (whose usefulness, he had long since decided, was practically infinite). By the time he crossed the room again, Christopher's mother had fled and the sense of drama was already abating. It was just a bloody nose, after all. There was some similar injury almost every week. Paula took the wipes and set to work. When Charlie saw them turning red her eyes widened and fresh tears fell, but she didn't freak out as badly as Dooley had feared she might.

'They say there's only one thing that can cure a bashed nose,' Paula said. 'And that's ice cream. Did you know that, Dooley?'

'Oh, yeah,' he said, pleased to have a helpful role to play. 'Everyone knows that. It's the first thing doctors learn when they go to doctor school.'

'Drawbry?' Charlie said. Paula released the wipe that she had pressed to the girl's nose. 'Strawberry?' Charlie repeated.

'I think that would be best,' Paula nodded. 'There's a coffee shop up the street. I'm pretty sure they have ice cream. Will we head up there?'

'Yes,' Charlie said, solemnly. 'And let's hurry quickly.'

Paula looked up at Dooley and Nicola. 'What about you two? Come with?'

Dooley hesitated. Coffee with… a woman? He didn't know anything about Paula's relationship status but he was pretty sure *he* was married. It seemed inappropriate. On the other hand, it was only a cup of coffee. What was this, 1850? Why shouldn't he go for coffee with whomever he pleased? The truth was, he didn't even fancy Paula. Or at least, he didn't fancy her a lot. Her mouth had always struck him as being unnecessarily wide. Good bod, though. You had to give her bod points. Excellent boobage.

'Dooley? Are you having a stroke?'

He snapped out of it. 'Sorry, yeah. Coffee – sure.'

Charlie was an impressive little girl, Dooley decided. There was no moaning, no acting up for extra sympathy. She was reasonably cheerful on their walk to the coffee shop and as soon as the ice cream showed up, was restored to her default setting of constantly active, constantly smiling. The only behaviour Paula had to check was her determination to call at every other table in the place and say a sunny hello to its occupants. He remembered his own attitude to childhood mishap, which was to milk every bump and scrape for all it was worth. Would Nicola be the same? He hoped not, partly because he knew he would be helpless in the face of her tears. He'd wind up buying her a pony every time she sustained a graze. He explained all this to Paula, who refused the compliment on her daughter's behalf.

'Nah,' she said. 'You'll see. It's nothing to do with bravery. They just can't concentrate on anything at this age. There's too much new information coming in. If this building went on fire and we got rescued by Mickey Mouse himself, Charlie would forget about it by lunchtime.'

He nodded at Nicola, who was having a snooze in her buggy. 'Not a lot of information going in there,' he said.

'Stop, I'm trying not to look at her. She's very cute and all, don't get me wrong, but I'm getting awful jealous of that nap.'

'Yeah. I could do with forty thousand winks myself.'

'At least you have… What was your wife's name again?'

'Julie.' He guessed that this meant Paula was alone but wasn't sure how he should respond. 'So, you, uh,' he said, after a pause during which it became clear that she wasn't going to elaborate, 'you don't… have anyone?'

'Nope. It's just us.'

'I see.'

'Charlie's dad and I aren't together. Never were, really. He's not an especially brilliant human being.'

Charlie returned from her latest walk and installed herself on her mother's lap, where she became immediately obsessed with her cardigan's zip.

'Right. It must be so hard doing all this on your own. I don't know how you do it. And then there's Neil, my God…'

Neil was one of the very few other men who ever showed up at Gymboree, which he did at irregular intervals. He was a widower. Dooley didn't know the details. He only knew that Neil's wife had died when their son was just a matter of months old.

'I know. Poor Neil…'

'The women at Gymboree are all very protective of him, aren't they? It's sweet.'

'We do love to see a man looking after a child.'

'And the tragedy part doesn't hurt.' He froze. 'Oh! I didn't mean—'

'I know.'

'Honestly, I wasn't trying to be funny. Or belittle him. Or the women. Or anything.'

'I *know*. Still.'

'Still?'

'Well. I don't want to sound like a bitch.' She half-swallowed the last word for Charlie's benefit.

'Okay, you have my full attention now.'

A smile half-formed and quickly died, like a match not quite catching fire. 'I'm not saying I don't have huge sympathy for the guy. Of course I do. But he doesn't have a choice, does he? He has to knuckle down and look after the kid. Personally, I'm more impressed with you.'

'Oh?'

'You've got Julie. You don't *have to* be the one who looks after Nicola. But there was a conversation at some point, I presume, when you decided that she would work and you'd do the baby-raising.'

'Yeah. Lots of them, actually – conversations. Julie's career is just way—'

'What I'm saying is, Neil, great and all as he is, has had full-time child-minding thrust upon him. You volunteered. And modern and open and equal as we all pretend to be, that's still a pretty rare situation. I think it's admirable.' She raised her coffee cup with both hands and took a long sip, apparently satisfied that she had made her point. Dooley pretended to adjust the position of Nicola's stuffed giraffe for a moment. He needed a distraction, something that would stop him from agreeing – or at least, stop him from agreeing too quickly.

'I love looking after Nicola,' he said, noncommittally.

Paula popped a chunk of blueberry muffin into her mouth and swallowed it almost immediately. 'Do people take the piss?'

'Sorry?'

'Your friends and that. About you being the stay-at-home one?'

'Oh. I got jokes about feather dusters and aprons, yeah. When I quit work, a few of the blokes gave me a make-up kit.'

'Dickheads.'

'Well, on the plus side, I hardly have time to see them any more.'

'Yeah. I know that song.'

'Know it a lot better than me, no doubt.'

She shrugged but said nothing. Dooley didn't think she wasn't being coy. She genuinely wasn't interested in talking about herself; she wanted to hear about him and his 'situation'.

'I suppose if I did get a night out with my old gang, we wouldn't have much to say to each other,' he said. 'I mean, some of them are dads themselves. But they do other stuff too, like hold down jobs and go to gigs and know who the Taoiseach is. The only thing I'm up to date with is *In the Night Garden.*'

'Ugh. The bloody Pontipines.'

'I *hate* the Pontipines.'

'I hate all of them. Upsy Daisy, the Tombliboos—'

'Makka Pakka.'

'He's the worst. I hope the Ninky Nonk falls out of the sky some day with him on board.'

'You mean Pinky Ponk. The Ninky Nonk is the train. The Pinky Ponk is the airship.'

'Right, right. Whatever. So long as he dies horribly.'

'Maybe it'll go up in flames one day, like the Hindenburg.'

'Oh, the humanity!'

'Or whatever the hell Makka Pakka is.'

Charlie looked up, all smiles, and said, 'Makka Pakka?' She had abandoned her zip in favour of a tiny plastic frog that she had retrieved from somewhere on her person. Dooley and Paula exchanged a look. *Oops.*

'We were just saying how great he is,' Paula said. 'He's your favourite, isn't he?'

Charlie darkened and shook her head emphatically. This suggestion had greatly offended her. 'No. My favourite is Upsy Daisy. UPSY DAISY.'

'All right, keep your hair on.'

'My *hair?*'

Paula responded with a kiss on the cheek and this, apparently, was closure enough for Charlie. She went back to hopping the frog over and back across a spoon.

'So,' Paula said to Dooley. 'That's it, huh? Your whole life is kids' TV and Gymboree?'

'Pretty much. Well – usually. I do have a bit of a project going on at the moment.'

She feigned awe. 'A *project*, no less.'

Dooley felt a little embarrassed. 'That might be overselling it a bit. I'm making a sort of a… Well, it's a bar, a pub, whatever you want to call it. In the garage.'

'Ah. So you're a raging alcoholic.'

'Actually, I'm more of a heroin kind of guy. But Julie doesn't approve of that.'

'Well, that's very old-fashioned of her.'

'I know!'

Two tables over, an old woman said something that amused

her companion greatly – almost amused her to death, it seemed to Dooley. The second woman's high-pitched laughter was so loud that he felt obliged to let it fade away before saying anything else. When relative silence was restored he said, 'Tell you the truth, she doesn't approve of the pub thing either.'

'Oh? Why not?'

Julie had brought up the 'pub thing' a couple of times since their initial row. She was sorry if she'd given him the wrong impression, she said. Of course she didn't think he was unmanly, by comparison with David or anyone else. And *obviously* she didn't expect him to start climbing mountains or anything of the kind. All she had been trying to say was that it would do him good to get more fresh air, and holing up in the garage scored no points in that regard. Dooley accepted the apology and offered one of his own, allowing that he'd possibly been oversensitive and short-tempered. They would have moved on, free and clear, if not for the fact that Julie still wasn't happy about his plans. It was obvious. Even after the clear-ups and apologies, she made a couple of disparaging remarks and cracked the occasional joke, all the while protesting that she didn't care either way. *Those* jokes hurt, much more than anything the lads had ever said. One of them featured the term 'playing house'. There was no need to tell Paula that, though, he decided. Why give her the image?

'I'm not sure. Maybe she thinks I'm being selfish.'

'Hm.'

Dooley felt his stomach lurch. He was shocked by how disappointed he felt. 'What, you agree?'

'I didn't say that.'

'You didn't say otherwise.'

'Actually, I… Never mind. It's none of my business.'

'No, go on. Please.' He squirmed, regretting the 'please'.

'I just think, y'know, since you've given up so much to take care of Nicola…'

She was apparently reluctant to go any further. But he wanted to hear it from her own lips. It wouldn't count if he finished the thought for her. There was something of a stand-off. Eventually, Paula took the hint.

'If it was me, I'd probably conclude that you deserve to spend time working on something for yourself.'

And there it was – approval, not just from another woman, but from another mum. Dooley felt like he'd done a shot. He joined his hands and tapped the thumbs together, thinking. *Yeah*, he told himself. *Go on. Why not?*

'Maybe it's not about selfishness, though,' he said. 'Maybe she thinks it's, I dunno... not... manly.'

'Really? It's hardly a *girly* activity. Making yourself a pub.'

'It's not the end-purpose of the thing, though. I'm guessing. It's the pretending. She's made the odd crack about... playing house.'

'Dooley. You're staying home to look after your daughter, and doing a great job. That's plenty manly. The best kind of manly. You could make yourself a wendy house and have dolls' tea parties every night and you'd still be more of a man than some I could mention.'

'*Yes*,' he said and only just stopped himself from thumping the table. 'I mean... thank you.'

Paula pulled a face. 'Shit. Feels like I'm getting into personal territory where I don't bel—'

'Don't worry about it. What am I going to do? Go home and tell her "Well, Paula, who you've never met, is all for the idea, so nyah"? Relax.'

'Okay.'

'I am filing this away, though. Just for me. A bit of reassurance.'

'Okay.'

'I get all excited, full of plans, y'know, but I can't talk to Julie about it. If I try, she just rolls her eyes and changes the subject to avoid a row. I was hoping to get a pool table, originally, but I just don't have the room. But then I thought—' He stopped himself. 'Ah, you don't want to know. It's boring.'

'I'll tell you what,' she said. 'Get more coffee in and maybe another couple of those muffins and you can talk my ear off. I'll just stuff my face and say, "That sounds great!" every so often.'

Dooley pretended to become emotional. 'That's all I've ever wanted,' he whispered. He got up and rejoined the queue.

'The name of the game, yeah, is Capture the Flag,' said the scrawny man. He was tall, maybe six-two in Deirdre's estimation, with the approximate proportions of a biro. She knew that he'd provided his name at the outset but it hadn't stuck. Her mind was racing too fast to catch such trivialities. A single fundamental question was repeating on a loop in there, drowning out all potential input: *Does it hurt? Does it hurt? Does it hurt?*

'You all look like reasonably intelligent people,' Scrawny continued, to some polite laughter, 'so you'll have worked out, yeah, that there are flags and the objective is to capture them.'

The previous year's company awayday had involved go-karting. Deirdre had loathed every bumpy, terrifying second of it. Despite everything life had repeatedly taught her, she'd allowed herself to hope that this year's 'fun activity' would be something a little more genteel. But no. Frigging *paintball*. They were somewhere in Coolock at a joint called Last Man Standing (even the name annoyed her, with its casual sexism and suggestion of authentic violence). It wasn't the pastoral setting she'd been envisaging. The play area – or 'battlefield', as Scrawny seemed determined to call it – was an old car park, or what looked like one, at least. There were concrete barriers scattered around it, as well as some water-filled barrels, a clapped-out old wreck of a bus and the carcass of a van that seemed to have ended its days aflame.

'Okay,' Scrawny said. 'Rules.'

Deirdre leaned forward and did her best to pay attention. The teams would be based at opposite ends of the battlefield. Each base would have a flag. The idea was to grab your opponents' and return it to your base while preventing them from doing the same. If you got shot, you were out. If you got shot while carrying the flag, you dropped it where you stood, and then you were out. There were a few more ifs and buts, which Scrawny ran through at speed. Then he joined his fingertips in front of him and adopted a serious expression.

'I've gone through the rules of the game quite quickly because we've only got a few minutes here and I want to get onto the important stuff. The important stuff is to do with safety. It's no big deal if you don't drop the flag in exactly the right place. It's a very big deal, yeah, if you lose an eye. So, please, listen up.'

To his credit, his safety talk was thorough and detailed – but it was not at all comforting. Deirdre didn't like the way he continually referred to the prevention of 'serious' injury. The implication, she soon realised, was that while serious injury could be avoided, non-serious injury could not. The answer to her fundamental question was clearly *yes – yes, of course it hurts.* As Scrawny issued his warnings and related his horror stories, she glanced around at her colleagues. All of the men (and the company was 90 per cent male) had the same stupid macho looks on their faces. Deirdre felt sure that some of them must be faking it and was irritated to find that she couldn't tell which ones. Some of the women seemed nervous but only in a giggly, *tee-hee, what have we got ourselves into?* kind of way. No one looked the way she felt, which was common-or-garden terrified. She looked down at the paint-spattered overalls she'd been given and tested the structural integrity of her face mask. Was it too late, she wondered, to feign illness? Probably. She might get out of paintball but she'd never hear the end of it.

'Right, then,' Scrawny said, clapping his hands together. 'Anybody have any questions?' A pause. 'No? Okay. Off you go then. Get out there and earn some glory.'

They began to troop outside, cracking jokes and jostling each other like schoolchildren. Deirdre hung back, hoping that some last-minute disaster – an earthquake, say, or a plague of locusts – would force the event's cancellation. Two of her colleagues sat chatting amiably, in no real hurry to rise from their seats. Mr Fallon and Louise. The former had declared himself too old and slow to take part. The latter had been excused on the grounds that her unborn baby might not take kindly to being hit in the face by a paintball travelling at 200 feet per second.

'Good luck, Deirdre,' Mr Fallon called out when he saw her looking over.

'Go get 'em,' Louise added. 'I'm sickened jealous.' She patted her bump, as she did after almost every pronouncement.

Deirdre gave them a watery thumbs-up and followed the others.

An hour and a half later she was crouched behind a concrete barrier, trying to get as low to the ground as she could without actually lying down. A few feet away, on the other side of the chain-link fence that separated Last Man Standing from a patch of undeveloped land, sat a fat ginger cat. They had been staring at each other for some time now. Deirdre felt mildly hypnotised. She could hear the shouting, grunting, swearing and occasional laughter that told her the game was still in progress. It seemed unbelievable to her now that there had ever been a time when she wondered if getting shot with a paintball would hurt. She'd been so naive. You might as well wonder if getting hit by a car would hurt. The first impact of the day caught her on the left thigh with such force that she didn't even cry out. She was too astonished. This was something people did for *fun?* In the next round, when she was hit right between the eyes and everything went black, her initial impression was that she had actually died. It was only when she saw a patch of ground in the lower left of her vision that she realised she'd merely been blinded by the paint. She did her best to clear her face mask as she jogged to the sideline and was not at all impressed when another shot struck her on the ass before she made it. It was probably an accident – you weren't supposed to shoot someone more than once – but that was cold comfort. Getting hurt was only part of the misery, of course. Every time she swallowed her fear and emerged from cover she had to disgrace herself by showing the whole company her version of running. They were all laughing at her, she was sure of it. *Waddling.* No doubt that was the word they were using in their own heads and would use again later in the pub when they put those heads together. *Jesus, did you see Deirdre Dunlop waddling about out there? I shot her every chance I got just to put her out of her misery. Didn't take a lot of skill – it's not like you could miss, ha ha!*

During those first few rounds Deirdre had found herself glancing with ever greater frequency towards Louise, who was standing well out of the way behind some hoarding. She seemed to be having a ball, chatting to Mr Fallon and laughing every time someone cried out in pain. Despite that, she didn't stick around. After a while, Deirdre saw her retreat back inside where there were seats and magazines and a coffee machine. Envy overwhelmed her, so intense that it made her knees tremble. Her perception of the paintball experience changed in an instant. It wasn't just an irritation that, however awful, would soon be over. It was yet another diabolical scheme that the universe was using to rub her infertility in her face. She became simultaneously furious and achingly sad. Now, hunkered down in a staring competition with a cat, she had turned reflective. This sort of reaction was a recent development. She didn't mind – or at least she understood – when the sight of a mother cuddling her baby in a coffee shop set her off. That was perfectly natural. That was to be expected. But it wasn't healthy, surely, to obsess so feverishly over the little perks of pregnancy itself. Just the previous weekend, she'd had to hide her face from passers-by in a Tesco car park having been reduced to tears by the sight of a man helping an expectant mother with her shopping. Not long before that, it was someone giving up a bus seat – and that was in a *movie*. But the real killer was Louise. She could barely type an email without someone appearing at her shoulder and telling her she shouldn't be doing that in her condition, before offering to go make her a cup of tea. She'd been deemed 'brave' – brave! – for tackling a single flight of stairs every day at work. Her opinions on the temperature in the office sent colleagues scrambling for the thermostat, each hoping to be the one to restore her to a state of relative comfort. And now, look. She was getting out of paintball.

Deirdre hadn't mentioned any of this to Leo. They'd barely spoken since he started work on the garage. But even if they'd been getting along fine she wouldn't have brought it up. It was too petty. And so she stumbled on, feeling merely upset when she envied women with baby bumps and halfway unhinged when she envied the special attention they received. It didn't help, of course, that she understood how scornful any mother-to-be would be if they knew what she was thinking. *Special attention? Perks? You think that the occasional cup of tea makes up for the heartburn and nausea and exhaustion? The aching back? The tortured bladder?* Unsurprisingly, piling guilt on top of the envy, which itself was piled on top of desperation, didn't do much good.

A shot whizzed by, breaking her train of thought and

reminding her of how uncomfortable she was. The strategy of simply hiding had enabled her to avoid being hit for several minutes now, but it was playing havoc with her knees. Could she stretch her legs, she wondered, without exposing any part of her body to enemy fire? She was still working out the details when the ginger cat suddenly flattened its ears and then bolted.

'Deirdre!' a muffled voice called. A body slid in beside her. 'Deirdre, there are three left alive of us but only two left alive of them. We can do it! Come on! Get up! We must go forward!'

It was Jadwiga. Deirdre's first thought was *I bet she hasn't been hit even once, the skinny bitch.*

'I'm grand here, thanks,' she shouted through her mask.

'What?'

'I'm grand here.'

'What?'

'*Fuck off, Jadwiga, I'm not going out there.*'

'But the game! We can get their flag!'

'I don't care about their fl—'

She felt a thump in the back, as if someone had planted their foot between her shoulder blades. Even before the sting arrived, she saw a second shot hit her companion on the shoulder. As Jadwiga cried something foul in Polish, Deirdre twisted around to see who had shot them – not that it made any difference – and saw Liam Fallon gleefully sprinting away. She could tell it was him because of his shaved head. (He thought it made him look like Bruce Willis, she knew for a fact. It didn't. It made him look like Nosferatu.) Although this shot didn't hurt any more than its predecessors, Deirdre found herself enraged afresh. She'd been beginning to hope that she would make it through to the end without further assault upon her person. And she probably would have done, if stupid Jadwiga hadn't come over all *Saving Private Ryan*. She swore violently and began to struggle to her feet. The minibus would be arriving soon to take them to the pub for lunch. She'd been dreading that part of the day almost as much as this bullshit – she would end up sitting beside Louise, she just knew it – but now she was beginning to see an upside. Pubs, if memory served, had vodka. She emerged from behind her cover and saw that the other surviving member of the opposing team was Francis Fallon. There was a general reluctance to shoot the boss's sons, it seemed; they'd made it through most of the previous rounds unscathed too. Liam had already collected the flag and was running back to base with it. This terrible game was over, at last. Deirdre pulled her face mask off and pushed back the clump of damp hair that clung to her forehead like seaweed on a rock. And then, on the far side of the playing area, beyond Francis, there was sudden activity. Jim Kenny, the company accountant and apparently the last remaining member of Deirdre's team, leaped out from behind the burned-out van. Deirdre saw him raise his gun and in what seemed like the same instant felt a tremendous smack on her left ear. Conscious thought went out the window. She dropped her mask and started running (*waddling*). Francis issued some words of concern as she went by but she didn't respond.

'For fuck's sake, Deirdre,' Jim shouted when she was close enough for communication. 'What did you take your face mask off for? We're not finished!'

She slowed now as she approached him. Her breathing had become shallow and laboured. She was oddly conscious of a bead of sweat running down her back.

'Are you all right? I think it just clipped your ear, did it?'

She stopped when there was just a few feet of ground between them. Not once in the ten rounds they'd played had she managed to hit anyone with a paintball. But those targets had been far away, moving and shooting back. Jim was right in front of her, stationary and entirely passive. She raised her gun to hip level and shot him in the balls. The noise he produced was neither a scream nor a roar. It was rounder and softer than that, as if he was singing underwater. She hit him twice more before he hit the ground, although neither shot could match the accuracy of her first. One hit him in the abdomen. The other, the wildest of the three, struck his knee. Should she hit him again, she wondered? She felt vaguely tempted but it suddenly seemed like a strange thing to want to do. Jim wasn't a bad stick. Why should she hurt him? The question had yet to resolve itself when she felt her gun being roughly snatched away.

'What the fuck?' Francis said, throwing her weapon out of reach like a cop on TV. 'Deirdre? *What the fuck?*'

Liam arrived then, and just behind him came half a dozen others, Mr Fallon among them. No sign of Louise, Deirdre thought. Still inside relaxing, no doubt. As Liam began attending to Jim, she ran her hand over the wet mess at her ear and then held it up close to her face. She saw blue paint. No blood, which was a surprise. The world had seemed blurred and distant in the short time since she'd been hit. Now it suddenly swam into focus again – into hyper-focus, actually. Everything in her immediate surroundings, the texture of the concrete, the splashes of colour on Jim's overalls, the shrieks and shouts of her advancing colleagues, all of it seemed supernaturally clear.

'Deirdre?' Mr Fallon said sternly. 'What did—'

'I shouldn't even be out here!' she yelled. 'I should be inside with Louise! Relaxing!'

He looked back where he'd come from, then peered at her again, evidently puzzled.

'I'm not sure—'

'*I* should have a shopping helper! *I* should have a seat on the bus! It's not fair! *None of this is fair!*'

She knew that none of this could possibly make any sense to him but she felt powerless to offer any more clarity. It was as if she was watching someone on a screen, willing them to do a better job but unable to directly intervene. She was crying too, she suddenly realised. When had that started? She had no idea. Mr Fallon stepped closer and put his arm around her shoulders.

'Come on with me,' he said. 'We'll take a little walk.'

He started moving and she allowed herself to be escorted. The small crowd of her colleagues parted to allow them through. She could feel the awful weight of their stares and their silence as she passed.

'I'm so tired,' she said softly, and her boss tightened his grip on her.

Everybody's staring at me, Redmond thought with considerable alarm. *Why is everybody staring at me?* He cleared his throat and straightened his back.

'Rise and shine,' Margaret Hanley said. 'It's a beautiful morning. I trust you slept well?'

'Sorry?' he said, blinking rapidly.

There were snorts and one or two muted giggles from his colleagues around the meeting room table. Margaret, at its head, remained impassive.

'You nodded off, Redmond,' she said. 'Either that or you had simultaneously closed your eyes and gone deaf. I've been saying your name for a while now.'

'I wasn't asleep,' he whimpered. *Don't say you were resting your eyes.* 'I was just resting my eyes.'

More snorts and giggles, louder this time.

'I'm a little offended,' Margaret said. 'I'd always thought you all looked forward to our little meetings. I thought they were the highlight of everyone's week. Now I find that it's a struggle for some of you to stay awake.'

This was her to a tee, Redmond thought. She never lost her temper or said anything that was objectively nasty (unlike, for example, Bill), and yet she retained the power to regularly infuriate. It was all in her tone. She had the lofty and weakly sarcastic air of a schoolteacher who'd been stuck with a class of no-hopers and could only retain her sanity by amusing herself with small jokes at their expense.

'Rough night with the kids,' Redmond said. 'My apologies.'

'No need to apologise,' Margaret said, smiling thinly. She glanced around at her team. 'Let's just agree, going forward, that maintaining consciousness will be a priority for all of us.'

She returned her gaze to Redmond, who wondered if he was supposed to literally voice his consent. He made a noise that was somewhere between a cough and a hum, and hoped that would suffice. The meeting got back on tedious track. It lasted for another 40 terrible minutes. When Margaret finally closed her notebook and declared that they'd covered everything for another week, no one moved. It was if they couldn't quite believe it was over.

'That means you can go now,' she added and fluttered her fingers in the direction of the door.

Like statues coming to life in a fairytale, her team creaked and groaned their way to their feet and made their way out. Redmond fell in beside Declan, who gave him a pitying look.

'Tough night with the kids,' he mocked in a low voice. 'Tough night with the PlayStation, more like.'

'No, really,' Redmond said. 'I'm operating on about four hours sleep here.'

'They say Maggie Thatcher used to get by on four hours.'

'Yeah, well she wasn't doing this shit, was she? I'd imagine that running wars and whatnot is a bit more interesting than corporate insurance.'

They returned to their desks. Redmond saw that in the little over an hour that he'd been away, he had received 22 emails, nine instant messages and four voicemails. A brief scan of his inbox told him that only a handful of the emails were trivial and that at least three promised serious additions to his workload. He reached up and massaged his right temple, where a headache was beginning to form. His computer issued a terse bleep then, and he saw that a tenth instant message had arrived. It was from Margaret. If he had a moment, could he pop in to see her? He replied in the positive, pushed his chair back, and hauled himself upright. *Oh goody*, he thought.

Margaret hadn't always had an office of her own. Until quite recently, she'd occupied a cubicle along with the rest of the troops, a fact that she never lost an opportunity to underscore. How could a team leader lead, she would muse, looking perplexed, if they were tucked away on their own somewhere? It made no sense! And then old Joe Keating retired, thus freeing up the pokey office that he had occupied since Jesus was a boy and where he was rumoured to spend a good portion of the day getting quietly arseholed on gin. Joe had barely left the car park before Margaret annexed the room, claiming now that it would be to everyone's benefit if she had a space to call her own. How could a team leader lead, after all, if she had no privacy in which to mull the difficult strategic choices that went along with her position?

Redmond loathed having to go in there, and not just because it usually meant trouble of some sort. As a general rule, he tried to avoid giving too much thought to his career. The job was never fun, but it was doable so long as you didn't look too far ahead. You could consider moving to Bill's team, for example, but thinking about where you might be a decade hence was… unwise. Visiting Margaret reminded him that this was the sort of office he himself could expect to occupy one day *if things went really well.* It wasn't a punishment, being squeezed into a little box like this one, with its too-harsh lighting and its chipped desk – it was a reward.

'Come on in,' Margaret called out when he tapped gently on her door. She rarely used any other form of words when inviting entry, although he had once heard her issue a cheery 'Yo', a choice that suited her the way, say, a pair of Converse All Stars would suit the Pope. He went in and took a seat without waiting to be asked. There was a knuckle-rap in the offing, clearly, and he wanted it over with as quickly as possible.

'Hi,' he said.

Margaret was typing something and continued to do so for a moment. Then she finished with a flourish and placed both palms flat before her.

'So. Redmond.'

'I'm sorry about the meeting,' he said quickly, hoping to head her off at the pass. 'I really did have a shocking night with my boys.'

He wasn't lying. Luke and Aidan had tag-teamed him in the small hours, taking turns to wake each other up and making a tremendous fuss every time. Nancy hadn't stirred, and he hadn't requested her help. It was possible, he supposed, that she'd genuinely slept through the whole thing. But if so, it was a first.

'I believe you,' Margaret said. 'I have kids. I know how it can be. But still.'

'Still?'

'Still. I'm concerned. About your level of commitment.'

He shrugged. 'I'm *tired*, that's all there is—'

'It's not just the meeting today, though, Redmond. It's not just today. You seem… I don't know… bored.'

'Margaret, we work in insurance.'

She tucked in her chin. 'You think the insurance industry is boring?'

'You mean you don't?'

He smiled and felt his features freeze as Margaret failed to follow suit.

'I'm sorry?' she said.

'A joke. Just a little joke.'

She shook her head and exhaled. 'You see? This is exactly what I'm talking about. You're literally falling asleep in meetings, you applied for a job on a different team, and now you tell me to my face that you think your job is boring.'

When he decided to go for the position on Bill's team, he had debated whether or not he should tell her. The internet was no help. There were as many voices saying an internal application was none of a current manager's business as there were saying it was unthinkably rude not to keep everyone informed. In the end, he concluded that it would do no harm to tell her. At the very least, it would look like ambition. Now that was beginning to feel like a mistake.

'Margaret! I nodded off because I'm knackered. I said the job was boring as a *joke*. And if I wasn't happy here, I'd be applying elsewhere entirely, wouldn't I? Not to Bill.'

She tapped her pen against her teeth for a moment, considering. 'Maybe,' she allowed.

'Honestly. Everything's fine. I'm perfectly content. There's nothing wrong with my commitment levels. You don't need to worry.'

He briefly wondered if he had protested too much, but then Margaret's expression softened.

'Maybe I've overreacted,' she said.

Redmond spotted an opening. 'Happens to us all,' he said in his slickest salesman tone. 'Have you considered getting yourself insured against future overreaction events?'

Margaret found this feeble line delightful, as he had known she would. Jokes at the expense of insurance were bad. Jokes *about* insurance were fine. His cheeks flushed with shame as she sat back and chuckled.

'Go on,' she said then. 'Forget I spoke. Do me a favour, though – try to get a good night's rest tonight.'

'It's my number one priority,' he said, and took his leave. As he walked back to his cubicle, he suddenly felt overcome by exhaustion. It was nothing to do with his lack of sleep. This was something deeper. He tested the word 'metaphysical' in his mind, and rejected it as too wanky. Plus, he wasn't sure he was using it correctly. How nice it would be, he thought, to have a team leader with a normal person's sense of humour. Someone who would laugh along about how boring the job was – it was *famously* boring, for fuck's sake! – while understanding that you still wanted to keep it, because your kids insisted on eating.

It had been a shitty morning, all told, but lunchtime was coming up fast. A treat, he decided. What he needed now was a nice treat.

'Creative T40 Series II's,' Redmond nodded to the man behind the counter. 'Yeah. Great speakers. I've had them for ages.'

'Nice.'

'Really nice. Got them here, actually. And they're still working fine. I just feel like upgrading.'

The assistant's name, according to his shiny badge, was Amit. Why were shops like this one always staffed by Indians, Redmond wondered? Was it a matter of policy on the owners' part? Had they realised that everyone thought Indians were tech-savvy and hired accordingly? Or were Indians, for whatever reason, the only ones who ever applied for the jobs? He checked himself. Was it racist of him to even wonder? He thought not, but he'd found as he grew older that the ground was shifting under him when it came to matters of cultural sensitivity. Everyone had older relatives who occasionally silenced the room with some shocking pronouncement. It was frightening to get even a small glimpse of how they got to be so cringe-inducing – not by being bad people, necessarily, but by simply failing to keep up.

'Have you got something in mind?' Amit asked. 'Or just a budget, maybe?'

'Nope, nothing particular in mind. But I would like to get a subwoofer this time. Budget-wise... I'm thinking something that could well give my wife a heart attack when she sees it on the credit card statement, but won't actually kill her.'

Amit smiled politely. 'I'm going to need you to be more specific than that.'

Redmond gave him a number.

The drive to Blanchardstown shopping centre from work had taken more than the ten minutes Redmond had imagined it would. But on the plus side he was all done in PC World well ahead of schedule (as soon he heard the Bose Acoustimass 3s, it was game over). If traffic was halfway decent he could expect to be back within his allotted lunch hour, even allowing for the Big Mac he planned to stuff into his face. Or should he make it a Whopper? He was pondering the issue when Nancy came around the corner with the boys. He saw her before she spotted him. A shot of adrenalin coursed through him and he caught his breath. He had to consciously remind himself that this was his wife, not some long-dreaded assassin. Something similar went through her mind, he imagined; he saw her flinch and momentarily stop pushing the buggy.

'Well, hello there,' he said as she drew near. Aidan barrelled towards him, arms raised over his head, like a footballer who'd just put a volley into the top corner from the edge of the box. Redmond dropped his shopping bag and scooped him up, tickled him, then bent low again to do the same to Luke. His back complained. He ignored it. 'This is, uh, a surprise,' he smiled at Nancy. 'You're a bit out of your way, aren't you?'

'Argos,' she said. 'I wanted to get the hair straighteners I told you about but they didn't have them at the one in Santry.'

'Ah,' Redmond said. 'Right.'

'You don't know what I'm talking about, do you?'

'I do, yeah. Hair straighteners. Argos.'

She shook her head and said (to herself more than him), 'Never listens.'

'I do listen, Nancy. Hair straighteners! Argos!' He did his best to keep his tone under control but he wasn't at all sure that he'd succeeded. It didn't help that he was lying. He'd never heard the words 'hair straighteners' coming out of Nancy's mouth in his life. As far as he knew.

'Anyway,' she said, giving up, 'what has you out of the office? Buying me a surprise gift?'

She had seen the PC World logo on the bag, surely. So why was she asking? Just to annoy him, he supposed. This was how almost all of their conversations had gone lately. Poke, reaction, counterreaction. He was as guilty as she was. He knew that. He wasn't denying that. Still, it made no difference when he was the one who got poked.

'Speakers,' he said cheerfully. 'Thought I'd treat myself.'

'Treat yourself...'

'Yes. Treat myself.'

'Right.'

'Yup.'

'The noise coming out of the garage is pretty loud as it is. You want to make it louder?'

'That's mostly coming from the TV. These are for the computer.'

'What? How does that help your case?'

Aidan squirmed in his arms. 'Down, Daddy, down.' Redmond complied. She had him there. Arguing back had become so natural to him that he occasionally forgot to make sure he wasn't talking nonsense.

'Look,' he said, hoping to sound like he did, in fact, have an excellent point that she was simply failing to grasp, 'if I'm being a little heavy on the volume sometimes, all you have to do is let me know. I'll turn it down.'

'Gee, thanks.'

Now it was his turn to shake his head defeatedly. 'Okay. Whatever.'

'How much did you spend, then?'

He'd been hoping he'd be able to smuggle the speakers into the house without her noticing. She made a big deal of never setting foot in the garage these days so she might never have spotted them, once installed. Despite his bravado with Amit, he'd been hoping that she wouldn't notice the hit on the credit card either. Now he was faced with owning up before he'd even taken the things out of the bag.

'They were reduced,' he said. Another lie. 'Twenty per cent off because there's a new model.'

'How much, Redmond?'

'Three hundred. Three hundred-ish.'

He braced for impact.

Her eyes closed for a moment. 'Another three hundred. This is on top of the hundred for the giant bean bag and sixty for the lamps and… You know what? Never mind. Just… never mind. Forget it.'

'I—'

'I've told you before, but no doubt you've forgotten this too, so I'll tell you again: I'm going out tonight with Julie from next door. Dinner and drinks.'

'I know,' he said. It was the truth this time.

'Just making sure. Right, we're off.' She started moving.

'Hang on, hang on. Jesus, can I say goodbye to the boys?'

'Yep.'

He got a high five from Aidan and vigorously shook Luke's hand, eliciting a squeal of delight. 'Just us, tonight,' he said. 'Just the men. We'll have a big ol' party.'

'In the garage?' Nancy asked. Redmond straightened up and looked at her. He was surprised to find that he didn't want to snipe back. On the contrary, he suddenly wanted to be conciliatory. *This can't go on, how did we get like this?*, something along those lines. But the words wouldn't come, so he just watched in silence as she walked away.

Leo had never thought of himself as a creative person or – except in matters musical – someone with particularly good taste. He saw other guys on the street who struck him as well dressed, for example, but when it came time to go clothes shopping for himself, he had no idea how to replicate what they'd done. Most of his shopping trips finished ahead of schedule with the purchase of yet another band T-shirt. Similarly, he could nod appreciatively at some of the work in the home makeover shows but when a room in his own place needed to be painted, he shrugged and reached for the magnolia. Despite all this, he had somehow convinced himself that it would be different this time. He would stand in the centre of the garage, swivel 360°, and instantly see how the space (they always called it a 'space' on the makeover shows) could be transformed. This turned out to be a long way from the truth. The luxuriously appointed 'music room' of his rapidly escalating fantasies manifested in reality as little more than a garage with a record player and an armchair in it. To think that he'd once believed he might have it in him to soundproof the place… There were *cobwebs* he hadn't got around to destroying yet. One thing he was pleased with, however, was the storage situation. There was a rickety old shelving unit against the back wall – it had been there when they moved in – that turned out to be exactly the same depth as a vinyl LP. It was big enough to accommodate his entire collection, with quite a bit of headroom to spare. He no longer needed to extract records with the very tips of his fingernails and greatly enjoyed the sensation of flipping through the sleeves when he had no particular choice in mind. It was like being in a record shop that only stocked music he loved. He was browsing among the Ls – LCD Soundsystem, Led Zeppelin, Leftfield – when he heard voices on the other side of the door that led into the kitchen. His heart skipped. *Burglars*. Frantic and already shaking, he looked around for something that might serve as a weapon. There were no obvious candidates; he hadn't done a good job decorating the place but he'd been pretty thorough in his clear-out. The door began to open. He grabbed *Houses of the Holy* and adopted the pose of someone about to launch a frisbee. Maybe he could Oddjob the guy in the throat. It was (marginally) better than nothing and might buy him the couple of seconds he would need to escape through the garage door.

'Jesus *Christ*,' he said when he saw Deirdre standing there. She looked awful, he noted parenthetically. 'You scared the shit out of me! What are you doing home? Are you all right? What happened to paintball?'

Deirdre made no reply. She turned on her heels and went back into the kitchen. Leo carefully put the album back in the correct spot and followed her. He hadn't laid eyes on his wife's boss in a couple of years and didn't recognise him at first.

'Leo! Hello. Eddie Fallon.'

He extended a hand. Leo stepped across and shook it. Deirdre, he couldn't help but notice, had carried on out of the room. He heard her footsteps on the stairs and something inside him did a long, slow roll.

'Mr Fallon, of course. What's wrong? What happened? Is she okay? Did she get hurt?'

'She's fine. Well, no, she's not *fine*, I mean…'

'What?'

'Would you mind if we sat down?'

Leo didn't like that. He gestured and they sat. The table was still covered with toast crumbs from breakfast. Somehow, despite everything, this made it through to strike Leo as a shameful state of affairs. He'd intended to clean up but had found himself wandering back to bed instead. Fallon shifted the position of his chair and sighed deeply.

'I'm not sure where to start.' He smiled awkwardly and then sighed again. Leo wanted to grab him by the throat and tell him to start *anywhere* but restrained himself. 'We're having our company awayday today, as you know. Paintball this morning, pub lunch, bit of brainstorming in the afternoon.'

'Yes.' *Get on with it, for fuck's sake.*

'Well, lookit, long story short, bottom line, not to put too fine a point on it, Deirdre seemed to have a bit of a, um… a bit of a mini… uh… mini… breakdown.'

'What? What's a mini-breakdown? What do you mean?'

'She started crying and she couldn't stop. This was after a bit of an incident with a colleague. Jim. I think you should get the details from her.'

Leo pushed back his chair but Fallon raised a hand. 'Please, if you don't mind. Not just yet.'

'There's *more?*'

'I think it would be best if Deirdre took some time off. A couple of weeks, a month, even, if she needs it. I'll keep paying her, of course. I know you're currently, ah, between jobs yourself.'

Leo felt himself blushing. 'Yeah. Well… Yeah. Thank you.'

'Oh, Lord, listen, here's no need to thank me. I'm very fond of Deirdre. She's such a sweetheart. I hate to see her being so stressed by… all of it.'

'All of what?'

'You know. I don't want to overstep—' He puffed out his cheeks. 'The baby thing. I'm talking about the baby thing. It's not my place, as a mere employer, to know about it, I appreciate that. But I do. It seems to be all linked to this min… incident.'

Leo could think of no suitable response. After a few seconds of appalling silence, Fallon tapped the table with his fingernails and got to his feet. 'Look, I should get out of your way.'

They walked to the front door. It was only there that Leo found his voice again. 'Thanks for taking her home.'

'Don't mention it.'

They parted. Leo closed the front door, gathered his strength, and wearily climbed the stairs. Deirdre was curled up on their bed with a pillow pulled over her head. He sat beside her and rested a hand on her leg.

'Are you okay?' No response. 'Deirdre? Please. Talk to me. What happened?' When she still didn't reply he gently removed the pillow. She looked catatonic. He lay down beside her.

'There's paint on your ear,' he said, brushing her hair back. 'Did you get hurt?'

'It's fine.'

'I thought you had helmet things for paintball.'

She sniffled. 'I'd taken it off. I wasn't thinking straight. Thought the game was over. Jim Kenny hit me. By accident. Wasn't aiming at me.'

'Right. Your boss said something had happened with Jim.'

'Did he tell you that I… hurt him?'

'Who? Fallon?'

'Jim. I hurt Jim.'

'Did you? How?'

'I shot him in the balls.'

Leo fought to keep his expression under control. 'I see.'

'From really close.'

'Okay.'

'I just walked up to him and shot him right in the balls.'

'Is he all right?'

'I don't know.'

'Can't imagine he would be, though.'

'No. I suppose not. Mr Fallon took me away. I was crying. A lot. And I kept on crying. A lot.'

'Do you know why?'

'I just… I felt really stressed out and weird.'

'Because?'

'Leo, I feel stressed out and weird *all the time*.'

Her whispered emphasis of the last three words reminded him of the little boy in *The Sixth Sense* who saw dead people with similar frequency. He congratulated himself on not mentioning this. 'I know, honey. But maybe there was—'

'It was Louise.'

'Ah.'

'Possibly.'

He took that to mean *definitely*. 'What did she do?'

'She got out of paintball. Because she's pregnant.'

'So it was about babies.'

'What else is there? Maybe I would have got set off even if paintball had been fun. Which it certainly wasn't. But waddling around in front of everyone…'

'You don't waddle, Deirdre, come on.'

'… getting shot on the arse, getting shot on the ear… I kind of lost it.' She slapped a hand over her eyes. 'Poor Jim, oh my God. They're all going to hate me. Or think I'm mental. Or hate me *and* think I'm mental. What am I going to do?'

'For a start,' Leo said, 'you're going to take some time off. As long as you need. They're going to keep paying you.'

He expected her to protest and was already marshalling his counterarguments when she nodded and said, 'Yes. That's good.' It threw him off a little. He tried not to let it show. 'And we've got IVF to look forward to.' This took some saying. He couldn't think of anything he'd ever looked forward to less.

'Counselling first.'

'I know, yeah. Look, the main thing right now is to get you rested and feeling well. And after that... we just keep on keeping on.'

Her expression softened, just a little. For the first time since she arrived home she didn't look like someone who'd just been bereaved. 'Yes. Thank you.' She reached across and placed her hand on the side of his face.

'I love you,' he told her.

'I love you too.' He couldn't remember the last time they'd said it. 'Why don't you take a nap now? Can I get you anything? Cuppa? A sandwich? Have you eaten anything?'

She scooched closer. 'There is something you can do for me, actually.'

'Name it.'

'Sex.'

He almost laughed. There had been no mention of the subject since the night when he decided to move his music stuff into the garage. But this was hardly a good time, was it? She didn't want it for its own sake, he was sure, or as a way to celebrate this thaw between them. She was feeling desperate and wanted to take yet another swing at getting pregnant *immediately*. It couldn't be healthy, surely, to go from 'mini-breakdown' to sex? That was one factor. The other was this: she looked a right fucking state. Truth be told, she didn't smell so great either. If he hadn't known better he would have guessed that she'd just done a punishing workout but had been mugged before she made it to the shower. No, this was a bad idea. He would have to explain, possibly focusing more on the first factor than the second.

'Eh...'

She saw his hesitation and her eyes watered. Panic gripped him. Christ. He couldn't have her mini-breaking down all over again on his account.

'Is this instead of a sandwich or as well as?' he said and started unbuttoning her shirt.

For as long as she could remember, Julie had been the sort who was showered, dressed, made-up and otherwise entirely ready for a night out way before she needed to be. As a teenager back in Sligo, and later as a student in Galway, she was bewildered by her friends, unable to understand how they could be so lazy and disorganised, always tearing around trying to find lipstick or a scarf as the taxi driver leaned on the horn outside. These days, her social excursions were so few and far between that she quite enjoyed sitting around waiting for the appointed hour – it served as a pleasant reminder of her wilder (or at least less tame) days.

'When are you leaving?' Dooley asked.

She looked at her watch. 'About 20 minutes.' She'd already been sitting there for 15. By her standards this was practically a last-minute rush. They were parked in front of the television. One of the shark channels. Nicola was down.

'Just you and Nancy?'

'Yeah.'

'This is a new thing, is it?'

'What – going out?'

'Going out with Nancy. I don't remember you ever going out before, just the two of you.'

This was true. A few years back, after Nancy and Redmond moved in, they'd all gone out for dinner together, had a reasonably good time, declared that they must make it a regular thing, and then never bothered again. Dooley and Redmond had gone for an occasional drink since then but the girls never had. The tricky part now, Julie thought, was to provide a convincing explanation for their sudden change of heart.

'I don't either,' she said, pretending to think it over. 'No… I think you're right. First time.'

'So what's the occasion?'

'No occasion.'

She said it casually, eyes still on the TV. The fact was, she'd bumped into Nancy outside their local petrol station earlier in the week. They'd exchanged a few sentences – updates on their kids, complaints about the cost of living, the usual banalities. As they were about to part, Julie made some throwaway comment about the enormous sack of crisps that she'd just bought for Dooley's stupid play-pub (as she'd taken to calling it). Nancy sympathised with her, and apologised too. She'd heard about Dooley's endeavours in the garage and knew that Redmond had given him the idea. Twenty minutes later, they were still standing there. Julie understood that the name for what they'd enjoyed in the interim was 'bitching session', and presumed that Nancy knew the same. But neither of them used those words. They parted saying how much they'd enjoyed their 'girly chat' and promising to follow it up with a 'girly night out'. Afterwards, Julie worried that Nancy was just being polite and wouldn't actually call. When arrangements were finally made, she almost punched the air like someone in a commercial who'd been given a loan by a friendly bank that wasn't like all the others.

'Just dinner, is it?' Dooley asked.

'I'm sure we'll go for a drink after,' Julie told him. 'So don't wait up, if that's what you're wondering.'

She didn't want to ask about his own plans for the evening because she knew damn well what the answer would be. He would be in his play-pub, faffing about. She honestly had no idea what he did in there. As far as she could tell, he wasn't even boozing. A quick scan of the bins told her that he was having a beer a night, and sometimes not even that. If anything, he was becoming addicted to crisps… The wounds from their initial row about the garage had healed after a day or two and she had now more or less given up on the idea of talking him out of there. All she asked was that he didn't let his new obsession interfere with his parenting responsibilities. And, to his credit (she supposed), it hadn't.

'If you're going to be out in the garage,' she said, 'don't forget the baby monitor.'

'I won't.'

'And try not to make any noise.'

'I never do.'

Julie looked at her watch. Nancy had two kids to deal with before she got away, and she was leaving them with Redmond, who would no doubt require elaborate instructions and last-minute coaching. She'd be late, probably.

'Gymboree today, was it?' she asked Dooley.

He seemed to startle, as if he'd been nodding off when she spoke. 'Yeah. That's right.'

'Did she have fun?'

'As much as she ever has, yeah. She's still too young for it but what the hey.' They watched the sharks in silence for a little while. 'Any excitement at work?' he asked then.

She shook her head. 'Nope. David got a new car. That was the day's big news.' She tensed. It had just slipped out, a genuinely innocent response to his question. She hadn't mentioned David's name since the evening of their row. There was no chance, she guessed, that Dooley would let it go without comment.

'Yeah?'

To her surprise, his tone was quite neutral. She was encouraged. 'Yeah. An Audi something or other. Silver.'

'Nice. No recession for some.'

'Nope. Gorgeous yoke. Sporty but really comfy inside.'

'Inside?'

Oh-oh. 'Well, I sat in it, y'know.'

'Just you?'

'And David. Obviously.'

'No, I mean, were you the only one to sit in it or did everyone get a go?'

She bristled. 'What's that got to do with anything?'

'Why are you being so defensive?'

'I'm not being defensive. If you must know, I was the only one who got a spin.'

In his best *ladies and gentlemen of the jury* voice, he said, 'So it wasn't just a sit-in? It was a *spin*.'

'Jesus, Dooley.'

'Wow, cruising around in his sports car. God, that's so much cooler than a "play-pub", isn't it?'

'I didn't say it was a sports car, I said it was sporty. For fuck's sake. And I never even mentioned the stupid pub. I don't know why you've got this thing about David. Do you think I'm banging him, is that it?'

She meant it half-jokingly but was frightened by the way it sounded. For a moment, the blood seemed to reverse course in her veins.

'No,' Dooley said. 'I don't think you're banging him...'

There was clearly a second half to this thought but he left it unsaid.

'Look, you asked me if there was anything new at work and the only thing I could think of was that – David got a new car. Big deal.'

'Okay.'

'Okay?'

'Okay.'

She was happier than ever to be going out. Although she seemed to have got away with her slip-up, it would be good to get out of each other's way, to remove any possibility of further friction. In fact, she pondered, it might be best if she retreated back upstairs until Nancy called for her. She could pretend that she wanted to adjust her make-up or try something else on.

'Paula thinks I deserve my man cave, by the way. Paula from Gymboree?'

Julie's mouth dropped open. A short crack of a laugh burst forth from it. 'Excuse me?'

'I said, Paula from Gymboree thinks I deserve—'

'*Excuse* me?'

He pouted. 'I'm just saying.'

'Holy shit, Dooley. So, you're not only weirdly obsessed with David Flynn, you're going to start mentioning other women as a, what, as a... I don't even know. Are you trying to make me jealous? Is it some sort of... revenge? I honestly...' She trailed off, shaking her head. They were looking at each other but now Dooley snapped his head back to the television. Julie continued gazing at the side of his face. The trace of humour she'd found in the moment was quickly evaporating. Suddenly, his ridiculous outburst seemed like a deadly serious development.

The doorbell rang.

'Shit. That must be Nancy. Early. I have to go.'

He kept his eyes on the sharks. 'See ya.'

She stood but felt reluctant to leave – not on this note.

'Go on,' he said. 'I don't want her ringing the bell again. She'll wake Nicola.'

Julie hesitated for another moment then said goodbye and headed for the door. She didn't kiss him goodnight. He hadn't returned her goodbye and she was afraid that he might actually retreat from physical contact.

Nancy said, 'Three. Hundred. Euro.' She was pleased to see genuine shock on Julie's face.

'No.'

'I'm not kidding you.'

'You are, you're kidding me.'

'I'm not. I'm not kidding you.'

'Three hundred Euro.'

'Three. Hundred. Euro.'

'For speakers for a computer?'

'Computer speakers.'

'But you can get them for a tenner.'

'I know. I know that.'

They simultaneously shook their heads, each of them lost in sad reflection. Dinner had been a huge success so far, Nancy thought. She'd assumed that Julie ate out a lot more than she did, even if it was only at lunchtime, and had been nervous about suggesting a restaurant. The one she'd chosen was an Indian place, old school. It looked like it hadn't been decorated since 1978, the Yelp reviews said, but the food was fantastic. And they were right. Everything was delicious. The lamb jalfrezi was not the source of Nancy's current high, however. She was marvelling at the sensation of discovering that someone who had been a mere acquaintance, and not a particularly well-liked one at that, could turn out to be so agreeable and insightful. To think that she had spent all this time metaphorically and sometimes literally rolling her eyes in Julie's direction when all along the girl was quite frankly best friend material. It was like suddenly realising that the horrible old painting you'd tossed in the attic was in fact a Monet.

'You should spend three hundred quid on something for yourself,' Julie said. 'Just to restore balance to the universe.'

'That did occur to me, actually. But I couldn't even think of anything I wanted. That's pathetic, isn't it? Besides, I don't want to lose the moral high ground.'

'Well, that's the place to be, no doubt.'

Nancy raised her glass. 'To the moral high ground.'

They clinked and drank. For the first time, conversation lulled. They'd spent a large part of the evening complaining about their husbands and their silly man caves, but that subject seemed to have been exhausted. What now, Nancy wondered? Was it going to turn awkward?

'I think I'm all done with this, actually,' Julie said then, gesturing at her korma.

'Oh? I thought you were enjoying it?'

'It's lovely. I just want to leave room for dessert, that's all.'

This was a phenomenon that Nancy had never understood. Leaving *room*? The whole point of going out for dinner, surely, was to misbehave, gastronomically speaking. You ate everything that wasn't nailed down. If that meant you were full by the time dessert arrived, so be it. You ate that too, without a second thought. But this wasn't a helpful train of thought. Tonight wasn't about the ways in which she and Julie were different. It was about solidarity.

'This is so stupid, but I've been really nervous about the food because the restaurant was my suggestion.'

'Huh? Why?'

I dunno, I just… I imagine you eat out a lot with work and all and I was afraid the place wouldn't be up to snuff.'

Julie turned down her lips and shook her head. 'Nope. I doubt I have dinner in restaurants any more than you do.'

'But business lunches and all that.'

'Once in a while, I suppose. But my lunches mostly come from the Spar down the street from the office.'

Nancy theatrically slapped her hands over her ears. 'Don't tell me that! Let me have my fantasies! I need someone to live through, uh, what's the word…'

'Vicariously.'

'Vicariously!'

Julie shrugged. 'Sorry. I'm a pretty poor candidate for that.' She poured more wine for them both, draining the bottle. 'Would I be right in guessing that you miss work, Nancy?'

'Sometimes. Like, from the moment I wake up until the moment I fall asleep. Plus, I sometimes dream about it.'

'So what's stopping you?'

Nancy took an unseemly gulp of the Shiraz. 'I kinda painted myself into a corner on that score.'

'How so?'

'Eh. I always made such a big deal of…' She realised that what she was about to say could lead to trouble. 'Just to be clear, this isn't a dig at you or anyone else, okay?'

'I'm nervous now.'

'It's all right, there's a "but" coming at the end. I always made such a big deal of my choice, my belief, which was that children need their mothers 24/7 in the preschool years. I took a very traditional view of it. And I wasn't shy about expressing it, to friends, family, colleagues, anyone. But now, I'm not so sure. To say the least. Is it really better for the kids to have their mother around all the time when she's so frustrated and exhausted and, to be blunt, fucking pissed off? Wouldn't it be better for them and for everyone to have a mum who wasn't around all the time but was happy and relaxed and engaged when she was? I want to *miss* them. I never get a chance to *miss* them.'

Julie's expression was difficult to read. But she didn't look pleased. Nancy braced herself.

'You know what I find interesting about all this?' Julie said. 'I find it interesting that you felt you couldn't just say that to me. You had to give me a warning and then promise me a "but". Why do we do that? Women? I do it myself. "Please understand, please, *please* understand that I'm not saying you're a bad woman or a bad feminist or anything because you want to stay at home but for me – and this is just me, I'm only talking about myself here – I sort of, kind of, after a lot of deliberation, decided to go straight back to work. Sorry. I'm so sorry. Please forgive me." It's ridiculous.'

Nancy hid behind her wine glass for a moment. Julie had missed what she was really trying to say – that she'd been such a pill about the correctness of her own choice that it was hard to go back on it now.

'We do that, don't we?' she said. 'Always apologising for ourselves.'

'All day long. I wouldn't judge you for choosing to stay at home any more than you would judge me for going straight back to work.'

For the sake of plausible deniability Nancy made a sound that was neither confirmation nor contradiction. In fact, judging other women for going straight back to work was the very thing that she'd been trying to confess. That ship had sailed now. A change of subject was required.

'Would it look bad,' she said, leaning in, 'to order more wine at this point in the meal?'

'I don't know… I was thinking maybe we could go on somewhere for a drink afterwards?'

'Oh, so was I. I meant, just to keep us going until we get there.'

Julie sat back and narrowed her eyes. 'All these years I've lived beside you, Nancy, and I never once noticed that you're the devil.'

Nancy looked at her lap, pretending to be ashamed, then looked up again and caught the eye of a passing waiter.

'You ever have the one where there's extra rooms in your house?'

Julie shook her head. 'I think that might just be you.'

'No, no, it's a thing. I looked it up. Sometimes it's your own house and sometimes it's a new house that you've just bought. You think you know every inch of it but you keep finding rooms that you had no idea were there.'

'Nope. New one on me. What does it mean?'

Nancy cocked her head, thinking. 'Shit. I've forgotten.' She laughed. Julie joined in. They were at that stage now – laughing at things that weren't remotely amusing. After leaving the restaurant they'd stood on the street debating standard pub options before concluding that, since they were all dressed up and all, they might as well go somewhere with a little class. In Nancy's opinion they had overshot the mark with this particular wine bar. Even in her best jacket and least-worst trousers she felt scruffy and cheap. There were several women in her immediate eyeline who either were or could have been fashion models. Julie fitted in better, of course. Nancy was amazed to find herself relatively unruffled by that.

'It probably means that you're not tidying up enough,' Julie said. 'Or that you're tidying up too much.'

If anyone had told Nancy before she left the house that they would wind up discussing dreams and their possible meanings, she would have assumed that their night out was going to be a disaster. On the contrary, it seemed that they'd moved on to this notoriously awful subject because they'd talked about everything else under the sun: old boyfriends, America's obsession with guns, Prince William's recent wedding, beloved childhood toys, the pros and cons of decentralised government, *The Good Wife*, the possibility of human extinction, Matt Damon...

'This has been a hoot,' Nancy said. 'Hasn't it?'

'It has. A veritable hoot.'

'I can't believe we never did this before.'

'I know. And let's face it, we probably wouldn't have if we hadn't started moaning about the boys that day.'

Nancy was glad that someone had said this out loud, and that it hadn't been her. 'Did you, uh… did you worry that we wouldn't have anything else to talk about tonight?'

'*Yes.*'

'But it's been so much fun!'

'And so therapeutic!'

Nancy almost raised her glass but decided against it. They'd clinked over so many things already that it was beginning to feel ridiculous. 'What *is it* with them? Men.'

'In general? Or are we getting into bitching about the garages again?'

'The second one. But let's try not to bitch. Or *just* bitch, at least.'

Julie looked at her wine and put down the glass as if it had somehow offended her. Nancy guessed that the alcohol was catching up with her. She didn't feel entirely stable herself. 'I honestly don't know. But I know they've all got it – this weird need to carve out a little space somewhere. When I was a girl my dad used to take the papers out to the car every Sunday afternoon. He'd sit there on his own, reading, and listening to the radio.'

Nancy had been taking a drink and almost choked in her haste to respond. 'Oh my God! So did mine! What the *fuck?*'

'I used to wonder what my mother thought about it. Because it wasn't a compliment, was it?'

'Christ,' Nancy said. 'It never even occurred to me to wonder what mine thought. If she was here now, she'd say that was typical.'

'If we'd had a garage or a decent garden shed, maybe he would have squirrelled himself away in there instead.'

'No doubt. Holy shit, I can't believe I've never made this connection before. If we were playing at the front of the house and Dad saw us coming over to the car, he'd look us right in the eye and wave us away, with one finger, like this.' She performed the gesture. 'Not in a nasty way or anything, he did it with a smile. But still.'

'It's some primitive thing in them, like, way deep. I don't think it's an accident that they call them man *caves.*'

'Right.'

'We should get them some animal furs to wear when they're in there.'

'Yeah. One day we'll peek in and they'll have painted bison on the walls.'

Julie reached for her glass then changed her mind and sat back, looking suddenly troubled. She had definitely reached her limit, Nancy concluded.

'Y'all right there, Julie? Maybe we'll make the next one a water.' No response. 'Julie?'

'I'm fine,' she said in a tone that clearly signalled the direct opposite. There was more going on, apparently, than mere limit-reaching.

'What is it?' Nancy said.

'Nothing.' From out of nowhere, her eyes had dampened. Nancy felt bewildered. Had she fallen asleep and missed something? Weren't they laughing just a moment ago? Was it something she'd said? The bison crack? Did Julie have a thing about *bison?*

'Come on. You can tell me. Sure we're old friends at this stage.'

Julie dabbed at her eyes with her little finger. 'It's just...' A long pause. A swallow. More dabbing. 'It's just that we're laughing and making jokes about the thing with the garages, but it's not that funny. Really. Not in our house, anyway. When I left Dooley tonight we were hardly speaking. I hated the idea when he told me about it and we had a big falling-out. But he dug his heels in and kept going with it, so I just stopped complaining. Still not happy, but keeping quiet about it, y'know? For an easy life. But it isn't working. He seems to *want* to fight about it. It feels like it's all tied in...' She stopped herself and stared straight ahead. 'Tied in with other stuff.'

Nancy waited for a moment, then gathered that it was her turn to speak. She really had nothing to offer by way of advice.

'I don't suppose it will help much,' she said, 'but it hasn't been all polite joshing with us either.'

'No?'

'No. Nope. Far from it.'

A slow nod from Julie. 'You know what? Sorry. I'm sorry. I

shouldn't have said anything. Can we just forget I spoke? Please. I'd really prefer not to get into it.'

Nancy flashed a micro-smile. 'Sure. What do you think? Will we make the next one a water, try and get our puff back?'

'If you don't mind… I think I'm done. Let's call it a night.'

'Oh. Okay. If you're sure you're all right?'

'I'm fine. Honestly.'

They gathered their stuff in silence. Once out on the street they spoke again but restricted themselves to banal observations about their immediate environment and feeble jokes about their level of inebriation. Nancy was relieved when they found it easy to get a taxi and further relieved when its driver turned out to have a great deal to say about which politicians should be executed and which should merely rot in prison. When they got home they hugged on the path outside their houses, assured each other that they'd had a great time, and vowed to do it again soon.

5

Nancy had a theory about doctors' waiting rooms. She believed that they were subject to strict regulation by the Department of Health, not for cleanliness or comfort but for cast. There was a document somewhere, she felt sure, that laid it all out in black and white. *Each surgery waiting room must have one old man with rheumy eyes coughing into a hankie, one skinny woman in a tracksuit who seems to be on the verge of tears, one pale teenage boy who looks as if he might actually die before he sees the doctor, and preferably three but no fewer than two haggard mothers, each of whom should have preferably three but no fewer than two children.* She'd been attending this surgery for almost a decade but the theory was a relatively new one. It had come to her one dark afternoon the previous winter when she'd been sitting there for two hours and had run out of normal things to think.

This morning the waiting room was falling short of the imagined standard. There was an old man but no skinny sad woman and no death's-door youth. There were *three* haggard mothers, however. If there was a sudden inspection, Nancy reflected, perhaps that would make up for the other failings. She caught herself following this line of thought and shuddered with embarrassment, as if those around her could see the poverty of her mental life.

'Ah, he looks miserable, the wee lamb,' said the woman on Nancy's left. She was the most recent arrival. Two kids, girls, identical twins, eight or nine, each of them with their nose in an actual paper book. She was looking at Luke, who was in full health.

'He's grand, that one,' Nancy said. 'It's bucko here who's not well.' She leaned back a little to let the woman see Aidan.

'Oh, sorry! I thought—'

'That's all right. He does look miserable. It's just his face.'

They both looked at Luke in the buggy for a moment. He stared back angrily.

'My throat's sore,' Aidan croaked by way of explanation. Nancy didn't for one second doubt that it was but she was beginning to grow weary of the constricted rasp he'd been affecting.

'You poor thing,' the woman said. 'My little girl has a sore tummy.' Her daughters both looked up briefly, stared, then returned to their books in a manner that reminded Nancy of *The Shining*. Neither claimed ownership of the sore tummy. Nancy thought about asking which one was ill but didn't bother. It seemed rude.

The receptionist half-stood so she could see over the counter she worked behind. 'Nancy Cole? You can go on in now.'

She was new, this one, or new-ish, anyway. A perky twenty-something. Nancy still missed sweet old Mrs McCardle, who had retired a few months back. She wouldn't have used the full name; Nancy was one of what she called her 'unfortunate regulars'.

'That's me,' Nancy said to the woman. 'Good luck.'

She stood and got the boys organised.

Doctor Foley was an elegant woman in her sixties. She always struck Nancy as being fundamentally unflappable. You could lift your shirt to reveal that your abdomen was covered in testicles and Doctor Foley would calmly assure you that she'd been seeing this sort of thing a lot recently. Aidan's sore throat was the result of a viral infection, she declared, so there would be no antibiotic treatment. Nancy was relieved to hear it. Every time she saw a poster or leaflet about declining antibiotic effectiveness, she felt that she personally was being chastised for past excesses. But she could hold her head up on this one, knowing that she had done everything she could to help her sick child but would not be contributing to the inevitable superbug apocalypse.

For as long as Nancy had been attending Doctor Foley, every appointment had ended with a few minutes of amiable chit-chat. The question that opened proceedings was always the same: 'And how is life in general?' The fact that it never varied led Nancy to believe that it wasn't something special between the two of them. Everyone got it. Some patients, no doubt, used it as an excuse to score free psychological counselling, but not Nancy. She always replied with pleasant banalities and made sure to enquire about Doctor Foley's own family (her children were all high-fliers – a UN translator, another doctor and a literal rocket scientist). It was soothing somehow, particularly when one of the kids was ill and the world seemed cruel and dangerous, to end the encounter like old friends who had bumped into each other on the street. Sometimes they produced phones and shared photos. Today, when business was concluded and the question was asked, Nancy took her usual approach. Life in general was fine, she reported, before listing a number of ways in which the recent good weather had enriched their lives. Doctor Foley nodded and smiled. Then she said, 'You look awful.' Nancy thought she had misheard.

'I'm sorry?'

'I'm saying that as your doctor, you understand. And because I've known you for so long.'

'I look… awful?'

'I could have said "tired" or "stressed". I chose "awful" to get your attention.'

'Well, it worked.'

'Are you looking after yourself?'

'Yes.'

'*Are* you?'

'Yes.'

'Because I see a lot of mothers in here who put their health on hold when they have kids. They go without sleep and proper food and downtime because they think that's the way it's "supposed" to be and, anyway, who cares because it's not forever, right? It'll all be normal again in a year or so. But it never gets normal again. And after a few years they collapse in a little heap.'

'I'm not going to collapse in a little heap. Okay, maybe I'm feeling a bit… Things have been a bit…'

'I'm listening.'

Doc Foley was old school, verging on old-fashioned. How

many times had she congratulated Nancy on her 'bravery' in giving up a career to look after her boys? This wasn't the time or place for a full confession. She couldn't reveal the disease. But she could complain about the symptoms.

She fixed her gaze on the doctor. 'Do you know what a man cave is?'

'Old movies' was a term that had always given Deirdre the warm and fuzzies. In her mind's eye the very letters themselves had a gentle orange glow, conjuring images of open fires, cosy slippers and the like. That was all ruined now. She'd spent almost every waking minute on the sofa since the paintball incident, floating glassy-eyed from channel to channel. Mornings were for makeover shows and documentaries about factories. Evenings were for soaps and quizzes. In the afternoons, she tended to settle on whatever quote-classic-unquote films happened to be showing, hoping they would lift her mood, if not to the ceiling, at least off the floor. Every single one so far had been abysmal. At first she suspected that the fault was hers and that nothing could have impressed her, way down there in the depths of her dressing gown. But she soon decided that, no, the problem was with the flicks themselves. Saying you liked old movies, it had slowly dawned on her, was as ridiculous as saying you liked new movies. They weren't all charming and graceful. The ones that broadcasters tossed carelessly into the afternoon schedules were anything but.

Today's offering on BBC Two was well down to the standard she had come to expect. It was a western, 1950s, she guessed. Everyone was called either Becky or Billy and said things like 'Gather the menfolk, there's a fire at the ol' Morgan place!' They all looked impossibly clean and attractive, sporting ribbons and neckerchiefs in bright primary colours. None of them was covered in mud or was missing teeth, which, Deirdre suspected, might have been more in keeping with the period. She understood that audiences had simpler expectations back then, but still. It was hard to imagine that anyone had ever enjoyed sitting through this sort of bilge, with its paper-thin story and no-dimensional characters.

'This is rubbish,' she said to Leo, who was half-asleep beside her.

He stirred and squinted at the TV. 'Hm? John Wayne, is it?'

Deirdre turned to look at him. It was a source of ongoing mystery to her how someone could apparently know everything about music and nothing – really, *nothing* – about movies. One night, long ago, when she told him how much she liked *When Harry Met Sally*, he asked if that was 'the one with Tom Cruise and Jane Fonda trapped on the ship'.

'No, Leo. It isn't John Wayne. John Wayne was much taller than this guy. And he didn't have mutton chops. And he wasn't bald.'

Leo made a noise with his lips and went back to dozing.

'Do you think you'll hear anything today?' she asked.

'Dunno. Maybe. Might be a bit early.'

He had attended a job interview the previous day – only his third since being made redundant. Deirdre was trying not to focus on that troubling statistic but rather on her hopes for a positive outcome. Frankly, she had been wondering of late exactly how much effort he was putting into his job search. Being at home had given her a chance to do some spying and, fair play to him, when he wasn't fussing over her, he was trawling the web or tinkering with his CV or scanning the newspapers. It did occur to her that he could have been faking it, but she pushed the thought away, and concentrated on feeling bad about having doubted him.

'So,' Leo said then. 'What about going to the doctor?'

'Not today,' she said, as she did every day.

'I'm starting to think you're never going to go.'

'Well... Maybe I won't.'

He didn't reply for a moment. On TV an Apache got shot and fell off his horse, the actor quite clearly coming close to losing his wig. Then: 'You don't think it might help?'

She shrugged and sighed, then sighed and shrugged. *Come on,* she told herself. *Out with it. You might as well.* 'Look, Leo. The thing is… The thing is, we have our IVF session coming up. The counselling session.'

'So?'

'So I don't want to go into that as someone who's just been to the doctor because they had a freak out in front of their colleagues. Okay? Just let me get this over with, then we'll see.'

'You want to let on to the counsellor that everything's fine when it clearly isn't? Is that it?'

She wanted to say, *Yes,* of course *that's it.* But the urge passed.

'No. Not at all. It's just to do with my own mindset, going into the thing. I just want—'

His phone rang. He peered at it.

'Oh. This is the recruiter.'

'Well, *answer* it.'

He did so. 'Hello?… Speaking… Hi, Derek, how's things?… Did you? And?… Right… Right… Ah… Oh, well… Sure… Yes, please do… Okay, thanks… Bye.'

'That didn't sound good.'

He tossed his phone to one side. 'Nope. They went another way. More experience.'

'That's a pity.'

'Yup.'

'There's always the next time. You just have to keep look—'

'I know what I have to do, Deirdre.'

He'd been on eggshells around her the whole time since paintball. This was as close as he'd come to a harsh word.

'I'm sorry,' he said. 'I didn't mean to snap at you.'

'That's okay. It was hardly snapping.'

He settled back on the sofa and was semi-comatose again in seconds. Deirdre fidgeted. He would love to be in the garage right now, she knew, flipping through his records and making a mental list of the ten best bands to come out of Birmingham in the 1980s or somesuch. She was glad that he was making this sacrifice to keep an eye on her – but she knew that 'sacrifice' was the word for it.

'Leo?'

'Yeah.'

'You don't have to sit with me all the time. If you want to go and listen to music, I won't mind.'

He did his best to seem casual but she felt his leg twitch. 'Uh. Maybe. I might. If you're sure you'll be all right by yourself.'

'I'll be fine.'

He waited a decent 30 seconds or so before stretching and getting to his feet. 'Okey-doke, then. I might just duck in for half an hour.'

'Go for it.'

He strolled off to the garage as casually as he could, which wasn't very.

One Saturday afternoon when Redmond was ten years old he went for a kickabout in the park with a few of his friends. They finished playing at around four then went to the shop for sweets. Strolling home with a Milky Way in each hand, he was in fine form. He'd scored six of the goals in his team's 15-12 victory and had got a big laugh with his impression of Mr T. There would be chips for tea later and *Diamonds are Forever* was showing on ITV. All was right with the world. But as soon he opened the front door of his house – before he'd even stepped across the threshold – his good mood evaporated. Something was badly wrong. He just knew it. At the time he put it down to some sort of spooky premonition, but looking back he suspected it was an atmospheric anomaly, an unusual stillness, perhaps, or a strange pattern of low-pitched sounds that his conscious mind wasn't sensitive enough to register. It soon transpired that his grandmother had dropped dead while giving out to a neighbour about his dog's incessant barking. Several aunts and uncles had gathered in his living room to whisper and mutter. Redmond loved his granny and he was devastated by her death. But his lasting memory of those terrible few days wasn't of the funeral mass or the graveside or even the sight of his father crying actual tears. It was of the eerie moment at the doorstep, of the certainty that something was wrong and the nauseating dread that enveloped him in those few seconds before he found out what it was. *That* was what he hoped to never experience again. And that was precisely what he felt when he stepped into his own house after work. His first, unbearable thought was that something had happened to one of the boys. He stepped down the hall, heart thumping, teeth clenched.

'Nancy?' he said in a hollow voice.

And then he heard a laugh. Aidan's. Relief swept through him like a hit from a bong. He shook his head, smiling at his own silliness. The front room was empty, though. So was the kitchen. There may not have been a tragedy unfolding, but something was definitely up. He stood by the kitchen sink and peered out into the back garden. No one there either. And then he heard a thump coming from the garage. He crossed the room and pulled open the door. Aidan was sitting on the sofa, colouring. Luke was in his bouncer, bouncing. Nancy was dismantling his gaming setup. A number of expressions rushed from Redmond's brain to his mouth where they jostled and elbowed for position. The one that finally burst forth, at some volume, was 'Nancy, what the fuck are you doing?'

She stopped what she was doing – unplugging his new speakers – and said, 'Don't swear.'

'I—'

'What does it look like I'm doing?

'It looks like you're losing your mind.'

'I'm not, though. Far from it.'

'Nancy. Stop. Nancy, stop. Look at me.'

She did so. Pulled back her shoulders. Lifted her chin. 'I took Aidan to the doctor today. She wasn't too concerned about him. But she *was* concerned about me. She said I'm extremely stressed out. She said I'm putting my health at risk. She said I had to take steps to look after myself better. So that's what I'm doing. I'm taking steps.'

'The *doctor* told you to pull my gaming set-up to bits?'

'Not specifically.'

She started wrestling speaker cables again, apparently satisfied that she had explained herself perfectly. Redmond's anger gave way to fear. Was this some sort of breakdown?

'Nancy,' he said softly. 'Please. Leave that. Let's go and have a cup of tea, talk this over.'

'Talk what over? All of this crap is going on eBay. That's all there is to it.'

She had apparently been in here for quite a while. Some of his gear – the older consoles, a couple of shelves' worth of discs – had already been dumped into large bin bags. They were lined up against the garage door. Redmond had assumed she wanted him to haul them back up to the spare room.

'Wait, wait. You think you're *selling* it?'

Fear and anger swapped places again. He put his hands on his hips and stared at her, breathing hard.

'This is insane,' he said. 'Am I dreaming? It's like a dream.'

'No more discussions,' Nancy said. 'This is all going. End of.'

'Nancy. This stuff is important to me. You can't just get rid of it. Be reasonable. If you want to talk about cutting down, we could—'

'That's not the point, for fu… That's not the *point*. It's not about how much gear you have in here. It's about *you* being in here.'

'This again? Jesus Christ! I'm out there all day long—'

'Here we go. Here we go with the "all day long" speech.'

'It's not a "speech", Nancy, it's the truth. I work really—'

'You care more about your precious me time than you do about your family.'

They had both been struggling not to shout in front of the boys. Now, Redmond found that he had to take a moment to compose himself.

'That's a ridiculous thing to say,' he whispered, overcompensating. 'It's ridiculous and it's very hurtful. I don't know what's going on with you, but I wish you'd stop lashing out at *me*. Nothing is more important than my family. Nothing. I don't see, Nancy, honest to God, I just don't see how you get from me having a hobby to me not caring—'

'A *hobby*.'

'Yes, a hobby.'

'It's not a hobby, Redmond, it's a whole other existence.'

'Oh, my God. It's just a little man cave, Nancy.'

She snorted derisively and stepped closer. 'If you like your precious man cave so much,' she said, almost into his ear, 'then why don't you fucking live in it?'

She picked Luke up and dragged Aidan to his feet before storming off into the kitchen, slamming the door behind her. Redmond stood perfectly still for a moment. Then he began to empty the bin bags and get things back to normal.

'You kind of expect the odd dirty look,' Dooley said. 'Maybe even a nasty remark, now and again. But an actual, honest-to-god *fight*? That's new ground.'

'Unprecedented,' Paula agreed. They were in the coffee shop again. Neither of them had suggested it out loud. They'd just sort of drifted there after Gymboree as they jabbered back and forth about the morning's dramatic events.

'That woman's always looked a bit crazy to me. The one with the ponytail?'

'Gemma'.

'Right. Gemma. There's something about her smile. It always reminds me of The Joker.'

'I dunno. The Lizzy one's a bit of a weapon too. I bumped into her one day, just brushed against her, really, and she *rounded* on me like a frigging badger, teeth bared. Nothing happened, though. I could practically hear her counting to five in her head, like she'd been on a course.'

Dooley wasn't entirely clear on the sequence of events; he'd been wrestling Nicola into her cardigan when it all kicked off. All he knew from subsequent conversations was that Gemma's son and Lizzy's daughter had fallen out over possession of a plastic guitar. Their mothers had stepped in to settle the dispute but someone must have said something inadvisable. Matters escalated quickly and the pair of them wound up rolling around on the floor, slapping and snarling and grabbing fistfuls of hair.

'Who won, do you think?'

Paula pretended to give it serious thought. 'I would have said it was a draw, more or less, but Gemma got that one last swipe in as she was being dragged away, didn't she? It didn't connect very well but it showed heart, I thought.'

'Commitment. Will to win.'

'Yeah. I'd have to give it to her on points.'

Charlie held up the small sketch pad that had occupied her since they'd arrived. 'Look, Mum. Look? Look what I did.'

'That's beautiful, honey,' Paula said. 'It's a flower, is it?'

'A flower? It's a clown. It's a *clown*.'

'I knew it was a clown,' Dooley said. 'It's the best clown I've ever seen anybody draw. Easily. By a mile.'

Charlie grinned, gave her mother a filthy look, and went back to doodling.

'Such a pro,' Paula said. She reached across to Nicola's high chair and gave her knee a little shake. 'You're one lucky lady, aren't you? Daddy has nothing to learn. No, he has not.'

'I can't remember the last time I saw two adults fighting,' Dooley said. 'Outside a nightclub back home, probably. When I used to go to such places. Back in the 1920s.'

'I always hated nightclubs.'

'*Did* you? I mean, I did too, but I always assumed women sort of naturally liked them.'

'Why the hell would we?'

'Because of the… socialising, I suppose. For blokes, back in my day at least, a nightclub was just a really expensive pub with too-loud music where you failed to get off with girls.'

'Oh, I bet you got off with plenty of girls.'

He didn't quite know how to respond to that. After a moment, he muttered, 'If only.'

'Speaking of pubs, how's yours? Still at it, are you?'

'Yeah. I am. I wouldn't get me started on the subject, if I were you. I am ridiculously pleased with myself about it.'

'Is that right? Did you get more… stuff?'

'It's not so much that I got a lot more stuff – although I have picked up a few things – it's that I've been much cleverer with the stuff I have. Lighting, Paula. It's all about lighting. I got some pointers on the web, dropped a few quid in Ikea, and boom. Transformation. Sometimes I walk in there and… Well. I told you not to get me going.'

'It sounds cool. I'd love to see it sometime.'

Dooley jolted, realised he had done so, and began adjusting his position in his seat in an attempt to disguise it. Was she being serious? She wanted to see his pub? She couldn't possibly. Christ, was this a *come-on*? No, that was ridiculous. She was staring at him with one eyebrow slightly raised, amused, it seemed, by his shock.

'Really?' he said. 'Um… why?'

Paula's shoulders popped up and down. She tucked away a loose strand of hair. And looked him right in the eye. 'I think it would be interesting,' she said.

Dooley struggled to keep his tone breezy. 'Sure. Some time. Yep. Sure.'

She was still looking at him intently. Staring, really. And then she broke it off. 'So, do you think Gemma and Lizzy will have a rematch next week?'

He seized on this change of topic and ran with it, barely pausing to breathe in case she said something else terrifying. The rest of their time in the coffee shop was a lurid blur.

Julie was two minutes away from the office when she had her mind made up, once and for all, by a couple of empty parking spaces on her left. The idea of taking a sickie had been there from the moment she opened her eyes that morning. It had the quality of something carried over from a dream. But she'd swatted it aside without giving it much consideration. Maybe it was the word itself. 'Sickie.' She associated it with slack-jawed third-raters phoning the office at 9.30 and trying to sound hoarse when it was perfectly obvious that they had simply been liquefied by a hangover. Sickies were for losers. And yet, after preparing for work as normal, she had hesitated before turning the key in the ignition. Just once? Couldn't she relax her standards just this once? She wound up driving off because she couldn't stand the thought of being cooped up with Dooley all day, much less being cooped up with him and pretending to be ill. She hadn't gone very far, however, before it occurred to her that she had fallen foul of a false dichotomy. It wasn't a straight choice between work and home. She could avoid both. But she banished *that* thought too, and kept driving. She was a senior account manager at a respected advertising agency, for God's sake, not Ferris Bueller. The whole idea was ridiculous. And then, providing one last ping in her mental ping-pong, the parking spaces came into view. *A perfect spot for turning around*, they said. *It'd be so easy. Call work from the car. Head off shopping. Go on. It'll be our little secret.*

'Fuck it,' she said, and executed a flawless U-turn.

Shopping lost its appeal almost immediately. Julie had never been a browser; she liked to know what she was looking for and to find that something with brisk efficiency. She'd imagined it might be different today, since she was apparently breaking long-held rules, but no. Five minutes in a hilariously expensive shoe shop and then half an hour in a department store proved more than enough. She got herself a takeaway coffee and sat by the pitiful little fountain in the middle of the shopping centre, wondering what to do next. She hadn't called the office in the end, opting instead to email a few key people, explaining that she was feeling 'under the weather'. The dismissive vagueness of that phrase, she hoped, would lead her colleagues to conclude that she was being brave in the face of some unspeakable viral invasion. It was slightly thrilling at the time, she had to admit, to instigate what amounted to a minor fraud. But the last vestiges of giddiness had deserted her somewhere between the perfume counter and kitchenware. All that remained now was mild embarrassment with an undercurrent of dread. She had just one idea for how to kill the time and that was to go to the cinema.

It would get her up to lunchtime, at least, at which point she could find somewhere quiet and linger over several courses. She took out her phone and checked the listings. The only film she could even begin to imagine herself seeing was a romantic comedy, and even that looked pretty appalling. It wasn't a genre for which she had much time. She was all for romance, in theory, and liked a laugh as much as the next person, but somehow she never found herself enthralled when rom and com came together. The merest glance at this one's promotional artwork told her that it ticked all the usual dreary boxes. The leads were impossibly gorgeous but looked troubled and helpless. No doubt they had never managed to find 'the one' and were beginning to give up hope, at the age of 26. They would each have a single close friend, Julie knew. His would be a little bit fat and/or slovenly but would have a heart of gold. He'd be envious of his pal's good looks and would desperately wish that *he* could get a chance to be bored of bedding models. Hers would be caustic and brittle to everyone else but would get all soppy when trying to convince the heroine that, no, she really was beautiful on the outside as well as the inside and that one day some special man would see it. The leads wouldn't get along at first but would go from mutual apathy, or possibly even loathing, to frenzied passion over 15 minutes of screen time. Then something would happen to put their fledgling relationship in jeopardy. The friends would step in to offer beer and spa days, respectively. Some sort of ticking clock would be introduced – a job offer in another city, say – leading to a frantic conclusion in which the hero would be obliged to sprint to an airport departure gate or the top of a tall building. Somewhere along the way it would snow, so they would get to look cute in bobble hats.

The movie would be terrible by every objective measurement. But it was 118 minutes long and, right now, that was what counted.

The film was about halfway over when Julie began to cry. At first she allowed herself to believe that she had been moved by the caustic friend's fear that no one would ever see past her wicked sense of humour, which she had developed as a shield and hoped to one day swap for better looks. She didn't even try to stop the tears, since the cinema was 95 per cent empty and there was no one around for several rows. But she could only fool herself for so long. The truth became undeniable. She was crying out of disgust – with herself. For the first time in her adult life she was taking a sickie, and why? Because she was under a lot of pressure and needed an unscheduled break? No. Because the company had been treating her badly and she felt like performing some tiny act of revenge? No. Because she'd been putting in long hours and wanted some extra time with her husband? *Please*. She was taking a sickie, and watching this colonoscopy of a movie, because she no longer trusted her boss to keep his hands off her. Or, perhaps more accurately, she no longer trusted herself to keep her hands off him.

In retrospect, telling Dooley about David's new car had simply been part of her effort to convince herself that the whole thing had been perfectly innocent. And, on one level, it had. Nothing had happened between them. But it was *weird*. She'd called it a spin but that was inaccurate; he'd driven her down the road a little and then parked 'for a chat'. She couldn't tell if she was being seduced or abducted and tried to stare straight ahead while concentrating on the new car smell. Things were bad between David and Caroline, it turned out. They were barely being civil to each other. He wasn't looking for advice, this time, he was merely reporting the news. It felt like a preamble. *Any minute now,* she told herself, *he's going to pat my hand or brush my leg or just say to hell with it and stick his tongue down my throat. And if he doesn't, I might.* But the moment passed. Or rather, the 20-odd minutes passed. David talked, Julie listened, and both kept all of their limbs and lips where they should be. And then he drove her back. She felt as if she had juggled with chainsaws and emerged unharmed. But she knew that every new day at work would see her juggling again, and again, and again. It was possible, she supposed, that there had always been something between them. Some little fizz. But it had changed recently. There was no point in pretending. With David and her, it was no longer a question of if, but when.

6

Deirdre and Leo had been holed up in the house almost 24/7 for more than a week. The latter had nipped out to the Little Spar for essentials a couple of times but they hadn't done a major grocery shop. She didn't feel up to it, and he didn't want to leave her alone for any significant amount of time.

On Saturday morning, she frowned into the barren cupboards and decided that an expedition could no longer be postponed. She still didn't think she could face Tesco, though. In her imagination, the lights were unbearably bright, the babble unbearably loud. She had a word with Leo. They decided to compromise and walk together to the Big Spar. It was his choice, really. The selection at the Little Spar was awful, he insisted. Deirdre knew that he couldn't care less about the range of available toilet rolls. He just wanted her to push herself beyond doing the bare minimum. Nevertheless, she pretended to be swayed by his argument. A good selection was important, she solemnly agreed.

It felt strange to be out and about again. Strange, but not entirely awful. When they were most of the way home, each swinging a plastic bag, she realised that the sense of panic and dread she'd been expecting had simply never materialised.

'Maybe it's time to go back to work,' she said.

Leo looked at her, surprised. 'What? Why do you say that?'

'Dunno. Just… I dunno.'

They walked another few steps. 'All we did was go to the shop,' he said then. 'And you hardly spoke the whole way.'

'Neither did y—'

'I'm not complaining. I'm just saying. Where's the rush?'

'There's no rush. No one's *rushing*. I've had a week off. More than a week.'

'And Fallon said you could have—'

'I know what he said.'

'So why don't you take—'

'All right, Leo, listen. Listen: I don't want to be the weirdo.

Okay? At work. I mean, I *know* I'm going to be the weirdo, but I don't want to make it any worse than it has to be.'

He hesitated. 'No one's going to think you're a weirdo. They'll understand. Everyone goes through—'

'I heard that, Leo.'

'What?'

'That little pause. You know I'm right. You know they've all been talking about me – talking about nothing else, probably – and the longer I stay off, the worse it's going to be when I go back.'

'That's not how we're judging this, though, is it. We're judging this by whether or not you feel *well* enough to go back.'

'I do!'

'Since when? Since we went to Spar for milk?'

'I'll be fine, Leo.'

'Deirdre, come on. It's—'

'Fine enough to go to work, at least. Maybe.'

They were back in their cul-de-sac now.

'I don't want to argue,' he said softly. 'And I can't sit on you, can I? I can't stand at the door with my arms folded and block you getting out. But I'm against it. For the record. I'm against it. Okay?'

'I didn't say definitely, did I? I'm thinking about it, that's all.'

'Give it another week. At least. One more week. Please.'

There was a kind of desperate tenderness in his last syllable. She felt tears forming and blinked them away, knowing that he would take their arrival as proof of her fragility.

'Let me think about it.'

She took his hand and gave it a little squeeze.

'Dooley's hard at it,' he said.

For a moment, she had no idea what he meant. She thought this was some sort of slang that she'd never encountered before, possibly something to do with erections. But then she followed his gaze to the house across from theirs, where Vincent Dooley was mowing the small strip of grass that served as a front garden.

'I hate to see people working on the outside of their houses,' she said. 'Reminds me that ours is a disgrace.'

Dooley spotted them and called out over the drone of the mower.

'What was that?' Deirdre said out of the corner of her mouth.

'I don't know. Just wave.'

They both did so. Dooley shouted something else. Once again, it was indecipherable.

'*What?*' Deirdre said. 'We should go over.'

Leo squeaked out a 'Nooo' but she was already crossing the street. Dooley seemed pleased. He killed the mower and stepped down to meet them on the footpath.

'Well! Hi, Leo. Hi, Deirdre, isn't it? I'm Dooley.'

'I know,' she said, shaking his offered hand. 'I've met Julie. We couldn't hear you.'

He cocked his head. 'Sorry?'

'We couldn't hear you? Over the mower?'

'Oh. I was just saying hello. Nice day. That sort of thing.'

'Right. So, how's the pub?'

He glanced back towards the garage as if to check that it was still there. 'You heard about that?'

'I did. You inspired this one' – she jerked a thumb at her husband – 'to take over ours.'

'No way!'

'Yup.'

Dooley looked to her left, awaiting an explanation. After what seemed like a full minute, Leo said, 'The records.'

'Nice!'

Leo shrugged. 'Nothing special.'

'Not how you saw it in your head, huh?'

'Not really.'

'I know that feeling, mate. You look at the websites, see what other people have done, and you get all excited. I pictured mine being party central, like in one of those beer ads when a bar just springs up in a log cabin or something? But it's only ever me in there.' He frowned. 'It's kinda sad, actually.'

'Well—'

'Hey! I know – why don't you come over? You can be my first customer.'

'Um. Maybe some—'

'Good idea,' Deirdre said. 'You don't have anything on tonight, do you?' She meant this as encouragement to Dooley and hoped that Leo wouldn't think she was being sarcastic.

'That's true,' he said slowly. 'I don't have anything on tonight.'

Dooley smiled and clapped his hands together. 'Sweet. Come over tonight and we'll sink a few. Yeah?'

'Yeah,' Leo nodded. 'If you're sure.'

'We'll say, what, 8.30?'

'Okay.'

'Right. I'll get back to it. Nice to meet you, Deirdre.'

'You too,' she said. 'Don't let him have Southern Comfort. It doesn't agree with him.'

'Not an issue. I haven't got any. I'm not exactly well stocked in there. Don't get your hopes up.'

'I won't,' Leo said miserably.

They said their goodbyes and parted. The instant the mower started up again, Leo said, 'Thanks a lot. What did you do that for?'

'It'll be good for you,' Deirdre said. 'Get you out of the house for a while.'

'I don't want to leave you on your own.'

'I'll be fine.' She took his hand again. 'Don't worry about me. Worry about yourself. It's not good for you to be cooped up all the time.'

'I *like* being cooped up.'

'So? I like chips. Liking something doesn't mean you can have it all the time.'

She felt quite pleased with that, and chose to ignore her husband's bitter pout.

In the first few weeks of their parenting careers, Julie and Dooley took every possible opportunity to 'do stuff' with the baby. They cooed and pointed in the zoo, they pretended to be excited about unnecessary boat trips, they hauled the pram to the top of some pretty major hills, and when imagination or energy failed them, they strolled around the park. On the day when Julie finally found the courage to wonder aloud if there was any point to all this since Nicola wasn't exactly taking videos, Dooley raised his hands to the heavens and thanked God. He'd wanted to ask the same question but thought Julie might get angry. They talked it over and concluded that what they'd been doing, subconsciously, was showing off. It was nothing to do with giving their infant a good time; it was about letting the world know that they had reproduced. They agreed to dial it down – but they still took Nicola to the park now and again. It became their pet phrase for any form of subtle and socially acceptable bragging. The neighbour who conspicuously washed his new car outside the house, for example, was seriously taking Nicola to the park.

This afternoon, they had decided to ignore the local facilities, which were nothing to get excited about, and strike out for the impressive expanses of Phoenix Park. This seemed, on the face of it, to be a declaration of intent about the length of the walk they were planning. But Julie knew that they would leave the car near the coffee shop, wander around a little, and then agree that a chocolate brownie would hit the spot, each of them pretending that they would prefer to keep walking and were only going along with the brownie thing out of deference to the other. And so it proved. They were lucky enough to get seats beside an old lady who was on her own, which meant that Nicola got a fine showing-off. Old ladies were easily the best bet in this regard, and this one played the role to perfection. She was liberal with her compliments to the point of being embarrassing and even treated them to some speculation about who baby most resembled, which was still catnip to them both. When she left the café, they sat in happy silence for a moment. As taking-Nicola-to-the-parks went, this had been a doozie. And they hadn't thrown any jagged remarks around, Julie reflected. Not one. There had been some heavy silences, but that was to be expected. On top of all this, for the first time ever, Nicola seemed to take genuine pleasure in being in out and about. They were on the point of packing up and heading home when Dooley glanced over at the queue of punters by the till and cocked his head. He adopted the expression of a man who's seeing something for which he is sure there's a logical explanation, even though none is leaping into mind at the moment.

'What's wrong?' Julie said, following his gaze. He seemed to be staring at the tall man who was, in turn, staring behind the cashier's head at the chalked-up list of prices.

'That guy looks…'

He didn't finish the thought. But then the man in the queue seemed to sense that he was being stared at. He looked over and pulled the exact same face that Dooley had just pulled.

'Who is it?' Julie asked.

Dooley said, 'Christ, it is him.'

'*Who?*'

'Ethan. A guy from high school.'

The man in the queue shook his head and briefly smiled, then went back to ordering.

'You're kidding,' Julie said. 'Small world, huh?'

'Yeah. Too bloody small.'

Ethan paid up and started towards them, smiling widely now. 'I'm sorry for staring,' he said when he arrived at their table. 'You're the spitting image of my old mate, Dooley. But there's no way you could be him because you seem to have a wife and a baby, and Dooley was like kryptonite to women.'

Dooley stood. 'Hello, Ethan. It's been a long time.'

Ethan put his tray down and they shook. 'It sure has. My God, I hate to think.'

'This is Julie,' Dooley told him, 'and this is our daughter, Nicola.'

'Julie. Wait… Julie Dooley? Perfect, I love it! Nice to meet you. Gorgeous baby.'

In the time between that line and his sitting down – a duration of perhaps a second – Julie decided that she didn't like him. 'Gorgeous'? What kind of compliment was that? The slice of pavlova on his tray looked 'gorgeous'. That old lady had spent a couple of minutes on Nicola's eyes alone. What kind of person met a beautiful little baby and measured out a single word of praise? It wasn't good enough. And what was the kryptonite crack about? It wasn't just a slur on Dooley, it was insulting to her, too. Did he think she'd been desperate? Without wishing to be conceited, had he got a good look at her?

'Have a seat,' she said, hoping he would catch the sarcasm. It wasn't a tremendous surprise when he did not.

'What brings you to Dublin, then?' Dooley said. 'Just a holiday?'

'Yeah. My wife's idea. Sam. She's always had a thing about Ireland. I'd introduce you but she's back at the hotel with the boys. We've got twins. Just turned seven, the little buggers. I thought I'd leave them to it for a couple of hours, check out the big park all the websites recommended. Bit rubbish, isn't it? There's nothing here.'

Julie bristled afresh. 'That's kinda the point, I would have thought.'

'I live here,' Dooley said. 'Met Julie when I was backpacking and just upped sticks.'

'Yeah? Good for you.'

He seemed profoundly uninterested, Julie thought. There was a moment's silence. Ethan poked experimentally at his pavlova and apparently decided, without even tasting it, that it wasn't for him.

'You always said you wanted to get into construction, didn't you?' Dooley asked. 'I remember because you were the only bloke I knew who had a plan.'

Ethan sniffed. 'Started out in construction, yeah. But I run a business of my own now. Landscaping. Small, y'know, but we're doing okay. What about you?'

There was a tiny pause before Dooley replied. A stranger might not have even noticed it. But Julie did.

'I stay at home with Nicola,' he said. 'Julie's in advertis—'

Ethan leaned in. 'You *what?*'

'I look aft—'

'Holy shit, you're a house husband!'

Another little pause. 'That's right. If you want to put it that way. I prefer stay-at-home dad.'

At this point, Ethan began to giggle. That was enough to

irritate Julie. But when he hid behind his hand like a schoolboy who'd heard a rude word in the company of adults, her irritation turned to fury. She wasn't sure why that made it worse. It just did. She considered telling him to fuck off and leave them alone. But it wasn't her place, she decided. She'd known the guy for less than a minute. Best to let Dooley handle it.

'Yeah, some people laugh when they hear,' Dooley said. 'Doesn't bother me.'

'I'm sorry,' Ethan said, not looking in the least bit sorry. 'I just got this image of you with a feather duster, mincing around… It all makes sense though.'

'Does it?'

'Yeah, yeah, yeah. I mean… you were never exactly the sporty type, were you?'

Dooley shook his head. 'You've lost me, Ethan.'

'And you were a bit of a dancer, weren't you?'

'I have no idea what—'

'There was a school talent show one time and you had a whole routine worked out. Did it onstage, all on your lonesome.'

'I remember,' Dooley said. 'But what has that got to do with looking after my daughter?'

Ethan gave him a look of disbelief, bordering on shock. 'Jesus, Dooley, I'm joking. I'm taking the *piss*, mate.' He nodded in Nicola's direction. 'Excuse my language.'

The appropriate reply to this, it seemed to Julie, would not be hard to find. Something about having heard all the jokes and no longer finding them funny. It wouldn't hurt to add that being a good father was nothing to be sneered at. You might finish up by pointing out that having been an unsporty youth who danced at a talent show was hardly an indication of closeted homosexuality and that, furthermore, giggling about such things had stopped being acceptable decades ago.

'Yeah,' Dooley said. 'All right then.'

Julie found a spot on the wall and stared at it.

'Are you all right?' Dooley asked when they left the café half an hour later.

Julie was pushing the buggy back to the car and had immediately opened up a lead on him. 'Yes.'

Dooley picked up his pace and drew level. 'You were very quiet in there.'

'I'm fine.'

They walked in silence for a while. 'So, that's Ethan,' Dooley said then. 'He's a horrible prick, isn't he? I never liked him way back when and he seems to be getting worse with age. Like a shit wine.'

Julie's stride stuttered. 'You think so?' she said.

'Dickhead. Always was.'

'Hm.'

'Nobody liked him. Nobody in my gang, anyway.'

'Hm.'

'And he has the balls to talk about *my* parenting situation? The big scandal when I was a kid was him getting someone knocked up before he'd even left school.'

It was a struggle, but Julie kept her tone neutral. 'Did she have the baby?'

'She did, yeah. But her family told him to stay away, which he very happily did. He pissed off to Melbourne for a year or two. No child support, and certainly no daddying.'

'Hm.'

'You're saying "hm" a lot, Julie.'

'Am I?'

'Yes. What is it?'

'What is what?'

'What is it that you're desperate to say but won't or can't?'

This was quite perceptive of him, she had to admit. 'I just thought... Never mind.'

'*What?*'

'I just thought you would have stuck up for yourself a bit more. On the duster front. And I didn't even know about him running out on a baby. That's serious ammo.'

'So, what, you think I should have brought that up? Probably the most traumatic thing that ever happened to him?'

Julie laughed, or at least cackled. It sounded nasty. She knew it did. 'Dooley, you've just finished telling me what an arsehole you think he is. And you're the one who brought his child into it.'

There was no doubting what he was going to say next. He was going to say something about David and how she obviously thought he would have handled it all in a more manly fashion. But he didn't say that; he didn't say anything. She knew he was thinking it, though. And she knew he was right. They got to the car, put Nicola in her seat, and drove home in unbroken deathly silence.

Leo was quiet all day. When they sat down in front of the TV after dinner, Deirdre offered several conversational gambits but none of them led anywhere. She assumed at first that he was worried about her going back to work. But when she told him she'd decided to give herself a few more days, he barely reacted. This was about Dooley, she realised with a mental snap of her fingers. He *really* didn't want to go over there. Just as she was wondering how to bring the subject up without aggravating him, he turned to her and said, 'I'm not going'.

'Not going where?' she said, for the sake of it.

'Dooley's. I don't feel like it.'

'How come?' He didn't reply. The excited hoots of the game show audience suddenly seemed deafening. 'Leo?'

'I just don't want to, Deirdre. Can we leave it at that?'

She chose her words with care. 'I meant what I said earlier about being stuck in here too much. It's not good for—'

'I'm not going. Can we drop it? Please.'

'You don't like him?'

'He's all right.'

'What, then?'

'Nothing.'

'It's not like you have something better to do, is it? What's your plan otherwise? Sit here watching this rubbish with boring old me? Play more records that you've already heard 500 times?'

The last sentence just slipped out. She held her breath, hoping she hadn't stood on a mine.

'I think I might have an early night, actually.'

'Leo! It's ten past eight.'

'I know.'

'Are you not feeling well? You're spending a lot of time horizontal.'

'I'm fine. Just tired is all.'

'So you're going to leave the guy hanging? You'll have to go over, make some excuse, at least.'

'If I go over, he'll drag me in there. I know he will.'

'You can't just not show up.'

He made a noise with his lips. 'Will you go for me?'

'Ah, Leo!'

'Please.'

'What if I say no?'

'He'll probably come knocking. And I'll be in bed. So you'll wind up having to talk to him anyway.' He got to his feet. 'Please. Tell him I'm sick or whatever.'

Before she could think of a suitable response he was moving, and then he was gone. It was all so sudden. She sat there in a daze for a few minutes, then got up, grabbed her keys, and set off for Dooley's.

Maybe he really was just tired, she told herself, several times.

In the normal course of events, playing *Left 4 Dead* in co-op mode was well up there on Redmond's list of the finest things in life. Shotgunning the festering heads off zombies was a tremendous amount of fun in any circumstances (obviously) but when you found yourself partnered up with someone who knew what they were doing, it became something else entirely. The thrill of working together to cut through a horde of the blood-crazed undead was sometimes so overpowering that he heard himself giggling like a child. His partner tonight, HotStepper89, claimed to be new to the game, which made the skill and sense of judgement she displayed all the more impressive. And yet, he wasn't enjoying himself. Not even a little bit.

'Agh, stupid fuckin' bots,' HotStepper moaned in an English accent that he couldn't quite place – Leeds, maybe? 'Get outta the way!'

Left 4 Dead, as the name implied, was built for teams of four. When fewer than that number of humans were available to make up a team, computer-controlled players – bots – filled the gaps. They were rarely much help. HotStepper89 hated them so much that Redmond wondered if, somehow, a member of her family had been hurt by one.

'Right!' he said. 'Boomer! Right!'

Boomers were enormous zombies who waddled about projectile vomiting bright green bile that burned on contact. On the plus side, they exploded in a highly satisfying fashion when shot.

'Got it,' HotStepper89 said, swinging around. She hadn't finished these two syllables before the boomer burst into pieces, showering the area with bloody chunks.

'Sweet,' Redmond said.

'I *love* shooting those fat pricks.'

'Me too.'

'Not because they're fat, mind.'

'Sorry?'

'I'm saying, I haven't got a thing about fat people or anything.'

'I didn't think you had.'

'Okay.'

Redmond switched weapon to a Molotov cocktail and absent-mindedly torched an advancing trio of infected. What was all that about? Had he said something to make her think *he* was fat? Probably not. He was just feeling sensitive. Paranoid, even. And no wonder.

'Shit,' HotStepper89 said then. 'I'm really sorry, but I have to go. My baby's woken up.'

'Oh. Right. Not to worry.'

'I thought I had another hour at least.'

'That's okay. Babies trump zombies.'

'Yeah. All right, I'm off. See ya.'

'Good night.'

She left the game and a second later, so did Redmond. He put the controller down and glanced at his phone to get the time. 2.13am.

Nancy never believed him when he said that huge numbers of women played video games. She thought it was an activity for little boys and men with the limited mental capacity of little boys. If he told her about playing with the zombie scourge HotStepper89, not just a woman but the mother of a baby, she would assume he was making it up to score points. For the thousandth time, he pondered how everything would be different if Nancy were a gamer. He wouldn't have painted himself into the corner he currently occupied, for a start. In fact, he would never have had the garage idea in the first place. It was all her fault.

He moved the pizza box that had housed his dinner and lay down on the sofa. There was no question of stretching out – even a man of average height would have had to dangle his feet over the armrest. Instead, he tucked his legs up until his knees almost touched his chin and bent his neck, making a flattened S of his body. Over the previous two nights, he had learned that this position felt deceptively comfortable at first but soon became irritating and then downright painful. Still, it was his only real option. The duvet he had commandeered from upstairs was lying in a heap on the floor. He snatched at it and did his best to make himself cosy. It was some consolation, he supposed, that this shitstorm had kicked up in high summer and not in the depths of winter.

He shook his head. Jesus Christ, had it come to this? Trying to convince himself that it wasn't so bad living in his garage, really, because it wasn't currently freezing? He had effectively separated from his wife and was mocking the very notion of 'family' but on the bright side, look, no icicles? In a matter of seconds, a kind of panic enveloped him. He threw the duvet back and sat up. This was madness. Madness. And it wasn't Nancy's fault. It was *his* fault. Obviously! He'd been stubborn and then he'd been stupid and now he was being stubborn again. He had to talk to her, right now. To apologise. To make it right. The longer he delayed, the harder it was going to be. He stood. Shoes? Did he need shoes? He was fully dressed but it didn't seem right to go grovelling in his socks.

Hm. *Grovelling.* That was what it boiled down to, wasn't it? Whether he went in shoes or socks, fully dressed or buck naked, he would be offering her his throat. She would make him suffer now and then hold it over him for the rest of his life. Even though, when you got right down to it, he hadn't done anything all that terrible. Being stubborn was hardly a crime. And – *and* – she'd been pretty stubborn too. Why was it up to him to debase himself?

He sat down again. And then he lay down again. No. There would be no grovelling. Not from him. Nope.

In Nancy's dream, she was stuck on a tropical island with maybe a dozen other women. They were taking part in a reality show, she believed, although no one else seemed to think so. Every time she mentioned hidden cameras or the satellite phone they surely had for emergencies, someone would round on her and bark that this was all real and she would do well to either help or shut the fuck up. She found it hard to shut the fuck up and harder still to help. Every last one of the tasks they needed to perform was beyond her. When she tried to start a fire, she created a huge explosion that left several of her companions dead (one of their heads became lodged in a nearby tree) but, somehow, no lasting flames. When she tried to catch fish, they pretended to be struggling in her makeshift net, then grew wings and flew away, laughing. When she went to fetch fresh water, her buckets passed the most painstaking inspection then miraculously developed holes on the long trudge back to camp. Worst of all were her attempts at building a shelter. None of the other women was living in luxury, exactly, but they had all made something to keep the rain out and themselves off the insect-ridden floor, at least. No matter how hard she tried – and it felt, in dream logic, that she did nothing else for about a month – Nancy could only manage to lean some sticks together and cover them with a few half-rotted leaves. No one offered to share their accommodation. On the contrary, they giggled themselves to sleep as she wept and shivered in what was essentially the open air. Redmond could help, she knew, if only she could find him. He was on the island somewhere. She was sure of it. But this was another point on which all of the others were unanimous. There was no Redmond on the island. There was no Redmond anywhere. She had imagined him.

And then she was in the sea, wading out. It was night, but the moon was full, and brilliant, hanging in the clear sky at five times its normal size. Despite the lack of clouds, a ferocious storm was raging. The thunder was deafening, the lightning both awesome and impossibly constant. There was so much rain that it was difficult to breathe. She kept going, slowly and deliberately putting one foot in front of the other on sand as hard as concrete. As the water came up to her abdomen, she marvelled at the lack of waves. For all the violence of the storm, the sea was like a pane of glass. She kept going. Up to her shoulders. Up to her throat. Up to her nose.

Nancy woke up and clutched the edge of the duvet in both fists, panting for breath. A few seconds passed as she convinced herself that she was neither drowning nor stranded anywhere but her own bed. She got up on her elbows then and looked at the alarm clock on her bedside locker. 5.22am. A terrible time to wake up. If she didn't get back to sleep immediately, there would soon be no point in trying. She lay on her back, blinking and sighing, feeling more alert with every passing second. Was Redmond sleeping well, she wondered? He couldn't be remotely comfortable down there. The thought gave her no pleasure, which was annoying, because she really wanted it to. This was the third night of the fiasco. At first, it made her feel angry. Then it made her feel worried. Now she wasn't sure how she felt. Disgusted? It was as good a description as any.

The fucking idiot. She ground her teeth.

7

'I dreamt about her last night,' Declan said to Redmond. 'Again.' They were in the kitchen at work, waiting for the kettle to boil. As usual, it was taking forever. Redmond was fond of saying that you could heat water just as efficiently by shaking it.

'This is Aoife you're talking about, I presume.'

'Who else?'

Who else indeed, thought Redmond. Aoife was a new hire, straight out of university, where she had excelled – president of this, founder of that – to an extent that made her new colleagues nervous. She seemed pleasant enough, if a little humourless. Physically, she wasn't unattractive, but she was nothing special either. Declan, for unfathomable reasons, had decided that she was sex incarnate.

'You're not going to give me any details, are you? Because I really—'

'It was an S and M scene, this one. Which is not normally my thing.'

'Declan, I'm begging you.'

'Weird you should say that, because there was a lot of begging in the dream. I was tied up, right, against…'

'Honestly, I don't—'

'… a wall on a sort of crucifix thing and Aoife comes in a sort of Catwoman outfit? With a little short whip? And she comes over, all slinky, and—'

'Hi, Aoife.'

Declan's eyes emerged briefly from their sockets. He spun around to find that he had been had. 'You *bastard*.'

'Sorry. I was desperate. I had to do something before you planted an image I could never unsee.'

Declan gave up and, for the third time, checked the kettle to make sure it was on. 'So, how's Nancy these days? Still being unreasonable?'

'Let's talk about your dream again.'

'That good, eh?'

Redmond hesitated. It might sound ridiculous if he said it out loud. On the other hand, Declan was already invested in the drama. It wasn't like telling a random stranger on the street. He decided to go for it.

'There has been a development.'

'Yeah?'

'I'm living in the garage now.'

'Just you and all your games. Good stuff.'

'Yep.'

Declan's smile froze. 'Fuck me. You're not serious, are you? You're serious? Are you being serious? Oh my God. You are. You're *serious.*'

'I came home and found her bagging up all my gear. To *sell*, Declan. On *eBay*. There was a row. She said I should live in the garage if I like it so much.'

'And, what, you said, "Right, then, I will", like an eight-year-old? Jesus Christ, Redmond.'

'What was I supposed to do? Let her get rid of my gear?'

'I don't see how you get from saving your stuff to fucking living with it. Are you, like, guarding it or something?'

'No. I'm just…' He couldn't think of a good way to end the sentence. It hung in the air between them.

'Holy shit,' Declan said. 'How long has this been going on for?'

'Um… a week.'

'Fuck. Me. Have you got a bed, even?'

'Sofa. Dragged a duvet and a pillow downstairs.'

'How could *you* possibly fit on a sofa?'

'I can't. I don't.'

Declan had been staring at him with his head cocked to one side. Now it suddenly flipped to the other side. 'Wait a minute, you've got *kids*. What are you telling them?'

'They're too young, they haven't even noticed.'

'So, is this how it's going to be forever? I mean, what's the endgame here? What's your exit strategy?'

Shit, Redmond thought. 'Exit strategy' was the very phrase that had occurred to him as he dangled his legs off the end of the sofa that first night. He didn't have one and couldn't imagine getting one any time soon. It couldn't be a good sign that Declan had spotted this flaw as soon as he heard what was going on.

'I must say, I expected a bit more support,' he said. 'You were the one who was egging me on with this shit.'

'Come on, man. I said you should stick up for yourself. I didn't say you should ruin your whole fucking marriage.'

There was a good comeback to that, Redmond felt sure. He just couldn't put his finger on it right away. Rather than reply, he spun away from Declan and leaned against the counter, arms folded.

'COME ON,' he hissed at the kettle.

'It changes, doesn't it?' Paula said. 'Over the years. When I first started going to pubs I wanted them lively and full of good-looking boys. That was all I cared about. Christ, we used to hang out in some awful shitholes. I presume you were the same? Decent music and plenty of loose women, right?'

Dooley nodded. He hadn't said anything for a while. But that seemed to be okay with her. She had barely paused for breath since they'd started walking.

'Then,' she went on, 'somewhere in your twenties you start caring about the state of the toilets and how many people have been stabbed there in the past couple of weeks. All part of the great circle of life.'

During the week, he had pondered what he would say if she mentioned visiting his pub a second time. Truth be told, he had pondered little else. Some days, he told himself she was just a friendly woman who was interested in seeing the man cave he kept banging on about. And she was lonely too, most probably. That was all there was to it. It would look weird if he tried to brush her off again. Weird and rude.

Other days, he warned himself that it was all a ploy. *Of course* she didn't care about seeing his pub. What woman would? The very idea was laughable. She was using it as an excuse to get him alone in private, at which point she would drop the pretence and her underwear. He had allowed himself to be flattered by her apparent interest in his project and now he was heading for disaster.

Just this morning, however, the matter had been settled when he remembered that – *duh* – they would have the kids with them. In all the (many, many) times he'd imagined how a potential visit might play out, he'd never once placed Nicola and Charlie in the picture. As soon as he had done so, a weight had lifted. When the subject came up, as they were gathering their stuff together after Gymboree, it had been pretty easy to say, 'No time like the present.'

'So,' he said, finally finding his voice. 'What's your idea of a good pub these days?'

She laughed. 'There is no "these days" with me and pubs.'

Dooley found further comfort in this. She was a single mother, tied to the house. In the absence of a proper social life, checking out a fake pub in a garage constituted a wild time. Nothing was going to happen. He would show her around, she would pay a few compliments, they would go their separate ways. Simple.

They rounded the last corner and entered the keyhole-shaped cul-de-sac.

'Here we are,' he said.

Either Paula was an astoundingly good actress – and Dooley had never seen any evidence of that before now – or she was genuinely impressed with the place. She loved the lighting. She loved the sofa and the beanbags. She loved the framed posters. She even loved the terrible bar, the few sheets of plywood he had knocked together as a stopgap and was only now admitting might be a permanent fixture. Most of all, she loved the 'darting area' (as Dooley heard himself describe the thin strip by the back wall) and cooed appreciatively as he described how he had co-opted a toy blackboard to help track scores. He didn't mention that he hadn't actually played against anyone yet and tried to disguise how pleased he was when she challenged him to a game. Better yet, she accepted his offer of a beer, becoming his first official patron; he'd wondered if he'd ever have one since Leo had cried off with a sudden attack of diarrhoea. He sipped on a Heineken himself, just to be social, and dearly wished he could knock it back, along with several of its colleagues. Although he was trying hard to keep it breezy, showing someone around his pub and having them actually *get it* was blissful. He felt giddy and sorely wished he could tell Julie about it later, just to see the look on her face.

Dooley was terrible at darts. He had assumed, based on the regularity with which he hit the laundry basket with socks, that he would be pretty decent. But no. His efforts usually missed their targets by some distance and quite often landed on the wrong hemisphere of the board. Compared to Paula, however, he was a laser-guided darting machine. They'd been playing for five minutes before she hit the board *at all*. She refused Dooley's suggestion that she should ignore the rules and stand a little closer but eventually did agree that they should play from 301, rather than the traditional 501. Given their respective skill levels, a game from 501 could take several hours. Charlie didn't seem remotely interested in this strange new activity at first but, after they'd been playing for a while, she suddenly insisted on having a go. Paula picked her up and let her throw a few from a metre away, at which point her enthusiasm evaporated as quickly as it had arisen. She reinstalled herself on the sofa and went back to performing an elaborate drama with her finger puppets. Nicola had fallen asleep on the walk home and was still in her buggy. Her head was hanging at an awkward angle but Dooley decided against making an adjustment. She would undoubtedly wake up and (how he hated himself for thinking this) ruin his moment.

'You know what?' Paula said after a while. 'I'm beginning to think that even 301 was too ambitious.'

Dooley checked the scores. 'You're on 206. I'm on 37 but I could be chasing that last double for a long time. Will we call it a day?'

'Might be for the best.'

It was his turn. He threw his darts in quick succession, not really aiming. 'Christ, look at that. Treble 19. That was my best dart.'

'Hm. Maybe the secret is not to aim.'

He smiled and nodded, not sure how to proceed. 'So. That's the pub.'

'It's great.'

'Yeah, cheers.'

'Really great.'

'Thanks.'

They locked eyes for a moment. She stepped closer. Then closer still. 'What about the rest of the house?' she said softly.

'Uh, the rest of the house? Did you want—'

'Aren't you going to show me the bedroom?'

Before he could even reply, her hand was on his chest, then snaking up behind his head.

'Jesus Christ, Paula,' he whispered. 'Is this a joke?'

She pulled his head lower and stood on tiptoe. 'I want you to fuck me,' she breathed. 'Now.'

It was so shockingly sudden. So shockingly unsubtle. And yet, he couldn't help but note, his fear that this would happen had been replaced by something else. It felt a lot like excitement.

He lowered his voice still further, almost to the point of inaudibility. 'What about the kids?'

'We can be quick.'

Before he could reply she peeped around him and said, 'Charlie, I'm just popping into the kitchen with Dooley for a minute. Be right back. Don't touch any of his stuff.'

Charlie grunted, lost in her own little world. Paula's voice had been chilling in its calmness. She was a good actress after all. So much for his people-judgement skills. He glanced at his daughter to check that she was still asleep and then allowed himself to be led towards the door.

Upstairs, everything was a weird blur. It was as if someone had rubbed a greasy finger over the lens through which he viewed the world. The bedroom itself looked different. Was that their duvet? Really? Had it always been that colour?

Paula was wearing a light summer dress. She raised it over her hips and neatly removed her underwear, then fell back on the bed, pulling him with her. They kissed, but not for long. There was no time for that, let alone any of the elaborate foreplay of which he was usually so proud. He got up on his knees and, with little elegance, lowered his jeans and shorts.

'What about—' he began but she was already waving a condom at him. Where she'd produced it from, he had no idea. He grabbed it from her and tore the packet open. The peculiar oily smell hit him before he'd even removed the contents. Julie was on the pill, and it had been a long time since he'd dealt with this unpleasantness. A possibility occurred to him: fumbling, followed by embarrassment, followed by functional disaster. He hesitated, just for a second – but that was long enough. Some unseen hypnotist snapped his fingers, and suddenly he was back in the room. Every muscle in his body turned to jelly.

'What?' Paula said.

'Oh, Jesus. No. No. No.'

'*What?*'

He dropped back to his feet and pulled his shorts up. His dick hadn't so much detumesced as shot back inside him like the head of a frightened turtle.

'Are you fucking kidding me?' she hissed.

'I can't. I won't. No. No way.'

Now that he wasn't going to act upon it, her state of undress seemed acutely improper. He turned away, as if he had entered the room by mistake. 'I'm going back downstairs now. Follow me when you're—'

'Jesus *Christ*,' she said.

He turned towards her again. They stared at each other, breathing heavily. Then he walked out and down the stairs. The self-loathing was coming in waves now, like a drug. He fought to retain control of his basic motor skills and threw the garage door open with a lot more force than he'd intended to use. Two facts struck him at once: Nicola was still sound asleep, which was good, and Charlie was missing, which was the end of the world. Clearly, she had either wandered into the kitchen and drunk bleach from under the sink or else wandered out onto the street and been flattened by a Tesco delivery van. And then he heard her voice. He dashed in and found that she'd relocated to the floor and had merely been hidden by the sofa. She was leaning against its side, hosting a conversation between a chicken and a sheep. The finger puppets bobbed in turn as they delivered their lines.

'Hello, Mr Sheep, what a lovely sunshine we have today... Yes, Mrs Chicken, it's the best day ever, let's go and get ice cream at the ice cream... uh... place.'

She looked up at him and smiled sweetly. He turned away, unable to meet her eye. Paula was coming through the door, beaming.

'Hi, honey, everything okay? Ah, lookit. Wee Nicola's still flaked out.'

He gawped at her. How could she be so calm? She pivoted to face him.

'Oh, Dooley! You forgot to show me your new coffee machine. Come on.'

She headed back to the kitchen. He followed, each step requiring a conscious effort. When they were alone again, she folded her arms and regarded him coldly.

'That was really embarrassing for me,' she said. 'Humiliating, actually. Do you understand? I feel *humiliated*.'

'I'm sorry about that,' he said. 'But I couldn't go through with it. I should never have left the garage with you in the first place. The whole thing was—'

'I don't get it. Because you're *married?*'

He surprised himself by laughing, albeit bitterly. 'Yes, Paula. Because I'm married.'

'That didn't stop you chatting me up multiple times, I noticed.'

'I wasn't ch—'

'It didn't stop you getting your cock out.'

He flinched. 'Look. I was weak. And I was tempted.' He

hesitated, unhappy at how melodramatic this sounded. 'But I came to my senses in time. That's the main thing.'

'Is it?' She tilted her head. 'Do you think your wife would see it that way?'

It was extremely important now, he told himself, that he take a long, slow breath and choose his words with care. He did both. 'Are you threatening to tell her, Paula?'

'I'm just saying… you might as well have gone through with it. There's "faithful" and there's "I stood over her with a massive hard-on flapping about but it's okay, I didn't put it in her". You follow?'

He wasn't at all reassured. 'But that's my problem. Right?'

'Sure. It's all yours. Enjoy.'

She walked back to the garage. Dooley leaned against the sink and splayed his fingers, watching them tremble. After a moment, Paula and Charlie came through the kitchen. They said their goodbyes, all smiles and bustle, then Paula announced that they would see themselves out. When the front door shut, Dooley went to fetch Nicola, hoping she'd still be asleep so he wouldn't have to look her in the eye.

The counsellor's name was Lauren. She was in her fifties, Leo guessed, slightly dishevelled, but with a kind face and an easy smile. Her office at the fertility clinic was low-lit and cosy; more like a living room than anything else. All three of them had armchairs to sit in. He held Deirdre's hand when they first sat down but it was awkward and began to feel like affectation. They seemed to realise this at the same moment and withdrew simultaneously, with no hard feelings.

'Let's all try and relax,' Lauren said. 'This isn't a test. I'm not here to judge you. It's just a chat about what's going to happen next, and how you both feel about it.'

'Great,' Deirdre said in a tone that Leo immediately recognised as faux casual.

'Why don't you talk me through your history so far?' Lauren

said. 'Did you always want kids? Was it something you explicitly spoke about when you got serious about each other?'

Leo was determined that he would do as much of the talking as possible to take the pressure off Deirdre. But she started answering before he could even part his lips.

'Oh, yes,' she said. 'You have to, don't you? We know a few couples who were married for a year before they found out that one or other of them didn't want kids. The thought of it... I mean, it's the biggest decision you can make. You have to know each other's intentions. We certainly did. We were talking about kids when we'd only been going out a few months.'

She giggled at the memory. Leo did his best to smile but it wasn't easy, because she was lying. They'd talked about having kids, sure, but only after they were engaged. And who were these couples they knew who never had the same conversation? He had no idea. Another lie, he suspected. This was not a good start. Something in his chest tightened up a couple of notches.

'You'd be surprised,' Lauren smiled. 'Not wanting kids is a lot more common than most of us realise. Some people, women especially, feel a kind of guilt about it, even though it's a perfectly valid choice to make. They don't want to say it out loud, which can lead to trouble, as you might imagine.'

'Not us,' Deirdre said. 'We wanted three, isn't that what we always said, Leo? Maybe even four. Of course, we'd settle for one now.'

Leo turned to face her, hoping she would catch his eye. She continued to look straight ahead at Lauren. They had never spoken about numbers.

'Mmm,' he said, not wanting to join her in the lie but not wanting to contradict her either. 'We never had any doubts.'

Lauren looked from one to the other, nodding. 'And you presumed, naturally enough, that it would just happen.'

'We sure did,' Deirdre said. 'You spend so long terrified that you're going to get pregnant by accident, don't you? You're afraid you'll conceive if you have a racy thought. It never really crosses your mind that it won't happen when you want it to.'

This drew a sympathetic laugh from Lauren. 'I hear that all the time. "If I'd known it was this hard to get pregnant I would never have bothered taking the pill."'

'Yeah, exactly.'

'So, how long was it before you started to suspect that it wasn't going to be easy for you to conceive?'

'I suppose—' Leo began.

'Probably about six months,' Deirdre said. 'I mean, there was no panic or anything. Not at that stage. But I had a bad feeling in the pit of my stomach.'

'And you came to us...?'

'After a year.'

'And then you had all those fun tests.'

'Ha, yeah.'

'How did you feel about that, Leo?'

His memories of the tests were extraordinarily vivid. The little room, the armchair just like this one, the sink, the coffee table piled high with dog-eared wrist mags. The variety of the provided stimuli had come as a great surprise to him. He knew there'd be magazines and had supposed it'd be pretty tame stuff – maybe a *Playboy* or two. But no, the selection was broad and, as a friend of his used to say, 'no holes barred'. There really was something there for everyone, from the predicted *Playboy* with its honey-toned Californians draped across sports cars to less celebrated titles featuring spotty-arsed fortysomethings dressed up as schoolgirls and bouncing enthusiastically on freakish cocks. He recalled saying 'What the fuck?' out loud to the empty room when he spotted, half-way down the pile, a two-year-old copy of *Hello!*. There were men out there, apparently, who couldn't knock one out to airbrushed perfection or grotesque anal assault but grew helpless at the sight of Joan Collins showing them around her living room. In the end, Leo had left the magazines to one side and relied solely on his imagination.

'It was fine,' he said. 'Deirdre had it a lot tougher than I did.'

'Oh, I was okay too. Didn't bother me.'

Leo was already losing count of the lies. Didn't *bother* her? She had cried endlessly about 'being on trial'. Nothing he could say was of any comfort. There were slammed doors and endless silences.

'But no obvious problems were found,' Lauren said.

Deirdre shrugged. 'Nope.'

Lauren tilted her head sympathetically. 'I often think that couples like you have it worse. If fertility tests find a definitive cause, that can be bad news, of course, but at least it's an answer.'

This was exactly what they had said to each other, over and over. It would be better to know. How could they take action if they didn't know what the issue was? Even if they'd been told that they could categorically never be parents, it would have been closure, at least. Anything would be better than this foggy limbo.

'I don't know about that,' Deirdre said. 'We still had hope. We could still keep trying. Which we did. A lot, ha ha.'

Leo bit the inside of his cheek and ordered himself not to call her a liar while they were still in this room.

'Well, that's true and I'm glad to hear you say it yourself. So – you've been trying and haven't had any luck, you've had tests and nothing has been found, you've, uh, redoubled your efforts, so to speak. And still no joy. Let me ask about your emotions at this point. Leo, can I start with you?'

He was relieved to go first. It gave him a chance to set the tone. 'It was tough. There's no point in denying it. Very frustrating. You start… y'know… you start seeing babies everywhere. And getting kind of… angry. How come that guy gets to be a daddy and I don't? That sort of thing. Which is silly, I suppose.'

'Not silly at all,' Lauren said. 'Completely normal.'

'It didn't help,' Leo said, feeling encouraged, 'that I lost my job on top of everything else.'

Deirdre stirred beside him. 'Let's stick to the fertility side of things, Leo. We're not here to tell our life stories.'

She had tried to keep her tone jovial but Leo heard the steel behind it and presumed that their counsellor had too.

'Well,' Lauren said, 'we're talking about how we felt, so anything that feeds into that is fair game, really. Losing a job is a very stressful event, Leo. Have you found something since?'

He shook his head. 'Nope.'

'Things have been so bad, though,' Deirdre said. 'In the market.'

'That's correct,' he said softly. 'It's been rough in property. Obviously. Since the crash.'

Lauren regarded him in silence for a moment. 'You still have to try, though, right? Have you found it difficult to get motivated?'

He gave it a moment's thought. What was she hoping to hear? Or not to hear? He wasn't sure. The best option was to tell the truth. 'Sometimes. A bit. Yes. Maybe a lot.'

'Sleeping too much?'

'Yes.'

'Avoiding company?'

'Yes.'

'Leo: do you think it's possible that you've been depressed?'

'Yes.'

He almost gasped. Had he really said that? For that matter, had he really thought that?

'Have you tried to get help from anyone?' Lauren asked after a moment.

He shook his head. The room seemed to have shrunk in the past few seconds. He felt warm and a little dizzy. There was a sudden tightness at his throat, as if he had overdone the tie he wasn't even wearing. Words assembled in his mouth but he had to consciously push them past his lips.

'No. I just… gave up. On it. On the job front. Ages ago, to tell you the truth.'

A horrible stillness enveloped them all. He stared at Lauren, afraid that if he looked to his left, he would see Deirdre hastily fashioning a shiv. Lauren looked back with a sort of kindly challenge in her eyes, hoping (he guessed) that he would say more but not wanting to push him. After a few seconds, she broke off in Deirdre's direction.

'Were you aware that Leo has been depressed?'

'Of course,' Deirdre said, 'but, as he says, it hasn't been too bad.

Just a bit down, you know. What with one thing and another. We talk it over. That helps.'

He almost lost it at that point. What was the point of this exercise if they weren't going to be honest? It was ridiculous. *But.* What if this really *was* some sort of test? What if he called his wife on her lies and Lauren cried 'Aha!' and produced a big red stamp marked DENIED? All he could do for now was make sure he told the truth himself.

'Maybe I've been feeling like a failure,' he said and then immediately wished he'd kept his mouth shut.

'Go on,' Lauren said.

'Um. Couldn't get my wife pregnant. Couldn't keep my job. Y'know. Useless.'

He was fully prepared for Deirdre to say that they had discussed all this at length and that everything was fine now. But she stayed quiet.

'You're probably going to think this is all I ever say,' Lauren smiled, 'but, again, that's perfectly normal. When babies don't come along when expected, people often blame themselves. They shouldn't, of course. But they do.'

Leo clammed up again. He had no idea where these declarations were coming from. He felt possessed. And... relieved? He swallowed, cleared his throat, shifted in his seat. Lauren seemed to notice that he was becoming upset.

'We can come back to this, Leo. Deirdre, let's talk about you for a moment. How have you coped, emotionally?'

Deirdre sighed. 'It hasn't been easy. Obviously. But I've tried to stay positive, to stay focused on the next step in the process. I've kept myself busy with work and all that. I've had the occasional bad day, don't get me wrong, but basically I've been fine. It's—'

'Oh, for fuck's sake!' Leo said. 'Stop lying! You've been lying since we got in here! You haven't been fine, Deirdre. You've been anything but. Crying every other day, obsessing about your weight, taking my head off every chance you get. You've just had two weeks off work with stress. Your boss told me you had a mini-breakdown. You deliberately shot a guy in the balls with a paintgun. Hello? You don't have to be Sigmund fucking Freud to see through that one. For Christ's sake, I'm begging you, tell the woman the truth.'

In that moment he really didn't care if Lauren brandished her stamp of denial. Enough was enough. But as the seconds dragged on and on he began to panic. He had ruined everything. Lauren would decide they were too unstable to be parents. Deirdre would never forgive him and would probably want a divorce. Having admitted to himself that he'd been depressed he would fall into a spiral and would end his days freezing in a shop doorway, homeless, alone, and utterly broken.

'Say something, Deirdre,' he begged when he could no longer stand the silence.

'He's right,' she said then. Her voice sounded almost comically small by comparison with the confident booming that had preceded it. It took him a moment to realise that this was merely her normal tone. 'I've been a mess. I'm terrified. I feel sick all the time. I lash out.' She swallowed. Cleared her throat. Swallowed again. 'We've never had any conversations about Leo being depressed, either. I suppose I knew he was. But I didn't speak up. I didn't have... room... for that.'

Leo didn't dare say anything. This was huge and he didn't want to ruin it. Lauren would respond, surely. But she didn't seem to want to. She just looked at Deirdre, nodding at a glacial pace, almost imperceptibly; the kindly challenge again. Time stood still. Then, at last, Lauren accepted that Deirdre had nothing else to add right now. She adjusted her glasses and said, 'I'm sorry to hear that you've been so down. Both of you. But you've taken big steps here today. Are you happy to keep talking to me?'

Leo risked looking to his left. Deirdre briefly met his eye, then turned back to Lauren and nodded.

'Yes,' she said.

'Definitely,' Leo added.

He reached across and held his hand out for his wife. It took some doing. He had no idea what he would say or do if she refused it. But she didn't.

By recent standards, Julie had enjoyed a pretty decent day at work. Her guilt at taking a sickie had propelled her to ever greater levels of industry on her return and she was, as she liked to think of it, Getting Shit Done. Better yet, David was temporarily out of the picture. He'd been busy on the day she came back and she hadn't bumped into him at all. And now he was away – a couple of days in London, attending some conference, then straight down to Cork to suck up to some clients. As she rounded the last corner for home she was looking forward to playing with Nicola and then collapsing in front of something truly mindless on the telly.

Deirdre thingy from across the street was just ahead of her on the pavement to her left, she saw, head down, hands stuffed into her jacket pockets. She had the form and demeanour of a woman who'd been caught in the rain, although it was a perfectly pleasant evening. Julie was about to give the horn a friendly little toot when, suddenly, and without even the metest glance in either direction, Deirdre started to cross the road. Shrieking, Julie stood on the brakes and brought the car to a halt just half a metre away from impact. Deirdre turned and looked at her, then slowly raised her hand in apology. 'Sorry,' she called out. She didn't seem remotely alarmed. Julie was nonplussed. Granted, she hadn't exactly been burning rubber, but still. There was no gentle way to get hit by a car. Most people would have been a little more energised by a near miss than this. She lowered her window and leaned out.

'Are you okay, Deirdre?'

'Yeah. Grand. My fault. Miles away.'

She turned and continued crossing the road. After a moment, Julie rolled the car forward until they were level.

'Is everything all right? You look a bit...' She couldn't think of a word that wasn't insulting and just let the sentence dangle in mid-air.

'Honestly,' Deirdre said. 'I'm fine. Thanks for asking. Thank you. Thanks.'

It was like talking to a machine that was doing its best to sound human, Julie thought. She wanted to be of some help – there was clearly something wrong with the woman – but had no idea how to proceed.

'If you're sure.'

'Yeah. See ya.' She extricated a hand from her pocket and performed a weak pantomime of a wave. Then she carried on her way.

Julie drove off.

'Would you like a glass of wine?' Dooley said. 'Dinner will be another half an hour.'

Julie was on her knees blowing raspberries on Nicola's forehead and trying not to get poked in the eye as the recipient thrashed about in delight.

'Um… okay. Thanks.'

Dooley finger-gunned her and said, 'Coming up', like a teenage waiter in a grubby pizza chain. He was being weird, she thought. From the moment she came through the door he'd been constantly hovering around her, asking how her day was, giving updates on Nicola's mood and health, smiling at nothing. It could be that he was trying to make amends, she supposed, to get things back to normal following their recent fallings-out. But it was all very sudden, if so. He had given no inkling that he wanted to sue for peace. The explanation could be something much simpler. Maybe he had broken something around the house and was radically overcompensating. She made a mental note to check the bins later.

'Oh, look, Nicola, look, Mrs Giraffe wants a cuddle. Will you give her one? Ah, lookit, she's so sad.'

She walked a stuffed giraffe through the air above the supine child, trying her best to make it look depressed.

'I wish someone would give me a big hug,' she said in what she imagined a giraffe's voice would sound like (a drunken sheep, apparently). 'A big hug from a beautiful little girl, that's all I want in the world.'

Nicola furrowed her brow, looking from toy to mother and back again. She had no intention of hugging anything.

'Oh well. Maybe some other time.'

Dooley returned with the wine. He held it before him like a ticking bomb, taking small, slow steps.

'Jesus,' Julie said. 'That's very good value.'

The glass was full to the point of overflowing. 'I was a bit heavy handed,' Dooley said. 'But so what? You only live once and all that.'

He handed it over and Julie sipped it down to a manageable level, then placed it out of the way of little arms and legs. 'Thanks.'

'Anything else I can get you?'

'What? No.'

'Okay, then.'

'Okay.'

They looked at each other uncertainly. Then Dooley swivelled and went back to the kitchen, where, he had assured her, something truly special was taking shape.

Long ago Julie had admitted to Dooley that every time a social conversation turned tediously foodie she wanted to stand up and declare that they could keep their quinoa and their goji berries, their chia seeds and their ethically sourced salmon – nothing made her mouth water like good old roast chicken and potatoes. Ever since then, it had been 'their' meal, in much the same way that *Before Sunrise* was their film and (for farcically convoluted reasons) 'You Can't Touch This' was their song. Dooley had worked hard on perfecting his methods over the years and was now something of an authority on this one small corner of the culinary landscape. His roast potatoes, in particular, regularly approached the status of art. The fact that tonight's were slightly dry had caused him significant distress.

'I'm sorry,' he said, for the third time when they'd been eating for ten minutes. 'I don't know what went wrong. They're a disaster.'

'No,' Julie sighed, 'they are *not*. They're lovely.' She had grown weary of talking him down on the subject. His dismay was not only overblown, it was further evidence that something was up.

'I was thinking,' he said then, 'maybe we could tuck in to *Breaking Bad* later? If you're up for it. Supposed to be great.'

'You're not spending the evening in the garage, then?' She only just managed to stop herself from adding 'for a change'.

'Not tonight. No.'

'Dooley, did you set fire to our wedding album or something?'

He froze. For a moment, it looked as if he was experiencing some sort of medical emergency. 'What? Wedding album? Why—'

'You're being suspiciously nice, that's all. I'm just wondering what's behind it.'

He seemed deeply shocked by this. His mouth opened and closed a couple of times. As he struggled to provide an answer, Julie was engulfed by self-loathing. There was nothing suspicious about his niceness. Dooley was nice all the time. If there was anything unusual about him today, it was that he was being *extra* nice in an attempt to build bridges after a rare difficult patch in their marriage. Why was she being so cynical? The answer to that one was obvious, of course. She was being so cynical because of her own guilt over David. The fact that nothing had happened between them was irrelevant. She had been unfaithful in her mind, and Dooley knew it.

'I'm sorry,' she said. 'Don't mind me. That'd be lovely.'

Simultaneously, they reached out to tickle Nicola in her high chair. All three of them smiled – Nicola at the tickles and her parents at the coincidence. Something shifted in Julie's mind. It felt like a stuck zip suddenly giving way. There was nothing inevitable about her sleeping with David. She was an intelligent, confident woman, not some dizzy wench in a cheap bodice-ripper. The choice was hers to make, and she would choose wisely.

Her marriage was as strong as ever. All was well.

Aidan had endured a few bad dreams recently and, out of nowhere, had decided that he was now afraid of the dark. Bedtime had become a bit of a struggle.

'Light on,' he said, as Nancy tucked him in. 'The big light. Up there.'

He wriggled an arm out from under his duvet and pointed at the ceiling.

'That one's too bright, Aidan. You can have your Spider-Man light.'

'No! The big light!'

'Shhh! Please! You'll wake Luke.'

'The Spider-Man light is rubbitch!'

She sighed and closed her eyes. Her head ached and she felt exhausted, as if she was coming down with flu. She wasn't up for this.

'What does Mammy always tell you, Aidan? About the dark? Can you remember?'

'Tell me again.'

'There's nothing there when it's dark that isn't there when it's bright.' This was the line her father had always spun in her childhood. She'd never found it remotely comforting but had appreciated the effort. Aidan had never before even deigned to respond. But this time, he did.

'No,' he said. 'No good. A monster could be not there at the day and then sneak in at night-time when you can't see him.'

This was a better argument than any she'd ever put to her dad. Through her irritation and exhaustion, she felt a faint glow of pride.

'If any monsters try to sneak in,' she told him, 'sure wouldn't Spider-Man get them for you? He'd have them tied up in a web in no time.'

Aidan looked at the Spider-Man night light, then back at Nancy. His expression said, *Bitch, are you drunk?* 'It's just a light. It's not the real Spider-Man.'

'Okay,' she said. 'Okay. I give up. I'll put the big light on. Good night.' She kissed him on the forehead, then checked on Luke. Fast asleep. She tiptoed over to the door and hit the light switch.

'Yay!' Aidan yelled. Luke woke up and began to cry.

She had to spend another half an hour in the boys' room. Aidan dropped off fairly easily but Luke turned purple with fury every time she moved more than a metre away. While she comforted him with various coos and whispers, she heard muffled noises coming from the kitchen, followed by the unmistakable beeps of the microwave being set to task. Redmond was nuking one of the frozen meals-for-one that he had bought and stuffed haphazardly into the bottom drawer of their freezer. He would slop it out onto a plate, then disappear back into the garage. If she'd been down in the kitchen herself he wouldn't have spoken to her – might not even have acknowledged her presence. She had tried talking sense into him, of course, but had made no progress. No matter how gentle her approach, the result was always the same – a shouting match. So she'd given up. They just crept about the place in silence now, except when the kids were around, in which case they both acted their asses off, laughing and talking and clowning without ever addressing each other. It was insane. The whole thing was insane. What was he hoping to achieve? How long did he plan to keep it up for? Did he think this was normal? Was he suffering some sort of episode? Did he need a doctor? All of these questions and many others like them had been met initially with anger and then with stony silence.

Downstairs, she found that he'd left almost no trace of his incursion into enemy territory. A lone spoon, recently washed and now drying on the draining board, was the only clue that he'd been there. It was like being haunted, she reflected, as she made herself a cup of tea. Haunted by a spirit who is unable to remain completely hidden because it occasionally needs the toilet or the shower or the microwave. She took her tea into the living room and curled her legs up beneath her on the sofa. The TV was off, as it always was these days. She couldn't remember the last time she'd watched something meant for adults, or listened to the radio, or read a magazine. It was as if some battery inside her was on its last legs and all nonessential activities had been shut down. *If you like your precious man cave so much, why don't you fucking live in it?* Even now, so many days later, the line kept popping up in her mind. Every time it did she wondered if she'd brought this on herself. Had all of this been predictable and avoidable? The self-doubt never lasted more than a few seconds. Who takes that sort of thing literally? She was married to a child. That was all there was to it. The worst part was that he had done lasting, possibly permanent, damage to her respect for him. Even when this all blew over, which surely wouldn't be long, how could she ever look at him the same way again? She found herself envying Aidan. There was no one around to offer her words of comfort and assurance, no matter how ridiculous. Her only option, she realised, was to reach out to Julie again. She grabbed her phone and sent a text: 'Fancy another girls' night out? Dinner?' That sounded nice and light, she hoped. Her hands had trembled as she typed it – they were always trembling these days – but she'd avoided using terms like 'I'm begging you' or 'Please help, I'm losing my mind', which was good. The reply came after a few minutes. It said, 'OK. Let's invite Deirdre from across the street this time.' This wasn't ideal. Nancy wanted to unburden herself to a semi-stranger, not chit-chat with a total stranger. But it was better than nothing.

'Sure!' she replied. The exclamation mark was a nice touch, she thought.

8

Thunk. Thunk. Thunk.

Dooley's darts formed a large triangle covering most of the board. He had aimed them all at the same spot.

'Twenty-two,' he told Nicola, who was watching him from her bouncy chair. 'Terrible.'

In the days since Paula's visit, the thought of going into his pub again had made him feel physically sick. But earlier this morning, as he kissed Julie goodbye, the urge to fall to his knees, confess all, and beg her to forgive him had been almost overwhelming. It was time to act, he decided. Take the bull by the horns. Get back in there. Try to restore some normality. It didn't work. Not by a long way. After pottering around for a little while, doing nothing in particular except trying not to throw up, he concluded that he should engage in some specific activity. Hence the darts. If anything, it was making him feel worse. His occasional asides to Nicola were sticking in his throat.

A possibility occurred to him, in a sort of whisper at first, growing louder with every passing moment. *The pub has got to go. The pub has got to go. The pub has got to go.* The words began to take on the quality of a meditative chant. Would undoing all his hard work actually make him feel better, he wondered? Or would it just be a form of self-flagellation? And how would he explain himself to Julie? She was already suspicious of his clumsy efforts to please her. What if she found him dismantling the pub and demanded to know why he was being so fawning? He wasn't sure that he could hold up in the face of direct questioning. Besides, the *bedroom* was the scene of the almost-crime. How come he was able to sleep in there, feeling admittedly wretched, but no more wretched than he did in, say, the bathroom, while being in the garage was like being chewed in the maw of some rancid beast? The answer came to him as soon as the question was formed. It was because the man cave had been instrumental in his undoing. If he hadn't been so desperate for validation on the subject, he and Paula would never have bonded, she would never have come over, and he would never have wound up waving his old man at her.

He plucked his darts from the board and planted himself with his back to the far wall.

Thunk. *The pub has got to go.*

Thunk. *The pub has got to go.*

Thunk. *Paula is going to squeal.*

Nancy was having a bad morning. Worse than usual, even. Aidan and Luke had been horribly cranky, and seemed determined to play with only the noisiest and most irritating of their toys.

'I want ice cream!' Aidan suddenly roared from the floor, where he had been listlessly banging a drum with a talking Elmo.

She looked up from the magazine that she had been staring at but not reading. He had been most vocal on this subject all morning.

'Aidan, I've told you again and again. We haven't got any ice—'

The doorbell rang. It would be a salesman of some kind. But still – a grown-up. He would demand nothing from her apart from her custom, which she could easily refuse. And by the time she returned from the doorstep, Aidan might have found something to occupy himself with, especially if she made it her business to drag the encounter out.

'Mammy!' Aidan screamed. He was literally bouncing with rage now. 'Mammy, I want—'

'There's someone at the door, Aidan, hang on.'

She stood, scooped Luke up into her arms, and went out into the hall. When she opened the front door she realised in under a second that her caller wasn't a salesman but a religious maniac. He wasn't wearing a suit or any kind of ID, for a start, and he must have been pushing 70. Retirement age, at least. But the real giveaway was the fact that his hands were behind his back. In Nancy's experience, a doorstepper who wouldn't show his hands was preparing to reveal that they were holding something with Jesus on the cover.

'Hello, there!' the old man said, smiling broadly. 'And hello to you, little soldier.' He patted Luke's back. 'How are you on this beautiful morning?'

I think I'm going crazy, thanks, Nancy thought. *How are you?* 'Grand.'

'I've been walking around the neighbourhood asking people a very simple question. If you have a moment, I'd love to put it to you too.'

Luke issued a tremendous fart and wriggled uncomfortably. Nancy pretended it hadn't happened and hoped the Jesus freak wouldn't either.

'Hit me,' she said.

'Well, it's very simple,' the man said. He had one of those pointy Adam's apples that bobbed up and down when he spoke. 'My name is Seamus, by the way. The question is this: do you fully understand that God loves you?'

'Nope.'

Seamus wasn't in the least bit put off. 'I could take that in a couple of ways,' he smiled. 'Maybe you mean "That's news to me, please, tell me more". Or maybe you mean "Go away, you silly oul' eejit, I have better things to do".'

'I just don't believe in God. Sorry.'

'So it's the "Go away" option. Okey-doke.' He produced his leaflets from behind his back. Sure enough, there was a suspiciously Caucasian Jesus smiling atop a fluffy cloud. 'Maybe, if you had time, you might give this a quick read some—'

'You give up awful easily, Seamus. I didn't say you had to go away.'

For the first time, his smile faltered. 'Maybe I don't have the energy I used to have,' he said. 'I was never really the foot-in-the-door type, anyway. Counterproductive.'

He proffered a leaflet. Nancy took it. An idea occurred to her. The words were out of her mouth before she could assess it.

'Would you like to come in for a cup of tea?'

Wow, said a voice in her head. *This is a new low.*

'That's very kind of you,' Seamus said. 'But no, thanks. I'd better keep going.'

Scratch that, the voice said. *We have a new new low.*

'Okay, if… Okay.'

'Enjoy the rest of your morning,' Seamus said. He gave Luke another pat on the back and was gone.

Nancy said goodbye to his back and ducked inside again. She'd only been gone for a couple of minutes. It seemed unlikely that Aidan would have abandoned his ice cream campaign. She braced herself for more shouting – but the living room was empty.

'Aidan? Where are you?'

She shifted Luke further up onto her shoulder and tried the kitchen. He wasn't in there either, but the door to the garage was open. She found him making a duvet and pillow fort on the sofa where his father was sleeping.

'How did you get in here?' she asked him. 'Was the door open?'

'Not open,' he said. Only the top of his head was visible. 'But you *could* open it.'

Redmond had been keeping the door locked since the day he'd caught her binning his gear, so this lapse in security afforded her first glance at his new living conditions. It was not an impressive sight. Despite how she felt about the general concept of his man cave, she had begrudgingly admired the neatness and precision with which he had arranged his equipment. Everything was just so. Everything was still just so but now there was a layer of domestic mess on top of it all. There were mugs and bowls and plates all over the place and the floor was littered with chocolate bar wrappers and empty crisp packets. Clothes were strewn across every item of furniture and the air was grimly stagnant. This was a surprise. Redmond was not the kind of man who became helpless in the absence of a wife or mother. When she first started seeing him, she'd been pleasantly surprised to see that the tiny flat where he lived alone was a model of cleanliness and order. And later, when they started living together, he was much more likely to complain about a mess than she was. What was she to take from this, she wondered? That he was relaxing his standards and having a ball without her? No. She thought not. This was not a space in which someone was living happily. He was most probably miserable in here. She enjoyed a flutter of *schadenfreude* but it didn't last. If he was unhappy living apart from his family, then why the hell didn't he just admit as much and come back into the house? Was it possible that this was all down to stubbornness?

'Mammy,' Aidan said. 'I want ice cream.'

He wasn't screaming any more. That was good.

'Let's go and watch TV,' she said.

He didn't argue. Apparently, she had broken his spirit. Another proud moment.

Leo felt better. He didn't feel *good*. But he felt better.

He had taken Lauren the counsellor's advice and gone to his GP. He'd expected some sort of inquisition, followed, most likely, by a referral to a third party. Instead, the doctor had listened politely and then immediately written a prescription for an antidepressant. It would need six weeks to take effect, he said, but that was all right by Leo. Just buying the things in the chemist gave him a little lift. Both Lauren and his own doctor had advised him – and in the latter case, more or less ordered him – to take regular exercise. Out of pure habit, he started to protest about his nice long walks but on neither occasion did he follow through. Instead, to his own barely disguised amazement, he was giving running another shot. It wasn't going brilliantly, but it was going, and that was something.

He had taken one other significant step and that was to get serious about looking for a job. Essentially, this involved little more than actually doing the things he had always pretended to do. He imagined that Deirdre would be delighted about this, in particular, but she surprised him by expressing doubt. Was he sure he felt up to it? Shouldn't he wait until his tablets kicked in, at least? He waved her concerns away and grabbed the opportunity to once again enquire when *she* was going to visit the GP. This had been the only bone of contention between them in the last few days. That was pretty good going, Leo thought, given that halfway through their meeting with Lauren, he'd genuinely feared she might kill him. She said she didn't want to see the doctor because there was simply no need. Just getting it all out in the open was all the help she required. She was fine now. He wasn't buying it but didn't want to put any additional pressure on her. They were due to see Lauren again for a second session and, until then, he planned to make no sudden moves. A check-in couldn't hurt, though. He grabbed his phone and sat at the kitchen table. She took quite a while to answer.

'Sorry, Leo, hi. Sorry. The phone was at the bottom of my bag.'

'No problem. How's it going?'

'It's going much the same as it was when you called this morning.'

'Right.' There was weariness in her voice, he thought – she'd chastised him several times about his 'fussing' over her – but there was no real anger. He tried to think of some gentle enquiry he could make and dearly wished he'd rehearsed. 'So,' he said, 'did you have a nice lunch?'

He made a fist and punched his thigh. For fuck's sake. What was he thinking?

'I had lunch but I don't know if I'd call it nice. Mixed salad from the fridge in the petrol station. Didn't taste as good as that description might lead you to believe. And then I ruined it all by having a Snickers.'

'Sure, why not? You're entitled to a bit of choc—'

'I don't know why I bother trying to be good. It's pointless. Even if I do manage to make myself suffer through some horrible bunch of leaves, I always screw it up by, ha, ha, "rewarding" myself.'

Leo slumped at the table. He was furious with himself. If there was one subject he had to avoid, it was food. Despite her assurances that all was now well, there had been no change in her feelings about her weight. She was still evaluating every mouthful, still spending a good chunk of every evening pounding away on her exercise bike or rowing machine. He let her berate herself for a minute or more, not because he had no counterarguments, but because he knew that this wasn't a matter of logic or reason.

'I sent another couple of CVs,' he said when she ran out of ways to call herself weak and stupid.

'Yeah?'

'Yeah. Both terrible jobs, to be honest, but it'd be good to get some interview experience.'

'Good for you. Have you been for a run today?'

'I have. Three laps of the park.' It felt weird to tell the truth on this subject.

'Great. Listen, I have to go. Lots to do.'

'Right. Any unpleasantness since this morning?'

'No. I don't think there will be, ever. Not to my face, at least.'

'Okay. See you later. Take it easy.'

'Will do. See ya.'

They hung up. 'Unpleasantness' was the term Deirdre had settled on for any potential blowback from the paintball incident. So far, there had been none. On the contrary, everyone was apparently being extra nice. Deirdre wasn't convinced that this was the better option. They were treating her, she'd said on more than one occasion, like 'a harmless nutter'. Leo hadn't expected any different but didn't say as much. It was good that her colleagues were so understanding, he told her repeatedly, and the nutter thing was, um, all in her head. He resolved to add 'Unpleasantness' to the list of subjects he should make a point of avoiding, right underneath 'Food'.

A few minutes later, without consciously deciding that he would do so, he found himself wandering upstairs to the spare room. Deirdre used to refer to it as the gym, back when she first set it up. That term had fallen out of use fairly quickly, however. Leo guessed it was because of those TV shows she watched, the ones in which rappers gave little tours of their mansions. The mansions always had gyms, and they were always immaculate. Deirdre would fidget and sigh as MC such-and-such drifted past gleaming machines in a cavernous, brightly lit and extravagantly mirrored space overlooking a swimming pool. Deirdre's 'gym', by contrast, featured a stationary bike and a rowing machine, both of which had arrived from their eBay sellers covered in grime and missing crucial knobs. Discarded haphazardly in one corner were a collection of cheap resistance bands and small weights, which had seen almost no use. The room wasn't tiny but it was dark and it needed a coat of paint. It didn't overlook a swimming pool; it overlooked the back garden that would need a full week's work before it could be described as 'untended'. After she had stopped calling it a gym Deirdre had briefly flirted with 'exercise room', but even that had seemed too grand, Leo guessed. Now she didn't call it anything. When she went to use the equipment she simply said she was 'going upstairs'. Her tone was never cheerful.

He sat on the bike and idly pedalled, trying to put himself in her place. Mere seconds passed before he felt his mood take a nose-dive. He leaped off the thing as if it was electrified. His breathing became ragged, and not from exertion. Poor Deirdre. Stuck in here night after night, punishing herself for no good reason. Alone. It was no good. No good at all. Something had to change.

It was just after lunch and Julie was in the middle of an activity that was widely described as 'catching up on email'. She hated that phrase. It made it sound like a minor chore, something you could casually breeze through. In Julie's experience, 'catching up on email' was like 'catching up on chemotherapy'. This was promising to be a particularly bad session. She'd been ignoring everything that wasn't blazingly urgent for almost a week and had north of 400 messages waiting to be triaged. Ten minutes into the process her phone buzzed. It was a text. From David. 'Crisis,' it read. 'Don't want to put details in text. Meet me in the Westbury lobby at 3pm. Don't say anything, just slip out.'

This was it, she understood at once. This was his move. There was no crisis. What kind of work-related issue would require her leaving the office to meet him in a hotel? It was so transparent. Maybe that in itself was a test. Just showing up would be an indication of consent. But what was the alternative? To reply saying, 'I don't want to have sex with you, thanks, I've changed my mind'? She had no choice, really. So she took the only course available to her. She slipped out.

Twenty minutes later, she was on the doorstep of the Westbury. 2.45, her phone said. She was early but could see no point in standing around on the street. Quite apart from anything else, it would be just her luck to bump into someone she knew and then to babble unconvincingly about her reasons for being out of the office. She skipped up the steps, nodding at the doorman, who added to the general air of weirdness by being the spitting image of her late uncle Brendan. The hotel's lobby wasn't on the ground floor, but up a short flight of stairs. Julie was aware as she climbed them of a mild tremble in her legs and of feeling almost weightless. She was surprised to see that David was already there, sitting by the window with a tumbler of something that looked distinctly alcoholic. He spotted her at once and stood to welcome her.

'Well,' she said unsteadily as he gestured to her chair. 'This is all very mysterious. Is everything all right?'

He waited until she was settled, then he sat too. 'Thanks for coming, Julie. I know it's all a bit cloak and dagger. What would you like to drink?'

She looked at his glass. Whiskey, she saw, now that she was up close. 'I think I'll just have some sparkling water. Bit early for me. Plus, I have to go back to the office.'

He beckoned a waiter. 'Have a real drink. I won't tell anyone, I swear.'

Her certainty redoubled. This wasn't about work. This was about them. What else could it be? Unless he was dying or something. Did he look ill? No. As usual, he looked like a soap opera doctor.

'Sparkling water, please,' she said firmly, as the waiter arrived.

'Of course,' the man said, and spun away again.

'What's the crisis?' she asked David before he could make a remark about her choice of beverage.

He looked at her and kept on looking long after she had ceased to feel comfortable. 'I think you know that there's no crisis,' he said then. 'No work crisis, anyway.'

The wisest course, she decided in the moment, was to keep her mouth shut. David soon got the message that he would need to say more.

'There's something between us, Julie. I know you feel it too. I think about you all the time. Are you going to deny that you think about me?'

With some difficulty, she maintained her silence.

'The question is,' David continued, 'are we going to pretend that the feelings aren't there? Or are we going to do something about it?'

He reached into his jacket's inside pocket and withdrew something. A moment's dramatic pause, and then he placed the object on the table. A key card. Room 202. She glanced at it and then returned her gaze to David. She was determined not to appear girlish or easily shocked. With impeccably awful timing, the waiter appeared with her drink.

'One sparkling water,' he announced and set about fussing over its presentation.

'Thank you,' Julie said without looking up.

'You're welcome. Is there anything else I can get you?'

'Not right now.'

'Very good,' he said, like a butler in an Edwardian drama, and left.

David raised an eyebrow. 'I think it's your turn to say something now.'

Still she hesitated, choosing her words with great care. Then: 'This is very flattering. And I'm not going to lie. I've thought about it. About you and me. Things would be different if I wasn't married. But I am. So nothing can happen. I'm sorry.' She grabbed her glass and took a large gulp of water, hoping she didn't look too much like a nervous witness at a tribunal of enquiry. 'I hope you understand,' she added for good measure.

'You're married,' David said levelly, 'and I'm in a long-term thing. By the skin of my teeth, granted, but I'm still in it. Those are just facts. We work in advertising. We have arms and legs. We live in Dublin. We currently have other partners. All just facts. We need to decide whether or not those facts are relevant to the question at hand, which is: do we want this?'

She had seen him do this in countless meetings, both internally and with clients. The cool and reasonable tone, the apparent simplicity and transparency of his points. She wasn't about to fall for it. In fact, she was a little offended by his hope that she might.

'Please don't pitch me, David,' she said. 'My answer is thank you, but no thank you.'

'I'm not "pitching" you, Julie. I'm trying to make you see something.'

Now this, she thought, was downright patronising. 'I'm seeing everything perfectly clearly, thanks.'

He sat back, then immediately sat forward again. 'I don't understand. If you never had any intention of following through, what was all the flirting in aid of?'

'What flirting?'

He threw his head back and laughed at the ceiling. 'Are you kidding me? All the hair flips and arm-touching? The lingering glances and double entendres and all the rest of it? How many times have you found some reason to brush up against me in the last month? "Excuse me, David, I'll just squeeze through."'

She had flirted with him, of course. She knew that. But not in all the ways he had described. She couldn't recall any double entendres and if she had ever brushed up against him, even once, it had been entirely accidental. Worse, his imitation of her voice had not been a kind one. He wasn't coping well with her response.

'David, I already admitted that I had… wondered. So, okay, there may have been some flirting. But I don't think there was as much as you've imagined and even if there was…'

'Oh, I'm imagining things now, am I?'

'… even if there was, no promises were made. You can feel disappointed. But you can't claim you were cheated.'

'I never claimed I was cheated, Julie. You're making shit up now.'

His tone had grown ever harsher and was now bordering on hostile.

Julie reached for her bag. 'I think I should go,' she said. 'I hope we can put this all behind—'

'Wait, please. Wait.' He grabbed her forearm. 'Julie, please... I'm not... I'm not explaining myself very well. This all looks a bit sordid and... shabby. I see that now. And I'm embarrassed. I'm not, I'm not looking for a quick... This isn't... Julie, I'm in *love* with you.'

She physically jolted but recovered quickly. 'Come on, David. You don't really believe that.'

'I do. I really do.'

'Look, you're in a bad place with Caroline...'

'She means nothing to me. It's basically over.'

'... and you're not thinking straight.'

He stared at the table. For a moment, she was confident that she'd made him see sense. Then he drained his drink and held the glass with both hands, his knuckles whitening.

'Well. It's bad enough that you're rejecting me. But to have you mock my feelings...'

'David, come on. You sound like a 15-year-old.'

He looked up at her. His expression was so forlorn, so deeply wounded, that she had to stifle a snort.

'I never realised you were so cruel,' he said. His lower lip began to tremble.

'I certainly don't mean to be cruel,' she said carefully. 'If I thought for one minute that you were really in love with me, I'd be doing some serious sugar-coating. But we barely know each other, for God's sake. Outside of the office, I mean.'

'But we could get to know—'

'David, no. No. Nothing's going to happen between us. Just forget about it.'

'How can I *forget* about it? You're going to be at work every day, *reminding* me.'

Anger had crept into his tone again. She saw it all clearly now. He had no mechanism for dealing with rejection. Perhaps this was the first time it had happened to him. He was a spoiled child who'd been denied chocolate. As his lip tremble grew worse, she felt herself becoming mildly disgusted. She desperately wanted to get out of there before he let loose with actual tears.

'We're professionals,' she said. 'We can deal with it. Now. I'm going to go. I'll see you when I see you.'

She got to her feet and walked away, forcing herself to keep her pace gentle. The whole thing had taken a couple of minutes. Now that it was over, her mind was ablaze. There was no question of going back to work.

Suddenly, she wanted a real drink after all.

Deirdre had set herself any number of goals for her dinner with the neighbours but first on the list was *Don't make an entrance*. She was nervous enough without the added pressure of being spotted from across the restaurant bar and then appraised as she crossed the floor. Leo thought this was a silly notion ('No one's appraising you, Deirdre, this isn't *Antiques Roadshow*') and had urged her to show up on time, no more, no less. She regretted her response, which had been to express surprise. Didn't he want rid of her as quickly as possible so he could spend more time with his records? Not only was this accusation out of place in the improved atmosphere between them, it wasn't even fair; he was still spending every available minute with her. At any other time in the past six months her sharp remark would have led to a row or at least a storm-off. Tonight, however, Leo had simply retreated. She'd apologised at once but was still cringing now, an hour later.

In any event, she arrived at Le Joli Moineau – the fancy name did nothing to ease her nerves – a good 20 minutes before the appointed hour. The *maître d'* was on her in seconds, taking her coat and, it seemed, apologising personally for the fact that it wasn't as warm outdoors as it might be. Deirdre did some apologising of her own, claiming she was usually late for everything, ha ha, but tonight she was way ahead of herself. She felt silly saying she was sorry she'd be spending extra money in the establishment but couldn't stop herself, nonetheless. The *maître d'* assured her that his own timekeeping was the worst in the western world and, amid much flapping and cooing, showed her to the bar. She bade him goodbye and took a look around, scanning left to right in a manner that made her think of the Terminator. There were only a few tables, each of which was occupied. One of the seated patrons was Nancy. She was staring into a glass of wine and had the expression of a woman who was stuck on 25 Across. Deirdre felt irritated not to have arrived first, then realised that it didn't matter. There was no danger of appraisal here. It looked like she could march up to Nancy beating a Lambeg drum and still not be noticed. She cleared her throat and walked across.

'Hello! Hi! Hello.'

Nancy looked up. 'Oh, hiya. I was just... hiya.'

She was drunk. It was obvious. Not tipsy, not started-a-little-early, and certainly not merry – plain old drunk.

'Deirdre,' Deirdre said and stuck out her hand. 'We've never actually met. Properly.'

Nancy had a surprisingly firm, almost masculine handshake. 'Nancy. Obviously. It's piss-poor, isn't it? Not knowing your neighbours from across the street?'

'I—'

'That's not knocking you, now. That's knocking me. You're the one who moved in. I should have made an effort.'

Deirdre wasn't sure how to respond. 'It was nice of Julie to ask me,' she ventured. 'I—'

'Anyway. We can make up for it tonight. What would you like to drink?'

She started to get up but Deirdre gestured for her to stay put. 'No, no, I'll go, I'm on my feet. Would you... like anything?' *Please say no. Please say no.*

'No, thank you.' She put her hand over the top of her glass as if Deirdre had been about to top it up there and then. 'To tell you the truth, I had some wine at home and this isn't my first one here. So maybe I should... slow down for a while.'

'Oh, you must have arrived really early. I thought I was going to be—'

'I'm not an alcoholic or anything.'

Deirdre waited for a smile. None was forthcoming. 'We all overdo it sometimes, don't we?' she said. Nancy nodded glumly.

Not knowing what else to do or say, Deirdre nodded back and went to the bar. She ordered a vodka and tonic and hoped the barman would take 20 minutes to make it. Anything to avoid having Nancy to herself. Her drink arrived within seconds, of course, and she had no choice but to return to the table and take a seat.

'Seems like a nice place,' she said before Nancy had the chance to say something disturbing. 'Have you been here before?'

'Nah. But then I don't get out much with the kids and all. What about you? Have you ruined your life?'

'Sorry?'

'Kids. I haven't seen any. Unless you have them locked away somewhere. Which isn't a bad idea. I'm not here to judge.'

'No,' Deirdre said. 'No kids.'

Nancy pulled a face. 'I'm so fucking jealous.' This time she did add a smile, but it was clearly an afterthought. 'Joke! I'm joking. I love my kids. Despite everything.'

Deirdre threw some vodka down her throat. She had never been more desperate for a change of subject in her life. 'So,' she said as casually as she was able, 'how's your husband getting on in the garage?'

Nancy whipped her head around and glared at her. 'What?'

'In the... garage? He made himself one of those man cave things, didn't he? Like Julie's husband? And mine?'

'Oh, you just mean... how's he getting on in there, generally?'

Deirdre had no idea what else she could possibly have meant. 'Yes?'

'He seems pretty happy with it. I didn't know your, eh...'

'Leo.'

'I didn't know Leo had done it too.'

'Yeah, he has. For his records. Leo has a lot of records.'

'Fuck me, it's an epidemic. And it's all Redmond's fault. He was first.'

'Boys will be boys,' Deirdre said.

'Yeah. They will.'

There was real venom in her voice. Deirdre took another

serious drink. Neither of them spoke for a few moments. It was just about to turn from awkward to excruciating when Nancy said, 'So, do you work?'

'I do,' Deirdre said, delighted to be on safe conversational ground. 'I'm a PA at a plumbing supplies company… God, that sounds tedious, doesn't it?'

'No! It sounds pretty bloody brilliant to me.'

'Really?'

'Yeah.'

'I suppose it's okay. My boss is a nice man. The work isn't too hard. Commute isn't bad. Could be worse.'

'Damn right. Count your blessings.'

'Leo's been out of work. For ages now. He was in estate management. Looking after apartment blocks and what have you. The property crash put an end to that.'

'He'll find something. Just a matter of perseverance.'

'Yeah. What about you, can you see yourself going back to w—'

'Most days I can't see anything else.'

'Right.'

Another silence fell about them. This one made it all the way to excruciating.

Half an hour later they were seated opposite each other in the very centre of the restaurant. There was still no sign of Julie but the change of location had given them fresh conversational material, at least. They'd exhausted the subject of interior design – the room was pleasant but it had too many plants and not enough lights, they agreed – and were moving on to the menu when their third arrived.

'Sorry,' Julie said. She was out of breath. 'I'm late, aren't I? Shit.'

She crashed down heavily into her seat and began to wrestle with her ponytail, swearing under her breath. Deirdre had her suspicions immediately but when Julie turned to her and issued another apology, the smell of her breath settled the question beyond reasonable doubt. She was at least as drunk as Nancy was.

'Have you ordered?' she said, way too loudly.

'Calm down,' Nancy said. 'You're not that late.'

'Oh, good. I was… I got caught up. Time got away from me.'

'Have you been in work all this time?' Deirdre asked. She occasionally had to stay on an extra ten minutes herself, usually because a printer had jammed, but she suspected that Julie was some kind of high-flier. Maybe this was normal for her.

Weirdly, Julie hesitated, apparently unsure of the answer. 'Yeah,' she said then. 'We have a big presentation coming up – I'm in the advertising game – and there's just not enough days. Hours. Hours in the day.'

Unless the office had a bar, this was clearly a lie, Deirdre thought. If Julie's next sentence was 'I'm not an alcoholic or anything,' she would have no choice but to conclude that she had stumbled into some sort of support group.

'What's the presentation?' Nancy asked.

Julie shook her head. 'Very boring. You don't want to know.'

'I do, though,' Nancy said earnestly.

'It's a pitch, that's all. Pitching for business.'

'What's the product?'

Julie rubbed an eye and sighed. 'It's… an air freshener. A plug-in air freshener.'

'Do you think—'

'Can we not talk about this, Nancy? Please? I've been at it all day and I really don't want to—'

'Okay, sorry, *Jesus*.'

'Okay?'

'Okay.'

'Thanks.'

They all studied their menus. The atmosphere could only get worse, Deirdre thought, if one of them threw up on the table and, assuming they were having wine with dinner, that was perfectly possible.

'Everything sounds lovely,' she said in a pitifully cheery tone. 'Ooh, onion soup.'

All things considered, Deirdre thought later as she cracked the surface of her crème brûlée, it was going pretty well. It wasn't *fun*, exactly – Nancy was volatile, Julie was preoccupied, both grew steadily drunker still – but the conversation rarely flagged. There were some quiet moments when all three of them seemed to suddenly remember that they were strangers who just happened to live in the same cul-de-sac, but even then they were able to fall back on discussing the food, which wasn't great, given the asking prices. It would all be over soon, Deirdre told herself, and then she would never have to do it again. With a fair wind, she might even be able to look back on it and laugh.

And then Nancy said, 'It's weird, isn't it? We've gone through the whole meal without bitching about our husbands.'

Deirdre looked at her. Not even a smile. This was her defining characteristic, apparently – saying things that sounded like jokes but weren't. Deirdre had no idea how she was supposed to respond, so she stared at her dessert.

'They're not all bad,' Julie said quietly.

A pause. Then: 'Huh. You've changed your tune.'

'Well, I—'

'Last time we had dinner you matched me bitch for bitch, moan for moan.'

'You caught me on a bad day, Nancy. I said things I shouldn't have.'

'Oh? So everything's rosy in the garden again?'

Julie's mouth was a narrow slot. 'Things are better. Yeah.'

'Right. And how was this miracle achieved?'

'I don't want to get into it. Okay? Can we not?' She looked embarrassed. And then the embarrassment turned to distress. Her eyes fluttered and her lower lip trembled. Despite her own declaration that the subject was closed, she kept talking. 'I struck it so lucky with Dooley, really.' She choked and swallowed. 'He's done such a great job with Nicola. I know I complained about him having this pub thing in the garage but I shouldn't have. He deserves it. Not every man would do what he's done. And on the wrong side of the world, too.'

Deirdre drank some wine. She'd been taking it easy, given the state of the other pair, but she was beginning to wish she hadn't. There were going to be tears on her right. She could feel it.

'I feel so guilty about it,' Julie continued. 'He just wanted one little thing for himself and I gave him hell. He looks after Nicola all day, every day. It's not easy.'

'Damn right it's not easy,' Nancy said. 'He should try it with two of them. That's what I do, all day, every day. And what do *I* get?'

'Nancy—'

'I'll tell you what I get. I get a husband who not only thinks *he's* the one who deserves the "one little thing", he likes it so much he's fucking living in it.'

No one said anything for a moment. Deirdre couldn't stand it. 'What do you mean—'

'I mean he's *living* in it. In the garage. We had a row and I told him if he liked it so much he should move in there and he fucking *did it*.'

Deirdre looked to Julie, hoping she would take her turn. But she stayed mute.

'But... how?' Deirdre asked. 'How can you live in a garage?'

All at once, Nancy's energy drained away. It was as if someone had opened a valve and let some air out. Her shoulders slumped and her features softened. She not only sat back but slid down her seat a little until her chin was almost resting on her chest.

'Never mind,' she said. 'I shouldn't have said anything.'

At last, Julie found her voice. 'My God,' she said, to herself more than anyone else. 'I'm so grateful to have Dooley.'

Even Deirdre found this statement annoying. It was just so smug. But *Nancy*... Nancy seemed to immediately and comprehensively lose her mind. She sprang into life again, diving forward and slamming both hands on the table, hard enough to make the cutlery jump and cause gasps and mutters all around them.

'Well, aren't you just fucking marvellous,' she spat.

Deirdre was fairly sure she had never heard anyone use the word 'marvellous' in real life before. Why that should be the first thought to strike her as the evening finally pitched over the edge of a cliff was something she would have to ponder later, she told herself.

'Listen,' she said, 'why don't we all just—'

Julie cut her off. She no longer seemed to be in danger of crying. On the contrary, she had turned haughty. 'Nancy, I'm sorry things aren't good between you and Redmond. I am, honestly. But please don't take it out on me. Have some self-respect, for Christ's sake.'

'Well, that's something you're not short of, that's for sure,' Nancy said. 'You've got *oodles* of self-respect, haven't you? Can't get over yourself.' Her voice turned mocking. '"I'm in the advertising game." Fuck off.'

She drained her latest glass of wine. And then *she* burst into tears. 'I'm sorry, Julie,' she sobbed. 'I'm so sorry. I didn't mean any of that. Good for you. Fuck me... I think I'm losing it.'

Deirdre looked to Julie as if to say, *Do something*. Julie reached out and took Nancy's trembling hand. There were a lot of eyes on their table now. A couple of waiters were orbiting them at a distance.

'You're not losing it,' Julie said. 'You're just pissed and upset.'

Nancy's head was hanging low. Her face was a mess of fissures, like a scrunched-up ball of paper. 'I'm losing it,' she said again. 'I am. I'm going mad.'

'You're not going mad,' Julie said.

Deirdre decided to chip in after all. 'Definitely not,' she said, and immediately felt ridiculous. Should she reach across and take the other hand? It seemed a bit much. Then the hand turned to a fist and she put the idea firmly aside. There was a few seconds of silence in which the only sound coming from their table was Nancy's sobbing and sniffling. A bead of mucus appeared on the end of her nose and dangled precariously over her black cherry flambé. Then her eyes swivelled up.

'WHY ARE THEY ALL STARING AT ME?' she roared, causing both of her companions to briefly leave their chairs in shock. Then, as if to answer her own question, she got to her feet and ran bawling in the direction of the toilets.

'Should we follow her?' Deirdre said, pushing her chair back.

Julie shook her head. 'Let's give her a minute.' She caught a waiter's eye and scribbled in the air. He didn't need to be asked twice and took off, unable to conceal his relief. 'We'll get her out of here, get some air into her.'

'I don't understand… Her husband's living in the *garage?*'

'Apparently. I don't know what's going on, really. In her house or in her head. She should probably get out more, I can tell you that.'

The waiter arrived with the bill. He was out of breath. 'Was everything to your liking?' he said. His smile was fixed and phony.

'Yes, thank you,' Julie said, handing over a card. Deirdre began to scramble for her bag, but Julie stopped her. 'We'll sort it out later.'

The terminal was swapped back and forth. As it made its connection to the bank, the waiter bent low. 'Is your companion okay? Is there anything we can do?'

'No, thank you,' Julie told him. 'She got some bad news today. A relative. Sorry for the disturbance. I've taken it into account in the gratuity.'

'There was no need. We only hope your meal wasn't ruined.'

'We'll be back another time,' Julie lied with impressive fluidity.

The machine finished doing its thing. He handed Julie her receipt and said, 'Enjoy the rest of your evening as best you can.'

'Thank you, we will.'

As he walked away, Deirdre and Julie exchanged a *Ready?* look, then got up and picked their way between the tables, both staring straight ahead all the way. They got their coats from the cloakroom and started for the ladies.

'Actually,' Deirdre said then. 'Maybe we shouldn't crowd her. I'll hang back.'

She went to the restaurant's entrance and hid in the shade of an enormous palm. Through the glass front door she could see that there was some sort of commotion on the street outside. She didn't pay it much attention until Julie returned, shaking her head.

'Not there.'

'What?'

Julie shrugged. 'She must have taken off.'

Deirdre stepped towards the door, had an unpleasant thought, and then ran towards it. Outside, the pavement was thick with bodies. She pushed her way through and saw that there were maybe half a dozen people gathered in a circle in the middle of the road.

'What?' she heard Julie screech behind her. 'What is it? Is it Nancy?'

Deirdre could see now that, yes, it was. It was Nancy. The car that had struck her was blocking traffic, its hazard lights blinking innocently. A young man, presumably its driver, was leaning against it, not casually, but to stop himself from falling down. He was shaking from head to foot. Attempts were being made to calm him down, and they were failing badly.

Not far away, an ambulance siren wailed.

Dooley threw his phone onto an armchair and rubbed a hand over his face. Shit. Shit. *Shit.* Okay – no time for thinking. Nicola first.

He raced out into the hall and took the stairs two at a time, but softly. The bedroom door whimpered as he opened it. He winced at the sound but Nicola didn't stir. She looked so perfectly comfortable in her A-shaped sleep suit that it seemed like a crime against nature to disturb her. But that was just too bad. He picked her up and let her head rest against his upper chest, his left arm cradling her. With his right, he grabbed an extra blanket and a stuffed tiger. Downstairs again, he took his keys from the hall table and went out through the front door. Their journey was brief and horseshoe-shaped. At the top of Redmond's driveway he took a moment to settle on a form of words. And then, after transferring blanket and tiger to his baby-holding hand, he rapped the garage's metal door, three times, briskly. He heard movement within and then a muffled voice.

'Yes? Who is it?'

'Redmond, it's Dooley. Can you let me in, please?'

A pause and then the door began to open. Dooley stepped back to give it room to swing out. His first thought when he saw Redmond was that the guy looked like crap already, even before he heard the news. Living in a garage was clearly not conducive to good health. This wasn't really a surprise.

'Dooley… and Nicola?'

'Yup.'

'Did you ring the doorbell? I was just, uh—'

'Julie told me not to bother, said I'd find you in here.'

Redmond's lips pursed. 'Julie? Did she? Wh—'

'Listen: she just called me. A minute ago. There's been an accident.' For a moment, his tongue seemed to fatten in his mouth, leaving him dumb as Redmond blinked and swayed. *Just say it, dickhead,* he scolded himself. *Just say it, quickly and simply.*

'It's Nancy. She was hit by a car crossing a street in town. They've taken her to hospital. The Mater. I don't know if it's serious or not. You go on, I'll stay here and mind the boys.'

'Nancy,' Redmond said.

'Yes.'

'My Nancy.'

'Yes. She—'

'My Nancy has been hit by a car.'

'Yes. Redmond, don't panic before you have any information. Go on, mate. Get to the hospital.'

'But you must have some idea of how bad—'

'No. I would tell you if I knew anything. Julie said they just took her away.'

'Was she conscious?'

Dooley adjusted Nicola's position on his chest and exhaled. 'No.'

He heard a child's laugh then and took a moment to source it: the baby monitor in the corner. One of the kids upstairs was having a funny dream. Redmond had been remarkably calm so far – shock, Dooley guessed – but the news was beginning to land. He walked to the garage wall, hand over his mouth, leaned on it briefly, then crossed the floor to do the same on the opposite wall.

'Nancy…'

In a move that was so sudden and dramatic that Dooley briefly mistook it for an attack on his person, Redmond clutched the sides of his head. 'Oh my God. Oh my God. I've been *living* in here. In the fucking garage. Out of *spite*. We weren't getting on. If this…'

'Redmond—'

'… is serious, Jesus Christ, if she *dies*, that will be how we ended. Because I was too much of a prick—'

'Come on now, we don't even know—'

'She was so mad at me tonight. Earlier. I think she'd been drinking. Shouting about how she was going out and I could take the boys and she didn't care if—'

'Stop this. It's not helping. Get in the car and go.' Nicola began to stir. He rotated his hips, rocking her back and forth. 'Come on. Please. Move your legs. I'd drive you myself if I could.'

'But Luke and Aidan—'

'I just said, that's my problem. I'll look after them.'

'Thank you. Thank you.'

'Don't thank me, just go. Forget about everything else.'

At last, Redmond made moves towards leaving. He tore around the garage looking for his keys and eventually found them under a takeout pizza box. Dooley clapped him on the back as he passed.

'Good man. Off you go. Everything will be fine. You'll see.'

Redmond managed a nod, but he didn't look convinced as he walked unsteadily from his man cave. He got into the car and drove off. Nicola coughed, then buried her face in her father's chest, murmuring softly. Dooley put her down on the crumb-covered sofa and placed her teddy beside her. He closed the garage door as gently as he could and returned to pick her up, then unplugged the baby monitor. The living room would be his headquarters, he decided. No way was he staying in here. It was entirely too grim.

Julie and the woman from across the street, whose name turned out to be Deirdre, not Denise, were struggling with a vending machine in the short corridor that lead to Accident and Emergency. They saw Redmond approaching and stepped towards him, smiling. It had to be good news, he thought. But they had no information. They were merely smiling for the sake of it. The three of them took seats and they told him what they knew, which was precious little more than he knew. When they had finished pointing out that he mustn't think the worst and that everything would be all right, and he had finished saying 'Yep', 'Okay' and 'Uh-huh', they fell into silence that they rarely broke thereafter.

Redmond didn't have much experience of A&E departments but he suspected that this wasn't a particularly horrendous night. He had prepared himself for a war zone, but in reality it was just extremely busy. Although there were some obvious drunks, none were being particularly loud or offensive. Only one of them had sustained an injury that was obvious to the naked eye. Three rows away, a fiftysomething man, hugely overweight, was slurring apologies to his wife while holding a bag of frozen peas to an enormous lump on his forehead. Every so often, he removed the peas, which couldn't possibly be cold any more, and asked her to re-examine the damage, which she did with no obvious compassion and certainly no medical skill. Redmond could tell that there was comedy in her rough pokes and her withering looks but it bounced off him. It was like overhearing a conversation in a foreign language. *I will remember this,* he thought. *If Nancy dies. I will remember the fat drunk with the peas.*

Twice he approached the reception counter and asked if there was any news and twice the supernaturally calm woman behind it told him politely but firmly that there was no chance – zero – of her having information but not passing it on. Time passed. A lot of it. He was on the point of getting up a third time, knowing full well that it was futile, when a doctor appeared and beat him to it. After consulting with the receptionist, he caught Redmond's eye and beckoned him over. He looked like a teenager. A TV in Redmond's head ran the opening credits for *Doogie Howser, M.D.*, a show he hadn't thought about in years. *I will remember this too*, he said to himself. *The doctor who told me she was dead was Doogie frigging Howser.*

'Here you go,' Julie said.

'It'll be fine,' Deirdre added.

They smiled at him the way you might smile at a dog you were taking to the vet for the last time. His legs took some convincing but slowly, as if in pain of his own, he made it across the room to the waiting doctor.

'Mr Cole? Doctor Sullivan. Your wife is going to be fine. She sustained a concussion and she has a lot of bruising. The worst injury is to her right arm. She has a fracture of the right radius, a nondisplaced fracture – that means the ends of the bone are lined up. If you're going to have a fracture, that's the one to have. She's in a splint for the moment but when the swelling goes down, she'll probably be in a cast for a while. No need for surgery or anything overly dramatic, though. Nobody's idea of fun, any of this, but it could have been a whole lot worse.'

Redmond's voice didn't seem to be working. The world seemed to be tilting, first one way, then the other. When he could, he said, 'She's not going to die?'

The doctor placed a steadying hand on his shoulder and he realised he'd been reeling. 'Not from this, anyway. We'll need to keep an eye on her overnight but she'll be all yours again soon.'

Redmond felt sure that he was going to pass out, then felt sure that he was going to hug the man. He did neither.

'Thank you, Doctor Howser,' he said.

'Sullivan.'

'Shit, sorry. Doctor Sullivan. Can I see her?'

'You can. Bear in mind that she's had a blow to the head. Bounced it off the road, probably. And she's had medication for the pain. And she's... been drinking. So, y'know – she won't be doing any Sudokus in there.'

'Okay. Thank you. Thank you so much.'

'Don't mention it. This way, please.'

As he followed the doctor into the ward he turned and gave a joyous thumbs-up to Julie and Deirdre. They beamed back at him. The latter returned his thumbs-up. The former raised her eyes to heaven and patted her heart.

Nancy's temporary bed was right by the entrance to the ward.

'Now, Nancy,' Doctor Sullivan said. 'Look who's here.'

Her head was bandaged and her right arm was in a splint. One cheek was badly grazed. There were traces of blood under her nose. Her eyes seemed to have retreated back into her skull. Having been flooded with relief that she was going to survive, Redmond was now shattered afresh to see her in this dismal state. He began to cry. She blinked up at him. Her lips moved but if any words emerged he didn't catch them.

'Nancy,' he croaked.

Her lips moved again and this time he heard what she said. It was 'For fuck's sake'.

'I'll give you a minute,' Doctor Sullivan said and left them to it.

'How do you feel?' Redmond said, taking her good hand.

She stared at him for a moment. 'Brilliant. Thanks.'

'I thought you were dead,' he told her.

'Nope.'

'I thought you were dead and I was never going to get a chance to tell you how sorry I am.'

Her tongue emerged to moisten her lips. 'Sorry?'

'Sorry about the garage. About the stupid garage.'

'Oh. Oh?'

'I didn't know how to back down. I wanted to. I just couldn't, I couldn't say the...' He was sobbing now, his shoulders heaving, his nose streaming. 'Fucking *pride*.' He sniffed and dabbed his eyes with the back of his hand. 'I'll make it up to you. I promise I'll make it up to you. Anything. I'll do anything.'

She said something. Once again, he didn't catch it. He leaned closer.

'What was that? Say it again, honey. Anything at all.'

She squeezed his hand, hard. 'Swap,' she said.

He squeezed back. She was, as the doctor had warned, pretty

out of it. But her sense of humour was obviously intact. 'I would if I could. In a heartbeat.'

A slow shake of the head. 'No. *Swap.*'

'I don't—'

'*Swap.* You stay at home. I work.'

He blinked at her. 'You want… a job?'

'Job.'

Cogs turned. Pieces fell. Focus sharpened. 'Wait,' he said. 'Is that why you've been unhappy? Is that what's been *wrong?*'

She ignored the question. 'Redmond,' she insisted. 'Swap?'

He nodded for all he was worth. 'Yes. Yes. Absolutely. Swap. Anything. Anything you want.'

Leo was washing a cup in the kitchen when Deirdre finally arrived home. She had texted ahead so he knew that Nancy, the woman from across the road, wasn't seriously injured.

'So?' he said when she joined him. 'Quiet enough night?'

'Oh. My. God.'

'She's all right, though?'

'Broken arm is the worst of it, by all accounts.'

'Tea?'

'I will, yeah.'

He put the kettle on. 'Might have another one meself. You didn't see it happening?'

Deirdre sat at the kitchen table. 'I couldn't really talk earlier. Leo, it was a disaster. The whole night. She was already pissed when I arrived at the restaurant. Nancy. Pissed and pissed off. Only not just pissed off, like, *wired,* y'know? All intense. Moaning about the kids, her old job, her whole life, really. To *me,* a total stranger. I kept trying to turn the conversation to something light but every time I did, I got nothing but awkward silence. And then the complaining started up again.'

'Boozer, maybe?'

'I don't think so. I don't know. Maybe. I couldn't wait for Julie to get there because at least I'd spoken to her before but guess what? She showed up drunk too.'

'No way.'

'And she was in a funny mood too. Staring into space half the time.'

She filled him in on the rest of her evening, shaking her head every so often at this or that detail and more than once doubling back to emphasise a point by which he had been insufficiently impressed. When she had finished her account they drank their tea in silence for a little while. Despite everything, he was glad that she had gone. He hadn't seen her this animated in a long time. She was positively giddy. This was as good a time as any, he decided.

'Deirdre, listen—'

'You know… Oh, sorry. Go on.'

'No, you go on.'

'I was just going to say, you know what I kept thinking?'

'At the hospital?'

'No, earlier. In the restaurant.'

'What?'

'I kept thinking what a shitty advert those two are. For marriage. And having kids, especially.'

Leo frowned at her. 'You think so?'

'Julie and whatever trouble she's been having with her husband, Nancy and her… God knows what. Who does what, who deserves what, who's taken for granted, who works the hardest. Who needs more space, who needs more time.'

Leo was confused. 'What are you saying? Are you saying you don't want kids any more?'

'Ha! Christ, no. No. I'm saying, if we do have any… let's not end up like the neighbours.'

'Ah. Okay. Deal.'

She patted his hand and started to get up. 'Right, I'm—'

'Deirdre.'

'Yes?'

'I was thinking too. Earlier today.'

'Oh, yeah?'

'Sit, sit.'

She did so. 'This sounds serious.'

'Not really, no. Well... No, not really.'

'Spit it out, Leo, please. I've had my share of tension tonight already.'

'Okay. It's about the spare room.'

'What about it?'

He hesitated. Maybe this wasn't as good a time as any. He steeled himself. 'We've talked before about the exercise gear and I know it's not your favourite topic.'

'You got that ri—'

'Just hear me out, please. We always wound up fighting all those other times and I don't want that to happen again. Okay?'

A slow nod. 'Okay.'

'Which is not to say that I'm blaming you for those conversations going... badly. I'm not. I'm really not. It was my fault. I wasn't good at telling you why I don't like you being up there, night after night. It wasn't because I wanted the room for something else. Or because I didn't want you having something of your own. Or because I didn't want you losing weight. Or whatever. Whatever you thought.'

He could see that he had her attention now. 'What then?' she said.

'It doesn't make you happy,' he said. 'Just the opposite. It makes you stressed and miserable. And I want you to be happy. That's it. That's all. I want you to be happy.'

She became emotional. 'A baby,' she rasped after a few moments. 'That's what's going to make me happy. You know that. I'm sorry. I don't want it to be that way. But that's the way it is.'

On another occasion he might have snapped. But not this time. 'There's two answers to that,' he said. 'First of all, your weight has nothing to do with our infertility. You've heard that again and again. You know it's true. You know you're not even that much over. Never have been. And second of all, aren't you more likely to get pregnant if you're relaxed and happy? As opposed to stressed and miserable?'

Her lips turned down. She shook her head and was on the point of issuing some retort or, perhaps, outright denial. And then her features realigned. 'Maybe.'

'I think it's more than maybe, Deirdre. But there's something else I want to say. This business of me holing up in the garage with my records. That's... that's not good either. You upstairs, unhappy. Me in there, avoiding.'

'But you love listening to your music.' Her tone was a little suspicious.

'I do. But there's no law says it has to be a solitary thing. So here's my suggestion: you forget about exercising. And I forget about having a man cave. We turn the spare room into a... I don't know what the right description is. A place for us both to relax. Y'know... together.'

'Is this a sex thing? Are you talking about a... dungeon?'

'*No*, Deirdre. I'm serious. I can have my records in there and you can have, y'know, your... whatever.'

'My whatever?'

'I was thinking maybe knitting?'

'*Knitting?*'

'Or, I dunno, painting. Meditation. Flower arranging. Something that isn't sweating on an exercise bike and hating yourself.'

She gave it some thought. 'So, lemme get this straight. You see me arranging flowers in one corner while you belt out The Clash from the other?'

'I wouldn't be "belting out" anything. Quiet stuff, we could listen to quiet stuff. Relaxing.'

'So I'm arranging flowers and you're sitting there tapping your feet?'

'You don't think that sounds nice?'

'I think it sounds... weird.'

'Well, we wouldn't *have* to be in there together. It wouldn't be, like, a *rule*.'

'If we're not in there together, then what's the point?'

'Right. Fine. Forget about it. I'm sorry I spoke. I was just trying to help. Silly me.'

He pushed his chair back and started to get up. Deirdre grabbed his forearm.

'Wait.'

'What?'

'Thank you for… wanting me to be happy.'

'I want nothing else.'

She leaned in and they kissed.

'I haven't done any painting since school,' she said then. 'Who knows? Maybe I'd be good at it.'

'I bet you would. You picked a great colour for the downstairs loo.'

'I think there's more to it than that.'

'Well, let's find out.'

'Okay,' she said. 'Let's find out.'

When she arrived home from the hospital, Julie tottered around upstairs in a state of confusion and panic for a full minute before she remembered that Dooley and Nicola were next door. She didn't want to call in there, but she didn't want to go to bed alone either. So she went back downstairs to wait. It had been a few hours since she'd felt completely pissed, but she was still a long way from sober. Once or twice she caught herself nodding off on the sofa, which felt distinctly more comfortable than usual. She turned on the television and found an old episode of *Columbo*, hoping that would hold her attention. Then, after no apparent passage of time, she was blinking up at her husband's face.

'Hey,' he said. 'You were conked out.'

She made some vague sounds and struggled into a sitting position.

'Water?' she gasped.

'Hm?'

She cleared her throat. 'Can I have some water, please? Hello.'

'Oh. Right.'

He left for the kitchen and returned with a tall glass. She drank it down in four tremendous gulps.

'Are you okay?' he said.

'Yeah. Too much wine. How was Redmond?'

'Bit shocked. But glad she's all right. Obviously.'

'Did the boys give you any trouble?'

'Not a peep out of them. Nicola neither. She just barely woke up when I moved her in there and didn't bat an eyelid when I took her back.'

'That's good. I'll go and say goodnight.'

She started to get up but Dooley raised a hand, as if he intended to physically stop her.

'Hang on,' he said, then sat beside her. When he grabbed her hand, she felt a sudden sense of panic. Something had happened. Some other disaster.

'What is it? Tell me. What's wrong? Is it Nicola?'

'I just told you, she's fine. It's not that.'

'What, then?'

He swallowed, visibly. Was she imagining things or was he getting choked up?

'I've been thinking all night. About the accident and how quickly things can turn to shit and how much I love you and how fucked I'd be without you and... all that sort of stuff.'

She nodded. This wasn't it, she sensed. This was preamble. 'It's shock,' she said. 'Drama. Makes you go all philosophical.'

'I don't want to lie to you, Julie,' he said. 'Even if it's just a lie of... when you don't say a thing.'

'Omission,' she said, on autopilot. Her skin had turned cold and prickly. Deep dread.

'Omission. Yes. I want to tell you something that happened. With Paula, from Gymboree.'

Julie yanked her hand away from his. 'Oh my God,' she said and dropped her head towards her knees, as if trying to stave off a faint.

'Wait, wait,' he said. Then, all in a rush: 'Let me finish. Nothing *happened* happened. She was here. The other day. She said she wanted to see my pub. Brought her daughter and everything. But she got me alone, away from the kids, and, uh, she tried to, y'know… kiss me. I pulled away, we never even touched lips, I swear on Nic… I swear to God. And I told her to get out, straight away, which she did.'

Julie straightened up again. Of all the many different emotions that were vying for prominence in her mind, the one that was bouncing the highest was curiosity. 'Why are you telling me this?' she said.

He took her hand again, and she let him. 'It's been killing me. Simple as that. Even though nothing happened, nothing at all, I should never have been in that situation. It was stupid even to have her over here. I just wanted someone to show the place off to. I didn't know she… fancied me.'

'Where did it happen? This kiss?'

'Attempted kiss!'

'Whatever.'

'In the kitchen. She just sort of snuck up on me and went for it.'

'What did you say?'

'Just, I dunno, I just… Y'know, no, stop, what the fuck do you think you're doing. That sort of thing. She was very embarrassed.'

'And then she just left?'

'Yeah. I told her to get out but she was going anyway, believe me.'

'And what if she hadn't tried to kiss you? Were you going to tell me she was here?'

He made a noise. It sounded involuntary. 'Probably not. No.'

'So some neighbour could have said something about you and your female friend and I would have said, "What female friend?"'

He looked at the floor. 'I'm sorry. It was stupid. The whole thing was really stupid.'

'Wait, wait. She was here because you wanted someone to say something nice about your *pub*?'

'I know. I know. It's pathetic. If it's any consolation, I'm dropping the whole thing.'

'What thing?'

'The pub.'

'Huh? No more man cave?'

'No more man cave.'

'But I thought you loved it in there.'

'Eh. I loved the idea of it. But it never really worked. At the end of the day, I was just a bloke playing darts in his garage. With some nice lighting. And anyway, it makes me think of her lunging at me now, so it's ruined.'

Julie peered at him. 'Is she horribly ugly or something?'

'No. Just... normal. Why?'

The 'lunging' remark was the first thing he'd said that she found unconvincing. Even if he wasn't interested in this woman, he had his pride. An attempted kiss must have been good for the ego, if nothing else.

'I believe you didn't go along with it, Dooley. You don't have to pretend you almost threw up.'

His lips moved for a moment but he said nothing. Calculating, she supposed. Trying not to make it worse. She waited. And waited. And then she heard herself talking.

'You said a while back that I'm always going on about David at work.' He snapped around to look at her. His eyes were wide and unblinking. 'There's a reason for that,' she went on.

'Oh, Jesus,' Dooley said, almost inaudibly.

'Let *me* finish. He fancies me. I know he does. He doesn't make much secret of it.'

Dooley nodded briskly, two staccato inclines of his head. 'And do you... fancy him?'

She snorted in what she hoped was a convincingly horrified fashion. 'I certainly do not. I mean, he's good-looking, but... Ugh. No. Still. It plays on my mind. So if I've been mentioning him a lot, that's why.'

Dooley's posture softened. And then he stiffened again. 'Does he, like, *harrass* you? Has he put his hands on you?'

'No, nothing like that. It's all just looks and little comments. All totally deniable.'

'Because if he's touched you…'

'Dooley, he *hasn't*.'

'… I'll knock his fucking block off.'

At this, Julie laughed, slapping her hand over her mouth.

'What?' Dooley said. He looked hurt.

'Just that phrase,' she said. '*Knock his block off*. It's a bit 1950s.'

'Oh. Right. Well – I'll kick the shit out of him, then.'

It wasn't just his choice of words, of course. She'd laughed at the very idea of him threatening violence, least of all against David, who would presumably just snap him over his knee like a dry stick. Still. She loved the fact that he was up for it.

'You don't have to do anything to him. But thank you for offering.'

'So, what are you going to do about it? There must be someone you can complain to.'

'And say what? That I think my boss fancies me? If he hasn't done anything about it, what am I supposed to say? He notices when I've had my hair done and I can't take it any more?'

The lies were coming to her so easily. It was a little frightening.

'But it's playing on your mind, you said, and that—'

'I'll get over it. What am I going to do, quit? It'll be fine.'

'Well,' Dooley said after a pause. 'At least we know people still fancy us.'

They leaned in until their foreheads gently touched.

'Yeah. And we still fancy us. Don't we?'

'Definitely.'

They kissed, and it turned into something. Dooley stood and offered her his hand. She took it, and they went upstairs.

9

Redmond looked up from the toast that he was buttering with more haste than skill.

'Aidan. Stop that, please. It's going to go flying.'

The boy was stirring his Weetabix with enough force to make the plastic bowl spin.

'No,' he said. 'Can't make me.'

'Well, no, I can't make you stop,' Redmond told him, 'but I can take it off you. Come on, man. No Weetabix? That'd be *terrible*.'

Aidan adjusted his grip on his spoon and stirred harder still.

'All right,' Redmond said. 'That's it. Gimme.'

He approached the kitchen table but was too late. Aidan misjudged his angle of attack and the bowl was launched away from him. It skated across the table, struck Luke in the chest and clattered to the floor. Upside down, of course. Redmond's go-to tactic for this sort of occasion was to immediately clap and whoop, hoping to convince the offended son that he hadn't been hurt in any way but rather had performed some wonderful stunt.

'Yaaaay!' he cheered but it was already too late. Luke's meltdown was so sudden and total that it had the air of parody. He threw his head back and screamed bloody murder while banging his tiny fists on his high chair.

'Aidan!' Redmond snapped. 'I told you. Didn't I t—' He stopped himself. No. There would be no loss of temper. 'Not to worry,' he smiled. 'Come on, let's not get all upset.'

Nancy had taken a taxi to the hospital for a check-up. On Monday, she would begin work at her new job. She'd started the search the day after her accident, from her hospital bed, and was doing interviews within a week. The broken arm was no barrier, she insisted. If she showed up to an interview with a sling, everyone would be dazzled by her determination and grit. Redmond was horrified and attacked the idea on two fronts. For one thing, she had been through a traumatic event and needed to rest. And for another, wasn't it possible that potential employers would see fragility rather than strength? She would be 'that injured woman'. First impressions and all that. Neither of these points made any impact.

The truth was, he had begun to regret his blubbering bedside performance before he'd even made it home from Accident and Emergency that night. In subsequent days, when it became clear that she was deadly serious about holding him to their new arrangement, genuine panic set in. He would have to tell her the deal was off. She'd caught him at a vulnerable moment and he'd made a promise on which he couldn't deliver. Simple as that. Except it wasn't. Obviously. As her excitement grew, he came to understand that he would be risking his marriage and quite possibly his life if he tried to renege. He changed tack and attempted to broker a compromise. It was clear to him now, he told her in a lawyerly tone, that she needed to return to work. But perhaps they had been too hasty about this whole role-swapping business? What about getting professional childcare for the boys? He'd already looked into it and knew that, Ireland being Ireland, it would be breathtakingly expensive – but he felt he had to try something. To his surprise, Nancy's counterargument made little mention of the money issue. Her principal objection was an old one, slightly modified. She used to claim that children needed the constant attention of their mother in the first few years of life. Now, using all the same phrases and citing all the same sources, she said that they needed *a parent*. Either one would do. Redmond made a few more attempts to broach the subject, feeling like a man who needed to pogo across a minefield, but eventually gave up. There was still a good chance, he supposed, that she would find it difficult to get hired in this economy, grow frustrated and drop the whole idea until the kids were older. This proved to be a laughably inaccurate forecast. She found something suitable at the end of her first full week of looking. They wanted her to start as soon as possible. And so, feeling punch-drunk and disembodied, Redmond found himself not only handing in his notice but using up holiday time to cut that period shorter still.

At first, he wafted about in a dream-like fog, not trusting the very floor beneath him. The world had gone fuzzy. Everything *smelled* different. He constantly teetered on the edge of panic. No, he told himself every 20 minutes. Just no. This was bullshit. He would make some terrible mistake or, more likely, a series of terrible mistakes and the boys would grow up warped – if they got to grow up at all. The pressure felt epic, ungovernable, geological. And then it began to fall away. It was a while before he realised why. The answer was Nancy. She was a different woman. Constantly thrilled, constantly smiling. She cracked jokes. She played pranks. *She bought him a footstool for his gaming room.* It was like living with a lottery winner, he thought initially, but that analogy wasn't quite right. Her joy had depth; it was almost spiritual. What she most resembled, he concluded, was someone who had been life-threateningly ill before ultimately pulling through. And it was contagious. Her happiness made him happy, just as her misery had made him miserable.

With room to breathe, he began to consider the other upsides to the new arrangement. Most obviously, he wouldn't have to go to work any more. No more meetings. No more commuting. No more targets or conference calls or spreadsheets. The novelty would wear off, no doubt, but for now it was pretty sweet. Then there was the guilt – or rather, the lack of it. He'd always known that he was missing out on a lot of his sons' development by being cooped up in an office. It was unavoidable, he'd told himself, and nothing to feel remorseful about. He realised now – by virtue of its sudden absence – that the remorse had crept in anyway. Maybe he'd be a terrible full-time dad. Maybe not. Either way, he would know that he had given it his all.

Sometimes he caught himself staring into space, wondering how he and Nancy had ever arrived at the point where he was living in the garage. It felt like something that had happened to a different couple – a nugget of gossip he'd encountered, shaking his head in disbelief. Not that they had arrived at an unassailable Happily Ever After. There would be other bumps in the road, of course, long before he even went back to work. He knew that. The difference was, next time he wouldn't be such a dick about it. This was his solemn vow.

Luke wailed again.

'Daddy's coming,' Redmond said, and doubled back to the kitchen counter. He grabbed a cloth and set about cleaning up the mess.

The thing about having dipped your toe in adultery, Dooley was learning, was that you felt as if the trouble might recur at any time, like malaria. Even the simplest encounters with women felt risky. He couldn't so much as buy a litre of milk at the corner shop without wondering if he would suddenly lunge across the counter to throw himself on Mrs Davey, who was 60 if she was a day and reeked so strongly of cigarettes that he sometimes didn't breathe around her. It was this fear that he had become some sort of monster, rather than common-or-garden guilt, that plagued him most unbearably. The guilt may have been significant, but it was constant. You got used to it. Not so the fear, which came upon him randomly and without warning. This was partly why he'd been avoiding Gymboree. It was nothing if not chock-full of women. Of course, the main reason he'd stayed away, for more than a month now, was that one of those women was Paula.

In the first few days after their encounter – that was his latest word for it – he'd stumbled around in a daze, certain that she was going to show up at the house, screaming from the footpath that she loved him and would not be discarded like a used tissue. One afternoon while he was busy getting the garage back to its pre-pub state he became convinced, for no apparent reason, that she was standing behind him. He spun around, like a frightened teenager in a slasher movie, to find himself alone. When the days turned into weeks he began to hope that if he simply avoided Gymboree and went out as little as possible for the rest of his life there was every chance that he would never see her again. He'd hoped that telling Julie what had happened – or at least telling her the children's version of what had happened – would ease the pressure. But it just gave him something extra to feel bad about. Paula, he began to suspect, had been correct. He may as well have fucked her.

And then came the text. It arrived, as terrible luck would have it, while he was standing beside Julie in the kitchen. David had been missing from the office for a few days, ostensibly on sick leave – but word had just reached her that he'd been interviewing at other agencies. She was losing herself in speculation about his current position going up for grabs when Dooley's phone shivered in his back pocket. He plucked it out and gave it a glance. When he saw who had texted it felt as if every organ in his body made a bid to escape, some heading north, some heading south. He didn't even know how she'd acquired his number. Kay from Gymboree, maybe? His one consolation was that when Julie asked what was up, he had the presence of mind to turn his facial spasms into a look of perplexed irritation. Bloody phone company, he told her. Stupid promotions. A few minutes later he sequestered himself in the bathroom and read the text. Paula had noticed that he no longer attended Gymboree and assumed that she was the reason. She'd got the message, she said, and would stop going herself. He had her word. It was all his. She signed off with 'Goodbye, I suppose!' and a smiley. Dooley read it twice and then deleted it. She seemed sincere. You could argue, he now supposed, that Gymboree was exactly what he needed. If Paula wasn't going to be there then its other defect – the fact that it was almost all women – could be viewed as a positive. He couldn't avoid them for the rest of his life, after all. Wasn't it better to dive in at the deep end, as such? If he could cope with Gymboree, he could cope with all the Mrs Daveys in the world.

No one was surprised to see him return. He doubted, in fact, that anyone had noticed he was ever missing. He caught Kay's eye as he and Nicola took their place in the circle and lifted his chin in greeting. She waved hello but then mouthed the word 'Welcome', which made him think she was under the impression that he was new. Given the scarcity of men at this event – there were three this morning, which was a bumper crop – he found this to be somewhere on the spectrum of humbling to offensive.

'Good morning, boys and girls, mums and dads,' Kay said when everyone was seated. 'I hope everyone's in good form and ready to raise the roof.' A couple of the older children looked above them suspiciously. 'We're going to start today with one of my favourites. We won't do any dancing or running around for this one, mums and dads, let's just get our voices warmed up.'

She hit a button on her CD player and treated them all to a surprisingly funky version of 'Sing a Song of Sixpence'. Nicola was unimpressed and began to squirm and complain. Dooley sat her up straighter and tried to soothe her by singing with a little more gusto than usual. He was delivering the words 'dainty dish' when he saw Paula and Charlie joining the circle several places to his left. He choked on the nursery rhyme and squeezed his daughter so hard that she cried out. Paula caught his eye and blew him a kiss. He recoiled as if she had hurled a bottle. His instinct was to get up and run but he fought back against it. What if someone had seen the blown kiss? How would it look if he got up and legged it before the end of the first song? And what if she *followed* him? Tongues would undoubtedly wag. When the song ended, Kay announced that it was time for the kids to grab some instruments. In the ensuing chaos Dooley gathered his strength and crossed the floor to Paula.

'Hiya,' she said cheerfully. 'Look, Charlie, it's Dooley and Nicola.'

He couldn't bring himself to look at the little girl and was grateful when she paid him no attention whatsoever.

'Drums!' she said to her mother and tore off in pursuit of same.

'So,' Paula said then. 'How have you been?'

He had no interest in pleasantries. 'What are you doing here?' he growled. 'You told me you wouldn't come back. "It's all yours", you said.'

She shrugged. 'I wanted to see you.' A small smile. 'Your face… What is it you're afraid of, Dooley? Do you think I'm in love with you, is that it? Do you think I can't go on without you?'

He stepped closer. 'Keep your voice down, for fuck's sake.'

'No one's listening.'

'They don't have to *listen*, they can *hear*. And I don't know what to think, do I? I have no idea what you might... do.'

She rolled her eyes. 'Okay, look. In your kitchen that day, fair enough, hands up, I might have allowed you to think that you had something to worry about. From me. But I was just feeling hurt and upset. I'm not going to start stalking you, for fuck's sake. I'm not going to leave messages on your wife's phone or any of that movie crap. I promise. I wanted to make that clear. And, y'know... apologise for letting you worry.'

Was this reasonable? It sounded reasonable. 'Okay,' he said.

'And if it makes you feel any better, I really will stay away from Gymboree in future. Okay?'

'Okay.'

She sighed. 'You wanna know why I was interested in you? Because you're a good man. Unlike some I could mention. I should have known that'd be the reason why you'd never go through with it.'

'That's a laugh. A good man wouldn't have gone as far as I did.'

'Give yourself some credit. I think you're the only man in history to get that far and not follow through. I didn't know it was possible.'

'Maybe if my blood was a bit more red—'

'Dooley, quit it. *Quit it.* Quit this "real man" bullshit you torture yourself with.'

'You're saying, what, I should be proud of myself? Over this?'

'I'm not talking about this. I'm talking generally.'

He gave it some thought. 'You know what I've been thinking lately? I've been thinking I should go back to work. Get childcare for Nicola.'

'You don't want to do that.' It wasn't a question. It was a statement.

'No. I don't. But the idea keeps popping up.'

'Well, slap it the fuck down. You've got the rest of your life to do some pointless job you hate.'

He smiled and nodded that this was true. Of course it was.

'Anyway,' she said. 'I've said what I wanted to say. Looks like this is goodbye forever.'

'Please don't kiss me.'

She cackled. 'Jesus Christ, man. Get *over* yourself.'

'Sorry. Sorry.'

Charlie reappeared. 'Can't find a good drum,' she complained.

'Actually, honey, I've just remembered something. We have to go.'

'What? Aw!'

'I'm sorry. Silly Mammy. Come on. Let's go. Say bye-bye to Dooley.'

Charlie sighed and raised a hand. Dooley raised his. Paula mocked their solemnity by doing likewise. And then she spun away, trailing her daughter by the hand.

'See ya,' Dooley said to their backs.

'Nah,' Paula said, over her shoulder. 'You won't. Take it easy, Dooley.'

Deirdre, it turned out, had no talent whatsoever for painting. It was a good thing, she said as she surveyed her first efforts, that they hadn't spent much money on materials. Because these were… Words failed her. Leo worked hard to keep her spirits up but he couldn't quite bring himself to say that, no, her paintings were really good, actually. They most certainly weren't. Her bowl of fruit looked like a pastoral landscape. Her pastoral landscape looked like a bowl of fruit. Both looked like they'd been done by a ten-year-old in the back of a moving car. Instead, he concentrated on the relaxation angle. Who cared about the end result? He had been watching her as she painted and it was like seeing a muscle unclench. On no account was she to give up. She could always forget about trying to make her paintings look like something. Take the pressure off. Do shapes and colours, nothing else. Deirdre admitted that there was something pleasant about dragging the cheap brush over the even cheaper canvas. 'Relaxing' wasn't quite the right word. It was more… medical than that. 'Soothing', perhaps. And so she went abstract. At first, she judged these paintings harshly too. They were childish. They were silly. They were embarrassing. Leo remained gently encouraging. The flow of complaints slowed to a drip and eventually stopped entirely.

And so they settled into their new arrangement. There were times when Leo was up there alone, headphones on, music blasting. The room lacked shelving but he had arranged his records on the floor along three walls. It wasn't ideal but there was something old school about it that he quite liked. He was surprised to find how often he didn't bother with music and just read in silence or roamed the job websites. (He'd had no luck on that front yet, but he'd begun to feel quietly confident that his ship would soon come in. Nancy from across the street had scored a new job, after all, and by all accounts she was crazy.) Deirdre had the place to herself too on occasion, although she seemed to prefer it when they were in there together. And most evenings, they were. Leo enjoyed playing DJ, picking out albums that fitted the ambience they were going for and watching his wife paint in the soft light they'd spent an evening getting just so. Sometimes they barely spoke. Sometimes they chatted for hours. Home improvement was a favourite topic of conversation; specifically, what they were going to do with the front of the house when they had the money to de-crappify it.

They'd had another session with Lauren, their IVF counsellor, and had both wriggled with delight as she congratulated them on the steps they'd taken to improve their mental health. It was okay, she said, that Deirdre hadn't visited her GP. She was helping *herself*, and that was huge. Next thing they knew, they had the go-ahead to begin treatment. It was happening. They braced themselves. And then Deirdre missed her period. They did some calculations. The day of her paintball adventure? *That* was the one that had done the trick? They told themselves not to get too excited. It was probably a blip. That said, it would do no harm to get a pregnancy test. Leo sat at the kitchen table not drinking a cup of coffee while Deirdre went up to the bathroom. She returned in tears, and not the good kind. Things were bad for the next couple of days. They both became quiet. Leo's runs became longer. Deirdre spent a lot of time staring at the wall. But they didn't turn on each other. That was something, Leo told himself, as he tried not to imagine how much it would hurt if IVF didn't work either.

Six days after the negative test, Deirdre came home from work in a strange mood. He asked her if everything was okay. She pulled a face. It was odd, she said. Her period still hadn't arrived. And she felt... funny. Pregnancy tests were reliable, she knew that. But they weren't perfect. She'd bought another one that lunchtime. She had promised herself she wouldn't even tell him. Why get his hopes up? They weren't up, he told her. But she might as well try it now. Get it over with. She shrugged and trooped off to the bathroom. Leo started to set the table for dinner. When she came back down a few minutes later, she was pale as a stone and looked as if she might actually keel over. Her mouth was hanging open. The test stick was in her hand, which was shaking. She stepped towards him, eyes growing wider. He dropped the knives and forks and went to meet her.

'What?' he said. 'What is it? What? What?'

The End

Patrons

6/5against 6/5against
Moose Allain
Eilis Anglim
Keith Appleby
Liam Ashby
Nick Ayerst
Ruairí de Barra
Denis Beary
Brian Bilston
Marion Bolt
Eoin Bradley
Eileen Brassil
James Candon
Caroline Grace Cassidy
Ciaran Clissmann
Ciaran Colgan
Hilary Colyer
Debbie Comerford
Niamh Concannon
Gar Concannon
Charlie Connelly
Paul Connor
Dorothy Cotter
Aidan Coughlan
Laura Crawford
Caroline Crotty
Stewart Curry
Nick Curtis-Davis
Brian Daly
Shelley Davis
Tom Dawkins
Neil Delaney

Apo Demirkol
Allison Devers
John Donachie
Pat Donnelly
Joe Donnelly
Paul Donovan
Christine Doran
Eoghan Doyle
Darragh Doyle
Balázs Édes
Elaine Fitzgerald
Tara Flynn
Denise Gallagher
Liz & Gary
Niall Glynn
Luke Griffin
Tim Haines
Fiona Hanley
Ray Harman
Jane Harris
Nicholas Harris
Nick Harvey
Katy Hayes
Rudy Hellzapoppin'
Edward Hemsley
Edel Henry
Lesley Heyworth
Steve Higgins
Robert Hogan
Glen Holmes
Eithne Howard
Sheilagh Johnson
David Jones
David Jones
Morgan Jones
Wayne Kearns

David Kelly
Ella Kennedy
Ciara Kenny
Louise Kiely
Dan Kieran
Gonzo Knob
Sean Leahy
Jude Leavy
Mary Lee
Michelle Lewis
Susie Lovejoy
Margaret Lynott
Mike Lythgoe
Stephen MacCann
Paul Maclennan
Alan Maguire
Arthur Mathews
Olive McGovern
Warren McAllister
Cat McCabe
Paul McClean
Steve McCool
Sean McDonald
Cian McGarrigle
Siodhna McGowan
Aoife McGrath
Gareth McKenna
Anne-Marie McMahon
Eamon McNulty
John Mitchinson
Vincent Molloy
Paul Moloney
Marina Moore
Benjamin Juliàn Moran
Daniel Morris
Barbara Morrissey

Laura Mulligan
Dave Murphy
Ivar Musum
Jo Nicholls
Sian O'Connor
Gearóid Ó Cúin
Linda O'Hara
Pat O'Connor
Conrad O'Dea
Suzanne O'Reilly
Aoife O'Sullivan
Shane Owens
El Pablo
Eilín de Paor
Vasiliki Papantonopoulou
Rajesh Patel
Justin Pollard
Chris Randell
Haydn Reece
Eoghan Rice
Jennifer Robertson
Fergal Rock
Charlie Rowlands
Stuart Rutherford
Irene Ryan
Jeremy Ryan
Susan Ryan
David Sheehan
Richard Smith
Paul Smyth
Siobhán Meehan Smyth
Sean Staunton
Jennifer Stratton
Brendan Strong
Keith Sutherland
Anthony Tierney

Colm Tobin
Spike Van Der Schyff
Sally Vince
Sven Wallman
Carrie Walsh
Ben Walsh
William Whyte
Lisa Wilson
Laura Wright